VAMPIRATES

BLOOD CAPTAIN

JUSTIN SOMPER

SIMON &
SCHUSTER

London · New York · Sydney · Toronto

A CBS COMPANY

SIMON AND SCHUSTER
First published in Great Britain in 2007 by Simon & Schuster UK Ltd
A CBS COMPANY

www.vampirates.co.uk

Simon & Schuster UK Ltd
Africa House, 64–78 Kingsway
London WC2B 6AH

A CIP catalogue record for this book is available
from the British Library.

ISBN 9781416901020

1 3 5 7 9 10 8 6 4 2

Typeset in Garamond by M Rules
Printed and bound in Great Britain by
Cox & Wyman Ltd, Reading, Berks

www.simonsays.co.uk

To Jenny, Jo and Jonathan.
Blood is thicker than water!

CHAPTER ONE

The Crow's Nest

"Come on, Connor. You can do it!"

"Come on, buddy! Keep climbing!"

Connor Tempest grimaced. His legs felt simultaneously as heavy as lead and uncontrollable as jelly. It was a mistake to have paused halfway up. He'd been doing so well. He wanted to conquer this fear. It was time. Way past time. But the fear was deep inside him, weighty and immovable as an anchor caught beneath a rock.

He wanted to look down. He struggled to keep his head straight, knowing that looking down was the worst thing he could do. He felt his eyes being pulled like magnets down to the deck, many metres – *too* many metres! – below. And then down the side of *The Diablo* and deep into the ocean. When you stopped to think about it – and you should *never* stop to think about it – there was a very long way to fall.

1

"Don't look down!" Cate's voice sailed through the air, strong and certain. If only he could be as confident as the deputy captain always sounded.

"Come on, lad!" Captain Wrathe called to him. "You've taken on worse foes than a few metres of rigging!"

This was certainly true, thought Connor, his mind flashing with dark snapshots of the past three months. His dad's funeral. Nearly drowning before he was rescued by Cheng Li. Being separated from Grace. The death of his dear comrade Jez. His betrayal by Cheng Li, Commodore Kuo and Jacoby Blunt. The terrible night when he'd led the attack on Sidorio and Jez . . . no, *not* Jez, but the thing Jez had become. The memory of that night burned in him like a fire, as hot as the torches he had sent across the water to the deck of the other ship. As consuming as the flames which had engulfed his friend . . . the *echo* of his friend . . .

"Come on, Connor!"

It was Grace! Even though she was back on the Vampirate ship, it *was* her voice – as clear as anything. It gave Connor the extra fortitude he needed. After everything they had been through, he could no longer be defeated by this one remaining fear. This *ridiculous* fear of heights.

Carefully, he removed his right hand from the rigging. It came away with the indentation of rope deeply imprinted, red and raw, across his palm. He realised how tightly he'd been clinging on. The ship's bell rang. The surprise of it made him lose his balance for a moment but it was only the bell announcing the changeover of shifts. He steadied himself. It was now or never. He reached up to the next square of rigging and took a deep breath.

He didn't look down. He didn't look up either. He just kept his eyes focused on his hands and the squares of rope. Each square was the same as the last – a rope window framing a patch of sky. If he just focused on this, it was as if he wasn't climbing at all.

Suddenly, he realised that his legs were no longer shaking. Instead, they were moving steadily, seeking out the next foothold, finding their rhythm. His breathing had settled too. He was calm. He was doing this. Conquering the fear. It felt good. It felt *so* good.

He lost himself in the movement and it was only when he heard the sound of cheering from below that he realised he'd reached his goal. He looked up and his hand touched not rope but the wooden frame of the crow's nest. All that remained was to haul himself up onto the lookout point.

A coldness sliced through him. There was no ignoring the sense of how high he was above the deck. With no harness to protect him. It was madness to be up here. At the mercy of the swell of the waves far below. Once more, an icy wave of fear tore through his insides. He gritted his teeth, waiting for it to pass. The fear clung onto him, but Connor was not about to be defeated. Not now.

There was good reason to be up here. Someone had to man the crow's nest – to keep a lookout and give early warning of attack, or opportunities *to* attack! Coming up here was about protecting your mates. And in the three months since he'd joined *The Diablo*, these guys had become more than mates. Bart, Cate and Captain Wrathe were his new family. They'd never replace Grace, of course, but Grace had had to embark on her own journey. Besides her, everyone he cared about in the world was aboard this ship. When you looked at it like that, it made absolute sense to be up here, in a position to safeguard them. Effortlessly, he climbed up into the crow's nest.

As he planted his feet on the wooden platform, he heard a fresh round of cheers from below. The temptation to glance down was strong now. Resisting it, he looked straight ahead. As far as the eye could see, there was the endless sprawl of glittering blue ocean. His new home.

In the distance, he saw the outline of a ship, silhouetted against the afternoon sun. Attached to the crow's nest was a small telescope. Connor reached for it and looked through the glass out to the horizon. It took him a moment to find the ship but then he caught it in the circle of his vision. It was a galleon, not dissimilar to *The Diablo*. A pirate ship, perhaps. He zoomed in still further and raised the telescope to get a better look at the flag. Yes, another pirate ship for sure! It seemed to be heading around the bay, the bay that could be seen curving into the horizon behind the vessel. Connor grinned. He knew *exactly* where that ship was heading. To every pirate's favourite watering hole – Ma Kettle's Tavern.

As Connor replaced the telescope in its clip, a small bird

came to rest on the crow's nest. From its forked tail, Connor recognised it as a sooty tern. It gave Connor a quick glance then flapped its wings and took off again, soaring away into the blue. Connor watched the bird until it lost its distinctive shape, contracted to a black speck, then disappeared entirely. He smiled to himself. That's my fear, he thought. Gone now.

"Good goin,' buddy!" Bart high-fived Connor as he jumped down the last metre onto the deck.

"Very impressive," said the pirate at Bart's side.

"Thanks, Gonzalez."

"No, I mean it," the pirate replied. "Half an hour to get up there and straight down in thirty seconds!" He grinned.

Connor shook his head. He'd only started to know Brenden Gonzalez since Jez Stukeley's death. Gonzalez could never take Jez's place but he shared a similarly dry sense of humour.

"I'm really proud of you!" Cate said, stepping forward and – most uncharacteristically – hugging him. "I know how hard that was for you," she whispered in his ear.

"An excellent effort!" said Captain Wrathe, beaming at him. Scrimshaw, the captain's pet snake, was coiled about his wrist, and even he seemed to be looking at Connor with fresh admiration.

"Well, gather round everyone," called Captain Wrathe. "I think Mister Tempest's accomplishment is cause for celebration, don't you?"

There was a rousing chorus of "Aye, Captain!" from up and down the deck. Once more, Connor had a sense of belonging to a vast, extended ocean-faring family.

"Tonight, we shall visit an establishment by the name of Ma Kettle's!" cried Captain Wrathe.

There was much cheering. Bart and Gonzalez hoisted Connor up onto their shoulders.

"Put me down!" he cried.

"Oh, dear!" said Bart. "You haven't got a fresh attack of vertigo, have you?" He and Gonzalez laughed good and hard at that.

"No," said Connor. "Put me down! I have news for the captain."

"A likely tale!" cried Bart.

"It's true!" Connor persisted. "Put me down!"

"If you've news for the captain," cried Molucco Wrathe, "you may tell him from up there on your perch."

"All right," Connor said, still balancing on his mates' shoulders. "It's probably nothing to worry about. Just that when I was up in the crow's nest, I saw another pirate ship."

"In our sea lane?" boomed Molucco. The irony of his comment was not lost on the crew, who greeted his indignation with hearty laughter. They all knew that Captain Wrathe had little – or rather, no – respect for the system of sea lanes instigated by the Pirate Federation.

Connor nodded. "It's in our lane, but I don't think it's going to cause us any bother. It looked to me like it was just taking a short-cut to Ma Kettle's."

"I see," Molucco said. He reached into his blue velvet coat and retrieved his own silver retractable telescope. He extended it fully, then raised it to one eye, closing the other eye tight. "Which direction was it coming from?" he asked.

"North-north-west," Connor said.

One eye attached to the telescope, the other still closed, Molucco swung around and narrowly missed whacking Cate in the nose. Fortunately, the deputy captain had quick reflexes.

"Ah yes! I see." He fiddled with the telescope lens. "Let me get a better look."

For a moment, the captain was silent.

"Do you see it now?" Connor asked.

There was a pause and Connor was about to repeat his question. But then the captain spoke. "Yes, lad. Yes, I see it."

They could tell from his voice that something wasn't right. Cate stepped closer to the captain's side. Bart and Gonzalez eased Connor from their shoulders and returned him gently to the deck.

"What's wrong, Captain?" Cate asked.

He seemed too lost in his own thoughts to answer. As if in slow motion, he dropped the telescope from his eye and compacted it once more. He looked dazed.

"The day has come," he announced.

"What do you mean?" Cate asked. "Is there something we should know about that ship?"

"You'll find out soon enough," Molucco said. "Cate, I'm going to my cabin. Make sail for Ma Kettle's."

"But, Captain," said Cate. "If there's something wrong, I'd really like to know . . ."

"Just do it," Molucco said wearily, striding away across the deck.

"What's eating him, I wonder?" Bart said, when the captain had disappeared below deck.

Cate shrugged. "Like he says, we'll find out soon enough." She sighed. "Of course, it might be nice to get a heads-up once in a while. I *am* Deputy Captain of this ship . . . in name, at least."

"Chin up, Cate," Bart said, giving her shoulder a squeeze. "Don't take it personally."

Cate lifted her hand and removed Bart's from her shoulder. "That," she said, "is a highly inappropriate," she dropped her voice "but much appreciated show of support." Smiling, she turned to address the crew. "Chop chop! Change tack for Ma Kettle's. Now!"

Connor headed off along the deck.

"Where are you going at such a stride, buddy?" Bart called after him.

"I'm going to grab a shower," Connor said. "I'm all grimy after my climb and I want to freshen up for Ma Kettle's."

Bart gave him a knowing glance. "Freshen up, eh? That wouldn't be to impress any particular lady who might happen to work at Ma's, would it?" He grinned at Connor. "Hey, are you *blushing*?"

"No!" Connor said. "I must have got sunburned up on the crow's nest, is all."

8

"Aw," said Bart, "our boy sure is growing up fast!" He and Gonzalez grabbed Connor and ruffled his hair.

"Stop it!" cried Connor, breaking free from their clutches and darting inside to get ready.

It was always reassuring entering the familiar terrain of Ma Kettle's. If *The Diablo* felt like Connor's home these days, then Ma's ran a close second. Connor always felt a sense of expectation as he heard the great waterwheel sloshing overhead and made his way with his comrades across the threshold.

Connor, Bart and Gonzalez strode into the main bar. Several faces turned as they did so. Connor noticed that a couple of the serving girls gave him a smile. Blushing, he smiled back. He was still unused to the growing amount of attention he had been receiving of late. Being one of Molucco Wrathe's crew gave you instant celebrity status in the pirate world. Love Molucco or loathe him, it seemed you just couldn't help talking about him.

The bar was bustling with activity, as always. Crews from numerous pirate ships spilled out across the main bar area. Some were lucky enough to be welcomed beyond the velvet rope into the VIP area. Others sought out the private curtained booths up above. Connor saw Cate standing at the bar. She gave him a wave and beckoned the three of them over to join her.

"So did ya find out what's eating the captain?" Bart asked Cate as he, Connor and Gonzalez caught up with her.

"No." She shook her head. "No, he's barely said a word to me since he saw that ship."

"Where is he now?"

"Over there." She pointed. "No doubt telling Ma everything he doesn't see fit to tell me."

They looked over to a roped-off section of the tavern, where Molucco was sitting with Ma Kettle. She was nodding sympathetically, rubbing his shoulder with one hand and pouring him a hefty drink with the other.

"They *are* old friends," Bart said to Cate.

"Yes," Cate said. "But I'm the deputy captain. I'm supposed to know some of what's going on in his head." She sighed. "Of course, you know what this is really about, don't you? He blames me for what went down on *The Albatross*. It's fair enough. Lord knows, I blame myself."

Connor hung his head. It was hard for all of them to move on from that fateful day – from the apparently easy victory that had turned into a nightmare for them all. It was the day that had ended with the death of their friend and comrade, Jez.

"Hey," Bart said. "We were all caught unawares by that."

"Yes," Cate said. "But *I'm*—"

"We know," said Bart. "You're *Deputy Captain!*"

Cate shook her head. "I was going to say that I'm not supposed to be caught unawares by anything."

Connor could see the hurt in her face. He wished he could say something to make her feel better but he felt a little out of his depth.

"Now look," Bart said. "Young Tempest here conquered a major fear today and we're supposed to be celebrating. So can we all put a smile on our faces and get a bit merry?"

"Amen to that," said Gonzalez, grabbing some drinks from a passing serving girl.

"My but you're pretty!" Gonzalez said. "Are you new?"

The girl blushed, shook her head and continued on her way. Bart laughed. "That's little Jenny, you drongo," he said. "Haven't you seen her before?"

"Can't say I have," Gonzalez said. "But I'll be looking out for her now! Little Jenny!"

Hearing her name, the girl glanced over her shoulder. Gonzalez raised his tankard in salute. "Ah, she's like a little angel, that one."

Bart shook his head with a smirk. Cate came over to Connor. "I'm sorry about before," she said. "You did good today and you deserve a celebration."

"It's OK," Connor said. "I know things aren't easy for you."

"No," Cate said. "But those are my problems. And I shouldn't have bothered you with them."

"Yes you should," Connor said. "You might be Deputy Captain, but first and foremost you're our friend."

Just then, there was a loud cry across the tavern.

"Molucco Wrathe!"

Connor, Bart, Cate and Gonzalez turned. Across the room, they saw Molucco and Ma freeze and then look slowly round. The voice boomed across the room again.

"Molucco Wrathe!"

A tall, imposing man strode across the room into the centre of the light. A striking woman and gangling boy followed some steps behind. Connor could tell by the man's clothing he was a captain. There was something strangely familiar about him.

"So *that's* why the captain was all worked up!" exclaimed Cate.

"What do you mean?" Connor asked. "Who is that?"

"That's Barbarro Wrathe," Bart said. "Molucco's brother."

CHAPTER TWO

The Expedition Party

The chill night air licked the deck of *The Nocturne* as the galleon rested in the waters of a small cove at the foot of a vast mountain. So vast was this peak that it was impossible to see just how far it stretched into the air, however much Grace Tempest strained her neck backwards to look. It didn't help, of course, that it was pitch black, save for the sliver of moonlight which fell unhelpfully across the other side of the deck. To most ordinary people, it would seem incredibly foolhardy to embark on an expedition up icy, unknown mountain passes in the middle of the night. But, Grace reminded herself, not one of the people embarking on this expedition could be termed "ordinary". Indeed, some would say it was stretching things to even describe her travelling companions as "people".

As she leaned backwards in vain, Grace felt the woollen beret slipping from her head. Feeling an immediate

13

resulting chill, she pushed the hat back into position and resumed an upright position. The beret, like the rest of her outer clothes, had been loaned to her by her friend Darcy Flotsam, who now stood beside her on the deck.

"Are you sure you're warm enough, Grace dear?" she inquired. "I could easily pop back into my cabin and fetch you one of my furs. Just say the word!"

Grace shook her head. "I told you before, Darcy. I won't wear fur. No animal should have to die to keep me warm."

Darcy shook her head in disbelief. "But it's so soft and toasty! And it's not like the poor fox what made my coat is about to spring to life again any time soon. So where's the harm, eh?"

"No, Darcy," Grace said, firmly. "Not under any circumstances. This coat is quite warm enough, thank you."

Darcy smiled at Grace as they waited for the others. "I so wish I was coming with you," she said. "I don't think I'd enjoy the climb, it's true, but I'd do it to stay close to you and Lieutenant Furey."

"I know, Darcy, and Lorcan does too." Grace smiled at her companion. "But the captain seems to think that the less of us leave the ship the better."

They both looked towards the closed door of the captain's quarters. Inside, he was briefing his deputies on how to manage the ship during his absence.

"It's *very* rare for the captain to leave the ship," said Darcy, turning back to Grace. "It shows how much he cares for Lieutenant Furey that he would take this risk."

Risk? Grace hadn't thought of it in those terms before, but now she realised that with the recent turmoil on the ship and the rebellions following Sidorio's departure, it would indeed be a risk for the captain to leave the other Vampirates for even a few days. Sidorio had questioned the rules of the ship, in particular the captain's limiting of blood-taking to the weekly Feast Night. Though Sidorio had been banished and was now gone, he had left the seeds of discontent behind him. Others amongst the previously compliant crew were now asking why *they* could not take blood more often. Grace knew that the captain had exiled three more of the crew since Sidorio had left. They had joined up with the renegade Vampirate and embarked on a terrible spree of wanton bloodshed until they had all been destroyed – by her brother, Connor. Connor the hero.

It was strange to think of her twin in such a way. So much had happened to them both in the few short months since their father had died and they had left their home in Crescent Moon Bay. How naïve they had been then, thought Grace. They had thought that leaving would offer them an escape route. And, in some ways, it had. But their journey had thrown them both into dangerous situations, where their very lives were under threat. Now Connor was, to his sister's great discomfort, a pirate warrior aboard the notorious ship *The Diablo*. And, perhaps to her brother's even greater alarm, Grace was a regular passenger aboard the ship of vampire pirates, or Vampirates, called *The*

Nocturne. Both brother and sister yearned for the other twin to see sense and join them – to see that *their* choice of ship was the right one. But it was a tribute to their relationship that they had lately come to the understanding that each must go their own way, for now at least.

And so here she was, on the deck of *The Nocturne*, awaiting the captain and her dear comrade Lorcan, about to embark on an important mission to the top of the mountain and a mysterious place called Sanctuary. There, they would meet the Vampirate guru, Mosh Zu Kamal, and appeal to him to cure Lorcan of his blindness.

Glancing back up towards the mountain, Grace wondered just how long it would take to reach Sanctuary. It might prove to be a very arduous trek indeed. Already, she was concerned about how Lorcan would manage. It was not just a question of his blindness but the fact that he had recently grown so weak. Why, just a few days earlier, it had been effort enough just to get him up onto the top deck.

"My business is concluded." She heard a familiar whisper, and saw a new figure emerge onto the deck. Clad from head to toe in black, it was as if he had been sculpted out of the dark night itself. Others would be perturbed by the sight of this tall, imposing man with his leathery cape, which sometimes flickered with veins of light, like the winged sails of the Vampirate ship. They would be intimidated by the fact that he always wore a mask and never removed his hands from their dark gloves. Some might recoil at his voice, which did not go out into the air,

16

as other voices do, but instead arrived in your head as an icy whisper, never varying in volume or pitch.

But in her relatively short acquaintance with the Vampirate captain, Grace had come to know him as a wise and compassionate being – more humane than anyone she had ever met before, save perhaps her dear departed father. In a way, she realised, she had come to view the captain as a father figure.

"Let us go." Once more the captain's words arrived in her head.

As the captain walked towards them, Darcy suddenly threw her arms about Grace's shoulders. "Oh, Grace," she said with a sob, "we always seem to be saying goodbye, don't we?"

Grace nodded, smiling. She was a little surprised to feel a tear roll down her cheek. Sometimes, she forgot just what a good friend Darcy Flotsam had become to her. It was no longer sufficient to think of her as the ship's quirky but beautiful figurehead; a wooden sculpture by day, but a girl full of life by night. Darcy was as much flesh and blood and emotion as anyone Grace had ever met.

Grace wiped away the tear. "I'll be back soon, Darcy," she said. "I promise. Just as soon as Lorcan is on the mend, we'll return to *The Nocturne*."

Darcy nodded. And so they hugged once more and repeated their farewells, both hanging onto the pretence that Lorcan was sure to recover. Neither could bear to even entertain the alternative.

The captain gently leaned forward. "Goodbye for now, Darcy," he whispered, laying a gloved hand on her shoulder. "I know I can depend on you to obey the deputy and do your best for the good of the ship."

"Yes, Captain!" Darcy exclaimed, giving him a crisp naval salute.

Watching them, Grace pondered the word "deputy". She realised that she had no idea who the captain had left in charge of *The Nocturne* during his absence. She was aware of a certain hierarchy aboard the ship – Lorcan, for instance, now held the post of Lieutenant, as Sidorio had before him. But she had no clue as to who the deputy captain was or even who might be of senior rank amongst the crew. This was in marked contrast to her time aboard the pirate ship, *The Diablo*, where it had been crystal clear that the deputy captain was first Cheng Li and latterly Cutlass Cate. Grace was reminded that, in spite of her already deep attachment to several of the crew of *The Nocturne*, there was still much she had to learn about the Vampirates. Perhaps her time at Sanctuary would give her more of an insight. She fervently hoped so.

"Ah," said the captain, his whisper cutting through her thoughts. "And here come the final members of our expedition party."

He nodded as Lorcan made his way out onto the deck. He was dressed in a heavy army greatcoat he had borrowed from another member of the crew. A medal still hung over the front of the chest. It looked rather good, thought

Grace, wondering which conflict it commemorated and what noble and violent deeds had secured the honour. With his military boots, Lorcan cut a dashing figure. On his back was a small kitbag, filled with a few articles to make his stay at Sanctuary more comfortable. Across his eyes was the fresh bandage Grace had helped to apply earlier. It obscured the livid burns, with which she was now all too familiar, and shone dove white in the moonlight.

Lorcan was not alone, however. Beside him strode Shanti, his beautiful but vicious donor. Her high-heeled boots drummed on the wooden deck and she gripped a vanity case in a small, suede-gloved hand. So, she was coming along with them too, thought Grace. It made sense. If Lorcan was to fully recover then he'd have to start taking blood again. Shanti was his given donor and he'd need her close at hand when the time came. Shanti, Grace now noticed, was wearing a matching fur coat and pillar-box hat. She didn't need to think very hard to realise where *that* outfit had been procured.

Darcy's face flushed red at Grace's stare. Grace shook her head. Darcy was such a generous soul – but how typical it was of Shanti not to give a thought to what dead creature she might be wearing. The most annoying thing of all, though, thought Grace, was that Shanti looked so pretty in the outfit.

As the new arrivals reached the group, Grace and Shanti exchanged strained smiles. There was no love lost between the two and clearly neither could quite hide the displeasure they felt in travelling together. Close up, Grace noticed how much older Shanti looked, even from the last time she had seen her. She was still beautiful, there was no question about that. In some ways, she was *more* beautiful, as lines wove their way about her eyes and lips. This made her beauty seem more fragile and therefore more precious. To Shanti, however, the lines were abhorrent. The donors were only immortal whilst their given vampire was sharing their blood. As soon as this stopped, mortality wasted no time in reclaiming the donor's body. Since Lorcan had ceased sharing with her, Shanti had begun to age at an alarming rate. If he did not start taking her blood again soon, she would be in severe danger. She too might be growing weak. Grace shook her head. What an unlikely expedition party they were, she thought, looking from one face to another.

"Come on," said the captain. "Let's not waste any more time. Sanctuary and Mosh Zu await us. Come, my friends."

"Goodbye, dear Lieutenant Furey," Darcy said, hugging Lorcan tightly. "I wish you the most speedy recovery."

"Thanks, Darcy," said Lorcan, warmly. "You be a good girl while I'm away, you hear me?"

Grace was pleased that he had managed to muster some of his old cheek. That had been missing for too long. Shanti looked displeased, her lips pursed tightly. She was, Grace had noticed, remarkably possessive of Lorcan. Now she looped a fur-wrapped arm through the sleeve of his greatcoat. Grace lifted her own small pack onto her back, then took Lorcan's other arm. They followed the captain gingerly down the gangplank and onto land.

Behind them, mist rose from the dark waters, stealing its way gently but firmly up the sides of the ship. Darcy stood on the deck, waving to the departing travellers until the very last. Then the mist drew a curtain between them and *The Nocturne* disappeared from sight.

"And now a new journey begins," announced the captain.

Grace nodded. She wanted to say something enthusiastic, to generate some positive energy amongst the group, but catching sight of Lorcan's downturned mouth and Shanti's cold, sharp eyes, she could see exactly what they were both thinking. This might be their final journey. If Sanctuary and the mysterious Mosh Zu Kamal couldn't heal Lorcan, there was no further hope for either of them.

CHAPTER THREE

Brothers

The whole tavern fell silent as Barbarro Wrathe – flanked by his two companions – appeared at the top of the steps leading down into the main part of the bar. The woman and boy lingered on the top step as Barbarro continued his journey alone. In his hand was a cane, its head a bulbous skull with a jewelled snake emerging from one eye-socket and spiralling down the length of the stick. The cane beat out Barbarro's steady progress towards his brother.

As he reached the main floor, revellers on all sides moved swiftly away – whether out of fear or respect, Connor could not be sure. Barbarro's cane echoed against the floor. There were low murmurs. Connor watched and listened intently. He knew that there was an old grievance between the two brothers. Had Barbarro come back to settle a score? His face gave nothing away.

The person who seemed the least surprised – and the least

perturbed – by Barbarro's arrival, was Molucco himself. But, of course, Molucco had known that it was Barbarro's ship making its way to Ma Kettle's. He had been shaken when he'd first seen it from the deck of *The Diablo* but, in the intervening time, he had composed himself. Now, he calmly took a last draught of his drink, then rose up and stepped down from the booth where he and Ma Kettle were ensconced.

"Barbarro!" he boomed at full volume. "What a wonderful surprise!"

Barbarro did not respond but stood, waiting for Molucco, in the centre of the room. It made Connor think of two jungle cats taking the measure of one another – a real power play.

As the two brothers at last came face to face, Connor was struck by the strong resemblance between the pair. They were not quite the mirror image of one another, but you could certainly see they were cut from the same, flamboyant, cloth.

Barbarro was just a little broader and taller than Molucco. Dressed in a bottle-green frockcoat with gold braiding and tall boots, he cut a similarly dashing figure. His hands, however, were devoid of jewels – save for a gold wedding band. Barbarro wore his hair long like Molucco's but it was still a glossy black, with a thick streak of silver-grey adding both glamour and gravitas. He had a neatly-cropped beard and moustache. But his twinkling eyes were the perfect reflection of his brother's. Just when you thought you knew which colour they were, it shifted. First green, then blue. Purple, brown, then black. They were as changeable as the surface of the ocean.

"It's been a long time," Molucco said. All eyes in the tavern were upon him as he spoke. Then they moved hungrily to Barbarro to gauge the response.

"Too long, Molucco," said Barbarro, his voice as sonorous as his brother's. "Since last we met, I have lost one brother. I do not intend to lose another."

Now he extended his arms and Molucco stepped forward to embrace him. There was a chorus of sighs around the room as the men hugged. It appeared that the long-running feud was over. At least, thought Connor, *something* good had come from the terrible murder of Porfirio Wrathe.

As the two Captains Wrathe at last disentangled themselves, Connor saw Scrimshaw emerge from Molucco's hair and extend himself expectantly towards Barbarro. Connor had noticed how Scrimshaw often seemed to scrutinise people, as if on Captain Wrathe's behalf, but this was something different. Suddenly, he noticed a reciprocal movement amidst Barbarro's dark locks, and a second snake pushed its way through and extended itself towards Scrimshaw.

Barbarro glanced up with a smile. "It seems Skirmish is pleased to see his own brother."

"Yes," nodded Molucco gravely, "I venture he's missed him terribly these last few years." The snakes hissed conspiratorially together for a moment, then settled around

24

their masters' necks, where they could keep an eye on one another.

There was a ripple of laughter around the tavern. It served as an escape valve after the high tension of Barbarro's arrival. Connor took advantage of the break from silence to give Bart a nudge. "You didn't tell me Scrimshaw had a brother," he said.

Bart grinned. "I have to keep *some* surprises up my sleeve," he said.

As they spoke, the tall woman behind Barbarro stepped forward. She walked gracefully and was dressed in a regal coat, the same pale gold as the hair swept up onto her head.

"That's Barbarro's wife," Bart hissed.

"Trofie!" exclaimed Molucco.

"Did he say *Trophy*?" Connor asked. "That's an odd name."

"It's *Trofie* – F-I-E. Scandinavian, I think," Bart said.

"She's a lot younger than Barbarro," Connor said.

"Yes, I think this face suits her."

"What do you mean, *this* face?"

"Let's just say it changes from time to time," Bart said. "Snip, snip . . . if you know what I mean."

Trofie extended her right hand. It glowed as golden as the rest of her, all except for her ruby-red fingernails. Connor watched as Molucco bowed before his sister-in-law and kissed her hand. This didn't seem to entirely please her for, as Molucco stood up again, she reached into a pocket, pulled out a small handkerchief and wiped her hand. As she

25

did so, Connor was surprised to see the light bounce off it. Looking more closely, he saw that Trofie's right hand was made of metal. It was literally as gold as her hair. And what he had taken for red-varnished nails were, in fact, actual rubies. He had never seen anything like it.

"What's with her hand?" he asked Bart.

"Ah, yes," said Bart. "There are conflicting stories about that. The official version is that Trofie was captured and held hostage by one of Barbarro's rivals. He threatened to cut off her fingers unless she revealed the location of Barbarro's secret treasure cache. Story goes that Trofie kept her silence for five days. And every day, they chopped off one of her fingers. On the sixth day, Barbarro rescued her, killed her captors and took her to a surgeon who reconstructed her hand out of gold."

"Wow!" said Connor. "That's amazing." It made him sick to think of such wanton violence. "So what's the *un*official version?"

"Well," said Bart. "Trofie Wrathe likes a jewel or two and Barbarro Wrathe believes in treating her to whatever her heart desires. Rumour has it that she got to the point where she had so many rings she literally couldn't lift her hand. In the end it was a choice between her rings and her fingers."

"And she chose . . .?"

"She had her actual hand removed – apparently it's in safekeeping in formaldehyde somewhere in case she ever wants it back – and then had her rings melted down to create this new gold hand."

"Wow!" Connor said again. "Which version do you think is the truth?"

Bart shook his head. "Search me," he said. "Chances are, we'll never know. I certainly wouldn't dare ask her. She scares me." Bart shivered.

Connor turned his full attention back to Trofie. "I'm very sorry for your loss," he heard Trofie say to Molucco. Her voice was icily precise.

"Madam," answered Molucco. "The death of Porfirio Wrathe was a devastating loss to us all. To the whole world of piracy, in fact."

Trofie nodded. Then she looked back over her shoulder. Connor saw she was beckoning to the lanky boy who had come in with them. "Moonshine, come and say hello to your uncle."

The boy rolled his eyes and ambled forward. He was dressed casually in black drainpipe jeans and a leather biker-jacket. "Uncle Luck," he said. "How's it hanging?"

Trofie dug a golden finger into his ribs.

"Ow!" he moaned. "That hurt!"

"Show your uncle some respect!" she said.

But Molucco beamed. "No need for formality where family's concerned," he said. "Why, Moonshine, you've certainly had a growth spurt since last we saw you. You're as tall and thin as a mast."

Moonshine looked faintly displeased with this remark but then, thought Connor, he had the kind of face that looked faintly displeased, period. It wasn't helped by the smattering of acne on his cheeks or the livid purple scar that crossed one cheekbone.

Suddenly, as if becoming aware he was being watched, Moonshine glanced in Connor and Bart's direction. As his eyes met theirs, his face froze. The look he gave Connor and Bart was venomous. Where had *that* come from, Connor wondered?

"Connor!" Molucco called. "Cate! Come and meet my family."

Connor and Cate crossed the floor.

"This is our Deputy Captain," said Molucco. "Cate, you've met Barbarro and Trofie before."

Cate nodded, bowing before them.

"But I don't think you've ever met their boy, Moonshine. And the three of *you* have yet to meet Connor Tempest," Molucco said, reaching out an arm and pulling Connor towards him. "Connor's the newest member of my crew. He's only been with us these past three months but it's hard to imagine a time without him. Why, he's become like a son to me."

Connor blushed at Captain Wrathe's fulsome praise. Once more, he was struck by the captain's generosity of spirit.

"A son, eh?" said Barbarro, shaking Connor's hand. "That's high praise indeed from my brother. Connor, this is my wife and Deputy Captain, Trofie."

Connor waited nervously to see if she would extend her real hand or the golden one. It was the gold one which moved towards him. As he took it in his own hand, he felt something akin to an electric shock. It was as smooth and almost as supple as flesh but it was ice cold.

Trofie gave a small smile. "Hello, *min elskling*," she said. "We've heard about you."

"Really?" Connor said, surprised.

"Oh, yes," Trofie said, her face still holding the smile. "We're very well informed."

"This is Moonshine," said Barbarro. "Say hello to Connor, Moonshine."

Moonshine surveyed Connor for a moment, giving the clear message he'd as much like to shake hands with a pile of his own vomit. At last, there being no clear alternative, he extended his hand to Connor's. Connor noticed the blackened, chewed fingernails. They looked somehow familiar but he didn't know why. He and Moonshine shook hands very briefly. Moonshine's hands were as cold as his mother's but clammier.

"How old are you, Connor?" Barbarro asked.

"Fourteen, sir."

"Fourteen? Why, just the same as our Moonshine! Looks like you're set to be firm friends," said Barbarro, evidently blind to the looks of disgust now emanating from both mother and son. Connor saw that Trofie had wrapped her metal hand about her son's waist. The ruby "nails" glistened.

"Well," Ma Kettle said, taking charge. "You've all got much to catch up on! Come and sit up here and we'll uncork a bottle of oyster champagne to mark this auspicious occasion." She ushered Molucco, Barbarro and Trofie into the booth where she and Molucco had been sitting before.

"Not you young men, though," she said, firmly grasping Connor in one hand and Moonshine in the other. "You too, Bart," she called across the room. "You boys are going to check out my newest attraction."

"We are?" said Connor.

"Oh yes," said Ma, "you are!" She called over her shoulder. "Sugar Pie! Is the band ready?"

"Yes, Ma!" came a familiar cry.

The cry was followed by the appearance of Sugar Pie, Ma Kettle's beautiful assistant.

"Connor! Bart! It's been a while. How are you both?" Sugar Pie kissed them each lightly on the cheek. Connor vowed not to wash for a couple of days. Speechless, he beamed from ear to ear.

"And this is Moonshine Wrathe," Ma Kettle said to Sugar Pie. "Molucco's nephew."

Moonshine leaned in his cheek for Sugar Pie to kiss, but she took one look at his pockmarked face and gave it a quick pat with her hand.

"So, have you seen the dance-floor?" she said, spinning around. They hadn't noticed it before but now Connor saw that Ma had changed around the layout of the bar. The section beneath the gallery of curtained booths was now a dance-floor. It was made up of glass squares, like a chessboard, under which coloured lights pulsed in time to the music.

"I assume you know how to tango," Sugar Pie said.

"Absolutely," Moonshine replied, puffing up his

unimpressive chest.

"Excellent! Then you'll partner Kat," said Sugar Pie, pushing him towards the dance-floor where a tall, dark-haired girl was waiting. "And you, Bartholomew," she said, "you shall partner Elisa." Grinning, Bart strode out across the floor and took his dance partner in his arms.

"And you, Connor," Sugar Pie said, taking his hand, "you shall partner me."

The musicians played a small overture as she led him onto the dance-floor.

"Erm, the thing is, I really don't know how to tango," Connor stammered.

"That's why you've got *me* as your partner," said Sugar Pie. "I'll lead. All you have to do is cling on tight and let me do the rest."

"But I thought the man was supposed to lead," said Connor.

"Ha!" Sugar Pie laughed. "Not on *this* dance-floor!"

Suddenly the tango music began in earnest and Connor was swept across the floor.

"That's it," Sugar Pie said. "Just hold on tight and don't let go!"

Connor realised he had little option as she dragged him along the floor. He had fleeting glimpses of the others as they passed, like speeding light boats cresting the surface of the sea. Bart winked at him as he elaborately dipped Elisa until her tousled hair was skimming the floor.

"Focus!" Sugar Pie instructed, pulling Connor's face

sharply towards hers and staring at him with her disarmingly blue eyes. "That's better!" It did not surprise him that when the time came, it was she who dipped him, his head and shoulders falling backwards until he was looking up at the velvet curtains of the booths overhead. They were all tightly closed.

"Excellent!" Sugar Pie cried, pulling him upright again. "You're really getting the hang of this."

Dazed, Connor found himself being marched back across the floor. Now he could see Moonshine, dragging Kat along in a rather brutal fashion. In everything he did, Moonshine seemed to express unknown depths of anger. Twisting Kat around, Moonshine gazed directly into Connor's eyes.

The music came to a crescendo and Connor was left facing a look of pure hatred coming from Moonshine Wrathe. Connor frowned. How could you hate someone you'd only just met? He had a bad feeling about Moonshine's arrival. Barbarro might have come to heal old wounds but judging by the expression on Moonshine's face, a new feud might already be starting. Connor couldn't understand where the boy's animosity had come from, but this was going to end badly, he could feel it.

CHAPTER FOUR

Dark Journey

As the mist cleared, Grace saw only empty ocean. *The Nocturne* had disappeared. She felt a shiver along her spine. There was no going back now. Glancing first at the captain, then at Lorcan and Shanti, she wondered what challenges lay ahead for each of them before they next returned to the ship.

"*Now* what do we do?" asked Shanti.

"It's really very simple," the captain said. "Now, we climb the mountain."

"Well *yes*, but where are our mules? And lights? Surely, they've sent someone to guide us and carry our bags?"

Grace hated to find herself in agreement with Shanti but she felt these were all fair points. Nevertheless, it came as little surprise to hear the captain's whisper. "We'll make our own way. Everyone makes their own way to Sanctuary."

Shanti struggled to take this in. "But how? It's pitch

black. We can't. We don't even have a map, do we? My shoes . . . Lorcan will never make it."

Lorcan sighed. "Thanks for the vote of confidence," he muttered. Through the darkness, Grace reached out her hand and squeezed his.

"Well, it's true!" Shanti continued, undeterred. "We'd be much better off waiting for daylight."

"You're forgetting," said Lorcan. "I cannot walk in the light. The captain is the only one of us – the only Vampirate – who can do that."

Shanti didn't miss a beat. "If you're already blind," she said, "what more harm can the light do to you?"

This was a vicious barb, even by Shanti's standards. Lorcan had no answer for it.

"Let's talk no more about this," the captain said. "We're wasting time." With that, he strode off along the path, his cape sparking against the trees on either side.

Shanti looked to the others for support. "This is madness," she said. "Don't you see? We'll never make it."

"You might well be right," Lorcan agreed despondently. It was as if Shanti's sharp words had stripped him of any remaining shred of confidence.

"We have to try," Grace said, with grim determination. "We can't give up before we even begin. I don't think the captain would have embarked on this journey if he didn't think it was possible."

"What do *you* know?" Shanti said. "What do *you* know about *anything*?"

Shanti was so bitter, so angry with Grace. Grace knew that she blamed her for Lorcan's blindness and for the fact that he had stopped taking Shanti's blood. And though it made Grace uncomfortable to admit it, it was true that Lorcan had been blinded trying to protect her. So she did feel responsible for what had happened. But there was nothing to be gained by standing around blaming one another or apologising again. The captain had said that Lorcan's best chance of a cure lay at the top of this mountain. That was the one truth they all had to cling on to.

"I'm going to follow the captain," she announced. "Before we lose sight of him." She turned to Lorcan. "Are you coming?"

He nodded.

Grace paused for a moment. It was an awkward question but she needed to ask it. "Do you need a hand?"

Before he could answer, Shanti looped her arm through Lorcan's. "If anyone is to help him, it will be me," she said.

But Lorcan shook his head and removed Shanti's hand. "I can walk by myself," he said, stepping forward. In spite of the bandages around his eyes, his steps were firm. "Grace, you lead and we shall follow."

Shanti's face flushed scarlet and Grace could see she was thinking of some fresh complaint.

"Come on then," Grace said. "I can still see the flicker of the captain's cape along the path, but we'll lose him if we wait another moment."

*

35

It was strange, thought Grace, how quickly you adapted to the darkness. The shimmer of light in the veins of the captain's cape was not as bright as normal – just enough to tell her where he was, but insufficient to illuminate the way. And so she simply walked in his wake. Occasionally, a stray branch brushed her face or the top of her head but already her other senses were making up for the lack of vision. She noticed how her hearing had grown more acute, as if the volume had been turned up on her footsteps on the path. It was strange how easy it was to distinguish her own steps from Lorcan's heavy but firm tread and Shanti's brisker pace. Try as she might, however, she couldn't hear the captain's footsteps ahead of her. She knew he was there from the constant flicker of light, but how come she couldn't hear his footsteps?

She could smell the musty coat Lorcan was wearing and, behind him, the trace of Shanti's perfume – quite incongruous against the mountain air. Grace walked on, her feet marching out a steady rhythm, her mind in a meditative state. Suddenly she heard a cry from behind her.

"What was that?" Shanti's shrill voice pierced the air.

"What was *what*?" Lorcan asked.

"Something wet and furry just ran past me," Shanti said. "Didn't you feel it?"

"No," said Lorcan, unable to keep a note of amusement out of his voice.

"Oh, yes," Shanti said. "It's very funny, isn't it? Climbing up a mountain path so dark we can't see a step ahead of us, with wild beasts running amongst us." Her voice was spiralling higher and higher into hysterics.

"There, there," said Lorcan, calmly. "Don't trouble yourself, Shanti. If you did feel a wild creature, remember that this mountain is their home. I reckon it only came out to take a look . . ."

"*This* time," Shanti said. "Next time, it might attack."

"It was probably just confused," Lorcan said. "On account of your coat."

He couldn't restrain a laugh. Grace tried to resist joining in, but failed.

"Yes, yes," Shanti said. "You two have your joke. You enjoy yourselves. But you'll see that I'm right. This journey will be the death of us." She paused, then continued even more pointedly. "Those of us who aren't dead already."

Her words echoed around them, turning the mood dark once more, reverberating in the chill night air. It had grown colder, Grace noticed. At first, she had thought she was simply becoming better at dodging the low-hanging branches, but now she realised that the vegetation was growing sparser on either side. They were moving into a more exposed area.

She noticed too how the path was steadily becoming steeper, requiring more effort to climb. Her legs were feeling the strain. It had been a long time since she'd embarked on physical activity on this scale. If only I'd gone on the morning runs at Pirate Academy, she thought wryly. Looking ahead, she saw the captain had come to a stop.

Why? She wondered if he was finding it difficult too. She caught up with him and waited for the others.

"The path grows steeper here," the captain warned. Saying no more, he began walking on. The others followed. As the path turned, a shaft of moonlight illuminated the mountainside.

Shanti gave a small cry. Grace just shook her head. The light was meagre, but it showed the path continuing right up the mountain on a cliff-face so steep that the track had to zigzag back and forth. The path was cut into the rock and was barely a footstep wide, with a perilous drop.

"He cannot be serious," Shanti moaned.

"Is it bad?" Lorcan asked.

"It's steep," Grace said, looking up at the sheer, exposed rock-face. Her own heart was beating fast. She was OK with heights – unlike her brother – but this was something else. She had to agree with Shanti, this challenge could well be beyond them. And yet she had absolute faith in the captain. She couldn't believe he would have led them here to fail.

"It *is* steep," Grace repeated, "but we can do it. We'll just have to be very careful."

"It's a sheer drop!" Shanti said. "And the wind's getting up too. Can't you feel how cold it is? My face is numb."

Grace didn't think it would be helpful to point out to Shanti that as she was the only one dressed in fur, the others were feeling even colder.

"We can make it," she said instead. "The captain

wouldn't be leading us this way if he thought we'd fail."
Her words were gentle but firm. She looked ahead,
realising that the lights of the captain's cape were now
growing faint. She wondered why he had walked on so far
ahead of them. Why didn't he stay to help them?

"Come on," she said. "We can do this. Lorcan, do you
want us to hold on to you or would you rather walk
alone?"

"Let's try to carry on as we are for the moment," he said.
"If I need you to guide me, I'll say."

"All right, then," Grace said, turning to Shanti. "Do you
want to lead for a bit?"

"*Lead?*" Shanti seemed surprised.

"Yes," Grace said. "One of us needs to go ahead of
Lorcan and one behind. Which would you prefer?"

Shanti shook her head. "I can't do it, Grace. I can't climb
that path."

"You don't have a choice," Grace said, still calm. "I'm
taking Lorcan up that mountainside because the captain
tells me there's a chance he'll be cured of his blindness up
there. Not a certainty, but a chance. And yes, it *is* my fault
that he's blind and so yes it *is* my fault that he isn't sharing
with you and that you're growing wrinkly and old." She
couldn't stop the rush of emotions and words. "All of this
is my fault, Shanti – not yours, *mine*. But at least I'm
trying to make it better. If we can just get to the top of this
mountain, I think we can sort this out. So for Lorcan, and
for you – though I really don't like you very much – I'm

prepared to give this a try. Now, either you come with us or we leave you here, but as long as Lorcan is willing to climb with me, I'm going on."

Shanti was speechless for a moment.

"I'm willing," Lorcan said.

"Then I'll lead," Shanti said, stepping past Grace and striding up the path.

"Good work, Grace." She heard the whisper in her ear, realising with a start that it was not Lorcan but the captain who was speaking to her. How could he hear her from so far up ahead?

In some ways, Grace thought, it was a blessing that it was so dark. You could block out the fact that the path was bordered by nothingness on one side. You *had* to block out that fact, as much as you could. As long as you kept focused on the steadiness of your footsteps, and remained alert to the turning points, it really wasn't so bad. Shanti was taking the responsibility of leading very seriously and calling out to Lorcan every time he needed to turn. The captain had slowed his pace too, so that he was never very far in front.

Once more, Grace found herself totally absorbed in the rhythm of her movements. She lost track of how far they had come, how high they had climbed. All she knew was that they had to keep going. For however long it took. It was strange making a journey that seemed to have no end point but, in a curious way, it was also a relief.

A noise ahead of her drew her back from her musings. Lorcan had tripped, she saw, alarmed. He had fallen on the path, thank goodness. But his feet had sent scree tumbling down the mountainside.

"Are you OK?" Grace asked, reaching out a hand to him.

"Yes," he said, gathering himself on his feet. "I don't know what happened there."

"It's my fault," Shanti said. "The path is narrower and more broken up here. I should have said."

"It's OK," Lorcan replied. "No harm done." Grace could see his smile in what little light there was.

"Oh," moaned Shanti. "I can't see the captain. Has he gone on ahead? It's so hard to keep up!" She hurried along the narrow track, practically running to keep sight of the captain.

"Be careful!" Grace cried. "Not so fast!"

But Shanti wouldn't heed the warning. She was determined to catch the captain. As Shanti disappeared around the corner, Grace told Lorcan, "I've got to catch her up, to stop her. Wait here!"

"All right," he agreed, relieved to catch his breath.

Grace pressed on ahead. She hadn't got very far when she heard a cry, followed by something that sounded very much like crumbling rock. She felt a wave of dread even before she heard Shanti's strangulated cry. "Help!"

"Shanti!" Grace cried, striding ahead.

As she turned the corner, the sight that confronted her

confirmed her worst fears. Shanti was suspended over the side of the mountain, a sheer drop beneath her. The path had given way around her and all that was keeping her from the abyss was a precarious-looking shrub. A shrub which, by the looks of things, could uproot itself at any moment.

"Shanti!" Grace cried once more, crouching down and extending her arm. "Take hold of me. I'll pull you up."

Grace had never seen such raw terror as she saw now in Shanti's eyes. "No," she rasped. "Grace, I can't. You're not strong enough."

"Oh yes I am," Grace said, though really she wasn't all that confident. She and Shanti were of a similar weight. What if Shanti dragged her down rather than Grace pulling her up? Grace had to shut out the thought. She was going to do this. They were both going to be all right. She reached out her hand. "Come on, Shanti," she said. "All you have to do is let go of that plant and I'll catch you."

"I can't!" But as Shanti spoke, the shrub began to move. The ground was loosening again and, as Shanti closed her eyes and prepared for the worst, Grace reached out and grabbed her arm. "I've got you," she said. "I've got you." Now, all she had to do was pull her up onto the solid patch of path.

But as Grace began to pull, she had the grim realisation that she was *not* strong enough. Now what was she going to do? There was no sign of the captain and there was no way Lorcan could get here without someone leading him.

She felt a rising panic but was determined not to transmit it to Shanti.

"What's wrong?" Shanti asked. "I was right, wasn't I? You're not strong enough! We're both going to die!"

Now Grace faced a terrible dilemma. Either let Shanti fall into the void alone or be dragged down with her. She looked down the brutal drop. There was no way either of them could survive such a fall.

Suddenly, Shanti's weight became lighter. Grace wondered if she had managed to summon some unknown resources deep within herself. Then she saw that another pair of hands were reaching out to hold Shanti. Grace turned and saw a young man crouching beside her on the path. He was dressed in the robes of a shepherd.

"I'll count to three," he said. "Then we pull her up, OK?"

Grace nodded. The man smiled at her. It was a smile which instilled complete confidence and calm in her.

"One, two, *three* . . ."

Grace focused all her strength as they pulled Shanti up and onto the path. She lay on the ground, covered in dirt, sobbing. Grace's own heart was pounding. They had both faced certain death. If it hadn't been for the shepherd, it would have ended very differently. What a miracle he had been passing at that very moment.

"Thank you," Grace said, turning to the man.

But he was nowhere to be seen, gone as mysteriously as he had arrived.

She glanced down at Shanti. "Well done!" she said.

"I nearly died," Shanti said, twisting her head back towards the drop. "We both nearly died!"

"No," Grace said, reaching out and turning Shanti's trembling face towards her. "Don't look down. Don't look back. We must only look forward! Do you understand?"

Shanti nodded, too terrified to speak.

"Wait here!" Grace said. "Catch your breath. I must go and fetch Lorcan, then we'll all go on together."

"No!" Shanti cried out. "Don't leave me!"

"It's just for a moment, just to fetch Lorcan." Grace wavered. "All right, let's get you up on your feet first." She held out her hand and helped Shanti to her feet. The girl was hobbling. For a moment, she feared that Shanti had twisted her ankle or worse. Then she saw what was wrong.

"The heel has come off one of your boots," Grace said.

"Where is it?" Shanti asked.

Grace glanced over the mountainside. "It doesn't matter where it is," she said.

"But what am I supposed to do?" Shanti's voice spiralled into panic. "I can't go on, Grace. I've tried. Haven't I tried? I really have but I can't do this, not with one shoe without a heel." She slumped to the ground and pulled herself into a ball, sobbing.

Grace made a decision. She crouched down and took Shanti's foot in her hand. Grabbing the one remaining heel, she twisted it as powerfully as she could. It came off in her hand.

"What are you *doing*?" cried Shanti.

Saying nothing, Grace threw the redundant heel over the mountainside, to join its partner. Shanti looked at her with rising panic.

"Now, just stand up and see how you balance," she said to Shanti.

"I can't walk without heels!"

"The important thing is, how does your ankle feel? Do you think you've twisted it?"

"But my shoes!" Shanti continued.

"If you're really uncomfortable, we'll swap boots," Grace said. "I think we're the same size."

"You'd do that for me? But . . . but you said you didn't like me."

Grace smiled, in spite of herself. "I don't think you like me very much either, Shanti, but we're in this together. We have to work as a team." Her smile faded and she looked more determinedly at Shanti. "It's vital we get Lorcan to Sanctuary . . . for his sake and for yours. Whatever it takes."

Grace's words hit their target.

Shanti nodded gratefully.

"I'm going to get Lorcan now. He'll be worried about us."

But just as Grace set off, she saw that Lorcan was making his own way towards them. How had he negotiated that tricky and dangerous stretch of path alone? Grace had a sudden image of the shepherd who had helped them just now. Could it be?

"Are you both OK?" Lorcan asked.

"Yes," said Grace. "Yes, we're fine – aren't we, Shanti? Shanti had a fall but she's OK now. Aren't you, Shanti?"

"Yes." Shanti nodded, somehow getting the message not to give Lorcan any further reason to be alarmed. She paused. "Thank you, Grace. Why don't we swap places? You lead for a bit?"

Grace nodded and went to the front of them. She glanced up the dark mountainside. How much further did they have to climb? As the question formed in her head, she suddenly heard a familiar whisper.

"Not far now."

She glanced ahead, seeing the lights flickering on the captain's cape. He must have waited for them, or perhaps even come back for them. But if he had been so near, why hadn't he helped? It seemed there was more than one mystery to ponder on this strange mountainside. But as Grace began thinking further about it, she heard Lorcan call out from behind her.

"Snow!"

For a moment, it seemed a random word. Then she felt it too as the first snowflake rested on her nose. Ordinarily, it would have thrilled her, but not here, not now. A snow flurry was the very last thing they needed if they were ever to make it to the mountaintop.

Soon the path beneath Grace's feet was utterly white. A shiver passed through her. She realised she was being tested to her physical limits.

"It *can't* be much further!" she heard Shanti moan.

"Not long now," said Grace.

"So you keep saying!" Shanti whined.

"Look up ahead," the captain's voice whispered through the breeze.

"Where?" said Shanti. "I can't see anything."

But Grace could see it. There, in the distance, twin lights pierced the darkness. Two flaming torches stood like giant sentinels on either side of the gates. The gates to Sanctuary. They had arrived. At last.

"About time!" sighed Shanti, as she too noticed the light.

"What a whinger!" Lorcan whispered in Grace's ear. Grace smiled. Her thoughts exactly.

"Oh, Lorcan," she said, excitedly. "We're nearly there! What a journey it's been . . . now we're almost at the gates." She looked up ahead. "Can you see?" As the words left her mouth, she could have kicked herself. "Oh, I'm sorry," she said. "I'm so sorry, I didn't mean . . ."

"It's OK," Lorcan said. "Don't upset yourself, Grace. Why don't you describe it to me so I can borrow your eyes to see?"

"There are gates made of iron," she said. "They're twice as tall as you, I'd say. There are spikes along the top and below is an intricate circular pattern, a bit like a clockface or sundial. It's very beautiful."

And that was how they came to the end of their journey – Grace describing the ornate fretwork of the vast iron gates lit by torches as they finally arrived at Sanctuary.

Until they reached the gates themselves, and Grace fell silent. Suddenly the magnitude of their journey caught up with her. It wasn't just a question of how far they had come but the importance of what lay ahead. This was the place that would decide Lorcan's future – a future which she already felt was as deeply entwined with her own as the thick mountain vines were within the iron fretwork of the gates. It was impossible to separate one from the other.

CHAPTER FIVE
Another Kind of Dance

Above the dance-floor, where Connor even now turns his partner, is the row of curtained booths where those wanting – or *needing* – privacy, can go. As the tango music starts, all the curtains are closed. But the melody soon pierces one of the booths. A pale hand reaches out and gently pushes back the velvet curtain. Just a fraction. Then a nervous eye leans into the gap, glancing down to the chequered floor.

The sight of the dancers is heartbreaking. There is little finesse in their steps, but there is so much life down there. So much life in their faces and limbs. The papery hand, the nervous watery eye, would do anything for a drop of that life.

Three pairs of the dancers are familiar. Of course they are. And it is as if they are flaunting their aliveness before his eyes. Once, he would have been down there himself, but now something much stronger than a velvet curtain separates them. They are on one side of it, striding and twisting across the floor. And he is on the other side, reduced to the role of watcher.

The sound of footsteps. A voice – high and light – from outside the other end of the booth.

"May I come in?"

He has barely formed the word "yes" on his cracked lips, when the curtain opens and a serving girl pokes her head into the gloom.

"Good evening, sir. Are you in need of something to drink?"

He nods. Yes, he thinks. How well she puts the question. Yes, he is very much in need of something to drink.

She is watching him, waiting for more of an answer. She watches him, but she does not truly *see* him. How can she? It is pitch dark inside the booth.

"Your candle is out, sir. Here, I'll light it."

"No," he says. "No, I don't like . . . fire."

But his words are too slow and her hands are too swift. The candle is lit and now it grows and glows inside its glass. He shivers at the sight of it.

"You need something to warm you, sir. Look, you're shivering."

"What do you recommend?" he rasps, trying to keep the edge from his voice.

She shrugs. She has no idea of the danger she is in. "We've got everything you could wish for here. Rum, beer, wine . . . your choice, sir."

He looks at her. She's a pretty thing. A memory stirs. But he cannot be sure if he remembers her for herself or if she just has a certain look. Lately, this has been happening a lot. Faces merge. He finds it hard to distinguish one from another. That's why he must act before it grows worse. He glances down at the dance-floor once more. The music comes to an end and the dancers hug, congratulating themselves and each other on their prowess. After the merest pause, the tango begins anew. The partners swap but the dance continues. He lets drop the curtain and feels water in his eyes.

"Are you all right, sir?"

So, she's still here. Part of him wants to tell her to get out, to run away. But, of course, he does not.

"Yes, I'm . . . all right."

"Are you sure?" She steps closer to him, leaning in. "You look so pale. Like you've seen a ghost. I think maybe a brandy . . ."

"Yes," he says. "Yes, there's an idea. Fetch me a brandy." Let her go. Let her go, and he will take his leave too – before anything happens. Before any line is crossed.

The candle flickers. She slides the candle-glass along the table. Now, for the first time, she sees him properly.

"It's funny," she says. "You look so like someone I used to know. Well, not *know* exactly. Someone who came in here. Awful popular he was. A pirate lad."

"Really?" He wants her to go. He doesn't want to hear this. And yet he does. He needs her to stay.

"Yes, sir. You're the spit of him . . . You could be his twin."

A twin? He smiles at the thought.

"Terrible sad it was," she continues.

"What's that?"

"Terrible sad, what happened to him."

"What did happen to him?"

"Killed, sir. Killed in a duel on a pirate deck, they say."

"A duel." The word sounds so noble. Not like his memory of that day. The hot sword. The unleashing of his blood. The life gushing out of him. The dying of the voices around him until everything was cold and silent and lonely . . .

He is there again now. Not for the first time. And somehow, he cannot leave that place. Not yet.

"What was his name?" he asks. "This pirate lad – what was his name?"

"Why, sir, his name was Jez. Jez Stukeley." She smiles. "A handsome pirate."

He smiles too. Softly, he asks, "Do you think I'm still handsome?"

"I should be going, sir."

Yes, he thinks. You should have been gone long before now. But you stayed. And now the die is cast.

"Stay." As the word slips from his mouth, his hand grips her wrist.

"Ow! You're hurting me."

"I'm sorry," he says, softening his grip. "I'm sorry. I'm

not used to . . . company. I've been away for some time . . ."

"Have you been on a voyage, sir?" she says, her innate inquisitiveness pushing aside her fear.

"A voyage?" he says. "Yes, I suppose you could say that. I've been on one hell of a journey . . . Perhaps you could sit with me – just for a bit – and I'll tell you something about it?"

She looks torn. "I'm not supposed to sit down on my shift, sir."

"Please," he says. "Just for a minute or two? After all, what is time?"

"You don't half say some funny things, sir." She smiles. "All right, then. I'll sit just for a minute while you tell me about your voyage. And then I'll fetch you a— wait a minute!" She pauses. There is a sudden light in her eyes. "What did you mean . . . when you asked me if you were *still* handsome?" The pitch of her voice rises. "What did you mean by that?"

"I think you know," he says, as he pulls her towards him. "I think you know just what I meant."

It is early in the morning when Sugar Pie draws back the velvet curtain. She and the other servers are doing their rounds, throwing out the clientele who are reluctant – or actually unable – to budge.

The candle has long burned out and it is dark inside the booth. But Sugar Pie can smell death. As she makes out the figure collapsed across the table, a deep pain breaks in her chest and she falls to her knees.

"What is it?" asks the boy at her side.

"Go and get Ma," Sugar Pie says. Her voice is hoarse.

"But why? What's wrong? Let me see—"

"Go and get Ma," she says, more forcefully this time. The boy doesn't need telling again.

"Oh, Jenny," Sugar Pie says, surveying the wound on the girl's chest. "Poor little Jenny. Who did this to you? And why?"

"What's up?" Ma Kettle says, stepping inside the booth. Sugar Pie cannot find the words, so she simply moves aside to let Ma see for herself. "Oh no! Not Jenny!" Turning, Sugar Pie sees a tear fall from her boss's eye. She hasn't seen that in a while.

"Stabbed," Ma says, horrified. "Right here. Right under our noses."

Sugar Pie cannot look any more. So much blood. She glances down at the girl's face. And notices the strangest thing.

"Look, Ma," she says. "Look – it's as if she's smiling. In spite of everything."

Ma Kettle sighs. "She's gone to a better place, that's why. Our little Jenny Petrel has flown to a much better place."

Sugar Pie wishes she could believe that, but something tells her otherwise.

CHAPTER SIX

Arrival

The weary travellers passed through the iron gates. Ahead of them, a column of lamps illuminated an empty courtyard, its surface covered in a thin layer of ice, which reflected the velvet-black night sky. The courtyard was bordered by a walkway and low wooden buildings on three sides. As far as Grace could see, there were no doors or windows in these buildings – except for a pair of doors in the centre of the block facing them, on the far side of the yard.

"We made it!" Grace said to Lorcan, feeling her spirits rise once more. They were perhaps only moments away from meeting the great Mosh Zu Kamal.

"Yes," Lorcan said, his voice low and hoarse. "We made it."

Grace wondered why he didn't sound more excited. Now their strenuous journey was over, the rest should be plain sailing. Lorcan would be given into the care of Mosh Zu Kamal and the healing process could begin. Wasn't that cause for celebration? But Lorcan looked cold and wan and his face seemed utterly devoid of hope. Clearly, the climb had fatigued him more than he had let on. Even the captain looked tired. Now, the effort of their expedition was catching up with all of them. Perhaps, also, Lorcan was apprehensive about his treatment and what lay ahead. Grace squeezed his hand. "Don't worry," she said. "It's all going to be fine. You'll see."

Looking up, Grace saw that several figures were milling about. They were all dressed alike in matching crimson robes. Clearly, the new arrivals had been noted, for now two of the robe-wearers were striding towards them. As they reached the expedition party, they drew down their hoods. Grace saw that they were a young woman and man.

"Welcome to Sanctuary," said the woman in a soft, precise voice. "It is an honour indeed to meet you and to welcome you and your company to this special place." Her bright eyes surveyed the group. "My name is Dani."

Her companion smiled, warmly. "Good evening, Captain," he said. "Perhaps you remember me from your last visit?"

"Indeed I do, Olivier," the captain said. "How good to see you again."

Olivier shook the captain's gloved hand. "Mosh Zu is so looking forward to seeing you again." He turned to the others and said, "To those of you here for the first time, I should explain. We are two of Mosh Zu's assistants. But as you can see," he pointed at the other robe-wearers who were walking between buildings, "there are quite a few of us."

The Captain introduced each of his party to Dani and Olivier. The assistants smiled warmly at Grace and Shanti. When they came to Lorcan, Olivier clasped him by the hand. "You are brave indeed to make this journey, brother," he said.

"Brave, or foolhardy?" Lorcan asked, with a laugh.

Olivier squeezed his hand once more. "Just brave, I think," he said.

Behind them, the tall iron gates clanked shut. A lock was fastened. The sound of metal on metal echoed like a dull bell. The sound took Grace back to *The Nocturne*, to the tolling of the bells for nightfall and sunrise. The sunrise bell. The one Lorcan should have obeyed. The one he had ignored to save her. What a chain of memories a lock sliding into place could trigger.

"Come," Olivier said. "You're shivering. The air is biting cold here. Let's get you into the warmth."

He and Dani led them along the walkway, which had been cleared of ice, and around the courtyard. They came to the doors Grace had noticed earlier. Olivier pushed these open and ushered the travellers in. Then he turned to Dani. "It's OK," he said. "I can handle this from here. Aren't you due to deliver the flasks to Block 2 about now?"

Dani nodded and, bidding the others farewell, set off across the courtyard. Grace wondered where – and what – Block 2 was. And what flasks was Dani going to deliver? But she was soon distracted as she followed Olivier.

Inside, the light was dim but, as Grace's eyes adjusted, she saw they were in a long, narrow corridor, lit by more lamps, this time suspended on low chains just above their heads. The metal lamps swayed a little as the wind swept inside. The flames guttered, then settled again, as Olivier closed the doors behind them.

Olivier smiled. "Welcome to Sanctuary, my friends. You are now in the Corridor of Lights. Please, walk this way."

As they proceeded along the corridor, Grace felt her sense of anticipation rising. With every step, they were coming nearer to their meeting with Mosh Zu Kamal. She was intrigued to meet the great man – the one that the captain called his "guru" and who, he said, had mapped out the workings of *The Nocturne* so long ago. It was Mosh Zu, the captain had told her, who had helped him to make a refuge from the world and to welcome into it "the outsiders of the outsiders" – vampires who had been exiled from regular society and finally, in the cruellest twist, from vampire society itself, because they rejected the constant hunt for blood. It was Mosh Zu who had devised the system of donors, and who had helped the captain to train himself to feast no more on blood.

Grace was eager to meet and talk to him, but, she reminded herself, they had more pressing business here.

The most important thing was to heal Lorcan. That was why they had struggled up the mountainside.

They turned a corner and the corridor grew a little wider. It was a good thing too because, on either side, the walls were groaning with shelves covered in trinkets and photographs. There was not a patch of spare wall and Grace could see that, in places, the items on the shelves were packed three and four deep. It was like walking through a junk shop, or a shrine. It induced in Grace the same feelings of intrigue and sadness. Where had these things come from? Who did they once belong to? They were nothing but clutter now, but once they had meant something, perhaps everything, to someone.

As if reading her thoughts, Olivier announced, "This is the Corridor of Discards. These are the things which those who enter Sanctuary have left behind."

Grace was even more intrigued by this, realising that the items, like the vampires who sought Mosh Zu's help, had come from all over the world and from vastly different historic eras. Their discards made a strange collage of the world that had been left behind. Grace wanted to linger but Olivier and the captain maintained a brisk pace. The corridor turned another corner, this one devoid of possessions, Grace noticed with a twinge of regret.

"What's that smell?" Shanti's voice cut across her thoughts. Grace glanced at her, to find Shanti wrinkling her little upturned nose.

Olivier smiled at her. "It's butter," he said.

"Butter? Is someone making pancakes?"

He shook his head. "We use it to fuel the lamps here."

"It's sickly," Shanti said, wincing. "Can't you get candles up here?"

Olivier kept silent. Grace could see in his eyes that Shanti was trying his patience.

The corridor turned again, and Grace realised that their path was sloping down at an increasing gradient. "Are we going underground?" she asked Olivier.

"Yes," he said. "The main part of the compound is underground."

Of course, Grace thought. That way, the vampires could move about freely without fear of being exposed to the daylight. She was intrigued to see more of the place. The corridor they were walking along made her think of pictures she'd seen of people entering the pyramids of Egypt. But, from what Olivier said, she guessed that Sanctuary was more of an inverted pyramid, cutting down into the heart of the mountain.

Then Grace noticed something else. Suspended from the ceiling on a thin rope, between the lights, were ribbons. They hung down like cobwebs, different colours and lengths.

"What are these?" she asked.

"Ribbons," Olivier said, shortly. "We are in the Corridor of Ribbons."

"Yes," Grace persisted. "But what do they signify?"

"I think I should let Mosh Zu explain that," he said.

Grace looked up at the ribbons, fluttering above her. She could tell that there was an importance attached to these simple strips of cloth. All the more so, she realised, if she must wait for Mosh Zu to explain their significance.

As the corridor turned once more, Grace spied another set of doors.

Olivier pushed them open and Grace saw that the chamber beyond was squarer in shape and lit more brightly. The floor was tiled and there were chairs and tables in there – the first chairs they had seen since leaving the ship.

Shanti's eyes lit up at the sight of them. "At last! I'd kill for a sit-down."

"Be my guest," Olivier said, pulling out a chair for her and placing a cushion on it. "Make yourself comfortable. We shan't keep you waiting long."

Shanti sat down, sighing in pleasure as her small body sank into the silken cushion.

Grace eyed the chair beside Shanti enviously, but Olivier propelled her forward with a light touch. "Not much further, now," he said.

Grace looked at him quizzically. She saw that the captain hadn't stopped either, but instead was walking on towards another pair of doors. Grace realised that this chamber was only an anteroom.

"Come," Olivier said, opening the doors. "Mosh Zu is waiting to meet you."

Grace looked back towards Shanti. Was she to be excluded

from an audience with Mosh Zu? Shanti wasn't exactly Grace's favourite person, but it hardly seemed fair to exclude her. Especially after her particular ordeals on the journey. Grace looked at Olivier, then turned towards Shanti, who had removed her shoes and was rubbing her tired feet.

"Shanti!" Grace called.

"*Whaaat?*" came the answering whine. Grace took a calming breath. Shanti certainly didn't make herself easy to like.

"Put your shoes back on and come with us," Grace said.

"But Mosh Zu did not invite . . ." Olivier began.

"That's not fair," Grace said. "We all came here together. It was as hard for Shanti as it was for the rest of us, worse in some ways. She fell . . ."

"It doesn't matter," Olivier said. "Mosh Zu knows his mind. She is merely a donor. After I have taken you to Mosh Zu, I will take her to the donor quarters."

Grace was dismayed – at Olivier's dismissive tone but even more so at Mosh Zu's purported attitude to Shanti. The relationship between vampires and donors was interdependent. The captain had always talked respectfully of the donors and the gift they proffered to their vampire partners. There was, surely, no greater gift you could offer than your very own life-blood. Whatever you might feel about the character of an individual donor, you had to respect them. It surprised and angered her that Olivier and Mosh Zu would not do so. Her rising fury was stalled by the sound of the captain's whisper.

He nodded to her and addressed Olivier. "Grace is right," he said. "Shanti has earned her audience before Mosh Zu Kamal. Besides, Mosh Zu is a bountiful host and I'm sure he would want to welcome all of us to Sanctuary."

Grace saw Olivier flush even as he nodded. "As you wish, Captain."

It was a victory of sorts, Grace thought, but she still felt rather cross. She had liked Olivier initially but now she was rapidly cooling towards him.

But as Shanti joined them and the four of them followed him into the next room her anger melted away, easily replaced by other distractions. This room was larger than the one they had come from. Its floor was tiled but it was largely devoid of furniture and its decorations were basic – a few simple wall hangings. Grace's eyes settled on the shaved head of a man whose back was turned towards them. He was lighting candles at the far side of the room.

Behind her, Grace heard the doors of the room close. Olivier stepped forward.

"Your guests have arrived," he announced, then stepped backwards.

For a moment, the other man showed no sign he had heard the words. He continued lighting the candles.

At last, he turned and began walking towards them. He was dressed simply in a white vest and baggy brown cloth trousers, tied and folded over at the waist. His feet appeared to be bare.

Grace couldn't believe her eyes. She had expected the

guru of the Vampirates to be an old man. But Mosh Zu, if this indeed was he, was a young man. He stepped forwards, his face and body largely in shadow. Unless this dim light was deceptive, he was only a few years older than herself. And then some, she reminded herself. He might *look* to be in his early twenties but this was only an indication of the age he had been when he had died. Or rather, she reminded herself, when he had *crossed*.

"Mosh Zu," she heard the captain say.

"Captain," answered the man.

So this really was Mosh Zu. Grace couldn't help but feel a little cheated. She had expected a wise old man. She watched as he and the captain bowed before each other, then he stepped closer and they hugged. It was perhaps the most human thing she had ever seen the captain do, a reminder that, in spite of the clothes that covered almost all of his body, there was, if not a heart, then at least a soul alive within the armoured shell.

"And this is Grace," said the captain. "I believe she has a special gift."

"We have heard as much," said Mosh Zu.

Grace was surprised and flattered by their talk, but, as Mosh Zu turned his face towards her, she had another shock.

It was the face she had seen on the mountainside – the shepherd who had helped to rescue Shanti from her fall and then disappeared into the night.

He smiled at her, his dark eyes twinkling in the half-light.

"Welcome, Grace Tempest," he said, looking at her. She felt his gaze go deep into her. Then he turned and his eyes took the measure of the rest of his guests.

"I welcome you all to Sanctuary," he said. "May each of you find just what you need here."

"All *I* need is a good lie-down," Shanti muttered. For once, no one rose to the bait.

Grace looked at Lorcan. He was shaking. She took his hand in hers once more. She didn't dare speak, but she tried to send the words through to him. *It's OK, Lorcan. It will all be OK.*

"Yes," said Mosh Zu, smiling at them, beatifically. "Yes, Grace Tempest. You are quite right, I think."

Grace was startled, though not surprised. Of course it made sense that he should be able to read her thoughts, just as the captain could.

"Well," Mosh Zu continued. "You've had a long, tiring journey and it is growing light outside. Time for us all to sleep, don't you think? Let us show you to your rooms. We have a big night ahead of us tomorrow."

CHAPTER SEVEN

Night Watch

"What's up with that Moonshine kid?" Bart asked as he, Connor and Brenden Gonzalez strode out along the jetty, back towards the ship.

"He was certainly giving you two some funny looks," Gonzalez said.

"I know!" Connor said. "It was like he had a bone to pick with us, like we'd done him some wrong before. But how can that be? We've never even met the guy!"

"You know what?" Bart asked. "He looks like the kind of kid who's got a chip on his shoulder the size of *The Diablo* . . . not to mention that nasty spread of acne. Bit of a mummy's boy too! Did you see the way he hung around Trofie's skirts?"

Connor nodded. "*She's* a little scary," he said.

"More than a little," Gonzalez agreed. "Barbarro seems like a good man, though. I know he and Molucco are at odds but you can tell there's a basic decency about him. I liked him."

"Me too," agreed Connor. "I hope he and Captain Wrathe – *our* Captain Wrathe – can work out their differences."

Bart nodded. "You know what? Just sit those two down alone with a big bottle of rum and some dates for their pet snakes, and I reckon they'd be back on track by sunrise. But with Trofie and the squirt in tow, I don't know . . . I'm not sure *they're* really back to settle an argument so much as to start one."

"What do you mean?" Connor said.

"I'm not sure," Bart said. "I've just got a funny feeling in my water."

"That's what happens when you mix your drinks," smirked Gonzalez.

Ignoring him, Bart continued. "We'll just have to keep our eyes and ears open and see what goes down."

By now they had reached the ship and began making their way up the gangplank.

"Man, I'm going to sleep well tonight," Gonzalez said, as he jumped onto the deck. He yawned and stretched out his arms. "Are you boys coming to crash or hanging out on deck a while?"

Bart looked at him with a grin. "I think someone's forgotten we're all on the night watch. You'd better get some espresso down you or you're going to be as much use as a custard cutlass!"

"No, no," Gonzalez said, shaking his head. "I forgot, is all. Hold the espresso, I'll be fine!"

"What's that noise?" Connor asked, five minutes later.

"Check out Sleeping Beauty!" Bart pointed up to the crow's nest.

Above them, Gonzalez was slumped against the edge of the barrel in an unpromising contortion, one arm dangling limply over the side. Now Connor realised the strange whinnying noises were his mate's snores.

"How can he possibly sleep up there? Standing up?"

Bart shook his head. "I wouldn't exactly call that standing. Thing about Gonzalez is he can sleep pretty much anywhere, anyhow," he said. "Fat lot of use he is. Let's just hope the waves are kind to us tonight. Wouldn't want to wake our little baby!"

Connor was tired himself, but pleasantly buzzed by the events of the day. Days which began with conquering your fear and ended with dancing in the arms of Sugar Pie had much to recommend them. And then there was the arrival of Barbarro and his strange family. Whatever they were here for, it was intriguing to get to see the rest of Molucco's family at first hand.

He walked back up the deck towards the prow, looking beyond the ship's edge out in the direction of the horizon. It was a starry night and, as was his habit, he began searching for the constellations. There was Ophiuchus, the Serpent Bearer. Connor smiled to himself at the name, thinking of the two Captains Wrathe with the snakes in their hair. Perhaps in millennia to come, they'd name constellations after Molucco and Barbarro. But, for now, there was Ophiuchus. He remembered how he'd struggled to see it as a kid, and how his dad had reassured him. "Don't worry, Con. Most of the stars in this one are quite dim – just look for the shape of a teapot." Ever since, he'd always thought of this constellation as the Giant Celestial Teapot.

Looking out at the night sky, he thought, of course, of Grace. Where was she now? Was she gazing at the same stars? Maybe she was thinking about him? He missed her. He knew she had her own journey to make but he hated her not being around. He hoped she'd be back again soon. He was tired of saying goodbye to the people who mattered most to him – his dad, Jez, Grace . . .

"Penny for 'em."

Connor looked up and found Bart at his side.

"I was just checking in with Ophiuchus," Connor said, with a smile.

"Oh you was, was ya?" Bart said, nodding. "OK, I have to confess I have zero idea what you're talking about."

Connor grinned and pointed into the sky. "Otherwise known as the Great Celestial Teapot!"

Bart looked out into the sky, then back towards Connor. "You know what, Tempest? Sometimes I forget what a strange fruit you are!"

"Strange!" Connor exclaimed. "Who are you calling strange?" He squared up to Bart, tensing his body.

"Oh you want some, do you?" Bart said, amused.

Suddenly Connor shook his head. His eyes were wide and he was shaking uncontrollably.

"What is it, buddy? You look like you've seen a ghost!"

Connor took advantage of Bart's momentary distraction to hurl himself at him.

"Oh, you dirty . . ." Bart regained his composure immediately, standing up to his full height, with Connor clinging onto him.

Suddenly Bart grabbed Connor and lifted him up across his shoulders, spinning him around his head.

"Aargh! Stop!" Connor cried.

"Know what they call this?" Bart said. "The windmill! Can't think why, can you?"

"Stop!" Connor wailed. "I'm getting dizzy! And I feel . . . sick!"

"Say please!" Bart said, mercilessly spinning him even faster.

Connor was weak with laughter and dizziness. Finally he managed to push out the word. "Please!" he moaned. "Please . . . put me *down*!"

"Well, since you asked nicely!" Bart dropped Connor into one of the light boats. He landed with a thud and lay there, sprawled on the tarpaulin and rope, dazed for a moment. He still felt like he was spinning.

Bart towered over him, waggling his finger. "Now,

there's a lesson see, young Tempest. You may be growing faster than a macaranga tree but you're not ready to take on Bartholomew Pearce just yet."

Connor regained his breath, finally sitting up again in the light boat. He was trying to come up with a witty retort but no inspiration was forthcoming. Suddenly, he saw something which took away not only his words, but also his breath.

"What's the matter?" Bart looked concerned. "You're shaking again. Oh . . ." He grinned. "I get it. You can't play that trick twice in one night!"

All Connor could do was shake his head, his eyes wide with fear and incomprehension.

Behind Bart, a pale face loomed closer. A face he had never expected to see again.

Trembling, Connor pointed.

Bart turned.

There, standing on the deck before them, was Jez.

"How do, lads," he said. "How's about a smile for an old friend?"

Chapter Eight

The Healer's Art

"Follow me," Mosh Zu said. "Lorcan, your room is on the next level."

As they followed the path down still further, Grace realised that this was not so different from being on a ship and going down to the cabins. Perhaps, she thought, the underground nature of Sanctuary was not merely designed to prevent the vampires from exposure to the light, but also to prepare them for life aboard *The Nocturne*.

"Very good, Grace," said Mosh Zu. She had the feeling he was watching her intently, yet when she glanced his way, his face was not looking at her at all, only forward. She still couldn't get over how young he was . . . or, at least, how young he seemed. He carried himself with strength and vigour. The skin on his face was as smooth as a mask. You could, if you chose to, describe it as handsome. He was not at all as she had expected.

"Thank you," Mosh Zu said, smiling. "I shall take that as a compliment."

Grace blushed. She had grown used to the captain reading her thoughts, but now Mosh Zu too? He was a stranger to her. It made her feel exposed. Even now, he could be reading these thoughts. Where was she supposed to hide her secrets?

"Don't try to hide from me," Mosh Zu said. "It's good you are so open. Others' minds are like overgrown forests, full of writhing branches. You are uncluttered, like the fresh mountain air. Trust me, Grace, this is good. This is very good indeed."

She blushed once more, in spite of herself. If only he would direct his attentions elsewhere. Whether in response to this, or of his own volition, he did.

"Lorcan Furey," Mosh Zu announced, coming to a stop. "This is your room."

He opened up a small chamber. It was, like the other rooms they had walked through, dimly lit. There was a single bed in the centre of the room and a chair in the corner. Above the bed and on one of the side walls were hangings, similar to those in the hall above. They were, Grace supposed, where windows might have been.

"All the rooms are more or less the same," Mosh Zu said. "Plain and simple. I hope you will be comfortable here."

Lorcan found his way to the bed and sat down. He let out a long sigh and reached down to untie his boots.

"Some rest will do you good," Mosh Zu said. "Soon, the

sun will rise and you must sleep through the hours of light."

Grace watched as Lorcan's fingers struggled to find his laces. She was about to help him but a sudden instinct held her back. Somehow she knew that this was something he had to do for himself. She turned to Mosh Zu and saw that he was nodding at her. Had he read her thought or sent her his own?

"Are you going to examine his wound?" she asked out loud.

Mosh Zu smiled. "You are a step ahead of me, Grace." He turned towards Lorcan. They both watched as he eased off the second of his boots. "Let us get you settled on the bed, Lorcan. And then, if you'll permit me, I shall indeed examine your wound."

Lorcan nodded. "Of course, sir."

Mosh Zu shook his head. "There's no need to call me sir. I would much prefer you to call me Mosh Zu."

"All right," Lorcan said, with a nod.

"Come on." Olivier began bustling the others out of the room. "I'll take you to your rooms and we'll leave Mosh Zu in peace to make his diagnosis."

Grace was disappointed. She was so eager to know Mosh Zu's verdict on Lorcan's wound.

"I think Grace would like to stay while I examine her friend," Mosh Zu said. "That's right, isn't it?"

"Yes," she said. "If that's all right . . . I mean, with you too, Lorcan. I don't want to get in the way."

74

"It's fine by me," Lorcan said, reaching towards her and squeezing her hand.

"Well, if *she* stays, *I* stay," Shanti said, reaching out for Lorcan's other hand.

"No," Mosh Zu said softly but firmly. "No, I think not."

Shanti continued to grip Lorcan's hand. "I'm staying," she said. "Grace is nothing to him . . ."

Lorcan was about to protest but Shanti was on a roll. "I'm his donor. He's got my blood running through his veins. Or he would have if he stopped messing about and started feeding again."

"I'm not messing about," Lorcan said, wearily. "I have no hunger."

"No hunger!" Shanti snapped. "Well find some! What kind of a vampire suddenly loses his taste for blood? It's unheard of!"

"No." Lorcan shook his head. "You don't understand."

"Come on," Olivier said, putting a hand on Shanti's shoulder. "You're upsetting him."

"Get your hand off me!" Shanti said, tears of rage in her eyes. "I've every right to upset him. Lord knows, he's caused *me* enough upset!"

The captain had been silent until now, but now he spoke, his soft whisper like balm on the tension of the room. "Perhaps, Shanti, it *would* be better if you and I waited outside. We can hear Mosh Zu's diagnosis as soon as he has made it."

Shanti said nothing. Her hand slipped free of Lorcan's,

though as Grace watched, she wasn't entirely sure that this was of Shanti's own volition. There was a strange, beatific expression on the girl's face as she walked towards the door. They watched as she exited into the hallway. Olivier stepped out after her.

"Thank you, captain," said Mosh Zu. "You, of course, *are* most welcome to stay while I make my examination."

"It's all right," the captain said, with a shake of his head. "I'm sure Grace will prove an able assistant. I shall leave you to your work and wait with the others outside for your diagnosis."

Mosh Zu looked at him, then nodded as the captain walked out of the room. The door swung shut behind him. Grace felt a slight chill. Suddenly, she was incredibly nervous. The moment she had waited for – the moment they had all waited for, toiled up the mountainside for – was fast approaching. But what if Mosh Zu's examination only confirmed her worst fears? Maybe it was better to live in ignorance and hope.

"Let's take this one step at a time," Mosh Zu said, smiling reassuringly at her. "Now, Lorcan, are you comfortable there on the bed?"

Lorcan nodded.

"I'm going to put you into a light sleep," Mosh Zu explained. "It will help us to make a deeper connection. Is that all right with you?"

"Whatever you need to do," Lorcan said. Then he smiled. "Why, I nearly called you 'doc' then!"

Mid-chuckle, Lorcan's head suddenly hung limp. Grace saw that Mosh Zu's hand was resting on the back of Lorcan's neck. He had been so fast, she hadn't even seen him reach out and touch him. She was amazed, and intrigued, at how quickly he had put Lorcan "under".

"Would you help me, Grace?" he asked now.

"Yes," she said, wondering what she could do.

"Would you remove the bandages for me?"

This she could certainly do! She'd been changing Lorcan's bandages ever since returning to *The Nocturne*. Now, Mosh Zu gently raised Lorcan's head, allowing Grace to untie the knot she herself had fastened earlier. She carefully lifted the cloth from his face. As the bandage came off, they both looked down at the wound.

"You've seen this before?" Mosh Zu asked her.

She nodded. "Several times."

"Does it show *any* sign of improvement to you?" Mosh Zu asked.

She looked down. She could almost persuade herself that the livid colours of Lorcan's scar were lightening, but she realised that this had more to do with the soft light in this room than any change on his face. As much as she wanted to see signs of improvement, the wound looked exactly the same as always.

"No," she said, shaking her head, glumly. "No, I wish I could say different, but it's just the same."

"And, out of interest, what have you been dressing this with?"

"Just a touch of yoghurt," she said. "I wasn't sure what else to do. My dad always used to use yoghurt when Connor and I got sunburned. I remember it being very soothing on tender skin. They had some in the kitchen on *the Nocturne*, so I thought I'd try it."

Mosh Zu smiled.

"Did I do something stupid?" Grace asked, suddenly embarrassed.

He shook his head. "I'm not laughing at you, Grace. I was just thinking that you do, as I have been told, have something of the healer's art about you."

"The healer's art? Really?"

He nodded. Now, she was pleased.

"Do not be dismayed that the wound has not yet shown signs of healing. It will be a slow process for Lorcan. Vampire skin takes much longer to mend than mortal skin. Lorcan does not have the same quantity or complexity of cells running through his body as you do. The blood he takes is needed for more basic functions – the life force, if you care to characterise it as such. He needs the blood to help him heal, but it cannot easily be diverted to cure a wound like this. We have to direct it there."

Grace nodded, but then a dark thought came into her head. "But Lorcan hasn't been taking blood," she said.

"Quite so," Mosh Zu said. "Quite so. And that is a further challenge to the healing process. We must encourage him to start feeding again."

Grace nodded determinedly. She was prepared to do

whatever it would take to bring Lorcan back to full health. If he had to drain every last drop of blood from Shanti's small body, he would have to do so. Grace shivered at the thought.

"The yoghurt you applied has helped to ease his pain," Mosh Zu said. "But I'm going to prescribe a slightly more intensive treatment. I shall have Olivier make up an elder salve. You might find it interesting to watch him do this."

She nodded. "Yes please! So, you think he *can* be cured, then?"

Mosh Zu nodded. "There's no problem with this wound. No problem at all. It's just a matter of time. As long as we get some blood back into his system and apply the salve on a regular basis, you'll watch these angry burns fade away. He'll look as good as new."

"And he'll see again. He'll be able to see again!"

Grace felt elated. Mosh Zu was definitely living up to his reputation. They'd only just arrived at Sanctuary and already he knew how to set Lorcan on the road to recovery. Now Mosh Zu indicated for Grace to replace the bandages. Once more, he lifted Lorcan's head to make things easier for her. She tied the knot and then stepped back from the bed.

As she did so, Mosh Zu spoke once more. "I don't want to upset you, Grace. But whilst the surface wound is fairly easily dealt with, I suspect there are complications here."

"Complications? What kind of complications?"

"I'm going to perform a deeper examination," Mosh Zu

said. "You may find this distressing. It's up to you whether you wish to stay or step outside to join the others."

"No," Grace said, standing firm. "I'll stay." Whatever was going to happen, she wanted to be there for Lorcan.

"Very well," Mosh Zu said. "But I want you to prepare yourself."

Now he was frightening her. What was he about to do? All kinds of dark thoughts rushed through her fevered imagination.

"I'm going to put my hand on his thorax," Mosh Zu said, his calm voice helping to slow the rush of terrors in her head. "You know the thorax? It's the part of the body between his neck and diaphragm. It is a very important part of the body for a vampire." He turned to Grace. "Have you ever watched him share?"

She shook her head. "No," she said. Then she remembered. "Except, one time, I saw him and Shanti afterwards. They were sleeping."

"But you've not actually watched him, or any of the others, in the act of taking blood?"

She shook her head, cross with herself for feeling repelled at the thought.

"Well, when they feed," Mosh Zu continued, "they bite into their donor's thorax."

Grace was surprised. "I always thought that they bit their vict— I mean their *donor*, in the neck."

"Of course!" Mosh Zu said, his eyes twinkling. "Everyone thinks that. Why, even some of the vampires

80

themselves. They've read about it in books so, of course, it must be true! They like the whole drama of it. But much the best place to make the connection is through the donor's thorax, just over their . . . well, I'm sure you can work it out for yourself."

"Yes," Grace said, excitedly. "Of course! It's where the donor's heart is."

"Exactly," said Mosh Zu. "But now let us turn our attention from the donors to the vampires. The vampire's own thorax is important too."

Grace was puzzled. "But they – I mean *you* – you don't have hearts, do you?"

"Not in the same way that you do," Mosh Zu said. "Immortality is a gift – perhaps the greatest gift of all. But it comes at a price. There isn't a living pump in the vampire's body, sending blood throughout the body. That dies when the body dies its first death. But, all the same, something remains under the thorax. You could describe it as a well of deep emotion. I suppose you could even say that it's the closest thing we vampires have to a soul."

Grace was wide-eyed. Mosh Zu shrugged. "These are emotive terms. It's a matter of debate what we call it. But, as you will see, this point of Lorcan's body is a seat for the deepest of emotions." He extended his hand towards Lorcan's chest, then turned and paused. "Are you ready?"

She nodded once more, her own heart suddenly racing.

Mosh Zu placed his palm on the left side of Lorcan's chest. Lorcan did not react immediately. Grace wondered if Mosh Zu was able to feel or hear something that was hidden from her.

But then, suddenly, Lorcan opened his mouth and emitted a deep, loud scream. It was a terrible sound – one of the most terrible sounds she had ever heard. It seemed to come from the very depths of his being. She wanted to cover her ears and shut her eyes. But somehow, she refrained from doing so. Instead, she focused on Mosh Zu, who remained in position, maintaining his hold. As the scream eventually subsided, he nodded to himself.

"It's OK," Mosh Zu told her. "Try not to be alarmed. There's more. Yes, here we go again . . ."

Lorcan screamed again, loud and long. How could this *possibly* be OK? Grace watched as Mosh Zu maintained the contact between his hand and Lorcan's chest. Mosh Zu was utterly still, as if alert to the smallest of signals.

"All right," he said at last. "That's all for now." He removed his hand.

Grace felt shaken to her core. "He's in terrible pain, isn't he?" she asked.

"Yes." Mosh Zu nodded. "I thought this might be the case. You see, the wound around his eyes is only a distraction. The *real* wound lies much deeper. It's like a thorn embedded deep within."

Grace felt all her optimism suddenly drain away. "Can you . . .?" She hardly dared to ask. "Can you work on him? Can you remove the thorn?"

"I can try," Mosh Zu said. "It won't be easy, though. It is a delicate operation and one that we cannot rush. We shall not use surgical instruments. We shall use the healing arts. And I would be grateful for your help."

Grace was surprised but pleased. She had a certain foreboding at the scale of the work that lay ahead of them, but whatever it took to get Lorcan better, it would be worth it.

"We've made a start," Mosh Zu said, more brightly. "That scream was the beginning. I know how it must have sounded to you, but actually that was Lorcan letting go of some of this deep-rooted pain."

Grace frowned.

"You find that hard to believe, don't you? But, watch, I'm going to wake him now and you'll see that he is more peaceful." With that, he touched Lorcan's head once more and the boy stirred.

"How are you?" Mosh Zu asked him.

Lorcan smiled. "I feel a little better," he said, as if on cue.

Grace couldn't believe her ears. Mosh Zu turned and nodded at her.

"I'm very tired, all of a sudden," Lorcan said.

"Yes, of course," said Mosh Zu. "You need to rest. Us too. We'll leave you now, but I'll have Olivier check in on you from time to time. And there's a bell beside your bed — if you need anything, simply ring."

Lorcan nodded. As he did so, Grace stifled a yawn. She couldn't help it. Suddenly, she too felt incredibly tired.

Mosh Zu grinned. "Do you hear that, Lorcan Furey? Nurse Tempest has grown weary from ministering to you."

"She's very kind to me," Lorcan said.

"Yes." Mosh Zu nodded. "There is much kindness in Grace. And now I must find rooms for her and her weary travelling companions, don't you think?"

"Yes," Lorcan said. "I think you better had."

"Sleep well, my friend," said Mosh Zu. "Welcome to Sanctuary. I hope you will come to know deep peace within these walls."

Grace reached over and squeezed Lorcan's hand. "Sleep tight," she said. "Don't let the bed bugs bite."

But, as she turned and followed Mosh Zu out of the room, she realised that Lorcan had a whole lot more than bed bugs to worry about.

CHAPTER NINE

Strange Bedfellows

As Grace and Mosh Zu stepped into the corridor, Shanti rushed over. Evidently Lorcan's screams had broken through any sedative spell which might have held her back before.

"What's going on?" she cried. "Why was he screaming?"

"It's all right," Mosh Zu said. "I know it sounded distressing . . ."

"Sounded distressing? It *was* distressing! It was like hearing someone die in there!"

"Nobody died," said Mosh Zu, "I can assure you of that."

"Mosh Zu began his healing process," Grace added.

"What do you know about it?" Shanti lashed out. "I wasn't talking to you anyway."

"There's no cause to speak to Grace in that way," Mosh Zu said. "I know you're tired and upset and worried about Lorcan. But you must try to contain this sizeable rage you feel. Get some sleep and, if you have any further questions, when we gather again later I shall be pleased to answer them."

Shanti opened her mouth to speak, but Mosh Zu had already turned from her. "Captain, won't you come with me? We have much to catch up on," he said.

The captain nodded. Mosh Zu now turned to Olivier. "If you would please take Shanti and Grace to their quarters?"

"Yes, of course," Olivier said. He gestured for them to follow him along the corridor.

"Sleep well," Mosh Zu said. "And Grace, thank you for your help with Lorcan. Please try not to worry too much. His healing has begun."

Grace nodded and bade Mosh Zu and the captain farewell. She guessed they had a lot to talk about. She watched them walk away along the corridor, wondering at the many mysteries the two men alone were privy to.

"Come on then," said Olivier. "We'll go to the donors' block first." Grace caught the implication of his words. The sooner he was free of the troublesome Shanti, the better!

They took a turning off the corridor and began climbing back up again, though Grace didn't think this was a path they had travelled before.

"The donors' quarters lie at the top of the compound," Olivier explained to Shanti. "This gives you access to the courtyard and other grounds as you wish. And you'll find the food provisions plentiful here. Breakfast will be served shortly."

"Breakfast?" Shanti exclaimed. "I don't need breakfast! I need my bed."

"Of course," Olivier said, with some amusement. "But you will keep the donor hours while you are here. It's simpler that way."

As they talked, they entered a corridor, where people were already moving around.

"Good day, Olivier," said a man as he passed.

"What's this?" said a less pleasant-looking girl. "Newbies?" She looked Shanti up and down. "Isn't she a bit old to be starting out?"

Shanti returned the woman's stare. "Who are you calling a newbie?" she said. "I've been travelling on *The Nocturne* for quite some time."

"As if!" the woman spat back at her. "You wouldn't look like that if you did. Don't you remember the lessons? Once you start sharing, you become immortal. Forever young – *preserved*. Look at you. It would be like preserving a dried prune!"

"That's enough!" Olivier said.

Grace could see that Shanti, though defiant, was upset. She knew that every fresh line on Shanti's face – and there were several new ones since their journey – was like a stab in her heart. Lost in reflection, she suddenly realised that the trainee donor was now looking *her* up and down.

"Now *that's* more like it. You look like your blood is nice and fresh," she announced. She reached out her hand and pinched Grace's face.

"Ouch!" It was like having a bird peck at your cheek.

"Oh yes," the woman said, withdrawing her fingers. "You'll make someone a very nice donor."

Grace shook her head. "I'm not a donor," she said.

"No dear. Of course not."

Olivier placed a firm hand on the woman's shoulder. "Grace is telling the truth. She is not a donor, merely a guest. Shanti, however, *is* a donor and she has indeed been travelling on *The Nocturne*. And now we have clarified these matters, perhaps you might leave us and allow me to take these weary travellers to their rooms."

In spite of his politeness, his voice was steely. The woman knew she had been outmatched.

"*Bien sur*, Monsieur Olivier," she said, curtseying before him. "Toodle pip, ladies! I'll be seeing you."

As she sauntered off down the corridor, Olivier opened a door. "Here you are, Shanti. This will be your room."

It was, as promised, little different to Lorcan's.

"We'll leave you," Olivier said, stepping back into the corridor.

"Wait!" Shanti said. "When shall I see you again? Where is Grace's room?"

"You're a donor," Olivier said. "These are your quarters. You'll be alerted at mealtimes. Talk to the trainee donors, get to know them. They're not all like that one!"

Like that one! Even if she *had* been repellent, couldn't he give her the respect of addressing her by name? Grace found herself angry with Olivier once more.

He seemed blissfully unaware of the fact. "Come," he said. "I'll take you to your quarters, Grace."

As he did so, there was a low wail from the neighbouring room.

"What was that?" Shanti asked.

Olivier shrugged. "Some of them find it hard getting used to the idea of giving blood. You know how it is. You'll be able to help them, I think."

"No!" Shanti said, her face paler than ever. "Please, Grace, don't leave me here. Let me come with you."

"Impossible," Olivier said.

"No," Grace said, taking a decision. "Shanti, pick up your bag and come with us. You can share my room."

Olivier shook his head. "I don't think so."

But Grace was adamant. "Are we guests or prisoners here?" she asked. "Shanti is my . . . my friend, and I'm inviting her to share my room. If you have any problem with that, I suggest you summon Mosh Zu right now!"

Shanti looked so grateful she seemed about to cry. Olivier smirked.

"If this is your friend," he said, "I wouldn't want to be your enemy."

"No," Grace said, steelily. "No, I don't think you would. Now, please show us to our room."

Olivier sighed and began walking back along the corridor. "This won't work," he said. "She'll be waking during the day but you will be keeping to vampire hours – sleeping by day and rising at sunset. It won't work!"

"We'll find a way," Grace said.

"Thank you, Grace," Shanti said, tucking her arm in Grace's.

Talk about an unholy alliance, thought Grace.

They seemed to take the long way back, finding themselves once more walking down the Corridor of Discards and then the Corridor of Ribbons, before turning off to another row of doors.

"Here," Olivier said, without his usual forced politeness. He pulled open a door.

It was as sparse as the other rooms, with a single bed in its centre.

"Don't you have any with two beds?" Shanti said.

"This isn't a motel," Olivier snapped. "I told you this wouldn't work . . ."

"We'll make it work," Grace said, quietly. "Thank you, Olivier, for all your troubles."

"You're most welcome, Miss Tempest," he said. "And now I'll bid you farewell. Enjoy your room . . . and your company!"

He let the door swing shut behind him. They were on their own at last.

"Oh, Grace," Shanti said. "I can't thank you enough! I couldn't sleep in that other block. I just couldn't . . . Thank you! Thank you!"

"No problem," Grace said, feeling suddenly tired. Her head was starting to ache as much as her body. She had to sleep.

"Well then," Shanti said brightly. "I suppose now we just have to decide who's getting the bed tonight!"

"It's OK," Grace said, swiftly seeing how this was going to go. "You take it. I'm so tired, I can crash here."

"Well," said Shanti, lounging on the narrow bunk. "If you're sure, Grace."

"Yes, I'm sure." Grace took off her shoes and coat. "Perhaps, if I could just borrow one of the pillows," she said.

Shanti frowned. "I usually sleep with two," she said, uncertainly. "You could fold up your coat . . ."

Grace gave her a look.

"No, no, of course, here you are." Shanti passed over a pillow.

"Thanks," said Grace.

"Oh, and I got you something as a thank you," Shanti said.

Grace was puzzled. How had she got her anything in the time it had taken to travel from the donor block to here?

Shanti dipped into her coat pocket and produced two ribbons.

"One for you and one for me," she said, holding both ribbons up to the light, clearly trying to decide which was the prettiest.

Grace felt a sharp pain in her head. "Where did you get those?" she asked.

"Where do you think?" Shanti said. "In the Corridor of Ribbons! Well, it's not like they're doing anyone any good there, flapping about in the breeze. But I thought they'd be just the thing . . ."

91

Having made her choice, she pulled her hair back in a ponytail and bound the ribbon around it tightly, finishing with a neat bow. "There!" she said. "Perfect!"

Grace shook her head. "I don't think you should have taken them," she said.

Shanti looked at her dubiously. "They're ribbons, Grace. Trust me, I've pinched a lot more than ribbons in my time. Bet you didn't even see me take 'em!" She looked rather proud.

"No, I didn't," Grace agreed.

"Well," Shanti said, offering the other ribbon out on her palm. "Aren't you going to take yours? You won't mind me saying so, but your hair *is* a bit of a mess."

Grace looked at the ribbon. She had a bad feeling about it. Stupid really. It was only a ribbon. But she remembered how reluctant Olivier had been to explain the ribbons – preferring to leave Mosh Zu to do so. Clearly, they had some significance but all Shanti saw was pretty cloth, like a magpie. Still, she wasn't going to get any peace unless she accepted the gift.

"Thank you," she said, taking the ribbon in her hand. Her head was aching so much now. She really needed to sleep. "I'll just put it here, under my pillow," she said.

"Suit yourself," said Shanti, plumping up her pillow.

Grace lay down on the bare floor and settled her tired head on the pillow. So this was Sanctuary – the place they had come so far to reach. It wasn't what she had expected. Nothing like it. But perhaps tomorrow would be different. She hoped so. She really hoped so.

CHAPTER TEN

The Lost Buccaneer

"Don't look at him," Connor said, grabbing Bart's shoulder. "Don't look at him and don't talk to him. It isn't . . ." He refused to even speak the name. "It isn't *him*." He remembered what the Vampirate captain had told him. "It's just an echo . . ."

However firm his words and tone of voice, Connor could not hold back the torment he felt inside. He could sense the same struggle going on inside Bart, as he gripped his friend's shoulder. He was relieved when, after what seemed like minutes of deadlock, Bart shook off his hold.

"It's no good," he said, glancing back at Connor. "He meant too much to me in life for me to shun him now." Turning away again, he took two steps forward and came to a standstill before Jez.

"Is it you?" Bart asked. "Can it really be you?" He reached out his hand but it froze in midair, as if he couldn't

93

yet face knowing one way or the other. "I held you in my arms as you died. I watched the life flow out of you. I bore your coffin and threw it into the ocean. After all of these things, how can it really be you?" Tears rolled freely down his face.

Jez stood still, speaking very softly. "It *is* me . . . or what little is left of me."

Bart shook his head, incredulously. "You sound so like him." Then he looked up at the moon. "This is so hard," he said. Connor couldn't be sure which of them he was speaking to.

"Won't you shake my hand, old buddy?" Jez said.

"Don't!" Connor implored Bart. "Turn away from him. It's some kind of trick. He's dangerous." He wasn't sure of his own feelings any more; he said the words more out of duty than belief.

He watched as Bart reached out his arm and met Jez's. As their hands clasped, Bart let out a sob. "It *is* you," he cried. "I don't know how it can be, but it's you." He removed his hand and lifted his forearm to wipe dry his eyes. "I half expected my hand to slide through yours," he said, dropping his arm again, "as though you were only a ghost."

Jez shook his head. "Just because you can see me and touch me, it doesn't mean I'm any more substantial than a ghost." Now, he looked beyond Bart, directly at Connor. "Please, Connor," he said. "Won't you come and shake my hand too? It would mean so much."

Connor realised he was trembling. "How can I shake your hand," he said, "when the last time we met, I tried to kill you?" His vision was blurred by tears. Through them, he saw that terrible night once more. He saw the flaming torch in his hand and Jez, standing on the burning deck, screaming for mercy.

"That's all forgotten," Jez said now. "Well, no, we shouldn't forget. But you had good reason to want to destroy me. I've done such terrible, terrible things. Why, lately, I've often wished to destroy myself." He hung his head.

Connor couldn't hold back any longer. He stepped forward and reached out his hand and felt Jez's touch. His hand was icy cold. For the first time, he allowed himself to look directly into Jez's face. It was pale and drawn. In life, he had always had a ruddy glow. In death – or whatever limbo this was – his skin had taken on a snow-white hue, shaded blue by the moonlight.

Suddenly he felt a shiver. He was holding the flesh of a dead man. His former friend was now a vampire. Grace seemed to have no trouble engaging with vampires, but this was new territory for him. He had so many questions.

"I know this is a shock for you both," Jez said. "More than a shock. If you knew how many times I've been on the verge of approaching you, but then shied away. After everything we went through together, I couldn't bear the thought of you rejecting me . . ."

"We're not rejecting you, buddy," Bart said.

95

"No," said Connor. "But what can we do for you? What do you want from us?"

"Mostly I just wanted to see you again," Jez said. "I've been so alone."

"What about Sidorio?" Connor could not help but ask.

"Sidorio is gone," Jez said, matter of factly. "You did kill *him*. You destroyed all of them but me."

Connor was surprised. How had Jez survived the fire? How had Jez survived when the mighty Sidorio had perished?

He thought of Sidorio's boasts . . .

"Fire only makes me stronger."

But it hadn't.

"Death cannot take me. Death cannot take back the dead."

But death *had* taken Sidorio and spared Jez. Connor's mind was racing. Could it be that the reason Jez had survived was because he was not yet made of the same stuff as the others? Perhaps he was not yet the "echo" the captain had spoken of. Perhaps too many traces of Jez's humanity still remained. Nevertheless, he had taken part in the brutal murder of Porfirio Wrathe and his crew. In his own words, he had done "terrible things". And, looking at him now, Connor reminded himself that there was much they didn't know about Jez's activities.

"What do you want from us?" he asked.

"I told you before," he said. "I need some company."

"No," Connor said. "There's something more than that. You want something from us."

Jez smiled. "I remember when you first came to *The Diablo*," he said. "And we trained you in swords. You were my back-up in attack. That was months ago, but it feels like years to me. And now you are changed. You've grown in stature. I hardly recognise you."

Connor frowned. "We've all changed," he said. "Some of us more than others."

"Well, you're right," Jez said. "I *didn't* just come back to hang out with you. I came to ask you a favour. And it's a big one."

"What is it?" Connor asked.

"Anything," Bart said.

"It's very simple," Jez said. "I want you to help me find my way back." He paused. "And if I can't, then I want you to kill me. Once and for all."

97

CHAPTER ELEVEN

Snow

Grace was having a hard time getting to sleep. She was dog-tired after the efforts of her journey to Sanctuary. Nevertheless, she couldn't seem to still her restless mind. She was so excited to be here – excited that Lorcan would now begin the path to healing and excited too to see more of Mosh Zu Kamal at work.

At least, she thought, she had adapted her circadian rhythms to that of the vampires – sleeping through the day and rising at nightfall. Though she missed the light, there seemed to be no other option if she was to really get to know them. She remembered her first days and nights aboard *The Nocturne*, when, shut away in her cabin, she had felt cut off from time. It was good to adhere to a rhythm, even if it wasn't the rhythm of your average mortal.

Beside her, Shanti groaned and twisted in her bed. In *Grace's* bed, rather. Having taken the only bunk, you'd have thought she'd have the decency to sleep quietly! But she was twisting and turning and sighing . . . it was as if she was having a bad dream. Grace contemplated waking her but decided on second thoughts that a sleeping Shanti, however disturbed, was mildly preferable to a wakeful one.

Grace settled herself back on the pillow. She needed more height under her neck, so she lifted the pillow and slid her pack underneath it. As she did so, she saw the ribbon Shanti had given her, lying on the floor. She scooped it up in her fingers and then lay back against the pillow. It was much better now the pack was underneath it. She wriggled to get the rest of her body as comfortable as she could on the thin blanket. She gently held the length of ribbon in her hand, letting it sneak about her fingers like a snake. As she did so, she felt her eyes grow heavy. Gratefully, she closed her eyelids and felt herself at last drifting into sleep.

She was soon in the midst of a dream. Though it was vivid, at first she was aware it was a dream. She was lying back, gazing up at the night sky. The sky was perfectly clear and full of stars, like a bale of cloth rolled out as far as the eye could see.

Something was digging into her neck. She raised her head and, twisting around, saw that her pillow was a saddle. Surprised, she rubbed her aching neck, then lay back down again. Nearby, she heard a whinny. She twisted her head once more and saw a horse standing not too far away, its reins fastened to a tree.

Seeing that the horse was all right, she smiled and settled back against the saddle. She lay there, looking up at the stars, feeling perfectly at peace with the world.

As she lay there, she felt something tickling her nose. Her first thought was that the horse was nuzzling her.

"Stop it, Whiskey!" she giggled, somehow knowing the horse's name. But the tickle continued, growing wetter. "Whiskey!" she exclaimed again, opening her eyes. But the horse was standing to her side, just where he had been before. She realised that the tickle on her nose came from flakes of snow. It was falling thickly, plump snowflakes dropping regally from the sky. The ground was already thick and white. Strangely, lying there, she felt no chill. She was too lost in the beauty of the falling snow, floating down like blossom over her until she was utterly covered by a thick white blanket.

Then, somehow, she was on the back of a horse – on Whiskey – riding through the snow. She wasn't alone either. Looking ahead, she saw the familiar shapes of her brother and father, right out at the front. Between them were other men on horses and a herd of cattle. She felt a sense of belonging here, the same sense of comfort that she'd felt lying in the snow before. Her family was here. Whiskey was here. This was home, right here on this horse.

"Permanezca allí, Johnny," called her father. "Subimos adelante."

Stay there, Johnny. We're going on ahead.

100

And somehow it wasn't strange to be called Johnny. She realised she was a boy. She looked down at her hands clasping the reins. Sure enough, they were a boy's hands – young but already callused from long enough spent working the reins. Well, this was a dream. Anything could happen in dreams. She could understand Spanish in dreams. She could even speak it.

"Si, Padre!" she called, settling back onto Whiskey's saddle as the horse ploughed on through the snow.

The ground was climbing fast and the snow growing thicker and thicker, swirling about them. She could only just see the men on either side of her.

"Nice riding, Johnny," she heard a voice of encouragement at her side.

"Just like his papa," said another gruff voice.

Then everything shifted. It was as if the earth was moving underneath Whiskey's hooves. She heard cries, from above and from all around. Human cries and the wilder lowing of cattle. She felt herself and Whiskey being jostled from all sides.

"Hold tight, Johnny! Pull back! Hold tight!"

She was doing all she could, but it was so hard. The snow was blinding now. It cut her off from the others. She gripped Whiskey's reins as tight as she could, but the horse was bucking her, trying to throw her. Holding tight, she realised with a start she was no longer riding through the snow. She was in the heat of the midday sun, sweat pouring down her brow, riding a horse – which wasn't

Whiskey – in a paddock. The red dust beneath her met the bluest sky she had ever seen.

"Look at Johnny go!" called a man from the other side of a fence. He was wearing a stetson and she realised she was too.

"If Johnny can't break her, nobody can," another man called to the first. Together, they watched her ride the bronco. She turned away, looking down at her hands. They were no longer the hands of a boy either. Here, gripping the leather ropes, were the hands of a young man.

There was cheering. The noisiest came from two fellows just over the fence. But looking up, she saw that she was no longer in the quiet paddock. Now, she was in a show arena and on all four sides a crowd was cheering for her. As she held tight onto the bronco, she caught a flash of a sign on a sweep of cloth. ". . . *County, Seventeenth Annual Rodeo*".

The cheers were so deafening, now she knew she must have won. But somehow, she didn't feel joyful at the prospect. It was like something was missing. The comfort she'd felt earlier – lying under the stars and then riding in the snow – was gone, and somehow she knew it wasn't coming back. *It's only a dream*, she told herself, *just a dream. I could open my eyes at any moment.* But she didn't. She held tight onto the reins and let the dream carry her from one rodeo ring to the next.

Everything began to speed up. She was riding, always riding. But now, she was journeying through the country. Through snow and sun, wind and rain. Sometimes on her own. Sometimes with one or more at her side. Sometimes with a herd of cattle between her and the next man. On and on she rode. She was growing tired. Soon, she'd have to stop riding and settle down for a long, long sleep.

The snow came down again. Thick and pretty as before. But this time, the snow made her feel sad and lonely, unbearably lonely. All around her was white, save for the dark grey silhouettes of leafless trees. She rode on, heavy of heart, the cattle all around her buffeted by the weather. Under the dark skies, the cattle seemed grey. Everything was grey now – funny how pure white snow could turn so ugly so fast. In the distance, she heard men talking. She couldn't hear the words but there was something in their voices that made her shiver.

"That's it, Johnny!" she heard the cry. "You're doing a great job! Just like always."

But though the words were reassuring, she felt nothing but coldness. She had the sense that everything was coming to a close.

Suddenly, she wasn't on the horse any more. She was back on the ground. Back in the snow, but it didn't feel comfortable this time. It didn't even feel cool. It felt like it was burning her. Above her was the night sky and, in spite of the snow, it was as bright and star-filled as that first time – which now seemed a long, long time ago. She realised that she was moving fast along the ground, being pulled by a rope. It hurt really bad. She prayed for it to end. And suddenly it did. The motion ceased and she was still once more, thick snowflakes dancing towards her. For a moment, it was beautiful and calm.

Then two pairs of hands reached for her and pushed her roughly. They were shouting things but other voices were shouting against them and the words were indistinguishable, so much white noise.

"String him up! Up next to the others!"

She felt something being hung about her neck. It was as if she had gone from being rider to horse. But these reins were too tight. Much too tight. She could feel her throat constrict. She opened her mouth to scream. Then, at last, she opened her eyes.

"Shanti!"

Shanti's face was bearing down over her, her eyes staring wildly into her own, blazing pure hatred at her. Glancing down, Grace saw that Shanti's hands were clamped to her neck. Shanti was strangling her!

"What . . . are . . . you . . . do . . . ing?" she managed to rasp out the words before Shanti's hands squeezed even more tightly.

In pure terror, Grace looked into Shanti's eyes. They were utterly empty.

"Don't fight it," Shanti said, in a voice as cold as metal. "There's no point in trying to fight it. I'm stronger than you. It's much easier if you just let go."

CHAPTER TWELVE
Seven Words

"Quick," Bart hissed to Jez as Molucco crossed the deck. "Jump into the light boat." For a dead man, Jez jumped fast.

"Connor!" cried Captain Wrathe, approaching fast. He was wearing an elaborate robe, with metallic threads and jewelled beads which glittered in the moonlight. His hair was even wilder than usual, jutting up in the air as straight as the ship's masts. Connor saw that it was pushed back from his forehead with what he at first took to be a scarf. Then he realised it was an eye-mask. This, Connor presumed, must be Molucco's sleeping gear. It was no less fabulous than his usual finery.

"Captain Wrathe!" said Connor. "We thought you'd settled into your cabin for the night."

"So I had, dear boy," said Molucco, his wild eyes roving the deck. Connor dared not turn around but prayed that

Jez was safely out of sight. Molucco shook his head. "I just can't get to sleep. Too many thoughts swimming around this old head of mine."

"Perhaps you'd like to talk about it?" Connor said, gesturing with his hand to direct the captain away from the light boat and towards the other end of the deck. Captain Wrathe nodded and began walking alongside him. Connor gave a quick glance over his shoulder and saw Bart give him the thumbs up. Phew! The danger was past.

"It was quite a jolt seeing my brother and his family again tonight," Molucco said.

"I'm sure." Connor nodded.

"Quite a jolt! You know that Barbarro and I haven't been on speaking terms for quite some time?"

"Yes," Connor said. "I had heard." Was Molucco about to tell him the origin of the fraternal feud?

"Death changes everything, you see," he said, fixing Connor with wide eyes. "You're only just beginning your life's voyage," Molucco continued. "But you'll come to know this, my boy. Death changes everything."

Connor was silent but he thought to himself that death had already changed everything for him and his sister. They would never have been at sea at all if their father hadn't died. Connor and the captain had now reached the midpoint of the ship. Connor looked out at the dark ocean beyond. His thoughts turned to his lost family — to his dead father and his dear sister, wherever she was now.

He was drawn back to the deck by footsteps.

"Ah, hello, Bartholomew," boomed Molucco. "How goes the watch?"

"Very quiet tonight," Bart said, with a reassuring nod. "Very quiet indeed, eh Connor?"

Connor nodded.

"Well, then." Molucco smiled. "Let's have a drop of rum, shall we?" He pointed to the nearby light boat. "From your private supply?"

Bart looked guilty but Molucco laughed. "It's a trick as old as piracy," he said, "hiding a cheeky flagon in a light boat. To keep the chill out of your bones and some fire in your belly during a long night watch. Come on, Bartholomew, quit blushing and fetch us each a snifter."

Bart lifted the tarpaulin and climbed into the boat. He passed Connor the bottle and three enamel mugs. Smiling, Molucco took the bottle from Connor's hands and poured a hefty slug of rum into one of the mugs. He passed this to Bart, then poured a similar amount into the other mugs as Connor held them before him.

"Come on," said the captain. "Let's have a seat up on the poop deck."

They walked up to the top section of the deck and sat down under the wooden canopy behind the ship's wheel. Above the wheel hung a lantern, its light sending a soft glow over the surrounding area. As Connor sat down cross-legged beside Bart and Captain Wrathe, he thought how, at this moment in time, there was no hierarchy between them. They were just three pirates taking a break while their ship idled in tranquil waters.

"A toast," said Molucco, lifting his mug. The others raised their mugs aloft too, as he declared, "A short life but a merry one!"

"A short life but a merry one," echoed Connor and Bart. The three men clinked their mugs together. The toast was one Molucco had used before, Connor remembered. It summed up his view of a pirate's life in just seven words.

Connor winced as he took the smallest sip of rum. He still hadn't gotten a taste for it. He hoped that the others wouldn't notice if he didn't partake of much more.

"Was it good to see your brother again tonight?" Bart asked Captain Wrathe.

Molucco nodded. "Oh yes," he said. "It was very good. Very good indeed. We had been at odds too long." He smiled, but the smile soon faded, and he took another swig of rum. "It makes me sad though, sad to think that the three brothers Wrathe will never be together again – at least not until the two of us join dear Porfirio in Davy Jones' Locker."

This, Connor knew, was pirates' slang for the bottom of the ocean. He imagined the three Wrathe brothers lying down there – in a grave marked by coral and algae, visited only by sea urchins and starfish. It was too grim a thought to ponder for long.

"I just wish," Molucco continued, "that Barbarro could accept that Porfirio is gone, and leave it there."

"Can't he?" Bart asked.

Molucco shook his head. "No. No, Barbarro is obsessed with revenge. And Trofie too. I understand it. Of course I do. I had the same hunger. But I told them. We have already taken revenge. I'll never forget that night we hunted down the ship of Porfirio's murderers . . . and destroyed it."

Connor would never forget it either. He guessed that none of the pirates who had put out to sea that night ever could.

"I told them about it," Molucco continued. "Told them how you, Mister Tempest, came up with the brilliant stratagem of fighting the fiends with fire. How the flames soared up to the very heavens and took all of those monsters down to their rightful dwelling place in Hell."

At these impassioned words, Connor thought of Jez. At this very minute, he might be hiding in the light boat but, from what he'd said earlier, Hell wasn't too far off a description of his existence now. As for Sidorio and the other vampires – whom the flames *had* consumed – perhaps they were indeed now dwelling in Hell itself. To Connor's mind, all that mattered was that they were gone and never coming back. It was a miracle that Jez had survived, but perhaps his goodness had somehow saved him. Connor thought a little more. Jez needed to be somewhere he belonged now – amongst his own. If they could just get him to the Vampirate ship, to seek the captain's help, maybe his suffering would come to an end.

Molucco frowned and interrupted Connor's musings. "But Barbarro and Trofie were not there and they do not understand. They want to know why Porfirio was killed and who the villains were who slaughtered him and his crew. I told them that we can never truly hope to understand why or who. That even if we did, it would not bring Porfirio back. Nothing can do that, save the dear memories we have of him."

"You're right," Connor said.

The others turned to him, perhaps surprised at the force in his voice.

"I mean that the battle is over. There are no enemies left to fight."

Molucco nodded, then fixed Connor with a look. "But there are other Vampirates, aren't there? Your sister is with them now."

Connor nodded. "Yes," he said. "But they were not responsible for what happened. You can't condemn a whole group of people because of the actions of a few."

"I don't know," Molucco said. "The way Barbarro talked, I think he'd happily hunt down every last Vampirate and slay each one."

Bart shivered. "I wouldn't rate his chances. Not after what we saw that night."

"Besides," Connor added, spurred on by thoughts of Grace, "it wouldn't be fair. It would be like killing every last pirate because of . . . because of how we suffered at the hands of Narcisos Drakoulis."

Molucco caught Connor's glance and held it. "You're right, lad. You both are. We don't want to tangle with the Vampirates again. If only I can make Barbarro see things our way. But he's as stubborn as a mule. And then there's his wife . . ."

"What they need," said Connor, emboldened perhaps by the rum, "is a distraction."

"A distraction?" Molucco said, his eyes suddenly sparkling.

"Connor's right," Bart said. "We need to come up with something that takes their minds as far away from death and revenge as possible."

"That," Molucco nodded, "would do us *all* some good. But what?"

They all thought for a moment, each taking a sip of rum. Connor winced as he swallowed it down. Then it came to him.

"A raid!" he exclaimed.

"That's it!" Bart slapped him on the back. "A good old pirate raid!"

"No," Molucco was as fired up as the others. "No, boys, not just another pirate raid. The mother of all raids. Yes! You've given me an idea." He looked fit to burst with excitement. "Quick, Bartholomew, fill up my cup and don't be stingy. I can feel an idea coming on . . ."

CHAPTER THIRTEEN

The In-Betweens

Was this part of the dream? In many ways it seemed more unreal than what had gone before, but looking up into Shanti's wild eyes, Grace knew at once that this was real. Shanti had never liked her and now, for some unexplained reason, she was trying to kill her.

As Shanti's hands pressed against Grace's throat, she felt her consciousness ebbing away. I'm going to die, she thought. I'm actually going to die here, in this little room. She felt sad. It seemed such a premature way to exit life. After everything she had been through – everything which she imagined lay ahead of her – to perish at the hands of a demented donor for no reason she understood was just grim.

She wanted to scream but Shanti's hands clasped her neck too tightly, rendering her vocal cords useless. In a moment, it would all be over. Somehow she had to make a sound. She began drumming her feet on the floor. Her feet were still bare and it didn't make as much noise as she would have liked. Was it enough? She swung her feet from side to side, hoping to make contact with something, anything. Preferably something large and breakable. But there was nothing there. Feeling her chances ebbing away, she continued drumming her feet on the floorboards, feeling no pain, only a growing sense of numbness.

Suddenly the door was pushed open and flew backwards. Shanti was flying away from her. Grace realised that two pairs of hands had grabbed the manic donor. It took a moment before she realised that Shanti had released her grip from her neck. It still felt massively constricted. She let out a breath. She had come so close to death. Only now did she allow herself to tremble. Only now did she feel the pain from pounding her feet against the floor. But it had worked. It had worked!

"I knew this was a mistake," Olivier said, gripping Shanti's hands behind her back.

"Let me go!" Shanti snarled at him, her head swinging, her teeth gnashing together. "Let me go or I'll kill you too!"

"You're not going to kill anyone, lady," Olivier said. "Here, Dani, take over from me while I check on Grace."

Olivier's companion stepped over to Shanti and slipped a pair of handcuffs over her small wrists. Still she bucked and wailed like a wild beast.

"Are you all right?" Olivier asked, lightly touching Grace's neck.

"Ouch! That hurts."

"I'm sorry," he said. "Your neck's a little raw. She really had a go at you."

"Yes." Grace nodded, and the action was painful. "But why? I don't understand. What's got into her?"

They both looked up at Shanti, who though held in Dani's clutches, was still seething and muttering in the vilest terms.

"It's very simple," Olivier said, walking over to her. "See, your friend Shanti took something which didn't belong to her." With that, he reached his hands into Shanti's hair and unfastened the ribbon she had knotted there. At once, Shanti calmed down. The fury drained from her eyes, her limbs ceased their wild movements and her voice faded into silence. She stood there, as limp as a marionette whose strings have been cut.

Olivier took the ribbon and rolled it around his wrist. "There," he said. "All quiet now."

Grace was dumbfounded. "It was the ribbon?" she said. "The *ribbon* did this to her?"

Olivier nodded. "Like I said before, it did not belong to her."

Grace scrambled up into a sitting position. "So Shanti meant me no harm? It was the ribbon. No, the *person*, who the ribbon belongs to?"

"I'm not here to answer your questions," Olivier said.

114

"Just to ensure that chaos does not break out again." He nodded to Dani. "Take the donor away to the donor quarters."

"No!" Grace protested, but Olivier gave Dani a look which left her in no doubt whose word was to be obeyed. Dani led Shanti away. The donor followed obediently, all strength apparently drained from her body.

"Perhaps you will understand now, Grace Tempest, that there are powerful forces here at Sanctuary. You would do well to listen to those of us who know of such things and not assume you can play hard and fast with the rules."

Grace felt suitably chastened but she was indignant at Olivier's manner. Did he feel threatened by her? Was that why he had to keep stressing his greater knowledge?

"Thank you," she said. "You saved my life."

"Yes," he said, with a smile. "Yes, I suppose I did."

"So now what?"

"So now, if you're up to it, you join me for breakfast. I'll wait outside while you get dressed."

"Breakfast?" said Grace. "But surely the vampires don't have breakfast?"

"No, indeed," Olivier said. "But since neither you nor I, to the best of my knowledge, are vampires, we will partake of some food."

"You're not a vampire?"

"If you continue to ask all these questions, we'll never get anything done." He sighed. "No, I'm not a vampire. I work for Mosh Zu. I'm not a donor, either, before you ask.

I'm like you. An in-between, I guess you'd call us, for want of a better term."

"An in-between," Grace repeated. It wasn't the loftiest of titles.

"Exactly," said Olivier. "Now, I'll wait outside while you get sorted. But do be quick. Saving damsels in distress always gives me a hearty appetite."

"So how long have you been here?" Grace asked as she and Olivier sat down to eat.

"Questions, questions. We have a rule here at Sanctuary. No questions."

"But how do you learn anything?" Grace asked.

"There you go again," said Olivier. "For you, everything is a question. Oh, it's not that I'm not as inquisitive as you, believe me. I hunger for knowledge. But I have learned, in my time with Mosh Zu, that it is better to let people open themselves up to you, in their own time. In that way, you will learn everything you want to know and more besides."

"But what if people don't *want* to open up to you?"

Olivier smiled and took an orange from a bowl in front of them. Deftly, he ran his fingers along the surface of the fruit and shucked away the peel.

"It's really just acquiring the knack of getting under the skin," he said.

"But, don't you . . ." Grace began.

"That's sounding very much like the beginning of

another question," Olivier said, as he divided up the segments of the fruit.

Grace sighed and shook her head, lifting a plum from her own plate.

They ate the rest of their meal in silence. It was only the two of them in the room and Grace wanted to ask if there were other "in-betweens" at Sanctuary or if it was just the two of them. But she realised she'd have to hold onto this question and await the information when the time was right.

"You've finished," Olivier said.

"Hah!" Grace said. "That was a question."

Olivier shook his head. "Not a question but an observation. You appear to have eaten everything on your plate. And so have I. Our breakfast is over and now I will take you to Mosh Zu."

"Mosh Zu has asked to see me."

Olivier shot her a frustrated look.

Grace shook her head. "Not a question," she said. "An observation. Anyone would think you didn't know that Australians often sound like we're asking questions, because our voices rise up at the end of sentences. It's called a High Rising Terminal, just in case you didn't know. There we are, I just gave you some information you didn't ask for. I think I'm getting the hang of this."

Olivier shook his head. "I can see you're going to be quite challenging company," he said.

"I'm sorry," said Grace.

117

"Don't be sorry," Olivier said, a smirk playing on his lips. "I enjoy a challenge."

Just then there was a knock on the door. Dani stepped inside. "Sorry to interrupt your breakfast," she said, "but the captain is preparing to leave." She looked at Grace. "He'd like to see you before he goes."

Grace stood up, surprised. "Yes, of course." She hadn't expected the captain to leave so soon. Had he had enough time to talk through all the things he had wanted to consult Mosh Zu on? Or was there another reason why he was hurrying back to *The Nocturne*?

CHAPTER FOURTEEN

The Typhon

The central of the three wishes had been lowered to allow Captain Wrathe and his companions an easy passageway from *The Diablo* to *The Typhon*.

"What exactly is a Typhon?" Connor asked as they passed the ship's sign.

"It's a mythological creature," Cate said. "A monster with a hundred heads and a hundred serpents in the place of legs. He was supposed to be able to create terrible storms."

"Nice!" said Connor.

He felt a little uncomfortable dressed in the stiff shirt, jacket and tie Molucco had loaned to him. Bart seemed to be having similar problems but that was possibly less because of the starch in his shirt and more because the velvet jacket, though stylish, was a tad on the small side for his broad shoulders. He squirmed as he walked. "Did we really have to wear these threads?"

"I think you've both scrubbed up very well," said Cate with a smile.

"Are you taking the mick?" Bart asked.

"Oh no," she said, the very picture of innocence. "It's nice to see you clean shaven, for a change, and smelling of lemons rather than sweat."

Connor was amused to see Bart blush. He noticed that though Cate had refused to "dress up", as Trofie had requested, she had nevertheless given her hair a wash and knotted a fresh bandana about her head. Now she nodded at Connor. "Make sure you keep that map-case dry," she said.

"Aye, aye," Connor said, giving her a mock salute with his free hand.

"Don't be cheeky, Tempest," said Cate, smiling indulgently.

Beyond the wish, crossing the deck of *The Typhon* was an actual red carpet. And, waiting on it, arm outstretched, a formally attired butler.

"Good evening, Captain Wrathe," the silver-haired servant said with a discreet bow. "Welcome aboard *The Typhon*."

"Thank you," Molucco said, sweeping past him along the carpet. "Well, I must say my brother and his wife do have some fancy schmancy ways. Anyone would think this was a cruise ship, not a pirate vessel! Next thing you know, we'll be throwing streamers over the side!"

Connor grinned as he and Bart followed Cate and

Captain Wrathe onto the red carpet. Looking up, he saw that Barbarro and Trofie were waiting for them at the end of the deck, standing side by side on the red carpet like royalty – pirate royalty. They were both dressed, as might have been expected, in rare finery. Barbarro wore a dinner jacket and trousers with a bright blue sash and a gold medal sweeping across his chest. At his side, Trofie resembled a swan, shimmering in a tightly-fitted dress of a diaphanous material, which glistened in the light of the moon and the lanterns set along the deck. She was wearing a necklace rather akin to a spider's web, with rubies at every connecting point. Connor couldn't begin to imagine how much it might be worth.

"Good evening," Molucco beamed, shaking his brother warmly by the hand. Skirmish and Scrimshaw popped out to greet each other. When their snake greeting was done, Molucco moved on and kissed Trofie on each cheek.

"Good evening, Molucco," she said, looking over his shoulder at the others. "And how nice of you all to make such an effort. I'm sure you don't get to dress up for dinner very often."

"Erm, no," Connor said, still fiddling with his collar. Meals on board *The Diablo* were generally a pretty rough and ready affair. If you bothered to shower before sitting down at the table, you were usually the object of much ridicule and ribbing.

"Welcome one, welcome all," said Barbarro cheerily.

Trofie clicked her fingers and the butler circulated

amongst the guests with a tray of tall glasses. "Champagne, sir?" the butler said, offering the tray to Connor. Connor reached out for the glass.

"Not while he's on duty," Cate said, handing the glass back.

"Come, come," said Molucco. "A few bubbles won't hurt the boy now, will they?"

"Quite right," said Barbarro. "Moonshine loves the stuff!"

Cate shook her head as Connor, caught between the captain and his deputy, took hold of the glass.

Barbarro turned to Trofie. "Where *is* our Moonshine?"

"In his cabin, I expect."

"I told him to be here on time!"

"Don't be such a grouch, *min elskling*. You know Moonshine. Always busy with something . . ."

"Busy doing nothing, more like," Barbarro snapped.

Trofie managed to maintain her fixed grin whilst hissing at her husband. "Not in front of our guests, dearest. Happy families, tonight. Remember?"

"Blowfish sashimi, sir?" The butler reappeared before Connor, holding out a large gold plate bearing tiny slivers of raw fish, arranged like the petals of a flower. In the centre of the plate was a shimmering pile of fish skin, and a small lime. Connor looked at the arrangement, thinking that it wouldn't have looked out of place in an art gallery. Eating it was another matter, however.

"Isn't blowfish poisonous?" he asked.

Trofie roared with laughter. "Are you worried we're trying to poison you, *min elskling*? If we were, I think we'd be a little more subtle about it, don't you?"

"Go ahead, dear boy," said Barbarro. "It's a rare delicacy." Beside him, Molucco nodded encouragingly.

Connor took a pair of gold chopsticks in his fingers and lifted a small sliver of fish to his mouth. It tingled on his tongue. At first, he wondered if it wasn't poisonous after all. Then, he realised that it was just the rare taste of the fish and its fiery dressing of lime, scallions and radish.

Trofie smiled. "Phew! Not dead yet," she said. "We'll have to try harder next time, eh?" She gave him a playful wink, but Connor found himself shivering. He still wasn't sure whether she was laughing with him or at him.

Thirty minutes later, after a second glass of champagne and another sliver or two of sashimi, Connor found himself relaxed and basking in the sense of wellbeing which radiated aboard the deck of *The Typhon*. It was clear that Barbarro and Trofie lived well and, in spite of Connor's initial misgivings, they were proving warm and generous hosts.

At last, Moonshine appeared on deck. Connor noticed that, as he did so, both his parents closed in on him as tightly as a clam shell – Trofie to adjust his bow tie and Barbarro to demand (none too softly) what *precisely* had kept him from joining them half an hour earlier. Connor didn't hear Moonshine's reply as behind him a gong was struck and the butler announced, "Captains, ladies and gentlemen, dinner is now served."

Barbarro turned and beckoned the others to follow him below deck.

"Marvellous," said Molucco, striding across the deck. "Those fish slivers have given me an appetite for some proper food." Connor grinned. You could take Molucco away from *The Diablo* . . . but he would always operate by his own rules.

"Say hello to Uncle Molucco," Trofie said, once more pushing Moonshine across the path of his uncle.

"Whatever," Moonshine said, apparently more concerned with pulling his long hair back down over his eyes.

"And here's Cate and Bart and, you remember Connor, don't you, darling?"

At that, Moonshine lifted his head and shook it so his hair flew back off his face. He stared at Connor, his eyes wild and bloodshot.

"Oh yeah, I remember Connor. Whassup?"

He reached out his hand and Connor assumed he wanted to shake it. As he did so, he felt a searing pain dig into his palm. What the . . .?

As Moonshine released his hand, Connor saw that his flesh was bleeding.

Connor winced and glanced up at Moonshine, then around to see if his crewmates had noticed what had just happened. But the lure of dinner meant that suddenly he and Moonshine were alone on the deck.

"Ooops," Moonshine said. "I'm so sorry. This must have

slipped out of my sleeve." He picked up a star-shaped *shuriken* – a jagged circular throwing weapon. One of its prongs was now wet with Connor's blood.

"What did you do that for?" Connor asked, scarcely able to control his anger and confusion.

"I thought it might help to jog your memory."

"My *memory*?" Connor said. "What are you talking about?"

"Don't pretend to be any dumber than you are," Moonshine sneered. "I'm talking about *Calle del Marinero*. Ring any bells, halfwit?"

Calle del Marinero. The Street of Sailors or *the Strip of Sin*, depending on who you listened to. That was where Connor had gone with Bart and Jez on shore-leave, a month or so after joining *The Diablo*. Nowadays, Bart and Connor referred to the trip as their Lost Weekend. Indeed, it was the stuff of legend aboard *The Diablo*. The self-styled Three Buccaneers had set out from the ship on a Friday night and, when it had returned for them on Sunday evening, the three young pirates had been unable to remember anything that had happened in the intervening forty-eight hours. Even more strangely, they had been discovered, dressed only in their underwear with mysterious matching tattoos. Two months later, Connor and Bart were still being ribbed about it. And yet they continued to remember nothing. It appeared, though, that Moonshine knew something more than them.

"Were you there?" Connor asked. "Did we meet there?"

Moonshine sniffed in disgust, and burst a zit on the side of his nose. "Give it a rest, eh, Connor," he said. "You know exactly what went down at *Calle del Marinero*. I had my bodyguards confiscated after that, thanks to you and your pals. Dad thought I was giving him a bad name. Well, I'll show him . . . and I'll show you. Expect payback very soon."

Payback? Wasn't a *shuriken* in the hand payback enough? What more did Moonshine have planned for him?

"Well, isn't this nice?" Trofie's voice was swiftly followed by her face, reappearing from the doorway. "Are you two young men becoming friends?"

"Yes Mother," Moonshine said, his voice as sweet as an overripe melon. "But Connor has had a little accident." He pointed to the gash in Connor's hand.

"Oh, no!" Trofie said, stepping forward to examine the wound. "You're bleeding!"

"I'll be fine," Connor said. "It's only a superficial cut."

"Come on inside and we'll fetch the sea-urchin salve," Trofie said. "It might sting a little, but it will staunch the bleeding. However did you do that? Oh, don't even tell me!" she giggled. "Boys will be boys!"

She ushered them through the door into a carpeted hallway with a massive chandelier.

Connor turned to Moonshine with a look of pure hatred.

"Get a move on, mutant," said Moonshine, giving him a shove. "I don't want to be late for din-dins."

CHAPTER FIFTEEN

Exeunt

"Ah Grace," said the captain. He and Mosh Zu were standing together in the corridor. They both turned as she and Olivier approached. "I'm returning to *The Nocturne*," he went on. "But, of course, I wanted to say goodbye in person."

Grace smiled up at him, but she felt suddenly nervous. She hadn't expected him to leave so soon. Part of her yearned to go with him. Of course, there was no question of her leaving Lorcan, but *The Nocturne* had become her new home. She was intrigued by Sanctuary, but it was not a comfortable place to her. Not yet. And she was impressed by Mosh Zu, but he was not the captain. He could never take the captain's place.

"It's OK," he said, a smile seeming to form across the mesh of his mask. He placed a reassuring hand upon her shoulder. "I'm leaving you in good company. I wish I could stay longer but I must return to the ship."

Grace nodded. She understood. Of course she did. She remembered Darcy's words: *"It's very rare for the captain to leave the ship. It shows how much he cares for Lieutenant Furey that he would take this risk."*

"And don't you worry," Mosh Zu said to the captain. "We shall take very good care of Grace and Lorcan."

"Would you like me to guide you back down the mountain?" Olivier asked. "I can fetch one of the mules if you'd like?"

The captain shook his head. "You've very kind, Olivier, but I always enjoy the walk. Besides, as usual, Mosh Zu has given me much to think about."

Mosh Zu smiled, self-effacingly.

"Well—" the captain began.

At that moment, they heard footsteps and then a cry. They all looked up along the corridor and found Shanti hurtling towards them at a rate of knots. She just about managed to come to a standstill before she could cause a mass pile-up in the corridor.

"Shanti!" the captain said. "It's good to see you. I'm just leaving to return to the ship."

"Take me with you!" she cried.

"But Shanti—" began the captain.

"Take me with you! Please, you have to take me with you! I hate it here! It's a loathsome place!" With each sentence, her voice became shriller and shriller.

"Please," Mosh Zu said. "Try to calm down. Tell us what's wrong . . ."

"Don't tell me to calm down!" she shrieked. "Horrors! Such horrors! I hate that donors' block. I won't stay here! I won't!"

The captain stepped forward. "Shanti, I'm very sorry if something's upset you, but surely you want to stay here, so that you can be with Lorcan."

"I won't stay here a minute longer," she responded hysterically. "I won't!"

"But Lorcan needs you," Grace said. "I know you're scared, but you have to face these fears. For Lorcan's sake."

"Why?" Shanti turned on Grace, her voice full of rage now as well as fear. "Why must I suffer so for Lorcan? We had no need to come here. We were fine on that ship. Until *you* came along. It's your fault we're here. For you, he went out into the light. That's when all his problems started. Actually, no, they started the day you came onto the ship!"

"Shanti!" said the captain. "There's no need to be so aggressive to Grace."

"It's no problem," Grace said. "She's already tried to kill me this morning. I can take a few insults."

The two girls stood before each other, Grace now as angry as Shanti. "You're so selfish," she said. "All we're asking is that you stay here and help us to persuade Lorcan to take blood again . . ."

"Not just blood," Shanti said. "My blood! My blood, you hear me? How dare you presume to get involved with this. If you really cared about Lorcan, you'd give him your own blood. But no, instead you act high and mighty like you're something special." She was warming to her theme now. "And the worst thing is, they *believe* you. They listen to *you* . . . They're think you're special. But I don't count for anything, not anything." Now, she broke down in sobs.

Once more, the captain stepped forward. "Shanti, you *do* count. You are vital to Lorcan's recovery."

Shanti shook her head. "I'm sorry," she said. "I mean him no harm – but I can't stay here. You've asked a lot of me. But this is too much. Too much, I tell you. Take me with you, Captain. Please take me with you!"

With that, she threw herself at the captain and, clinging on to him, broke into loud sobs that caused her small body to vibrate. Grace wasn't sure she had ever seen anyone in such distress.

The captain looked at Mosh Zu. "I think I had better take her back to the ship."

"You know the implications of that," Mosh Zu said.

The captain nodded. "I'll find a way to make this right," he said.

Mosh Zu frowned and shook his head. "What did I tell you before? You take too much upon yourself."

"I really don't see any alternative," the captain said.

"So you'll do it?" Shanti said, her eyes brightening. "You'll take me with you?"

"Yes, child." The captain nodded. "Now fetch your things. We must go."

"I'm not worried about my things," Shanti said. "Let's just leave!"

"All right," the captain said, as if comforting a small child. "All right. We'll go right now." He looked up at the others. "Olivier, if you would just open the gates for us?"

Olivier nodded. He began walking briskly along the corridor. The captain and Shanti followed.

Grace couldn't believe her ears. She could understand Shanti's fears but how could she abandon Lorcan like this? And how could the captain let her?

"Your head is raging with questions," Mosh Zu said.

"Yes." Grace turned to him when the others had gone.

"Walk with me, Grace," Mosh Zu said. "Let me try to answer them as best I can."

"How could she abandon Lorcan like that?" Grace asked.

Mosh Zu shook his head. "That's not what you're really asking. You're worried about Lorcan. You're thinking, how will he survive without his donor?"

"Yes." Grace nodded. Of course, that was exactly what she was thinking.

"We can deal with that," Mosh Zu said. "For now, we need simply to get Lorcan drinking again. But you're right, in due course we will have to find him another donor, at least for the time he is here, but possibly on a more permanent basis." He turned to Grace. "The relationship between a vampire and a donor is complex. You can't switch them around every five minutes."

As they walked on towards Mosh Zu's meditation room, Grace remembered her offer to the captain – that *she* become Lorcan's donor. It wasn't an offer she had made lightly and she had been relieved that it hadn't been necessary at the time. But perhaps it was now. If so, she would do it. She'd do anything to help Lorcan. Even that.

They had reached the meditation room. Mosh Zu pushed open the door and gestured Grace to follow him inside. "Please sit down," he said. "Perhaps you would like some tea to soothe your frayed nerves?"

Grace shook her head. "No," she said. "No, I'm all right." Then she jumped up. "I'll do it," she said. "I'll become Lorcan's donor. I'll do anything to help him."

"Yes." Mosh Zu nodded. "I believe you." He sat down on the cushions. "Grace, I appreciate this offer. I know that it is heartfelt. I know too that you understand the implications of what you are offering . . ."

"Yes," she said. "I do."

"But Grace, I think you have much more to give. I've said before, you have a talent for healing. If you were to become Lorcan's donor, your life would be more limited."

Grace smiled and shook her head. "How would it be limited? I'd be immortal."

Mosh Zu nodded. "Always one step ahead," he said. "Yes, you would be immortal, but do not confuse immortality with being free of limits. It's much more complicated than that."

But Grace was warming to her theme. "I remember what

you said," she went on. "You talked about immortality as a gift. Perhaps the greatest gift of all, you said."

His sharp eyes examined her. "For a vampire, yes. But for a donor, things are not quite the same."

"What do you mean?"

"The relationship between a vampire and a donor is interdependent. You understand that, of course?"

She nodded. "As long as the vampire takes the donor's blood, the donor remains ageless."

"Yes," he said. "And you've seen what happens when that bond is broken."

"You mean, how rapidly Shanti is aging?"

"Yes. The captain was wrong. It would have been much better if he had not let Shanti go with him."

"But you said Lorcan would be all right," Grace said, beginning to panic again.

"Lorcan *will* be all right. We will find a donor for him. But I'm afraid that Shanti's future is less clear . . ."

Grace suddenly saw what he meant. "Without a vampire feeding on her, Shanti will continue to age fast. Until . . ."

Mosh Zu nodded. By leaving Sanctuary, Shanti had effectively signed her own death warrant. And the captain had allowed her to do so.

"How could he?" she asked Mosh Zu.

"The captain was, as usual, acting out of exemplary motives," Mosh Zu said. "He didn't want to see Shanti so distressed. None of us did. And I suspect, too, that he thinks her presence here could cause Lorcan further tension. He knows that we can find other sources of blood."

"But I still don't understand why he let her go with him," Grace said.

Mosh Zu looked very serious. "The captain always thinks he can save them," he said. "That's the problem. He always thinks he can save everyone. But I'm worried about him, Grace. All this is taking its toll upon him. Things are changing fast in our world. You've seen the rebellions. This is only the beginning. We must be strong. We must prepare ourselves. But the captain does not see this. He is full of goodness, but he gives too much of himself away. Just when he needs to be growing stronger, he allows himself to grow weak."

Grace was stunned to hear such things. She had always thought of the captain as a heroic figure, utterly without flaws and weak points. To hear him described as being so vulnerable was disconcerting.

"You must not speak of these things with the others," Mosh Zu said. "Not even with Lorcan or Olivier. Not anyone."

"No," she said. "I understand."

"I'm talking to you," Mosh Zu said, "as one healer to another. You and I have much in common."

Grace was flabbergasted and deeply humbled. "But I have so much to learn," she said.

"We all do," Mosh Zu said. "And we had all better learn fast."

CHAPTER SIXTEEN

The Emperor

"We've come," said Molucco, "to propose a raid."

Immediately Barbarro became alert with interest. Spearing the last of his steak, foie-gras and caviar, he inquired simply, "A raid?"

"Your crew and mine," Molucco continued. "*The Typhon* and *The Diablo*. Working together, just like the old days."

Connor noticed that Trofie had set down her cutlery and was listening intently, her face resting gently on folded hands. "Do you have a specific ship in mind?" she asked.

Molucco smiled at this. "Not a ship," he said. "Something a little more unusual." He paused and took a draught of wine.

"Well?" urged Barbarro. "Spit it out, brother. The plan, that is, not my vintage claret!"

Completely composed, Molucco turned towards Cate

and gave her a nod. At this sign, she snapped open the case Connor had been carrying for her and began unrolling a large map. Connor and Bart rose from their seats and took hold of the corners of the paper.

"The Sunset Fort," Cate announced, "location: Rajasthan, India." With the tip of her épée she lightly tapped the map to mark its position.

Moonshine yawned. He was still working his way through a mound of pizza and chicken wings which he had been served in preference to the meal the others were eating.

Trofie smiled sweetly at Cate. "Thank you for the geography lesson, *min elskling*, but I think we're all well aware of the Sunset Fort."

"Excellent." Cate nodded, unfazed. "Then you'll know that it was built in the 1640s by Prince Yashodhan for his wife Savarna."

"Ted-i-ous!" muttered Moonshine. Then "Ouch!", as if someone had perhaps kicked him under the table. Sneering, he reached for another chicken wing.

Trofie smiled sweetly at Cate once more. "Actually," Trofie said, "Yashodhan built Savarna *two* palace forts. One to watch the sunrise, the other to view the sunset."

Connor raised his hand.

"Yes, Connor," Cate said.

"Question," said Connor. "Why two palaces? Couldn't they have watched the sun rise and set from the same fort?"

Trofie laughed at this and shook her head.

136

"Mor-on," mumbled Moonshine, just loudly enough so that Connor could hear.

Barbarro grinned. "Only a young boy, a boy who has not yet known true love, could pose such a question." He placed his hand over Trofie's golden fingers. "Why, I'd build a palace for every hour of the day – no, every minute – to honour my dear wife."

Trofie beamed. "Don't give me ideas, *min elskling*," she said, before planting a kiss on his cheek.

"Of course," said Cate, "the palace has quite a different occupant now." Everyone's attention turned back towards her. "The Sunset Fort has long ceased to be an ancestral home. For centuries, it was abandoned, and many of its peripheral buildings fell into disrepair. But the core structure remained sound and today the fort has a new resident. He calls himself merely the Emperor."

"The Emperor?" Barbarro was clearly intrigued. "The Emperor of where?"

Cate shook her head. "He's not an emperor in the conventional sense. He has no empire, beyond the fort itself. Nor does he seek one. He isn't interested in power as such. He isn't even interested in people. He's a collector of treasures. They're his whole world. Prince Yashodhan filled his fort with treasure to express his feelings for the lovely Savarna. But the Emperor loves only his treasures. He has spent his life amassing them from all over the world. It's an extremely rare and valuable collection. Pieces of art that were assumed to have vanished in the flood have somehow ended up there. Once, they were displayed in museums, art galleries and the homes of the wealthy. Now, they are hidden from view within the fort's vault . . ."

"I see where you're going with this," said Barbarro. "A raid on the fort! I like it!"

Cate nodded eagerly. "Yes, yes; you're on the map now. OK, so do you want the good news or the bad?"

Barbarro pondered for the moment. "Let's get the bad news out the way."

Cate nodded. "Originally the Sunset Fort was built, like its twin palace, on a high hilltop. However, when the floods came, four centuries ago, the waters rose. Today, the palace fort is surrounded by water on all sides. It used to be an arduous climb to its base. Now, the fort is almost level with the sea."

"All the better to reach by ship," said Barbarro.

"In principal, yes," Cate agreed. "But it's no easy voyage. The seas surrounding the fort are rough and subject to rogue waves. Many other pirate crews have tried to get to the fort and almost all have come to grief before even reaching the palace gates."

"It would take the very strongest of ships – and the most talented of sailors – to brave such waters," Molucco said.

"I hear you, brother," said Barbarro, his eyes aflame. "This is a job for the Wrathes, and no mistake."

Cate nodded. "The ocean was the first piece of bad news, but there's more. The vault at the Sunset Fort is one of the most inaccessible ever built. Well, Prince

Yashodhan didn't want anyone making off with the treasures he amassed for his beloved Savarna. The impregnable nature of the vault is one of the reasons why the Emperor chose the fort for himself. And, of course, the vault is now protected at all times by the Emperor's elite security force."

"We can expect a colossal fight, then?" Barbarro said. "I'm not sure about this." The others turned, surprised at his change of heart. "I don't shirk from a good fight," he went on, "but this sounds like an impossible situation. Even if we manage to break into the fort, and, by some skill and fortune, conquer this security force, we've still got to get the treasures and get out of there." He frowned. "Unless I'm missing something?"

Cate smiled. "You asked me to save the good news. Well, here it is! We're not going to have to break into the fort and we're not going to have to fight the security force. Indeed, they're going to help us."

"I don't understand," said Barbarro. "Does the Emperor have a rebellion on his hands?"

"How long is this riveting discussion going to go on for?" Moonshine moaned, tossing the last of his chicken bones over his shoulder. Immediately the butler stepped forward and removed the offending items in a gloved hand. Moonshine yawned again. "And when are we getting dessert?"

Connor glared at Moonshine. He'd like nothing more than to give him his just desserts.

"Be quiet, Moonshine!" snapped Barbarro, also clearly frustrated by his son's interruptions. "Go on, Cate, we're all listening."

"With the latest rise in sea level, the Sunset Fort has ceased to be a safe harbour for the Emperor and his treasures. The vault itself is in imminent danger of flooding. The Emperor has resisted taking action for as long as he possibly can. He loves the fort for its isolation. But now, he faces the possibility that one single rogue wave will wipe out his refuge and all he holds dear."

"And so . . ." Trofie snapped her fingers, "he's moving!"

"Exactly." Cate grinned.

"And I'll bet I know where he's going," Trofie said. "To the Sunrise Fort."

"Bingo!" Cate nodded, her eyes bright with excitement. "As you know, the Sunrise Fort was built on somewhat higher ground. The Emperor and his treasures should be safe there, at least for the rest of his lifetime."

"I still don't understand," said Barbarro. "Where do *we* fit into all this?"

"Isn't it obvious, *min elskling*?" Trofie glanced towards her husband. "This Emperor has to transport his goodies from the Sunset Fort to the Sunrise Fort . . ."

Barbarro still looked confused, so Cate continued. "He's hired a top-level security company to ship his goods from A to B, or from Sunset to Sunrise, if you like," she said. "He's paying them top dollar to ensure the safety of his treasures."

"I see," Barbarro said, smiling once more. "*We're* going

140

to intercept the removal company as it travels from one fort to the next."

"Not exactly," said Cate.

Barbarro and Trofie looked at her in equal confusion.

With a light cough, Molucco stood up to deliver the coup-de-grace. Beaming, he announced, "We're not going to intercept the removal company because we *are* the removal company." Turning to Connor and Bart, he gave them a nod. "If you would, lads."

The boys lifted an onyx casket onto the table. Molucco took a small key from his pocket and inserted it into the lock. With a light click, the casket opened and the room was suddenly suffused with light. Inside the casket was a nest of round, brilliant-cut diamonds, which caught the candlelight and reflected it back from every perfect facet.

"Such *beautiful* diamonds," Trofie said, her hand already outstretched, as if the casket was a magnet, drawing her towards it. The length of her arm shimmered silver in the light of the gems.

"Impressive, aren't they?" Molucco grinned. "It's the Emperor's first down payment," he said. "We're hired!"

"What do you think?" The captain of *The Typhon* turned to his deputy.

Trofie considered for only a moment. "Doesn't the Emperor own that diamond-encrusted skull?" she said. "I've always dreamed of adding that to my collection." She paused. "Let's do it!"

Barbarro turned back to Molucco. "It's an audacious

plan, brother," he said. "And we're in." He snapped his fingers. "Transom, let's open some more champagne. We must toast to our success in this venture."

There was great excitement amidst the group as everyone began talking over one another.

"I just hope it turns out better than Cate's last plan," said Moonshine. Somehow, his voice cut through the hubbub.

"Button it, Moonshine," snapped Barbarro.

"What's that?" Molucco asked.

"I was just saying I hope that Cate's strategy this time proves more successful than when you attacked *The Albatross*. That was a bit of a foul-up, to say the least."

Cate blushed fiercely. Molucco looked dumbstruck. Trofie frowned. Barbarro was incandescent with rage. "Go to your cabin, Moonshine!" he roared. "Now!"

Even Moonshine seemed a little taken aback by his father's fury. Ever the PR woman, Trofie smiled. "That's a good idea," she said. "Darling, why don't you take Connor and show him all your lovely things?"

"Whatever." Moonshine shrugged, stomping out of the dining room.

Connor turned to follow him. As he did so, he heard Trofie hiss at her husband, "Happy families, remember? We don't want Molucco thinking anything but good thoughts about Moonshine. After all, *min elskling*, he is the heir to *everything*."

"Right now, I'd sooner Molucco's fortune passed to that Tempest lad," Barbarro snarled.

"Don't talk nonsense," Trofie whispered, icily. "Moonshine is the rightful heir. That boy is nothing to us."

Connor wondered if she knew he could hear her. She suddenly seemed to become aware of his presence and turned around, her perfect smile in place.

"Are you still here, *min elskling*? Hurry along now. Moonshine is waiting for you, and we adults have many important *family* matters to discuss."

CHAPTER SEVENTEEN

The Welcome

"Hi! It's me, Grace. Can I come in?" She pushed open the door.

"Grace!" said Lorcan, stretching after his lengthy sleep. It was now past dusk. "Of course you can come in," he said, sitting up. "How are you tonight?"

"I'm all right," she said, hoping that she sounded convincing. The last thing she could face was bringing Lorcan up to speed on the tense scenes that had preceded the captain's – and Shanti's – departure. "More importantly, how are *you*?" she asked, brightly.

"None too shabby," he said. "I slept really well. Much better than I can remember. Maybe there's something special in the air up here!"

"Talking of air," she said, "maybe we can get you out and about later?"

"Do you think it's allowed?" Lorcan asked, surprised.

"This isn't a prison," she said. "It's a place of healing. I'm sure it's fine to go outside for some air. If you want to."

"Maybe later," he said.

Nodding, Grace sat down on the bed. As she did, she realised she was in danger of crushing a sheet of card.

"What's this?" she asked, pulling the card from underneath her and taking it in her hands. "There's a bit of card here. Did you know it was here?"

"Oh, yes," Lorcan remembered. "Olivier left it for me before. He said it's some kind of welcome message. He offered to read it to me but I was too tired before." He grinned. "Besides, I thought you might read it to me. I have a fonder liking for your voice."

"Of course," Grace said, smiling. Lorcan had a knack for making her feel better. All thoughts of Shanti began to recede. She picked up the card and began to read . . .

Welcome, wandering soul. Welcome to Sanctuary.

Everything you think you know is about to change.

You think you are a limited being. But you are no more limited than the sky or ocean.

You think there is only one path. There are many paths.

145

You think you cannot change. You can change.

You think you are too weary to continue your journey. You are about to regain the energy you need. You will never feel weary again.

You think the best times are behind you. The best times are spread out before you like the most beautiful of gardens.

You think that your existence is empty. We will enable you to fill that void.

Your time of wandering is over. At least, it can be. The choice lies within you. The fact you have made your way here – no easy or regular journey – tells me that you want to change.

You will be amazed at the changes you can make here. Now, you may feel chained to a hunger which never seems to cease but only demands more. You may feel lost in an endless cycle of hunting and hungering. This cycle produces a thick fog which prevents you from seeing what lies beyond it. You may fear there is no other way. There _is_ another way. We will remove the fog and open your eyes. Prepare to see things very differently.

146

There are three stages to your treatment here. There is no fixed time period for each stage or for your treatment as a whole. There are no expectations for you to fulfil. Stay as long as you wish to. Take as long as you need. Do not concern yourself with how quickly or how slowly others pass through the treatment phases. Allow yourself to progress at the pace which is right for you.

The gates of Sanctuary are never closed. They welcome whoever needs to come here. Equally, you may leave at any time. When things get tough – and they <u>will</u> get tough – you may be tempted to leave. Your treatment will make intense physical, mental and emotional demands upon you. These challenges may seem greater than any you have faced before – in life, in death or beyond. Know that you are up to these challenges. Embrace the struggle. You will be the stronger for it. Be assured that the time of struggle will come to an end.

You may feel that you are a very long way from being human. However long it is since you crossed, remind yourself that once you were human. Cling on to the best of what we might term human traits, whilst learning how to accept and nurture the rest of what you are.

147

There is greatness within you. Learn to recognise it.

There is peace within you. Learn to nurture it.

There is another way. You are about to discover it.

Many arrive here feeling that they have been given a terrible burden to carry. We will show you that you have been granted not a burden but a wonderful gift. Perhaps it is the most wonderful gift of all. Be prepared to unwrap it.

Mosh Zu Kamal

Grace felt quite emotional as she finished reading. She carefully set down the card on Lorcan's nightstand.

"Well, that's a lot to think about," Lorcan said.

"Yes." Grace nodded. She reached for Lorcan's hand and held it in her own. "This is a strange place, but I think you'll find the help you need here. Mosh Zu seems like an extraordinary . . . man."

Lorcan nodded.

"And I'm sure," Grace said, "I'm sure that if anyone can help you, he can."

148

CHAPTER EIGHTEEN

Moonshine's Lair

"My cabin's at the bottom of the ship," Moonshine said, as he led the way back along the corridor to the central staircase, which plunged down through the centre of *The Typhon*. "Ordinarily, the VIP cabins are on the top deck, but I wanted one down in the depths. And I always get my way."

With that, he climbed onto the stair-rail and let go, sliding down in ever decreasing circles. Connor watched him. In his dark clothes, Moonshine looked like a witch in flight. Connor climbed onto the stair-rail himself, deciding to follow suit. The ride was brief but exhilarating. As he jumped down onto the bottom deck, he saw that Moonshine was already striding ahead towards a heavily bolted door, with so many padlocks hanging from it they looked like Christmas-tree ornaments. Moonshine's pale hands began twisting the combinations to snap open the locks.

"My parents are very security-conscious," Moonshine said. "Besides, I really value my privacy."

Watching the mound of opened padlocks amass on the floor beside Moonshine, Connor couldn't help but think this was all a little extreme. But maybe, just maybe, it was justified – if the rumours that Trofie had been kidnapped were true. He wondered if he dared ask Moonshine for the truth about that – about his mother's metallic hand. Perhaps not yet.

At last, the door opened and a heady cocktail of incense, body odour and something animal assaulted Connor's nostrils.

"Welcome to Hell!" Moonshine announced, smiling, as he stepped into his room. He continued, without even looking at Connor. "And just so we're clear on this, the fact that I'm letting you in here doesn't mean we're friends or anything dumb like that. OK?"

"Fine by me," Connor said. "Fine by me."

Moonshine's room was vast – at least as big as Molucco Wrathe's cabin back on *The Diablo*. It was a room fit for a prince, and Connor supposed that that was what Moonshine was, a pirate prince. The thought of it, even without the noxious smell of the room, was enough to make him slightly nauseous.

The walls of Moonshine's cabin were painted black. A large iron four-poster bed stood in the middle of the room. Where curtains may have hung from a regular bed, metal chains hung from this one. As the ship moved, they clanked together. The sound would have been enough to give you a headache, even without the thrash-shanty music which Moonshine had flicked on upon entering the room, and which was now turned up to the max.

Connor had developed a deep hatred of thrash-shanty, especially when played this loud. The tune – if you could call it that – sounded somewhat familiar. But then, he thought, all thrash-shanty sounded the same.

The music sorted, Moonshine sauntered over to a vast pinball machine on the other side of the cabin. "Pirate Pinball," he said over his shoulder, by way of explanation. "My dad had it made for me. It's a one-off."

Connor shrugged. Hearing Moonshine speak and seeing the bounty in his cavernous lair, he got the sense of a spoiled brat who had never been told "no"; who had been indulged with whatever he wanted whenever he wanted it.

One entire wall of the cabin was lined with shelves, which were loaded with stuff. One shelf was home to several model ships. While Moonshine lost himself in Pirate Pinball, Connor stepped closer to the shelf to take a better look at his models. They were impressively detailed and very finely painted. Connor imagined a younger, nicer Moonshine slaving away over these ships long into the night. He saw what looked to be a replica of *The Typhon* itself. Beside it was another, slightly larger ship. He saw its name painted in tiny red script on the side of the vessel. *The Diablo*. Connor reached out for it . . .

Moonshine suddenly turned. "Don't touch . . .

anything!" he cried, twisting away from the pinball machine and stomping over.

Frowning, Connor set the model ship back on its shelf. "Sorry," he said. "But this is really good. How long did it take you to make it?"

Moonshine smiled and it was like storm-clouds suddenly parting to reveal the sun. "Aw, my dad and I made that ship together. It took us a whole weekend. We got so into it, we both fell asleep with paint brushes in our hands and Mum had to come down here with blankets so we could sleep like that . . ." He shook his head in reverie. "Happy days!"

Connor was surprised. This was an entirely different window into Moonshine's relationship with his dad.

But suddenly Moonshine's beatific smile was replaced once more by his default sneer. "And if you think that's true, Tempest, you're a bigger sucker than I thought. Do you really think that pirate captains have time to build model ships with their sons? Yeah, right. I did it myself – with a bit of help from Transom . . ." Seeing Connor's blank look, "Transom – our *major-domo*." Connor still looked blank. "Our head servant, dummy. The guy who gave you champagne and sushi before dinner."

"Oh, him." Connor nodded.

"Yeah, him," Moonshine said. "And don't start thinking that there's a special friendship between me and him or that he was like my substitute dad. He only came down with glue and paint brushes because my mum slipped him a nice fat bonus."

Connor was unmoved. "So you had a tough childhood?" he said, glancing around the room. Under his breath, he muttered, "Get over it." Poor little pirate prince, he thought. But, frankly, he didn't feel at all sorry for Moonshine.

He continued exploring the shelves, his eyes roving from a collection of rare seashells to a row of books on *Lives of the Most Notorious Pirates.* He noted *Volume 16: The Brothers Wrathe.* He was about to reach for the book, when he became aware of a fresh squeaking sound, which he managed to distinguish from the music.

Turning again, he saw that Moonshine was standing before a large cage, which had previously been covered in a black cloth, now discarded.

"Hello, my lovelies," Moonshine crooned. He reached into the cage and helped out two creatures from inside. When he turned around again, Connor saw that they were two largish rats, who, grateful to be free, were now crawling over Moonshine. Moonshine grinned. "I call them Flotsam and Jetsam," he said. "Flotsam's the one with the white patch. Isn't she pretty?" He paused. "They're twins," he said, smiling strangely.

"Really," said Connor, still trying to get the measure of his strange companion.

For a moment, Moonshine seemed quite transported by his pets. As they scurried up and down his arms, he looked more peaceful than before. He sat down in a globe-like chair which was suspended from the ceiling by a chain.

"What was *your* childhood like?" Moonshine asked, as he continued to pet Flotsam and Jetsam. The question took Connor by surprise.

Connor decided to take the question at face value. "It was good," he said. "My dad was a lighthouse-keeper. We never knew my mum. It was just the three of us – my dad, my sister Grace and me. We didn't have much but we were happy. We lived in the lighthouse . . ."

"Ah," said Moonshine, ruffling the fur under Flotsam's chin. He was very gentle with the rats, thought Connor. Moonshine looked up again, through the thick strands of his hair. "Happy days in Crescent Moon Bay! Shame that Pops died, eh? Bye, bye Dexter Tempest! Bye, bye nice Crescent Moon Bay!"

Wow! Connor hadn't seen *that* coming. Moonshine's nastiness was deeper than he'd anticipated. But he was more struck by something else. "You know about me," he said.

"We've done our homework," Moonshine said. "Trofie and I *always* do our homework."

Connor was beginning to see there was a strange bond between Moonshine and his mother.

"And how's your weirdo sister?" Moonshine continued. "Still consorting with the Friends of the Night?"

Connor just shook his head. He was determined not to let this strange boy wind him up. Moonshine continued, undaunted. "Looks like little Gracie got all the interesting genes in your family. Just my luck that I get saddled with the wrong twin."

"It's OK," Connor said, suddenly angry. "I can leave at any time."

"Yes," said Moonshine. "Yes, you can leave. You can go back to *The Diablo* and bed down in a hammock next to that himbo Bart. You can go back to your sword-practice and toadying to my uncle. But you'd better remember something, Tempest. As much as he might tell you you're the Next Big Thing, as much as he might flatter you that you're the son he never had, you're *not* his son. *I'm* the heir to the Wrathe fortune. Not you. Me!"

"Whatever," Connor said. "I'm not some kind of fortune hunter, if that's what you think."

"Oh no?" Moonshine said. "You mean you're actually here because you see Uncle Luck as some kind of replacement father figure?" He gave a hollow laugh and shook his head. "You'd better understand something. Molucco Wrathe isn't the doddery old seadog he'd have you believe. He's as sharp as my *shuriken*. He uses people. He makes them think they're part of the family and then he sends them into the line of fire. Your friend Jez, for instance—"

"*Don't*," Connor began, his voice cracking. "Don't talk about Jez."

Moonshine grinned. "Oh but I must, Connor," he said. "I must talk about Jez Stukeley, to illustrate my wider point. Molucco Wrathe pretended that Jez Stukeley was a prized member of his crew. But he still sent him into that duel with Captain Drakoulis' prize fighter—"

"He didn't send him," Connor snapped. "Jez volunteered."

"Same difference. Molucco let him fight when there was no way he could win. Molucco sent Jezzy boy to his death. And one day, for all his talk of you being the prodigal son, he'll do the same to you."

"No," Connor said.

"Yes," retorted Moonshine, just as emphatically. "Yes, he will. Because that's what we Wrathes do. We're users. Me. My parents. Uncle Luck. Why, even good old Uncle Porfirio. We're all the same. We'll tell you anything we feel like to get what we want. But when push comes to shove, we're only out for what we can get for ourselves."

"No," said Connor again. "That might be true for you and your parents, but Molucco's not like that. He saved my life. He's always looked out for me."

Moonshine laughed. "How long have you been on the scene, Tempest? Three months is it now? You know *nothing* about this world, nothing about this family. Well, don't worry. You'll soon see things differently. If Uncle Luck's being good to you right now, it's only because he hasn't worked out how to use you yet. But he will. He always does. We all do. If you really want to know what the Wrathes are, look at me. You might not like what you see, but I'm the only one of this whole crazed dynasty who tells it like it is."

Connor looked at Moonshine's acne-ridden, pockmarked face. He saw the livid purple scar. It wasn't a pretty picture, but nor was the one he was painting of his family. Suddenly, the noxious smell of the cabin was too much for Connor. The rich food and drink he'd enjoyed earlier in the evening began to repeat on him and he had a sudden fear of throwing up. He needed fresh air and fast!

Connor turned and walked briskly out of Moonshine's lair. He began climbing the stairs, two at a time. He found himself shaking, as if there *was* poison in his body. Perhaps there had been something wrong with the blowfish after all and it had just had a delayed reaction. No, he thought. The poison had come from Moonshine's mouth – the vitriol of a lonely, jealous, threatened kid. There was no truth in what he'd said. None at all.

Behind him, he heard Moonshine close and bolt the door to his lair. One lock clanked shut after another. How fitting, thought Connor, that Moonshine chose to reside down there, with his pet rats, in the putrid darkness of his vast cabin. What a loathsome creature he was. But, try as Connor might to dismiss Moonshine's words, some of what he said had hit home. The seeds of doubt had been sown.

CHAPTER NINETEEN

The Ribbon

"Are you able to lean your head back for me a touch?" Mosh Zu asked Grace.

She did so and he came forward to inspect her neck. "So Shanti departs, but she leaves her mark, eh?" Stepping back again, he smiled. "I don't think this wound will be too bad. I'm sure it hurts though. I'll make you up a salve. It should hasten the healing process."

"Thank you," she said.

"Well," he said. "You're very composed. Others might have been a little disturbed to wake up and find someone's hands about their throat." As he spoke he busied himself with a pestle and mortar, taking down jars of herbs and oils and adding a little of each to a bowl.

Grace watched him. "Trust me," she said, "I *was* disturbed. But I know that it wasn't Shanti's intention to hurt me." She paused. "It was the ribbon."

Mosh Zu nodded. "Yes, Grace. You are right. It was the ribbon. A good observation." He began grinding the herbs to a paste with the pestle.

"I know you don't like being asked questions," Grace said.

Mosh Zu looked up in surprise. "Why do you say that?"

"Olivier," Grace said. "He told me that there was a rule at Sanctuary not to ask questions." She smiled. "I think I'm going to struggle with it."

"Yes." Mosh Zu smiled, setting down the pestle and looking directly at her. "I see. Yes, I knew something was holding you back. I expected you to charge in here, brimming with questions. I know that's how I would be myself, on my first day in this intriguing new place."

Grace nodded. "I am. I mean, yes, I do have questions. But Olivier said that I was to wait for people to open up to me and not to ask . . ."

Mosh Zu nodded. "Well, Grace, here are some things you should know. Firstly, Olivier is a good man. He takes his duties here very seriously. He came to me when he was little older than you and he's become almost indispensable to me."

Grace noticed that Mosh Zu had said *almost*. This struck her as strange. There was something behind the word, as if he was giving her some extra information; but she couldn't quite decipher what it was.

Mosh Zu continued. "Secondly, he is right in so much

as it is better not to push those who come here for too much too fast. They come here because they have their own questions, which *we* can help them to answer. This must be our priority." He smiled at Grace. "But *you* may ask *me* all the questions you want," he said. "The rules, if you must call them that, do not apply between us."

Grace smiled. This was a great relief to hear.

Mosh Zu took a small glass jar and poured the contents of the mortar into it. "Here you are," he said, handing it to her. "Apply a little of the salve now, and then, if the wound is still raw, a little more before you sleep tonight."

Grace unscrewed the lid. It was a pungent mixture. She recognised some of the smells.

"Is there rosemary in here?"

Mosh Zu nodded. "Yes. Now, you don't need very much of it. That's it. Just a little on each side."

Grace applied the salve, then wiped her fingers on a cloth Mosh Zu passed to her.

"And now some tea and questions?" he said, smiling and indicating a circle of cushions in one corner of the room.

He poured her a cup of herb tea and another for himself, then sat down cross-legged on the cushions.

Grace watched as he lifted the tea-bowl to his lips. She was surprised. When you had been around vampires as long as Grace had, you looked for signs. If Mosh Zu was drinking tea, did this mean he wasn't a vampire? Was he an in-between like her and Olivier? Could the

Vampirate guru – to use the captain's own word – be an in-between?

"Yes," Mosh Zu said with a smile. "I see you are full of questions. Where shall we begin, I wonder?"

Grace was in no doubt. "Tell me about the ribbons," she said.

Mosh Zu sipped his tea. "Let's make this more interesting," he began.

Grace waited for him to continue.

"Why don't *you* tell *me* about the ribbons."

"I don't know about them," Grace said.

Mosh Zu took another sip of his tea. "You know more than you think."

Grace shook her head. "Olivier led us along the Corridor of Ribbons on our way to our room but he didn't explain about them. He said that you would."

Mosh Zu set down his teacup. "Let's consider what we know," he said. "Shanti took a ribbon from the corridor. Thinking that it was nothing but a pretty strip of cloth, she pulled it down and used it to tie up her hair. She fell asleep wearing it and the energy contained in the ribbon began acting upon her." He looked up at Grace. "Did you notice anything strange about Shanti's behaviour before you yourself fell asleep?"

"Yes," Grace said. "At least, she seemed very restless. She was tossing and turning so much, I almost woke her. I thought she might be having a bad dream . . ."

"And, indeed," Mosh Zu said, "that isn't far from the

161

truth. Certainly, the ribbon was controlling her thoughts. The dark energy contained within it was seeping into her head, changing her thought patterns."

Grace was wide-eyed. "You're telling me that the ribbon itself is evil?"

Mosh Zu shook his head. "Think about the sort of people who come here— vampires. You'll meet some of them soon enough. The vampires who come here are those who are tormented. Perhaps they have only recently crossed and they are struggling to accept their new existence, what I call the Afterdeath. Then again, they may have crossed long ago but still they are conflicted." As he sipped his tea again, Grace was hungry to know more.

"What are they conflicted about?" she asked.

"Many things," Mosh Zu said. "It might be about their hunger – we can work on that – or perhaps they still struggle to leave behind the light and embrace the darkness. Then again, there are those who find the idea of eternal existence to be overwhelming. We can help them work through all these emotions."

"But how does this link in to the ribbons?" Grace asked.

"When someone arrives at Sanctuary, no matter what afflicts them, we begin treatment in the same way. We work with them on the letting go of all their past hurts. Are you with me so far?"

She nodded.

"The more of their pain they can let go of, the better the chance we have of working successfully with them. And so

162

each of them is given a ribbon. Then we begin working to let go of all their bad experiences – all the pain they endured in life, and during death, and afterwards. And, equally, the pain they have inflicted upon others."

"So the experiences are transferred into the ribbons?"

"Just so," said Mosh Zu. "And when the patient is ready to move on to the next stage of treatment, we hang their ribbon in the Corridor of Ribbons. They are released from their past hurts, but the dark energy remains within the ribbon."

"But isn't it dangerous to keep the ribbons?"

"Evidently," Mosh Zu said, tapping his own neck. "But where else should this energy go? It must go somewhere. And, as much as I want each of them to free themselves from hurt, I do not want them to forget absolutely the road they have travelled. Sometimes they will need to be reminded. Sometimes we all need to be reminded."

"So the ribbon Shanti took contained a dark energy."

Mosh Zu nodded.

"Do you know who the ribbon belonged to? What experiences it contained?"

Mosh Zu nodded again.

"But you're not going to tell me?"

He smiled. "Why don't you tell me about the other ribbon?" he said. "The one she gave to you."

"You know about that?" Grace said.

"Olivier saw it in your hands when he rescued you. He picked it up and brought it to me."

Yes, Grace realised that, in the throes of the attack, she had forgotten about the ribbon. And now, Mosh opened up his own hand and laid it out between them.

"I'm sorry," Grace said, looking at the piece of cloth. "She gave it to me before we went to bed. I knew she shouldn't have taken it. She didn't mean any harm. I was going to make her take them back but events overtook us."

Mosh Zu shook his head. "I'm not angry with you," he said. "And not with Shanti either, as a matter of fact. You're right. She didn't know what she was doing. But tell me, what happened with your ribbon?"

"Well, it didn't make me want to kill anyone," Grace said.

Mosh Zu smiled. "No, it didn't. Isn't that interesting?"

"My dreams!" Grace said suddenly. "I had the most vivid dreams. Was that the ribbon? Did I somehow channel some of the experiences in the ribbon?"

"Perhaps," Mosh Zu said. "Perhaps you should tell me about your dreams?"

She thought back. The boy lying on the ground, looking up at the star-filled sky. The boy with the horse. Whiskey. And the boy was called Johnny . . .

She relayed the fragments of her dream to Mosh Zu. He listened patiently, encouraging her to take her time, to remember each piece as vividly and thoroughly as she could. When she went from Johnny breaking in the bronco at the paddock to him riding the horse at the rodeo, her memory started to fail.

164

"If you need help," said Mosh Zu, "take the ribbon once more."

She looked down at the red ribbon, curled about itself in a wooden bowl between them. It looked so innocuous, but as soon as she picked it up, she felt a sudden energy. Instinctively, she closed her eyes.

"That's good, Grace. Now, find your place. Find Johnny in the paddock."

Grace nodded. "I'm there," she said.

"Now what?"

"It isn't the rodeo," she said, puzzled. "He's riding other horses, breaking them in. He's in different places, with other people, but it isn't a big rodeo. And then he begins riding across the country – that's right . . ."

She opened her eyes again and let go of the ribbon.

"I don't understand," she said. "The rodeo was so clear before. I couldn't have imagined it."

Mosh Zu shook his head. "You didn't imagine it. It comes later. It comes after he dies."

Grace trembled. "After he dies." Of course.

"So, he begins riding across the country. Take it from there."

Grace continued Johnny's story. The rest of the dream fell into focus, right to the moment when she was lifted from the snow and felt a rope being fastened around Johnny's neck.

"And that's where I got to when I felt Shanti's hands on me. It was as if the dream and reality came together at that moment."

"That's not so strange," Mosh Zu said. "Your ability to channel Johnny's story is amazing. Do you feel ready to know how it ends?"

Grace wasn't sure. As she'd channelled Johnny's experiences, she hasn't just been watching them, she had felt his emotions, his hurt – the hurt he had somehow channelled into the ribbon.

"Perhaps you are not quite ready to take this step," Mosh Zu said. "Perhaps you do not think you are ready. But I think you are."

She wanted to know. She couldn't leave the story here. Taking a deep breath, Grace reached forward and took the ribbon into her hand once more. Again, she felt the sudden surge of energy within her.

"The vigilantes're fastening the noose around my neck," she said, falteringly. "And round the necks of my two compadres. And I'm tellin' them that it's not fair. I didn't do nothing wrong. I didn't know they was rustlers, the pair of 'em. And though they lied to me right up to that moment, now they start telling the vigilantes I'm tellin' the truth. I'm no rustler. I had no idea of their villainy. They know they're gonna die hangin' from that tree but they start beggin' for me to be spared. But the noose tightens. They lift me up. Now we're hangin' side by side, like a line of washing. And then the noose tightens and I'm hanging there looking out at the prairie, at the infinite roll of sky and stars. And I'm thinking, So that's it. Eighteen years old. I travelled all the way from Texas to South Dakota for

166

this. And then everything goes black, no – everything goes blank."

Grace opened her eyes, feeling the hot tears welling behind them.

"Here, let me take the ribbon," Mosh Zu said gently.

As he did so, tears began to fall down Grace's face.

Through them, she saw that Mosh Zu was smiling at her.

"You have such abilities," he said. "Don't you see? When Shanti wore the ribbon, all she took from it was its darkness, its violence. But you . . . you read his whole story."

"But whose story was it?" Grace said.

"You'll find out soon enough," Mosh Zu said.

CHAPTER TWENTY

Night Mission

"And what exactly *do* you need the light boat for at this time of night?" asked the pirate in charge of the night watch. Just their luck, thought Connor, that Lieutenant Nosey, a.k.a. Jean de Cloux, was on duty.

"It's a private errand for Captain Wrathe," said Bart, confidently.

"What kind of errand?" De Cloux was immediately suspicious.

"If we told you *that,* it wouldn't be private, would it?"

"I think I'd better check this out with Captain Wrathe," de Cloux said.

"Be my guest," Bart said, as relaxed as ever. "I'm sure the captain would welcome you disrupting his precious sleep to question his orders."

"Well . . ." De Cloux considered the matter once more. It was common knowledge that Captain Wrathe did not take kindly to being woken up, especially over trifles. "All right," he said, loftily. "I *shall* help you. But I'm going to have to check with Captain Wrathe in the morning."

"Understood," said Bart. "Quite understood. *Except*, as this is a private errand, the captain asked specifically that none of us mention it to him again or to any other members of the crew *at any point*."

Connor smiled at Bart's audacity, wondering if de Cloux would go for it.

De Cloux seemed to have taken Bart's words at face value. "He said that?"

"Yes," said Bart, preparing himself for the *coup de grâce*. "And he asked us to give you this." He reached into his pocket and retrieved a small package, which he dropped into de Cloux's palm.

De Cloux gave a sniff. "Is this what I think it is?" He prised open the small package. "Chocolate?" he said, in a faraway voice. "I've been dreaming of chocolate . . . dark, bitter chocolate . . ." He couldn't seem to stop himself from breaking off a square. As it melted in his mouth, his expression was one of pure ecstasy.

"He knew that," Bart said, sealing the deal. "And he asked us to give you this, to thank you for your silence."

"Captain Wrathe himself asked you to give me the chocolate?"

Bart nodded, very sombre. "From his own private supply." He paused and reached out a hand to de Cloux's shoulder. "What's more, he said that if you were able to

169

keep your silence, there *might* be a promotion for you before too long."

"Promotion?" De Cloux's eyes bulged in the lantern-light. He couldn't believe his ears. Nor could Connor. This had never been part of the patter they'd prepared. Bart was getting carried away with himself. It was all very well palming people off with contraband candy, but you couldn't go around promising people promotions.

Connor coughed to get the others' attention. "We should be going," he said. "Time's moving on."

"Yes." De Cloux nodded, carefully pocketing the rest of the precious chocolate. "You two get into the boat and I'll winch you down." He called over another pirate to help him.

"But where are they going to at this time of night?" the junior pirate protested.

"Don't be impudent, Gregory!" de Cloux said, bristling with authority. "It's the captain's own orders, so just help me out and keep your mouth shut for once."

"Yes, sir," answered the chastened Gregory.

Connor was grinning to himself as he climbed into the boat, careful not to step on Jez, who was still hidden under the tarpaulin. Bart passed over two lanterns to Connor, then he climbed in himself as de Cloux started to lower the boat towards the water.

"Remember," Bart said, as he gave the thumbs up to de Cloux, "mum's the word!"

"Mum's the word," repeated de Cloux, with an uncharacteristically good-humoured wink.

Moments later, the light boat slapped into the dark waters and Bart released the lines which held the satellite vessel to *The Diablo* and began steering the small craft away into the open ocean.

They had only travelled a few metres when a pale hand pushed back the tarpaulin and Jez's equally pale face appeared. His pallor still shocked Connor but the laugh was the same old Jez Stukeley laugh.

"Poor de Cloux," Jez said, between giggles. "He'll be waiting until Christmas for Captain Wrathe to ask him into his cabin to discuss his prospects."

Bart grinned. "He'll be waiting a sight longer than that. Still, it'll keep his silence."

"Thanks, boys," Jez said, sitting up beside them now that they were far enough away from *The Diablo* not to be seen. "Thanks for everything you're doing for me."

"All for one," said Bart, "and one for all." He grinned at Jez. "Didn't we always look out for each other? Just because you're dead, mate, doesn't mean you stop being one of the Three Buccaneers, eh, Connor?"

Connor shook his head and smiled. "You can't get away from us that easily!"

Jez beamed back. "And there was I thinking you'd let Brenden Gonzalez take my place."

"Gonzalez?" Bart asked, as he moved the tiller. "What makes you say that?"

Jez shrugged. "I saw you all dancing together, a few nights back, at Ma Kettle's."

171

"You were at Ma's?" Bart exclaimed, surprised.

"Yes," Jez continued. "I wanted to talk to you both then, but I didn't have the guts. I just sat there in one of those curtained booths, sneaking glances at you guys on the dance-floor. Gonzalez was with you then."

They continued on for a minute or more in silence. Then Bart's face suddenly turned as pale as Jez's. "Wait a minute," he said. "You were at Ma's the night that Jenny Petrel was killed."

"Jenny Petrel?" Jez repeated, blankly. Evidently, the name meant nothing to him.

"She was one of Ma's serving girls. You remember Jenny. Pretty as a summer's day." He frowned. "They found her in one of the booths above the dance-floor. No one heard anything. Little Jenny didn't scream. No one even heard her cry, over the tango music. But, when they found her . . . cuts all over her chest . . . she had bled to death."

Jez shook his head, sadly. "Poor Jenny," he said.

"So," Bart went on. "You were in one of the curtained booths where she was killed. You need to drink human blood to live now, right?" He sighed, deeply. "Don't you understand what I'm saying?" Bart looked gutted. "You did it, didn't you?"

"Me?" Jez reacted as though the suggestion was utterly absurd, let alone repugnant. Then his expression grew normal again, as he conceded, "I might have done." He paused. "I don't remember."

"What do you *mean*, you don't you remember?" Connor asked, appalled.

"How could you *kill* someone, and not remember?" said Bart.

"It's the hunger," Jez answered matter-of-factly. "When the hunger takes over, you have no choice but to feed it. It drives you, then it numbs you. Afterwards, your senses are dull for a time and you need rest."

Connor couldn't believe what he was hearing. Clearly neither could Bart. Earlier, as they'd set out in the boat, it had seemed just like old times. But however much they might pretend that nothing had changed, that this was just another crazy adventure for the Three Buccaneers, things *were* different now. A line divided him and Bart from Jez. Strangely, it hadn't mattered so much that he was a dead man, the living dead, a vampire . . . whatever you chose to call it. But now he had confessed to being a wanton murderer, and shown not an iota of remorse, not even a spare thought for his victim.

"I know what you're both thinking," Jez said. "I'm not stupid. Don't you see? I hate this thing I've become. I told you that before. I need help. I'll do whatever it takes. If I did kill that girl – and, yes, I probably did – well that's terrible. And it's terrible that I don't remember. But you don't understand what this hunger is like. I'm not in control of my own body any more – my own thoughts, my own needs. When the hunger comes over me, flows into me, there's nothing I can do to fight it."

Connor was somewhat reassured to hear these words. He's not a monster, he told himself. Not, at least, a monster of his own making – a monster who *chose* to do evil. He managed to smile weakly at Jez. "The Vampirate captain will help you," Connor said. "He'll know what to do."

Bart turned to Connor, suddenly all business. "OK," he said. "Let's finish what we started. How do we find our way to the Vampirate ship?"

"Do you know where it's anchored?" Jez asked excitedly.

Connor shook his head. "No," he said. "But I met the captain. And he told me that when I needed to find it, it wouldn't be hard."

The captain had told him a lot more besides, thought Connor. Like how to kill Jez – or the thing Jez had become. He had told him to attack with fire. But fire hadn't killed Jez, only Sidorio and the other Vampirates. How come Jez had been spared that night? Was it some residue of humanity that he alone of the vampires retained? Not enough humanity to prevent him from killing Jenny Petrel, Connor reflected. They had to get him to the Vampirate ship and seek the help of the captain, before he committed another atrocity.

He looked at his old ally, trying to get the measure of him. Jez stared back. As he did so, the contours of his face suddenly changed. His eyes had disappeared, as if his eyeballs had fallen down into a deep, dark well. Out of this darkness rose twin balls of fire. It was terrifying, yet mesmeric, to watch. Then, just as rapidly, the fire was gone again. Jez's eyelids flickered and he stared back at Connor with his old, familiar eyes.

"What's the matter, mate?" Jez said. "You look like you've seen a ghost." He giggled to himself. But Connor couldn't join in the joke this time.

"Your eyes disappeared, just for a second." He turned to Bart. "Did you see it?" Bart nodded, his own face taut with fear. Connor turned back to Jez. "Your eyes disappeared. And in their place was fire."

"Ah," said Jez, as matter-of-fact as ever. "That generally means I need blood."

"*You need blood?*" Bart repeated, his voice rising in pitch. "We're out alone in the middle of a dark ocean with you and you have a sudden fancy for blood! Remind me again, who came up with this brilliant plan?"

Seeing that Bart was bordering on hysteria, Connor took command of the situation. "How soon?" he asked Jez. "How soon do you need blood?"

Jez's eyes disappeared once more and the fires of Hell returned. "Need blood now," he said. "Need blood now."

CHAPTER TWENTY-ONE

The Ribbon Ceremony

Grace knocked on the door.

"Come in," Mosh Zu called from inside.

Grace squeezed Lorcan's hand before pushing open the door. The room was small and sparsely furnished.

Two other people – a man and a woman – were already sitting in the centre of the room. Beside them was an empty chair, presumably for Lorcan. As Grace led him towards the chair, she quickly glanced at the others.

The man was dressed in white from head to toe. His face was as pale as his clothes. The woman, in contrast, wore an elaborate ball gown. On closer inspection, Grace saw that it was in tatters. Her eyes travelled up to the woman's neck. Around it hung a diamond necklace, glittering in the soft lamplight. The woman caught her looking and smiled softly, her fingers touching the necklace. The man had already turned away, his eyes firmly fixed on the floor.

As Lorcan sat down, Grace noticed there were no other chairs.

"Should I go?" she asked Mosh Zu.

"No," he said. "I'd like you to stay." He glanced up at the others. "If that's all right with you."

The woman shrugged. "*Pourquoi pas?*"

The man said nothing, his eyes still glued to the floor.

"Take a seat on the floor, wherever you wish," Mosh Zu said to Grace. She nodded and sat down, cross-legged.

"We are all here, so we shall begin," Mosh Zu said. "I want to welcome you to Sanctuary. I'm so pleased that you have found your way here. You may stay as long as you need. You have, doubtless, wandered this world for a long time."

Grace's eyes travelled across the faces of the three vampires. She noticed that the woman was no longer smiling and the man dressed in white had at last lifted his eyes and was staring at Mosh Zu.

"I know how tired you must be," Mosh Zu said. "Sanctuary will help to take away that tiredness." He smiled at them. "We will work hard to remove the burdens you have been carrying for so long."

There was something incredibly soothing about Mosh Zu's voice, thought Grace. And, though he was not talking to her, she sensed that her own burdens might become lighter through her time here.

"I will not ask much of you today," Mosh Zu said. "For today marks only the beginning of a new journey for you.

A journey that, I hope, will bring you peace and a new beginning. Think of Sanctuary as a place to shed all that pains you."

He let the words settle upon the three of them. Grace saw the relief in their faces.

"Tell me your names," Mosh Zu said. "When and where you were born, and when and where you died. That is all I need at this point."

He nodded to the woman. She was, Grace noticed, still running her fingers over her diamond necklace.

"My name," she said, "is Marie-Louise, Princesse de Lamballe." She paused, as if expecting some congratulation or recognition. Mosh Zu said nothing, simply nodding and waiting for more. "I was born in Turin in 1749. I died in Paris in 1792. I was a companion and confidante of . . ."

"That's all we need, thank you," Mosh Zu said, cutting her off – but softly. Grace could tell from the woman's expression that she had been keen to tell more of her story. But now Mosh Zu nodded to the man dressed all in white.

"I'm Thom Feather," he said. "Born Huddersfield, 1881. Died Wakefield, 1916."

Unlike the princess, Thom Feather did not offer any further information.

"Thank you," said Mosh Zu, turning now to Lorcan. He stepped forward and placed a hand on Lorcan's shoulder. "And now you," he said.

"My name," he said, "is Lorcan Furey." Grace watched

him intently as he continued. "Born 1803 in Connemara, died 1820 in Dublin."

"Thank you," Mosh Zu said. "Thank you all for choosing to come here."

Grace wondered then how the others had heard about Sanctuary. And how had they found their way here? Had they, like the expedition party from *The Nocturne*, had to clamber up the mountainside? What other option was there? If so, how had Thom Feather's clothes remained so stark white? And how had the princess made it in such an impractical dress? This was something she must ask Mosh Zu about when the time was right.

"I have something for each of you," Mosh Zu said now. He took up a wooden box and passed it first to the princess. "Please take a ribbon," he said.

"Must I?" Strangely, the princess trembled.

Mosh nodded. "Yes," he said. "I know it has unfortunate associations for you, but you must."

What did he mean by that? Grace saw how surprised the princess was at his words. She watched as the woman lifted a green ribbon from the box and held it, trembling, in her fingers.

Next, the box was passed to Thom Feather. He looked inside it and gave a hollow laugh. "I suppose the white one is for me," he said, taking it out of the box.

Finally, Mosh Zu passed the box to Lorcan. Grace watched as Lorcan extended his arm and searched the air before him for the box. Mosh Zu waited patiently. When

Lorcan frowned, he placed his hand on his shoulder again. "There's no rush, Lorcan Furey. Take your time."

Lorcan's fingers finally found the box and took hold of the ribbon inside. "Well done," Mosh Zu said, closing the box and stepping back again.

"Now," he said. "I want each of you to make a fist and hold the ribbon tightly within it." His eyes passed over the three of them. "Good," he said. "Now, you must be brave. Next, I'm going to ask you to let go of your pain; wherever that pain has come from – whether it is from your life, your death or the Afterdeath. Don't force it. You probably won't be able to shed too much of it, at first. But we'll repeat this night after night. And in time, you will be free from these terrible burdens."

He smiled. "Now, as you focus on releasing your pain, maintain your hold on one end of the ribbon but let the other end drop."

He waited and watched as each of the three followed his instructions. Behind him, Grace watched just as intently. Could it be true? Could their pain really be travelling into the ribbons themselves? She could see the intensity of the expressions on their faces. Even though Lorcan's eyes weren't visible, she could see his determination in the set of his jaw.

She watched as Mosh Zu lifted his right hand. As he did so, something amazing happened. The three ribbons stopped hanging limply in the air and began seeking his hand, as surely as if a magnet was attracting them. The others noticed it too, raising their eyes in wonder.

"Don't focus on me," Mosh Zu told them. "Keep the focus on yourself. Shed the pain from your body and let it travel into the ribbon."

Grace watched as the ribbons grew tauter, as if Mosh Zu was reeling them in. She could see a pool of light gather around the edges of the ribbons. If she needed any convincing about the power of the treatment, she found it when she turned back to the vampires.

Grace saw that the princess was crying. Her eyes were still shut but tears were flowing down her cheeks. Grace turned to Mosh Zu. He did not meet her gaze. She realised he too must be channelling all his focus into the ribbons.

Then there was a terrible moan. Grace realised it was coming from Thom Feather. His eyes too were closed. The moan continued, low and long. She remembered his death date as 1916. But it was as if the pain of six hundred years was slowly leaving his body. At first the sound distressed her but, as it continued, she imagined a boil bursting deep within him and waves of distress at last beginning to break free.

As Thom Feather's moan at last began to subside, Grace turned her eyes to Lorcan. There were no tears on his face, nor did he make any sound. Grace frowned. She sensed that this was not a good sign.

She watched as, at last, Mosh Zu lowered his hand and his connection with the three coloured ribbons was broken.

Gradually, the princess opened her eyes. She was still

clutching the ribbon. With her free hand she rummaged in her dress and removed a lace handkerchief with which she dried her tears.

Now, Thom Feather opened his eyes. He looked shaken, as if he had just woken and was surprised by his surroundings. After a moment or two, he came back to himself, but Grace thought that already there was a new vitality to him.

Lorcan did not make any movement, but Mosh Zu seemed to sense that he too had done as much as he could.

"You have all made the first step," he said. "Whatever pain you have brought to Sanctuary, you will leave it behind here. Whether you are struggling with your hunger, or battling wounds old or new, or are simply tired – so very tired – of wandering, here you *will* find a new beginning."

Grace thought how tranquil his words were, like soft water lapping on a shore.

"Go now," Mosh Zu said. "Return to your rooms or, if you wish for air, take to the gardens. Spend time in solitude or, if you prefer, get better acquainted with each other, or those who came here before you. We will meet again tomorrow night. Keep your ribbons with you at all times and bring them along here tomorrow."

He smiled and turned. It was clear that the session was over.

"I have a question," the princess said. Her eyes swivelled towards Grace. For some reason, Grace found herself shivering.

Mosh Zu turned back to her. "Yes?"

"Blood," she said. "My need for blood is very strong. They said that you would advise us of the arrangements."

Mosh Zu smiled at her. "You will take no blood," he said.

"*No blood?* But that's preposterous!"

He shook his head. "You do not need it. I can tell. You must learn to distinguish between real need and habit," he said.

"But—" she began to protest once more. Once more Mosh Zu cut her off.

"When you truly need blood, we will address the question," he said. "Live with the anxiety. Allow your hunger to possess you. And then deny it. And watch it recede."

"I can't . . ." the princess began. "I am weak."

"No," Mosh Zu said. "You are very strong. You all are. Stronger than you realise. But soon you will know yourselves better."

He smiled. Then, to Grace's surprise, he simply walked out of the room and disappeared along the labyrinthine corridors.

CHAPTER TWENTY-TWO
Blood Tavern

"What are we going to do?" Bart asked as he and Connor gazed nervously at the fire burning in Jez's eye sockets.

The hunger was clearly growing stronger but Jez seemed to be doing his best to fight it. "Don't fear me," he rasped. "I won't harm you."

"Mate, you need blood, and we're all alone at sea with nothing but a drop of rum in my flask," Bart said. "You said it yourself. When the hunger takes you over, you can't control yourself. I think we have every reason to be afraid."

"Take me . . ." It seemed a great effort for Jez to force out the words. "Take-me-to-the-Blood-Tavern."

Bart looked at him, confused. "*Blood Tavern.* What are you on about, mate?"

In answer, Jez held out his arm and lifted his sleeve. Connor was shocked afresh by the whiteness of his skin.

It was almost translucent, pale blue veins swimming beneath its sheer surface. There, on the inside of his forearm, was the mysterious tattoo of three cutlasses they had all woken up with after their lost weekend in *Calle del Marinero*. But Jez was pointing above the tattoo to fresher ink. Not a tattoo, but what appeared to be a hastily scribbled note.

> Blood Tavern
> Limbo Creek
> Black door
> Lilith

"Take me," Jez said once more, his eyes aflame and his mouth seeming now to contort.

Connor shivered. He turned to Bart. "Do you know Limbo Creek?" he asked.

"Yes," Bart said. "It's not far from here." Already he was adjusting the direction of the boat.

Connor turned to Jez, who seemed to be trying desperately to contain his appetites. But his body seemed no longer his to control.

"How much time have we got?" Connor asked him.

Jez kept his face turned away but rasped once more, "Need-blood-now."

The night winds were in their favour and Bart made swift work of steering the light boat towards Limbo Creek.

"OK," he said. "We're here."

Jez was rocking to and fro, causing their small boat to do the same.

"We're here," Connor repeated, tentatively reaching out an arm to Jez. When Jez looked up, Connor had to tear his eyes away. With every passing moment, Jez seemed to be shedding another layer of his human visage.

"Have you been here before?" Connor asked.

Jez opened his mouth but, instead of answering the question, he simply repeated, "Need-blood-now."

Bart let out a deep sigh. "There's no point. You won't get any more sense out of him," he said. "We'll just have to find this Blood Tavern ourselves."

Connor agreed. "So we're looking for a black door," he said.

"Right now, any door would be a good starting point," Bart said, his voice heavy with frustration and anxiety.

They were now up close to the rock at the perimeter of the creek but, so far, there was no sign of any buildings or habitation at all.

"I don't ever remember seeing a building in this creek," Bart said, disconsolately.

Connor's heart was sinking fast. If they didn't get to the Blood Tavern soon, there was going to be a bad end to this. An end which would result in at least one less person returning in the light boat, possibly two.

"Wait a minute," Bart suddenly cried, pointing up the rock-face. "Could that be a door, there?"

"Where?" Connor couldn't see anything but the shadowy rock.

"Quick," Bart said. "Pass me your lantern!"

Connor did so and Bart held it up towards the rock.

There was a ledge and, above it, somewhat obscured by rough vegetation, the outline of a door.

"That *must* be it!" Connor said.

"It's black and it's a door!" Bart said, grinning. "It's good enough for me!"

Jez lifted his head and opened his mouth. It looked swollen. Connor hadn't noticed before how pronounced his incisor teeth were. They seemed to be growing. His gums were engorged and bleeding. Connor was greatly relieved when Jez closed his mouth again.

"There's nowhere to moor the boat," Bart said. "Connor, I'll have to wait here, while you go in with him."

"Me?" Connor said.

Bart nodded, squeezing his arm. "Go on, buddy. However bad it is, it can't be worse than the alternative."

Connor wasn't so sure. A blood tavern sounded a pretty bad place to be. He shivered in anticipation as Bart steadied the boat so he could step out onto the rocky ledge. "Here," he said, holding out his hand to Jez. "Follow me." He helped Jez to climb up onto the ledge. It was like leading a wild dog.

Once they were on the ledge, the overgrown plants formed a kind of arbour leading towards the black door.

187

There was a bell-pull at its side. Trying to calm his tide of nerves, Connor reached out and gave it a tug.

After a slight delay, there was the sound of sliding metal and a small opening appeared in the door. A pair of milky eyes glanced out. They fixed on Connor. He stared back, his heart beating fast.

"Well?" came a voice from inside.

"Is this the Blood Tavern?" Connor asked.

There was no response. The milky eyes stared out, devoid of all expression. Connor couldn't help wondering if they were the eyes of a blind person.

"This is Limbo Creek and this is the only black door. This must be the Blood Tavern. Please let us in. My . . . my friend needs blood . . . very badly."

The eyes showed not even a flicker of understanding. Then Connor remembered the final note on Jez's arm.

"Lilith," he said. "We're looking for someone called Lilith."

At that, the door creaked ajar, and an opening appeared in the rock. Connor ducked down and stepped inside, pulling Jez along with him.

The milky eyes of the doorkeeper seemed to hover in the darkness. He was dressed in dark robes. Saying nothing, he lifted a hand and pointed along a curving corridor. Connor could see a glow of light and hear voices up ahead.

"*Blood?*" Jez said, questioningly.

"Yes," Connor reassured him. "Blood. Very soon now."

He pushed on through the dimly-lit corridor until they

came to a small square vestibule. There was a glass booth at its centre – rather like the one at the Crescent Moon Bay Picture House – and Connor could see a woman inside it. Her hair was arranged in an unruly black beehive. Her eyelids were thickly caked with emerald-green glitter. It seemed somewhat incongruous to her surroundings and to her face, which was not in the first flush of youth.

There was someone ahead of them in the queue. He turned and Connor saw, to his horror, the same fire burning in this man's eyes. Another vampire. If it had felt dangerous out on the boat, when he and Bart had outnumbered Jez, it felt a lot worse here. In this strange place deep inside the rock, doubtless vampires outnumbered mortals. He watched as the vampire reached into his pocket and produced a stash of coins. Then Connor felt his own blood run cold. They were going to have to pay for the blood. Of course they were! Why hadn't he anticipated this?

"Room three," the woman in the booth announced, dropping the vampire's money into her till and pointing to a doorway, covered in red velvet. The vampire nodded and pushed through the doorway into the darkness beyond.

"Next!" called the woman from inside her gilded glass cage.

Connor stepped forward in trepidation.

"We need some blood," he said.

"You've come to the right place," the woman said. "A pint, a half-pint or a special measure?"

Connor looked at Jez, then turned back to the woman. "I don't know," he said. "It's for him, not me."

The woman looked Jez up and down and turned to Connor. "I'd say a pint."

"OK," Connor said, then asked the question he'd been dreading. "How much is that?"

It wasn't really a large amount. But it was more than Connor had on him.

"Do you have any money, Jez?" he asked.

Jez shook his head and then moaned, "*Blooooood*."

"No money, no blood," the woman said. "Sorry, dearie, but we're not running a charity here. Now step aside, there's others behind you in the queue."

Connor couldn't believe they'd come this far, only to be defeated. Sadly, he turned away. As he did so, the woman spoke.

"Wait! That locket you're wearing. I'd say that's worth something."

Connor turned back. "My locket?" His fingers fell on it. It was the locket he'd given Grace and that she'd left for him when she went away. It was a talisman for him, a way of keeping her close. "I can't give you this," he said. "I can't."

"Oh well," the woman said. "It was just a thought. Next!"

CHAPTER TWENTY-THREE

An Alternative to Blood

Olivier had a suite of rooms, though, from what Grace could see, each was as simple and monastic as the other chambers within Sanctuary. The door to his bedroom was ajar and looked as sparse as Lorcan's or her own, suggesting that the "staff" at Sanctuary enjoyed no more privileges than visitors or those undergoing treatment. Another door opened into a small office. This, she was not surprised to see, was fastidiously tidy. There was a chair and small desk, currently clean of any papers. Behind it was a shelf bearing a neatly ordered row of files and ledgers. On the wall was some kind of wooden unit with cards inserted into it. It looked like something you might find in a hospital or library. Grace wished she could get closer to see exactly what it was.

"Having a good nose round, eh?" Olivier said, fastening a simple apron over his robes and tying it at the waist.

"Sorry!" Grace said, blushing. "I can never resist exploring new places."

"No sweat," he said. "*Mi casa su casa* and all that."

Grace looked puzzled. "It means 'my home is your home'," Olivier explained.

"Ah," said Grace, stepping away from the office doorway and towards the wooden counter where Olivier was now setting down a large iron pestle and mortar.

This, the largest room within his suite, seemed to her like a cross between a kitchen and a pharmacy. It was dominated by the large counter. The wall behind it was lined from left to right and floor to ceiling with shelves. They groaned with a cornucopia of glass jars containing spices, bottles of oils, baskets of fresh herbs, fruits and vegetables, barks, nuts and other items which, for the moment, eluded Grace's powers of categorisation. A wooden ladder was connected to the highest shelf, enabling Olivier to climb up and fetch what he needed from the uppermost reaches. Each of the glass containers was labelled but he seemed to know instinctively where everything he needed was located. It was like watching a pianist, Grace thought, as Olivier's hands ranged across the shelves, swiftly selecting the various items he required, and placing them down on the counter, alongside the pestle and mortar.

"Pull up a stool, Grace," he encouraged, as he lined up the jars and bottles and prepared to set to work.

"Thanks," she said, doing so. "So, what's in this salve?"

"Ground ivy . . . wormwood . . . beeswax, from our own

192

hives . . . sunflower oil . . . green elder . . . ribwort . . . plantain leaves . . ."

As he named the ingredients, Olivier opened each container in turn and measured an amount into the iron bowl. He continued itemising further substances but Grace lost track, fascinated at how he seemed to know just what quantity of each ingredient to add, without the use of scales, measuring spoons or any other equipment.

Suddenly he looked up. "What's the matter?"

"Do you always make up your potions without measuring them?"

"I am measuring them," he said. "Just not with equipment. I've made this salve many times before."

"Very impressive," Grace said.

He shrugged. "Not really. It's a common enough remedy. Elder is the most important ingredient. Do you know about the magic powers of elder, Grace?"

She shook her head.

"Well, allow me to bring you up to speed," he said, crushing the various leaves and twigs. "In Russia, they believed that elder trees drove away evil spirits. And in Sicily, they used it to repel serpents and robbers! Serbs used elder at wedding ceremonies to bring the happy couple good fortune. And in England, people gathered elder leaves on the last day of April and hung them on their doors and windows to prevent witches from entering their homes. And here at Sanctuary, we use it to heal external wounds and bruises, like those around your friend's eyes."

He began pounding the mixture with the pestle. Grace watched as the disparate substances gradually coalesced into a creamy paste. She wasn't sure she believed in the folklore he'd just spoken of. Nevertheless, there was a certain alchemy in the way he had made the salve from its many constituents.

"It looks good enough to eat," she said, as Olivier set down the pestle.

"Best not to," he said, with a smile. He reached for a small, empty glass pot and spooned the salve into it. Then he passed it to Grace. "Here, take care of this. We'll deliver it to your friend later. I'll apply the first dressing but then it will be your responsibility to do so, twice a day – when he wakes and before he goes to sleep. More often if he requires it."

Grace held the pot of salve in her palm, pleased at the thought she could do something practical to help reduce Lorcan's pain.

Olivier took the pestle and mortar over to a deep sink and filled it with hot water to soak. Grace watched as he vigorously scrubbed his own hands. Then he moved over to a vast copper pan, which stood on an unlit stove.

"What's in there?" Grace asked.

"Come and see for yourself," he said.

She slipped down from the stool and walked around the edge of the table. The pan was still warm, though there was no heat under it. Inside it was a dense purple-red liquid, on which a thin skin had formed. Olivier reached for a ladle, broke up the skin then gave the liquid a stir. As he did so, a rather distinctive and none too pleasant smell snaked its way into Grace's nostrils.

"What *is* that?" she asked.

"Have a taste," Olivier said, ladling a small amount into a cup and passing it to her. Then he took a thermometer, dipped it into the pan and took a reading. "It's still a little warm," he said. "It's best drunk at around thirty-seven degrees Celsius."

Grace held the cup in her hand, looking down at the liquid. It was thinner than soup but thicker than fruit juice and there was something familiar about this particular shade of red. Suddenly, a horrible thought crossed her mind.

"Wait a minute. Thirty-seven degrees is body temperature." She frowned. "This isn't what I think it is, is it?"

"Taste it," Olivier said. "It's cool enough now."

She wasn't sure that she wanted to taste it. Not if it *was* what she thought it was.

"Grace, come on!"

She lifted the cup to her lips and, grimacing, took a small sip. It had a strange and rather bitter taste. The texture was very definite too. It seemed to linger in her mouth and on her tongue. Most liquid quenched your thirst, but this was drier. It made her long for a glass of water to rinse out her mouth.

"You like?" Olivier asked.

Grace shook her head. "Not much," she said. Then, she asked for the third time, "What is it?"

"Berry tea," Olivier answered at last. "We make it from a blend of seven wild berries. Many of them are quite rare but grow here on the mountain."

"That's a relief," Grace said. "I thought it might be . . ."

"You thought it might be blood," Olivier finished, unsurprised. "It's what we give the vampires during the first phase of their treatment here. Its texture is very closely aligned to that of blood, but more importantly, so is its biochemistry. It's very high in minerals and other nutrients."

Grace's mind was racing. "You feed the vampires an alternative to blood? But doesn't the deprivation from real blood weaken them?"

Olivier shook his head. "No, not at all. As you've seen on *The Nocturne*, vampires only need a relatively small portion of blood, taken on a regular basis, to survive. The quality of the blood they take is the important thing. Most of the vampires who check in here have been gorging on blood from multiple, often unknown, sources. A lot of it is junk. During the first phase of their treatment here, we need to get that blood out of their system and begin retraining their ideas about hunger. When we reintroduce them to blood, we focus on them taking it in a more measured way, from one known source."

"Their donor," Grace said.

Olivier nodded.

Grace was dumbfounded. "I didn't think they could digest anything other than blood."

Olivier nodded. "Oh yes. A vampire's digestion is undoubtedly different to a living human's. It would be pretty impossible for them, for instance, to digest solid food. The physiological explanation is kind of complex, but think of it this way. The body after death is rather like the body at birth. You wouldn't try to feed a newborn baby a steak now, would you?" He smiled. "Well, likewise, a vampire can only digest liquid. And yes, in the long term that liquid must be blood. But the beauty of this tea is that it is similar to blood in look and texture. It satisfies their immediate need. And, as I say, it also closely mirrors blood in terms of its chemical compounds."

Grace's head was spinning. "Could they survive on this instead of blood?"

Olivier shook his head. "Not indefinitely, no. At least, we don't think so. It's an interim measure. But it's a real wonder drug. Mostly, we use it to wean vampires off blood but, for instance, Mosh Zu tells me we're going to start Lorcan on it, to build him up to taking blood." He dipped the thermometer back into the pan and took another reading. "Ah! Perfect." He took out a tray of metal flasks and began unscrewing their lids.

"You said that you give the blood to vampires during the first phase of their treatment. What happens next?"

Olivier began ladling the tea into the flasks as he talked. "There are three phases of treatment here," he said. "The first phase is initiation and breaking down the extent of the addiction to blood. The tea plays a part in this, but there is a lot of more important psychological work to be done. The hunger for blood, the obsession with the hunt – these are as much mental and emotional needs as physical ones." He screwed the top on one flask and began filling another.

"The second phase is reintroducing them to blood, but in a new, measured way. During this phase, they will be given real blood, supplied by the donors on-site, but there will be no actual physical interaction between vampires and donors. The blood is supplied to the vampires in flasks, just like these." He screwed the cap on the second flask.

"It is only during the third and final phase of treatment that vampires and donors are paired up. Then, the sharing begins. That is the final preparation for joining *The Nocturne*."

Grace nodded. "So the ultimate aim for every vampire passing through Sanctuary is to join the Vampirate ship?"

Olivier nodded. "Yes, of course."

"But how come they don't run out of space?"

"*The Nocturne* has as much space as is required for all who wish to travel in it. And besides, some fail to complete their treatment here and return to their old ways. It's disappointing when that happens, but not everyone makes it." He screwed the lid onto another flask and moved on. "And then there's the occasional vampire and donor who complete the pairing stage of the treatment but elect not to join the ship."

"Where do *they* go?" Grace said, puzzled once more. This had not occurred to her as an option before.

"Wherever they choose." Olivier smiled. "Undoubtedly, theirs is the harder path, living amid human society and keeping their secret . . ."

"You really mean that out there, in villages and towns and cities, there are vampires living with their donors, amongst the rest of us?" Grace's eyes were wide.

"It's an intriguing thought, isn't it?" Olivier said, his eyes twinkling. "Why, you never know, they might be your next door neighbour! How would you know? Other than that one partner never seems to age, and the other is never seen to eat. But mostly, people aren't that observant. They're easily fobbed off with tales of fad-diets and beauty treatments.

Grace supposed there was no logical reason why two people could not live in "normal" society as vampire and donor. It was an astonishing thought.

"There," Olivier said, fastening the lid on the last of the flasks. "All done. The tea will keep warm in these flasks for another few hours. We'll do the rounds later, but now there are more pressing things for us to attend to."

He began laying out more pots, pans and knives on the table. Grace shook her head. Olivier's duties seemed never to be done. "What are you going to make now?" she inquired.

"Well, I don't know about you," he said, "but I'm starving. I thought I might just whip us up some lunch."

CHAPTER TWENTY-FOUR

Room Four

Connor saw the flames burning in Jez's eye-sockets. It was as if they were about to consume his face. "All right," he said, roughly wrenching off the locket. "All right, you can have it. Just get my friend some blood now!"

"No problem, dearie," the woman said, her hands clamping on the locket and pulling it inside her booth. "Room seven."

Connor led Jez to the red velvet door.

The woman interrupted her next transaction to call out, "You can't go in with him. Wait here. There's coffee and magazines."

Connor was half relieved. As Jez walked through the door, he turned and his face flashed normal again, just for an instant. "Thank you," he said. Then he was gone.

*

The half-hour that Connor spent in that waiting room was one of the strangest of his life. At first, there was a steady stream of vampires coming through into the anteroom and handing over their money, before being directed beyond the velvet-covered door. Connor did his best to avoid eye-contact with the clientele but he was aware that every last one of them clocked him as they came through. Perhaps they could sense he wasn't a vampire and wondered therefore what he was doing here. Or perhaps they saw him in more simple terms – as a convenient container of blood. He did his best to quell the rising panic induced by that thought. Reaching for a magazine, he turned the pages but found himself unable to focus on the content. All he could think about was this strange place, the curious path that had brought him here and the danger that hung heavy upon him.

Connor watched the latest arrivals out of the corner of his eye. Evidently, the vampires were all kinds of people. Men and women. White, black, Asian, Hispanic. Young, old and everything in between. What united them was the terrible hunger in their eyes. Few were in the extreme state of need that Jez had been in, but the same recognisable fire flickered in their faces. Each time he saw it, Connor thought of Jez's earlier words . . .

"I'm not in control of my own body any more – my own thoughts, my own needs. When the hunger comes over me, flows into me, there's nothing I can do to fight it."

Perhaps he had been too quick to judge Jez over his

attack of poor Jenny. Jez hadn't asked for this existence. He had died an early death as a pirate. Connor wasn't sure what lay on the other side of death, but if it was supposed to be peace then Jez had been denied it. Sidorio had intervened. Sidorio had brought him back into a new existence, a distortion of life. But now Sidorio was gone and Jez was left to carry his burden alone.

Connor wished that Grace was with him now. How could she be so at ease with vampires? His sister had depths of courage that he could only imagine. He reached up sadly to his bare neck, where the locket had hung half an hour earlier. He felt depressed that he had had to give it away so cheaply. As if he had somehow betrayed Grace. But what choice did he have?

"Do you want a coffee?"

He looked up to find the woman from inside the glass booth now standing before him. She was much smaller than she had seemed inside the booth, perched up on a stool.

"Coffee?" she repeated. "I'm on my break. And you look fit to drop."

"Yes please." Connor nodded, surprised by the offer and the smile which accompanied it.

Moments later, she returned with a tray and placed a warm mug in his hands. "Help yourself to cream and sugar." She took up her own drink, lit a cigarette and sat down beside him.

"You're not one of them, are you?" she said. "You don't belong in this world."

He shook his head. "No. I was just helping out an old friend."

The woman nodded, blowing out smoke in a perfect ring. "I could tell," she said. "There's something clean about you. Innocent."

Connor shrugged. He didn't like to say so but he felt far from clean right now. Something about this place made him feel urgently in need of a long, hot shower.

"What happens?" he asked. "Behind the velvet door. In the rooms. What happens there?"

There was a pause as the woman sipped her coffee and inhaled her cigarette, taking a tandem hit of caffeine and nicotine. "What do you think happens, dearie? The clients need blood. And my girls . . . and boys, they give them what they need."

In spite of himself, Connor was intrigued. "Your girls and boys . . . who are they? Where do they come from? What makes them want to do this?"

The woman settled her cigarette in an ashtray. "Well I don't imagine that any of them set out in life thinking 'Ooh, I know what I'd like to be – a blood donor for vampires!' But options are scarce around these parts. There aren't many opportunities to make money . . . not nowadays. What makes any of us do anything in this life, dearie? Cash. The need to survive."

"But giving blood," Connor said, "like this . . ." He shivered.

"What do *you* do?" she asked.

"I'm a pirate," he said.

"Oh, really?" She laughed, and it wasn't a nice laugh. "A pirate. There's a noble profession for you." Then her face softened and she smiled at him, a kindly smile. "Bless you. You really *do* think it's noble, don't you? You're that green."

He didn't understand her. What was she saying?

"Here," she went on. She reached into her pocket and took out the locket. "Have this back," she said, pressing it into his hand.

"No," he protested. "It's OK. We made a fair trade."

"Shh, boy." She closed his fingers around the locket. "You're one of the good ones, I can tell that. It wouldn't be right for me to take this. It's been a good night. I can take a small hit."

"Well, all right," he said. "Thanks."

"Oh look," she said. "Your friend's back at last."

Connor glanced up as Jez stepped through the red velvet doorway. It was the old, familiar Jez, smiling broadly. He looked restored, as if he'd woken from a long sleep and tucked into a hearty breakfast. He strode over to join Connor and the woman.

"Better?" Connor asked.

"Much," said Jez. "I feel like a new man. Let's get back to the boat, shall we?" He began heading out along the corridor.

"Well," the woman said. "Go on, pirate. What are you waiting for? Aren't you going after him?"

"Yes," Connor said, standing up. "Thanks for the

coffee." He paused. "I'm Connor," he said, "Connor Tempest. What's your name?"

"Lilith." The woman smiled. "My name's Lilith." She gave him a wink, then made a shooing motion with her hands. "Get out of here, Connor Tempest. Go back to the oceans where you belong."

He nodded and smiled, then turned and followed Jez out into the night.

As they closed the door behind them, they heard a voice from beneath the rock-ledge.

"Connor? Jez? Jump in!"

Bart had moved the light boat to directly beneath them. Connor jumped lightly down, followed by Jez. Immediately, Bart began steering the boat away from the creek. "Next stop, the Vampirate ship!" he said.

Back at the rock-face, another small boat edged out from the reeds, under cover of darkness. It had just one crew-member. A young crew-member, dressed in a beaten-up leather jacket, who smiled to himself and couldn't help but exclaim, "Well, well. This night just gets more and more interesting!"

Then Moonshine Wrathe set his sights on the small light boat and began to sail after it on the next leg of its curious voyage.

A little later that night, another boat sails into Limbo Creek. Its sole inhabitant is familiar with this place. He needs no map to find the black door. He gives the bell-pull a hearty yank. The milky eyes appear through the slit in the door, but he hardly registers them; says only one word.

"Lilith."

When the door opens, he strides inside, straight along the corridor into the vestibule.

She is sitting in the booth, filing her nails. He approaches and she looks up, surprised at first. Then she smiles perkily. "I heard you were dead."

He returns her smile. "Good. Then the rumour is out there. That gives me more time."

"The rumour's out there, all right," she says, placing down her nailfile. "And I'll be happy to keep it buzzing."

"Do that," he says, reaching into his pocket and pushing a wad of notes through into her booth.

"Someone's doing well for himself," she says, then holds one of the notes up to the light.

"All genuine," he assures her.

"I'm sure," she says. "Just have to check." She pauses. "Had that cohort of yours in earlier. The young one."

"Stukeley?" he says. "Excellent. Then all is going to plan."

"What are you up to, I wonder?" She giggles. "No, don't tell me. You know I'm a terrible gossip."

He nods.

"So, are you just here to chew the fat, or do you want some blood in those thick veins of yours tonight?" she asks.

"I'm hungry," he says.

"A pint? Two . . .?"

"Unlimited," he says.

"That'll cost you," she says.

"I know."

"There's the disposal of the body to think of. And hiring a replacement . . ."

He thrusts another stack of notes into the booth. "That should cover any *inconvenience*."

She takes the money and stacks it on top of what he gave her before. She thinks for a moment.

"Room four," she decides.

He nods, then turns and makes his way to the red velvet door.

"Try not to be too . . . messy," she calls after him.

He grins. "Nice to see you again, Lilith."

"You too, Sidorio."

CHAPTER TWENTY-FIVE

The Rec Room

Grace watched as Olivier carefully applied the salve around Lorcan's eyes. It still pained her to look at the livid burns across the centre of his face but she comforted herself with the thought that, with this treatment, the wound should start to heal. It would all be worth it – the day Lorcan opened his eyes once more and could look at her again, the way he used to. For a moment, Grace's thoughts slipped back to her first days on *The Nocturne*, when Lorcan's impish charm and twinkling eyes had kept her from going out of her mind.

"You see, Grace," Olivier said. "You only need a small amount. It's strong stuff." Then he addressed Lorcan directly. "I'm going to put some directly on your eyelids now. This will sting a bit, I'm afraid."

At even the gentlest touch of Olivier's fingers, Lorcan winced.

"I'm sorry," Olivier said. "I know it's uncomfortable, but it will get better."

Lorcan gave a small nod. "It's OK," he rasped.

Grace took Lorcan's hand and squeezed it. "I watched Olivier prepare the salve," she said. "The main ingredient is elder. He was telling me all about the magical beliefs people have about elder. Like in Sicily, they used to use it to ward off snakes and robbers!"

Lorcan smiled softly. "In Ireland too," he said. "Why, in Ireland, the elder is such a sacred tree, it's forbidden to break one twig. People think witches use elder boughs as magic horses. Imagine that!"

"There," said Olivier. "All done. That wasn't so bad after all, eh?" He took a fresh roll of bandage and some scissors from his satchel, then seemed to have second thoughts. "Actually, Grace, why don't you replace Lorcan's bandage? You seem to be getting pretty expert at it."

Grace nodded, taking the bandage and scissors and setting to work. Olivier watched her as she neatly fastened the new bandage about Lorcan's head.

"Excellent work," Olivier said. "You're very lucky, Lorcan Furey, to have such a competent nurse at your side."

"Don't I know it?" Lorcan said, smiling again.

Grace's heart leaped. Two smiles in short succession. She hadn't seen that from Lorcan in quite some time.

"Now, I also brought you something to drink," Olivier said.

Immediately the smile disappeared.

"I'm not thirsty."

"It isn't what you think it is," Grace said. "It's a substitute for blood. It's a tea made from seven wild berries that grow here on the mountain. It's full of minerals and other nutrients."

Olivier smiled. "That's right," he said. "We don't expect you to start taking blood again until you're ready. In the meantime, this tea will help you to gain strength."

Lorcan remained impassive. "I'm feeling tired again," he announced.

"That's no surprise," Olivier said. "If you feel tired, you must rest. That's why you're here. It's all part of the healing process."

"Do you want me to stay with you?" Grace asked.

"Yes." Lorcan nodded. "Yes, if you don't mind."

"I don't mind at all." She smiled and gave his hand another squeeze.

"I'm going to leave you two," Olivier announced. "And I'm leaving a flask of tea here on your nightstand. If you'd like some, ask Grace to pour it for you. No pressure, Lorcan, but if you can manage even a small drop of it, it will help to speed your recovery."

"All right," Lorcan said. "Let me sleep and we'll see about the tea."

"That's good enough for me." Olivier nodded and began collecting his things together and putting them back into the satchel. Standing up, he reached for the door.

"Grace, a word," he said, beckoning her out into the corridor. She followed.

"Let him sleep," he said in hushed tones. "But when he wakes, try to get him to drink some of the tea. Don't force him, but if anyone can get him to drink the stuff, it's you." He smiled. "Probably best not to tell him you found it disgusting!" he added.

Grace nodded.

"I'll check back on you both later," he said. "Oh, and I almost forgot. I have something for you."

He opened his satchel again and produced a book. He held it out to her.

"What's this?" she said, expecting it to be more information about Sanctuary, or perhaps a collection of recipes for herbal remedies. But, as she turned the book on its side and read the spine, she smiled.

"*The Secret Garden*! One of my favourites."

"I thought you might want something to occupy yourself with while he's sleeping," Olivier said.

"Thanks," Grace said. Once again, she found herself revising her opinion of Olivier. Her first impressions of him had been quite wrong. He really was quite considerate after all. She watched him pad off along the corridor, satchel over his shoulder, knocking on the next door along and disappearing into the next vampire's chamber. Then she pushed back the door to Lorcan's room. She could tell from his breathing that he had already fallen asleep. She sat down in the chair at the foot of the bed and quietly opened up the book. She had read it for the first time years ago and often since. The familiar opening was like a balm to her.

When Mary Lennox was sent to Misselthwaite Manor to live with her uncle . . .

With a contented sigh, Grace soon found herself lost once more in the story of poor Mary Lennox's arrival at the lonely house on the moors.

"What are you reading?"

The voice came out of nowhere.

Grace glanced up.

"What are you reading?" he asked again.

"How can you tell I'm reading?" she asked, disconcerted.

"Because I can hear you turning the pages," Lorcan said with a chuckle. "It didn't take a great deal of psychic ability to work that out."

"Have you been awake long?" she asked.

"I dunno." He shrugged and pushed himself up.

"Here," she said. "Let me rearrange your pillows for you."

"Thanks," he said. "You certainly do make a good nurse. I'm sorry to put you to so much trouble. It's not fair."

"Nonsense," she said. "You looked after me, remember? You rescued me from drowning, and then, on *The Nocturne,* you protected me . . . The least I can do is plump your pillows."

"All the same," he said, this time reaching for her hand, "I'm very grateful to you, Grace."

Out of the corner of her eye, Grace saw the flask which

Olivier had left on Lorcan's nightstand. He was in such a good mood she thought it might be the moment to mention the tea again. She was building up to asking him, but he spoke first.

"So are you going to tell me or is it some deep, dark secret?"

"What?" she asked, feeling guilty and not entirely sure why.

"What you're reading!" he said.

"Oh!" She smiled. "It's *The Secret Garden.* Olivier gave it to me. It's one of my favourites. Do you know it?"

"I've heard of it," he said. "But I'm not much of a reader. What's it about?"

"Well, there's this girl called Mary Lennox," Grace said, sitting down on the edge of the bed. "She's been living in India but her parents have died and she's sent back to England to stay with her guardian in this vast manor house. It's a beautiful but lonely place. Her guardian's wife died and he's still in mourning. The wife had a walled garden but, after she died, her husband locked it and buried the key . . ."

"It sounds sad," Lorcan said.

"It *is* quite sad," Grace said. "But I like sad stories. And it's very beautiful too."

"Would you read some to me?" Lorcan asked.

"Yes, of course I will," she said. She returned to the chair and opened the book at the beginning again. "Are you sitting comfortably?" she asked.

"What do you mean?" he said.

Grace smiled. "It's just something my dad used to ask Connor and I before he read to us," she replied.

"Ah," said Lorcan. "Well, yes, Miss Tempest, I am quite comfortable. So let's hear about this secret garden of yours."

Grace opened the book and began to read.

"I think I'd better leave it there for now," Grace said. "My voice is getting hoarse."

"It's a grand story," Lorcan said. "And you read it very well."

"Thank you." She looked up at him and smiled.

Lorcan yawned.

"Are you sleepy again?" she asked.

"No," he said. "Actually, I feel wide awake. I could do with getting up and about."

"Really?" Grace was surprised.

"Yes," he said. "Shall we go for a little wander?"

"Sure," said Grace. "Mosh Zu said we could go outside, didn't he?" Then she thought again. "Oh no – it's light."

"Well, let's go on a little exploration indoors then, shall we?" Lorcan suggested.

"Yes! Why not?" Grace was pleased that Lorcan was keen to get up and about. She couldn't help but think this must be a good sign. She closed the book, marking her place for later, then came over to help him out of the bedclothes.

"There you are," she said. "Swing your feet down to the ground. They left you some soft shoes."

"Slippers, Grace," he said. "Let's call a spade a spade, shall we? I'm an invalid, so of course they gave me slippers. It's OK. If you put them in front of my feet, I'll put them on."

She did as he asked and he pushed his toes into the slippers.

"Righto," he said. "Let's go on a magical mystery tour."

Grace glanced at the flask of tea on the nightstand. "Before we go," she began, "do you think you might try a drop of tea?"

He considered for a moment, then shook his head. "I'm not thirsty," he said. "Maybe later, when we come back."

Grace felt somewhat deflated, but at least she had tried. And Olivier had instructed her not to push Lorcan.

"OK," she said. "Are you ready then?"

He nodded. She pushed open the door and led him out into the corridor.

"Left or right?" she asked.

"You choose," he said.

She decided to go to the right. At first Lorcan was a little unsteady on his feet, but as she led him along, he fell into a rhythm. The dimly-lit corridor was deserted. All the doors on both sides were shut. It reminded Grace of being back on *The Nocturne*, when the vampires were sleeping; or after the Feast, when they were locked behind closed doors, sharing.

One corridor led into another. Grace was unsure whether

215

they could make a complete circuit if they kept going or if, like a maze, the corridor would lead them to a dead end or in a direction from where it would be hard to retrace their steps. Still, she kept going, unsure whether this was now a new corridor or one they had walked down before.

"It's very quiet," Lorcan said.

"Yes," agreed Grace. "The others must be resting."

"You see?" Lorcan smirked. "I've got more get up and go than the rest of them, even in this condition."

"Yes," Grace said. "Yes, you have."

As the corridor turned again, Grace saw an open door to one side, and the glow of light from within it. She must have paused because Lorcan asked her, "What is it? Why have you stopped?"

"There's an open door up ahead," she said.

"Well, what are we waiting for?" Lorcan said. "Let's investigate!"

Grace nodded, delighted that he seemed in such good spirits. She led him along the corridor to the fan of light that spilled out from the open door.

"Here we are," she whispered, hesitantly leading him inside.

"Well," Lorcan asked, also whispering. "What's the room like?"

"It's bigger than your room and mine," she said, feeling less nervous now that she saw the room was quite an ordinary one. "Rectangular in shape. There's a sofa and a couple of chairs around a low table. On one side of the sofa is a shelf of books, and boxes of games and . . ." She turned. "Oh, I'm sorry."

"What is it?" Lorcan said.

"There's someone in here," Grace said, her eyes meeting those of the good-looking boy sitting at the table. He nodded at her and returned her smile, his chocolate-brown eyes twinkling at her. In front of him was a chessboard. He seemed to be in the middle of a game, judging by the pieces scattered on either side of the board. But his opponent must have slipped out for a moment. "I'm sorry," Grace said, addressing the boy directly once more. "We didn't mean to interrupt you."

"No problema," he said. "It's nice to know someone else is awake and moving around here."

"How's the game going?" Grace asked.

"It's pretty level," said the boy, running a hand through his thick curly hair. "But then, the players are well matched."

He turned his eyes from Grace to Lorcan and, as he did so, Grace took the opportunity to get a better look at him. He was dressed in the same robes as Lorcan, so it was clear he was another vampire, undergoing treatment. But under the robe, she could see he wore a red neckerchief. This gave her pause, but her train of thought was interrupted as his eyes flashed back to her.

"I don't suppose either of you play chess?" he said, hopefully. "It gets really boring playing by yourself, even if you *are* pretty awesome at it."

"I play," Lorcan said, turning. "But it would be a little hard at the moment."

"Ah yes, I'm sorry," said the boy. "I hope you're not in too much pain." He looked back at Grace. His brown eyes were disarmingly wide. The openness of his stare drew her in. It was like a hand reaching out to her, pulling her towards him. It was inviting but, at the same time, she felt uncomfortable. No, not just uncomfortable. She felt fearful. As if some instinct was telling her not to get close to him. To turn around now, while she still could.

"How about you, little lady? Can I tempt you to a game?" His voice was as soft and melting as his eyes.

"We should probably get back," she said. "We all need some sleep—"

"No," said Lorcan and the stranger simultaneously, cutting her dead.

"No," Lorcan repeated. "I'm not ready to go back to my room."

"And I'm not about to lose the only good company I've had in weeks," said their new companion. "Sit yourselves down, folks. Make yourselves at home. It puzzles me, it really does, why so few of the others make use of this rec room."

Suddenly he shot his arm across the table. "I'm sorry," he said. "You didn't tell me your names?"

"I'm Grace," she said, "Grace Tempest." She took his hand and shook it, noticing two things. His grip was strong. And his hands were a little callused. Something in her mind clicked.

"Pretty name, Grace," he said. She noticed the trace of an accent. Now, her mind was spinning. He had said *problema* before. Not *problem* but *problema.*

"And this is Lorcan Furey," she said, trying to keep as level-headed as possible.

He shook Lorcan by the hand. "Good to meet you, Lorcan."

"And you are?" Lorcan asked.

"I'm Johnny," he said. "Johnny Desperado."

Of course! This was Johnny. The cowboy whose ribbon she had held in her hand. The one whose memories she had somehow tapped into in her dreams. The one whose lonely death, hanging from a branch above the snow, she had channelled. Grace froze, unable to take her eyes away from him. This did not escape his notice. Smiling, he gave her a wink. Without taking his eyes off her for an instant, he spoke once more.

"Well, are you guys going to stand on ceremony like that all night, or sit yourselves down and tell ol' Johnny something about yourselves?"

CHAPTER TWENTY-SIX

Lost

"So," Bart mused as he steered the light boat out of Limbo Creek. "Blood Tavern – a one-of-a-kind kind of place, or do they have a franchise?"

Connor grimaced. "It's all very well you making jokes about it," he said. "You didn't have to go inside."

"No joke," said Bart. "Serious question, mate." He turned to Jez. "Is it a unique establishment or are there blood taverns all over the place, if you know where to find them?"

Jez shrugged. "I don't know. I didn't even remember going there before. Only, when I was inside, it *did* seem familiar."

"Hmm," Bart said. "And what exactly goes on in there?"

Connor sighed. More than anything, he wanted to leave the world of the strange "tavern" behind him. He tried to turn his mind to Ma Kettle's. That was what a tavern *should* be – a place to drink and have some fun with your mates. Not a place where you went to drain another person's blood."

"Guess you two are gonna hold out on me, eh?" Bart said.

Jez nodded. "Since you didn't have the *cojones* to come in with me and Connor, I reckon we'll keep schtum." He sighed. "Besides, I really don't want to talk about it. I needed blood and I got some. End of."

"All right, buddy," said Bart. "I can take a hint."

"Just take me to the Vampirate ship," Jez said.

Bart glared at his old friend. "I'm not sure I like the new you," he said. " *Take me to the Blood Tavern . . . Take me to the Vampirate ship . . .* If you don't mind me saying so, buddy, since you died, you've got awful bossy. What's the rush anyhow? Aren't you immortal now? From where I'm sitting, you've got all the time in the world."

Jez shook his head. "That's just it," he said. "Maybe I'm not immortal yet. Maybe I'm not wholly a vampire. If there's a chance . . . *any* chance that the Vampirate captain can reverse the process, then I want him to do it. So, the way I see it, time is of the essence."

Connor spoke now. "But if the captain did reverse the process, wouldn't you be dead again?" He had a grim memory of Jez lying cradled in Bart's arms, bloodied and pale in the wake of the fateful duel.

Jez nodded. "I'd rather be dead than be this way."

"Is it *that* bad?" Connor asked.

221

"You have *no* idea."

Bart's face was a picture of gloom. When he spoke, his usually robust voice started to falter. "You can't die again. It's not fair . . . *on us*. We already lost you once. Then you come back—"

Jez's words cut across his friend's. "I'm *still* lost to you, mate. I'm lost to you and I'm lost to myself." Connor saw then the abject despair in Jez's eyes. In a way, it scared him more than the fire that had blazed there during Jez's blood-hunger.

"We need to get you to that ship," Connor said. "The captain will be able to help you. I'm sure of it."

"I hope so," Jez said. "I've never hoped for anything so much in all my . . . well, I've never hoped for anything so much."

"If only wishing were enough to get you there," Bart said. "I still have no idea how we're going to find it. What do you reckon, Connor?"

Connor looked around them. They were in the middle of the ocean. They could no longer see the land. Nor were there any ships in their midst. Suddenly, it all became clear to him. "Stop the boat," he said.

"What?" Bart asked.

"You heard me," Connor said. "Stop steering the boat. Let's just float here for a moment."

Bart shook his head. "I dunno. I'm out in the wilderness with two jellyheads!" Nevertheless, he obeyed Connor's command and brought the boat to a standstill.

"Now what?" he asked, sitting back down again.

Immediately, Connor heard his father's voice inside his head. He turned to Bart. "*Now,*" he said, "we learn to trust the tide!"

Bart looked at him curiously but Connor said no more. He simply settled back into his seat, leaning against the side of the small wooden boat.

They sat like that for a time, none of them speaking – the only noise the slap of the water against the side of the boat. The sea was unusually calm and the boat became a cradle, rocking three tired infants gently to sleep.

Until, with no warning, the water became suddenly choppy. Connor's eyelids had slowly drooped shut but now, instantly, they were wide open again.

Bart too was alert and glancing about. "The sea's getting awful rough awful quickly," he said, unable to disguise his alarm.

"Maybe," Connor said with a smile. Somehow he had expected this.

Bart looked at him enquiringly. "What are you thinking, Tempest?" he asked.

"Just wait," Connor said.

The force of the waves started twisting the boat. They began spinning around, slowly at first, then with increasing momentum. The motion was dizzying.

"What is this?" Jez cried. "Are we in some kind of maelstrom?"

Bart was unable to hide his own panic as their small boat

spun faster and faster. "You know they say that many boats have gone missing in the vi-cin-i-ty of Lim-bo Cree-eek . . ." The boat was spinning so fast now, it almost hovered above the water.

Connor shook his head, exhilarated by the ride. "Nothing bad's going to happen to us," he exclaimed, unsure where this confidence was coming from. "Be patient!"

"*Be patient?*" Bart roared, his voice fighting against the raging water. "*Trust the tide?* Are you sure someone didn't slip you something strange back at the blood pub?"

Connor smiled and shook his head. His hair was soaked through. So was the front of his shirt. But, glancing up again, he noticed that the dizzying movement of the boat was rapidly subsiding. Then the waves which had spun them around began pushing them forward with an equal force.

"What the . . .? What's going on?" Bart asked.

"It's the Vampirate captain," Connor said, with some satisfaction. "He's leading us to the ship."

It wasn't exactly a smooth journey across the dark ocean. They had no need to steer, only to hold tight. But their boat was small and all three of them had to cling on to prevent themselves from going overboard. For Connor, it brought back uncomfortable memories of the storm which had changed his life. At the same time, he felt somehow protected. He knew that the Vampirate captain was in control, just as surely as if he had been sitting beside them as the fourth passenger in the boat. He remembered something – that fleeting moment at Ma Kettle's when he had met the captain and shaken his hand. The strange sensation as the captain's gloved hand had enfolded his own and how he'd felt sure that he'd held that hand before.

Suddenly, Connor felt icy cold. He looked up, shivering, and couldn't see a thing. They were surrounded on all sides by a veil of mist. The boat seemed to have slowed, but perhaps this was only a visual deception. The mist rapidly became so thick he could only barely see his two companions. They were no more than silvery shapes – a ghost crew.

"I suppose," Bart cried, "that this is all part of the plan?"

"Yes," Connor called back, his voice echoing in the void. He found himself smiling at another sudden memory. The first – and only – time he'd seen the Vampirate ship, it had been ringed by mist. They must be close now, very close indeed.

The mist began to clear. As it did so, he realised that his senses had not been playing tricks on him. The boat *was* travelling more slowly. Which was a good thing, because you wouldn't want to collide with the majestic galleon which crested the waters only twenty or so metres away.

"There it is!" Jez cried, his face clear again as they broke through the mist. "That must be it!"

Connor nodded. There, before them, was the Vampirate ship. Just as he'd known deep down that it would be. The captain had said that he'd always be able to find it when he needed to. And he had told no lie. As their boat came up close, Connor glanced up at the prow of the ship, expecting to see the beautiful wooden figurehead he had glimpsed on the night of the storm. Her painted eyes had seemed to watch him, but now she was nowhere to be seen. The front of the ship, where she had been suspended, was empty. Connor grinned to himself, remembering Grace's tales. The figurehead came to life at sunset. It was well after sunset now. No wonder she had abandoned her lookout post for the night.

Connor was excited at the thought of seeing Grace. His head had been so full of other things but, now that he had reached the ship, he realised he needed nothing so much as to see his sister, to give her a hug and talk about old times. A great big dose of normality. Yes, that was what he could do with.

Coming up alongside the ship, he could hear voices on the deck and see the glow of lanterns up above. The ship's vast wing-like sails flapped slowly back and forth – their curious texture occasionally sparking with light. Connor turned to the others. Bart looked dazed. Jez's eyes glowed bright with expectation. Connor knew that the ship represented Jez's last hope. He sent up a silent prayer that the captain would be able to help his lost friend.

"So how d'ya reckon we get up on deck?" Bart asked.

Connor lifted their lantern and pointed to a rope ladder running down the side of the ship.

"What were the chances?" grinned Bart. "After you then, buddy. Youth before beauty."

Connor shook his head and reached for the rough twine of the ladder. As he climbed out of the boat, he turned to the others and smiled. "One for all," he said. Bart laid a hand on Jez's shoulder.

"And all for one," they answered.

Then Connor turned around and began to climb. He didn't even think of the height. Though the waters below were swirling and spitting at him, the ship was strangely still. It was as if, Connor thought, it was hovering upon the waters, rather than within them. Just as it had been when he'd seen it that first time. Just then, in his head, he heard a whisper – as soft and elusive as a trickle of water. *"Welcome, Connor Tempest. You took your time."*

CHAPTER TWENTY-SEVEN

The Vaquero

After a time, Grace realised that she was reading to herself. She looked over at Lorcan, wondering how long he had been sleeping. Oh well, she thought. He needed his rest. It was the reason they were here at Sanctuary. She hadn't reckoned on what a lonely place it might be.

She reached out to Lorcan's nightstand to find something to mark her place, then closed the book. Rising from her chair, she decided to take it with her. She could sense the sleepless hours ahead and she might have need of it. "Sleep well, Lorcan," she said, reaching forward to kiss his forehead before slipping out into the corridor.

She had a fancy for some air, so she followed the corridor up towards the courtyard. She stepped out through the central doors and, sighing, breathed in the cool, fresh air. It was a clear night. Perhaps she'd walk down to the gates and look down the mountainside.

But as she set off across the courtyard, she heard a cry.

"Hey! Little lady! Grace, ain't it?"

Turning, she saw that Johnny Desperado was sitting on the courtyard wall. Tonight, he was out of his Sanctuary robes and dressed, instead, in boots, jeans, a chequered shirt rolled up to his elbows and a Stetson. He lifted his hat and waved at her.

"Hello, Johnny," she said.

"Where's ol' Lorcan tonight?" he asked, helping her up beside him.

"Sleeping," she said, sitting down on the wall.

He nodded. "So, you had a touch of the lonelies, did ya?"

"Something like that."

"Well, I was feeling kinda the same, so I guess we're lucky we both craved a bit of fresh air."

She nodded. Looking down at his hands, she noticed once more how callused they were. Then above one of his hands, on the inside of his forearm, she saw there were markings. It looked like writing, but she couldn't be sure.

"What are you looking at?" he asked.

"What's that tattoo?" she inquired.

"Oh, that!" He extended his arm and held it steady for her.

"*The ride is far from over*," she read.

Johnny removed his hand and ran his fingers through his thick, unruly hair. "Reckon that tattoo just about sums up my story." He turned back to Grace, his eyes boring into her. "Don't you think so, little lady?"

"What do you mean?" she asked, a little alarmed.

"I mean, you know all about me, don't you? You had my ribbon. You read it. Mosh Zu told me. It's kind of a private thing, your ribbon."

Grace felt deeply embarrassed. She realised that she had trespassed into hugely private territory. "I'm so sorry," she said. "I didn't mean to. I was given your ribbon."

"It's OK," he said. "Ol' Johnny's not angry with you, Grace. Not a bit of it. Why, I'm just surprised — and flattered — that you'd sit with me, knowing my story and all."

"Why *wouldn't* I sit with you?" she asked, frowning at the thought.

"I done some real bad things, Grace," he said. "But there I go again. You know that already."

"Actually," Grace said, "it seems to me that you had some very bad things done to you."

He smiled. "That's how you see it? That's really what you think?"

She nodded, smiling back at him. Then she had an idea. "Would you tell it to me? In your words?"

"My story?" He shrugged. "But you know it already."

"No," she said. "I had a brief window into your life and . . . death. But I want to know if I was right. And I want to know more."

"You do?"

She nodded. "I'd love to hear it. I love hearing people's histories."

"Well sure, if that's what it takes to win your company for a while. Best get yourself comfortable though, little lady, because I've a good deal to tell you."

Grace smiled, drawing her sweater around her for added warmth as Johnny began to tell his tale.

"I was born in Texas in 1869. My given name was Juan, but the ranchmen always called me Johnny. I grew up on a ranch, see. Me, my dad and my brother Rico. I guess my mamma was somewhere around too, but I didn't spend too much time with her. They used to tease me that I thought the horses were my real parents. They reckoned I could ride before I could walk. See, I wasn't just any kind of cowboy. I was a *vaquero*! A Mexican cowboy – the very best kind of cowboy you can be! Horsemanship was in my blood – like my brother and my dad and his daddy before him. Rico and my dad, they trained me up. I took part in my first trail drive at the age of eleven.

"That was when my life took its first downturn. You grow up fast on a trail drive. You get used to foul, fickle weather, stampedes and death. Rico and my dad led that drive. We went all the way from Texas to Denver before this major stampede broke out. It was snowing badly. The cattle were goin' plain crazy. Rico and my dad did all they could to prevent it. But we were climbing a mountain, see, and the idiot cattle started throwing themselves off the cliff." He paused. "That day, we lost three hundred and sixty-one cattle and two horses to that abyss. Fell ninety-five feet to their death. We lost two men too . . ."

"Your brother and father?"

He nodded. "You shoulda seen their bodies, Grace. I've never forgotten that sight. Never will."

"What did you do then?"

"Ranchers are a bit like family see, so though I'd lost my dad and Rico – and soon after my mamma too (they say she died of a broken heart) – they took good care of me. Real good care of little Johnny. Even then, they knew I could outdo any one of them with my lariat. By fourteen years old, I was in demand on those Texas ranches. I was a bronco-buster by then. You know what that is? It means I broke in the meanest of the horses. It was fun for a while knowing I could run rings round men twice, three times my age. But bronco-bustin' is dangerous work for not enough pay and I wanted something better outta life. And that was my first mistake. Shoulda stuck with what I'd been given, even if it didn't amount to a whole lot."

"What did you do?" Grace was fascinated.

"I set off from Texas, riding the trail. And I never went home. I moved around the country. It wasn't all work, neither. There was time to play too. I had some crazy times. There were bullfights, cockfights, fiestas and street-fairs." He smiled and closed his eyes for a moment, and she knew that in his head he was right back there. When he opened his eyes again, they were bright. "The food at those street-fairs, Grace, you never tasted better – tamales, tortillas and dulcies. And whiskey! Lots of whiskey." He laughed. "Funny, 'cos that was the name of my first horse,

232

now I think about it." He paused for a moment, lost in his journey again.

"So that was my life, really. I'd ride the trail, make some money, then find a thousand ways to fritter it away. I gave rodeo-riding a go too, but that was before it became so big. In the end, I decided I needed the wide open spaces. And that was mistake number two.

"Guess I'm just a real bad judge of character!" He shook his head. "I was eighteen years old. Winter of 1887, it was. I was up in the South Dakota badlands. And I hear about this job going with two cattlemen tending a herd. They want a horse wrangler, they like my style and they put down good money – *real* good money – on the table. What could possibly go wrong? It looked like the best deal of my life. Turned out to be the worst."

He paused again. "Those winters of 1885 to 1887 were brutal. It was just one blizzard after another. Storms so harsh they killed millions of cattle on the Great Plains. Three quarters of the northern range cattle perished. It was the end of an era. They called it 'the Great Die-up'. It was the last of them long trail drives and round-ups. And it was the end of an era for me, too.

"It was a tense time. Cattle were dying left, right and plumb centre. Any cattle you still had, you prized them. And, like I say, these guys that hired me, they had a good-sized herd. Only trouble was, it was a stolen herd."

Grace gave a small gasp.

"I know. But you gotta believe me, I didn't know that

when they took me on. I didn't know it right until the end. Then it all came into focus. Why their money was so good. I was paying over my life to those two rustlers. And all the time I was working my butt off, tending to their cattle, we had vigilantes on our tail. Sent by the rightful owner of that herd to exact revenge."

Grace was pretty sure she knew what happened next. She hoped that he'd be sparing with the details.

"Those vigilantes caught up with us. They hanged both those cattlemen. I told 'em I didn't know the score. They talked about letting me go but, in the end, they decided they couldn't take that chance. Guess I couldn't blame them. They hanged me from the same tree."

The picture in her head was too vivid – just as it had been when she'd read Johnny's ribbon. But now, instead of looking out from the tree, she was looking at Johnny, hanging alongside the two rustlers who had cost him his life. It made her feel sick. "So you died aged eighteen," she said. "In 1887?"

He nodded. "It was a bad winter for cattle and for dumb vaqueros who shoulda asked a few more searching questions."

"So," Grace said. "What happened next? How did you cross?"

Johnny smiled at her. "You love all this, don't ya?"

"Do you think that's weird?" she asked.

He paused to consider for a moment, then nodded his head. "Yes, Grace. Yes, I think you're a definite freak."

She was cut to the quick for a moment, but then she saw the broad grin sweeping across his face. He laughed. And she laughed with him. And the laughter cut through any awkwardness that might have been between them.

"Way I see it," Johnny said, "you're interested in people. Interested in what makes people tick. We could all do with paying attention to that kinda thing. Why, if I'd paid a little more attention a ways back, well . . ." He paused, ruminatively, running a finger along his tattoo.

"I'm fascinated by these crossing stories," Grace said, pleased to be able to freely express her excitement. "Actually, I've started writing some of them down. I've been a bit slow getting started. I've got Darcy's – that's Darcy Flotsam. She's the figurehead on *The Nocturne*. She was a singer on a great ocean liner which crashed into an iceberg. During the crash, her soul became fused with the ship's figurehead."

Johnny beamed. "That's a great story!"

"Yes, and then there's Sidorio. He lived in Roman times. He was a pirate in Cilicia, this pirate stronghold, which threatened the Roman Empire. He and some accomplices kidnapped Julius Ceasar when he was a student." She paused. "You know who Julius Caesar was?"

"Hell, yeah," Johnny said. "When I was alive, the only names I knew were those of my friends and family. Maybe the odd rodeo star. But since I crossed, I've read a few books."

"OK," she said. "Well, Sidorio actually kidnapped

Caesar, when he was a young man on his way to university."

"Cool!" Johnny said. Grace was starting to see what Johnny meant about not being the best judge of character.

"What wasn't so cool," she continued, "was that Caesar turned the tables on his kidnappers. He had them all killed."

"Still," said Johnny. "If you're going to be killed by someone, might as well be by a great Roman Emperor."

Grace rolled her eyes. "Oh yes," she said. "You should have heard Sidorio on the subject. He wears it like a great badge of pride."

"Is he on *The Nocturne* too?" Johnny asked. "I wouldn't mind meeting him."

Grace shook her head. "Oh Johnny, you wouldn't have wanted to meet him. He was evil. The captain had to throw him off *The Nocturne* because he started to rebel. He wouldn't take blood in moderate quantities. He always wanted more. He killed his donor!"

"No!" Johnny's eyes were wide. Grace wasn't entirely sure if this was from shock or admiration.

"Yes," Grace said. "After that, he was banished. But he didn't go away quietly. He found others who felt the same way and they went on a rampage of violence. They killed a very famous pirate captain – the brother of the captain of the ship my brother's on."

"Your brother's on a pirate ship?"

Grace nodded.

"A brother who's into pirating and a sister who's into . . . into what, exactly?"

"Learning about things," she said. "You said it yourself. I like to know what makes people tick. Connor – that's my brother – Connor and I were born in a small town. We never knew much about the world beyond the bay. It's a long story how he came to be where he is and how I came to be here, but everything that's happened has given me the chance to see things I never even dreamed of."

Johnny smiled. "You can't do that," he said.

"Do what?"

"You get me to tell you my whole life story, then you dismiss yours in a few lines."

She shrugged. "I think yours is a whole lot more interesting."

"The grass is always greener," he said grinning. "It sounds like you and your brother are having an extraordinary time. And you're not even dead yet!"

"Maybe." She shrugged again.

"Maybe," he said, doing a pretty rotten impersonation of her. He swiftly returned to his own voice. "I like you, Grace," he said. "I like you and I want to know all about you. I told you my story. Now I want to hear yours!"

"All right," she conceded. "I'll tell it to you sometime. But not tonight. You must finish your story. After all, you only got to the part where you died." Her eyes were bright once more. "Tell me how you crossed!"

Johnny shook his head. "Honestly, Grace! I bet you were the kind of kid who loved creepy stories before bedtime."

She nodded. "Of course!"

"Well, actually," he said, "there isn't too much to tell. At least, I don't remember too much of it. I was, as you'll recall, hanging by my broken neck from that tree branch. I must have been hanging there for two, maybe three days. Believe me, the view had lost its appeal by then. The snow kept falling and what with the rigor mortis and the bitter cold, I was turning into a regular icicle. On the third day, this rider comes along the way. Only he wasn't any regular rider. He wasn't the usual kind of guy making his way through the Badlands. I'd lost my senses by this time, of course, so what comes next, well it's dependent on what he told me. And the way he tells it, he cut me down from the tree and carried me away on his horse. Thawed me out by the campfire, then gave me the kiss of life. Or the kiss of death, if you prefer to think of it that way. In other words, he was my sire."

"Why did he pick you?" Grace asked. "Why you, and not the other two men who were hanging on that tree?"

Johnny nodded. "I asked him the same damn thing. And he told me two things. Number one, there was something about me that reminded him of himself. And number two, that it just seemed like I had a whole lot more living to do." Johnny gave a laugh. "And he was right. And you know what, after that, things were a whole lot better. Me and Santos – that was his name. In life, he had been a *vaquero* too. Me and Santos forgot about the trail drives. Like I said before, they kinda died along with me that winter. But rodeo, well rodeo was taking off in a big way. And Santos and me had a grand ol' time moving from state to state, winning prizes, partying with all the pretty ladies . . ."

Grace shook her head. "You competed in rodeos as a *vampire*?"

"Hell, yeah!" Johnny said. "You could tell that some of them broncos had a suspicion. Animals have a keener sense of life and death than humans do. But them cowboys, them dumbass cowboys! They were completely in the dark."

Johnny grinned once more, then hung his head and fell silent for a time. Grace wondered if he was dwelling on the harsh facts of his life – and death. The silence weighed heavy between them. "Are you OK?" she asked, at last.

"Me? Oh sure, sure. I was just thinking about something about those crossing stories of yours," Johnny said. "Tell me another one." He paused. "Tell me Lorcan's." His dark eyes glistened in the moonlight.

Grace faltered. "I don't . . . you see . . . Lorcan's never told me his story."

"What?" Johnny looked askance at her. "That doesn't make sense. You two seem real close, yet you don't know his story?"

Grace shook her head. "Of course, I've always wondered

about it. All I know of his life is where he was born and where he died. The rest is a blank."

Johnny shook his head in disbelief.

"The thing is," Grace continued. "I think if I did know his story, I might be able to help him. Mosh Zu says there's something in Lorcan's mind that's stopping him from healing. If I could find out what that was, well maybe I could help him deal with whatever it is and truly begin his recovery."

Johnny smiled softly at her. "There you go. You're a lady with a plan."

"Yes," said Grace, shrugging. "But it's not as simple as that, is it? Lorcan's never been one to open up about himself. And now, especially, he's more guarded than ever. I wouldn't want to ask him."

Johnny nodded. "But you don't need to ask."

"What do you mean?" She turned to him, puzzled.

"You're good at reading ribbons, aren't you?"

She nodded, then watched as Johnny's eyes fell to the book she had placed on the wall between them. Poking out between the jagged pages was Lorcan's ribbon. Of course! She'd unwittingly employed it as a bookmark. Grace realised what Johnny was suggesting. Her heart began racing at the thought. At last, she might begin to crack the enigma of Lorcan Furey. Did she dare? Was it right? "No," she said. "No, I can't."

Johnny chuckled. "You didn't show any restraint in reading *my* ribbon. What's the difference?"

"That was an accident," said Grace. "I told you . . ."

Johnny pushed the book off the wall. As it tumbled to the ground, he reached forward and grabbed the ribbon. "Oops!" he said, cupping the ribbon in his callused hands. Grace looked at it, lying there, like a snake. What secrets did it contain?

Now, Johnny took the ribbon between his fingers and held it out to her. She shook her head. "I really don't think I can."

"The way I see it," Johnny said, "you don't got no choice. You want to help your friend and this is gonna tell you how." With that, he placed the ribbon around her neck and knotted it gently in a bow. Then, he jumped down from the wall. "I'm gonna leave you to your own devices now, Grace," he said. "But be sure to come and find me when you're done."

She said nothing, feeling a shiver as the ribbon settled on her skin.

"Hey," he said. "Don't look so worried. I'm sure it'll be just fine." With that, he gave a little bow, then placed the Stetson back on his head and strode away across the courtyard.

CHAPTER TWENTY-EIGHT

The Plea

The deck of the Vampirate ship was crowded and faces were quick to turn, conversation quick to halt, as Connor, Bart and Jez climbed onto the deck. Wordlessly, the vampires began moving towards them. Was it Connor's imagination or were they like a pack of animals, closing in for the kill? All eyes stared at them intently, taking the measure of the new arrivals.

At the front of the pack were two men – one rotund, the other tall – and a young girl.

"Who are they?" asked the girl.

"New donors, perhaps?" said the shorter, rounder of the two men. He was staring at Bart, his head tilting to one side to take in his full height. "He'd make a *very* good donor, too." Connor watched as the man's mouth opened and his sharp teeth became visible.

His taller companion laughed. "You can't just trade in

your donor. It doesn't work like that." He glanced at Connor, his eyes flickering with fire. "All the same, it's tempting, isn't it? I'm so very hungry tonight."

Connor felt like a piece of meat, thrown into a cage at the zoo. Were they in direct danger? Surely the captain would protect them.

"Who are they?" repeated the girl, stepping closer. She had a look of perpetual confusion about her. "Who are they?" Her little mouth fell open and now he could see her teeth extending like needles. Connor wasn't sure how much more of this he could endure.

Suddenly a fresh voice was heard across the deck. "Let me through! Let me through!" There was movement in the crowd. Connor watched as a woman forced her way between them and stood beside the confused girl. The newcomer had an altogether livelier air about her. She had wide, staring eyes and a short dark bob of hair. Connor had met her once before. He smiled with huge relief.

"Darcy Flotsam," he said. "That's right, isn't it? And I'm . . ."

She smiled back at him. "You're Connor Tempest. I remember you. Besides, your eyes are the exact same colour as your sister's."

He nodded. "Is she around?"

"She's not here," Darcy said. "She left the ship to go to a place called Sanctuary."

"Sanctuary?"

"It's a place where vampires are healed," Darcy

243

explained. "Grace went there with Lorcan Furey. You know of Lorcan?"

He nodded. He knew all about Lorcan. There was some bond between Lorcan Furey and Grace. He was the reason she'd found it impossible to keep away from the ship. It was like a crush but Connor knew that it was nothing so fleeting as that. It was something stronger. He didn't like it. He had nothing against Lorcan personally, but he wished the boy vampire had never come into his sister's life. But then again, if it hadn't been for Lorcan, Grace would have drowned. It was as if in saving Grace's life, Lorcan had claimed her for his own. What did he want with her? It made Connor's head ache.

"If you know of Lorcan," Darcy said, "then perhaps you know of his affliction? He is blind. They've gone to Sanctuary in search of a cure. The captain went with them, but he's just returned."

Blind? Could it be true? Now Connor felt bad. And his guilt was mingled with disappointment at the news that he would not, after all, be seeing Grace tonight. It had been the one bright point on a very dark horizon. Well, if he was not going to see her, they may as well get straight down to business.

"Actually," Connor said, "though I'd have liked to see Grace, it's the captain we've really come to visit." Connor indicated his travelling companions. "Darcy, these are my friends. This is Bart . . ."

"Pleased to meet you." Darcy gave a small curtsey and

shook Bart's hand. "Actually, I think I've seen you before. You came with Connor when he was on the ship that time before."

"Yes," Connor said with a nod. "That's right. And this is . . . this is Jez."

Jez reached out his hand to her. "Nice to meet you," he said, holding her small pale hand in his for a moment.

Darcy blushed. "And you too, sir. Jez, is it?"

"That's right," he said, smiling. He seemed nervous, thought Connor, as well he might be.

A fresh voice began to speak. But it was not one of those gathered on the deck. The voice was a whisper. Connor recognised it immediately.

"Bring them to my cabin, Darcy."

The captain's command was sufficient to pull Darcy together. She turned and cleared her throat to address the circling vampires. "You heard the captain. He wishes me to escort the guests to his cabin. Now step aside, please. That's right. Step aside!"

The vampires were slow to move but eventually a path opened up between their ranks. Connor tried not to meet any of their eyes. Already, he felt a deep sense of unease being aboard this ship. How Grace could deal with living amongst these creatures was a mystery to him. The sooner that he and Bart passed Jez into the captain's care and headed back to the living world, the better.

As they followed Darcy across the deck, he heard the

confused girl ask once more, "But who *are* they? I want one. I want the youngest to be my new donor."

"I do apologise for my fellow travellers," Darcy said, *sotto voce*, to the three lads. "They are at their most listless tonight. It's Feast Night tomorrow, you see, so they are entirely drained and incapable of even a good conversation right now."

"Feast Night?" Jez repeated, his eyes full of wonder.

"Yes," Darcy said. "It's the night when each vampire takes the blood he or she needs for the following week."

Jez nodded. Connor wondered how Jez felt about this new world, with its strange rituals.

Darcy led them to a doorway and, as they stood there, the cabin door opened. Darcy walked inside, beckoning the others to follow.

"Captain, I've brought your guests."

"Thank you, Darcy," came the captain's disembodied whisper. "You can leave us now."

She was clearly disappointed but as she exited the cabin, she reached out and brushed Jez's arm. "Nice to meet you, Mr Je— I mean to say, Jez!"

"Yes, and you too," he said, smiling at her. Once more, Connor sensed his nerves as he turned from Darcy to the captain. So much hinged on the captain's decision. For Jez, it meant the different between life and death or, at least, between a living death and oblivion.

Miss Flotsam walked out of the door and it swung closed behind her. The three lads found themselves momentarily in darkness. Connor's pulse was racing. But, he told himself, I know the captain. I've met him before. And he's looked after Grace. I have nothing to fear. And yet . . . and yet, this was a ship of vampires and here they were, in effect locked in a dark room with the leader of the crew.

"Come further inside," came the whisper. As they did so, they entered a candlelit section of the cabin. Connor could see the folds of the captain's cloak. He was standing, his back turned to them. Flickers of light traced the veins within the cape. Connor had seen this before but he knew how alarming it must seem to Bart and Jez. He wanted to comfort them but he dared not speak.

The captain turned to face them. As he did so, Bart gasped.

"My apologies," the captain said. "I forgot that though *I* have seen *you* before, Bartholomew, you have not seen me. Please, do not be alarmed by my appearance. You will become accustomed to it, I'm sure."

"I'm sorry, sir, you've seen me before?"

"Why yes," the captain said. "It was at *Calle del Marinero*, I believe. You were having . . . difficulties. I was able to help you."

Calle del Marinero . . . their "lost weekend"? Connor was stunned. "You were there?" he said, puzzled.

The captain nodded. "I was there. But let us not concern ourselves with that now. Connor, it is good to see you again. You look well."

"Thank you, sir."

"Doubtless you would welcome news of your sister," said the captain, reaching out a gloved hand and placing it on Connor's shoulder. "She is well, and seems to grow in strength and wisdom every day. We all have so much to learn from her."

Connor flushed with pride.

"I imagine that the choice she has made must seem strange to you," the captain continued. "But each of us must make our own way in this world and I think Grace is exactly where she should be."

Connor nodded. "Actually, I think so too, sir."

The captain nodded back and withdrew his hand. He moved past Connor and Bart and came to a standstill before Jez.

"This is Jez . . ." Connor began.

"There is no need to introduce us," said the captain. "I know who stands before me." He paused. "This is the one I thought you had destroyed. The one sired by Sidorio."

His words were cold. All the warmth he had shown Connor had drained suddenly away. Now he spoke directly to Jez. "There is much darkness in you," he said.

"Yes," Jez said, his voice faint.

"Why are you here?" the captain asked.

"I want to shed my darkness," Jez said. "I want to change what I've become."

The captain stood for a good while, observing Jez. As he did so, tears began flowing down Jez's face.

"I didn't ask for this," he said. "I accepted my death. But he found me and, as you say, sired me." He paused to wipe the tears on the back of his hand. "I've done some terrible things. Some that he made me do. Others because of the hunger. This terrible hunger, which I can't control." He began to tremble.

"And you think I can help you with this?"

"I have heard certain things, sir. That there are ways to reverse my condition. That I might become a mortal once more. That I might get my old life back."

"Yes," the captain said. "It *is* true that this can happen, but the way is paved with difficulties. I will not help you with that. I can take you to another . . ."

"It is *your* help I seek, sir," Jez said. "When I was mortal, sir, I heard Connor's sister talk of you, of how strong and merciful you are. How you give shelter to those like me—"

"No," the captain interrupted. "I give shelter to those who control their hunger. I can't take the risk of having you aboard the ship."

Connor couldn't believe it. Had they come this far only to be told no by the captain? Grimly, he remembered what Jez had said to them back on *The Diablo. "I want you to help me find my way back. And if I can't, then I want you to kill me. Once and for all."* He had to do something.

"Captain," Connor said. "Isn't there anything you can do to help him?"

"I didn't say I *couldn't* help. I said I wouldn't." The captain stepped back. "You should have destroyed him when you had the chance. It would have been better all round."

"But Captain . . ."

"No, Connor. I told you once before. He is not who you think he is. He is only an echo. He may talk like your friend and look like him, but there is too much darkness in him. We can thank Sidorio for that."

Jez cried out and fell to his knees. "I'm begging you, sir, help me! Sidorio is gone now. And all of his company. I am alone. So alone. Even when I am with my friends here, I am alone. There is a distance between us I cannot bridge . . . I beg you, sir . . ." His voice fell away into silence.

There was a long pause.

"All right," the captain said at last. "Get off your knees. Stand up."

Jez drew himself upright.

"I will allow you to travel with us, for a time. And, if you prove your worth, I shall take you to one who can help you with your onward journey. But do not expect any of this to be easy. There is much work to do and it can only come from you."

"Yes, Captain – *my* captain. Thank you."

"The best way of thanking me is by proving that there is truth in what you have told me. Disappoint me and you will leave this ship, never to return. Is that understood?"

Jez nodded. "Yes, sir."

"I'll have Darcy sort out a room for you. And a donor. I think I have someone who can fill that role."

Connor suddenly blanched.

The captain shook his head. "Not you, Connor. We are carrying an extra donor at the moment. Her name is Shanti. I think she will be a perfect match."

The captain's mood suddenly seemed to lighten. "Connor, Bart, would you like me to prepare a cabin for you?"

"No," Connor said, abruptly. "That is, I mean—"

Bart interjected. "I think what Connor is trying to say, sir, is that we should be getting back to *The Diablo* before we are missed."

"As you wish," said the captain. When he spoke again, it was not to them. "Darcy, please come and collect Jez, will you? I'd like you to take him to one of our spare cabins. He's going to be travelling with us a while."

In a few moments, Darcy had appeared inside the cabin, the door opening to admit her. She was beaming.

"Come along," she said to Jez, "and we'll get you settled."

"Thank you, Darcy," the captain said.

"Thank *you*, sir," Jez said to the captain. His relief was evident.

"Remember what I said, Jez. There are no more chances beyond this."

"Yes, sir!" With that, he hugged Bart and Connor in turn. "Thanks for helping me out, guys."

As Connor released Jez, he wondered what lay ahead for him. Would they ever see him again? He felt suddenly drained – by their reunion and by their journey back to the Vampirate ship. He had a certain curiosity to find out more about the place but he knew that it was not his world. Grace clearly thrived on its mysteries, but he preferred the more solid world of pirates.

"So it's goodbye once more," the captain said to him.

"Yes," Connor replied. "For now. I have a feeling we'll meet again."

The captain seemed to smile at him through the mesh of his mask. "Oh yes, Connor, we will meet again. And, in the meantime, I'll be watching you."

Though the words might have been forbidding to others, to Connor there was some strange comfort within them. He reached out and shook the captain's gloved hand. As he did so, he had a sudden vision. He was in the water and the hand was lifting him out of it, up to safety. Was that what had happened at *Calle del Marinero*? He tried to sustain the vision but it evaporated all too quickly.

As he and Bart walked back across the deck, his head was full of thoughts and questions about the Vampirate captain.

They reached the ladder back down to their small boat, then turned. Jez and Darcy were talking together on the deck. Connor heard them laughing.

"I think Jez is going to be OK here," he said.

"Reckon so," said Bart. "Always did have a way with the girls, that Stukeley! The captain seems tough but fair. And talking of captains, we'd better get some speed on before ours twigs we're missing."

Nodding, Connor climbed over the side and began descending the ladder. As he did so, he heard a familiar voice.

"But who are they? Who *are* they? I'm hungry. I'm *so* hungry."

Funny, he thought. *They're as curious about us as we are about them.*

Jumping back into the boat, he thought about the vastness of the dark ocean – so vast that it could shelter so many different kinds of people. Then, as Bart joined him, he pulled up the anchor and they sailed off once more, guided by the silvery sliver of a crescent moon.

CHAPTER TWENTY-NINE

Lorcan's Ribbon

The ribbon was clearly having an effect upon Grace. Ever since Johnny had slipped it around her neck, she had begun to feel drowsy. It was as if the ribbon was getting ready to talk to her – or rather, preparing her to listen. Slipping down from the wall, she decided she had better find a more comfortable spot. Ideally, she'd have gone back to her room but she sensed that there wasn't enough time. She could take the ribbon off again, but now the process had begun, she was eager to get on with it. She'd heard Olivier talk of a kitchen garden and a fountain on the other side of the courtyard. That sounded like a tranquil place to sit for a while.

The garden was just as Olivier had described it. In its centre was a circular fountain. The sound of running water was instantly soothing. Better yet, there were three benches around its circumference. Grace sat down on one, then decided she would be more comfortable lying down. She removed her sweater and bundled it up as a pillow. As she stretched out, her eyes closed tight and she found herself quickly transported into another place.

It was dark. It took her a moment to realise that she was underwater. Then she saw the body. The girl's body, floating in the water. Grace shivered. It was her own body. She was watching herself on the verge of drowning. It was riveting, but horrific at the same time. Her first instinct was to open her eyes but she knew she had to stay within this vision world, however unsettling.

She swam powerfully towards herself and reached out, taking the frail body and carrying it up to the surface. She could sense the weakness in her own limp body as she delivered it up into the night air.

Then she was looking down upon herself, sprawled out on a deck. Of course! She realised she was seeing her first meeting with Lorcan but from his point of view.

He looks down in wonder at the girl lying on the deck. The girl's eyes are closed. Is she dead already? No, she cannot be. He waits. At last, her eyelids flicker and she looks up at him. She looks up but she does not see him – she is too busy finding her way back into the world. But he sees her. And the sight gives him a jolt. Her eyes are as green as emeralds. He has seen eyes like this before. On three faces. Can it be? Can it really be true?

"You're going to get me into trouble," he says.

She looks confused, as if she can't quite understand him.

The strands of her auburn hair have settled over her eyes. He reaches forward and brushes them away. The sight of her hair in his pale hands triggers another memory. Hair just this shade. He shivers to think of the implications. But then the girl starts making sounds and he is drawn back into the moment.

She is shivering and, at first, the sounds she makes are incoherent. He realises she is desperately dehydrated. He reaches for his flask and offers her a drink. As she takes the water, he uses his free hand to tear off his jacket and bundle it under her head. Once more, he sees the auburn hair and feels the shock of recognition.

"Who are you?"

At last her words make sense to him. They provoke such a rush of thoughts and memories. Now, he is starting to panic. But, at the same time, he is intrigued, excited. This moment is a gift he had never thought to receive.

"The name's Lorcan," he says. "Lorcan Furey."

She wants to know where she is, how she got there. He answers her questions as best he can, choosing his words carefully. Then she mentions her brother. She speaks his name.

"Connor! We're twins. We're everything to one another . . ."

Twins. She has said the word now. And now there can be no remaining doubt. He looks at her and hopes she does not see the fear in his eyes. He is grateful, so very grateful, to hear the captain's whisper calling his name.

"Wake up! Wake up, I say!"

The vision becomes shaky. The girl fades from view. Then the deck disappears altogether, gone to mist.

"Wake up!"

She felt a finger prod her chest. "Oww!" Grace opened her eyes and found herself looking up at a woman's face. It took her a moment to come back to her senses, to realise she was in the gardens at Sanctuary and that she had seen the woman's face before, though not as angry as it appeared to be now.

"You're the princess!" she said, sliding up into a sitting position.

"That's right," said the woman, who Grace had watched during the ribbon ceremony. "I am Marie-Louise, Princesse de Lamballe."

Grace swung her feet down to the ground. "What are you doing here?" she asked.

"I'm sorry," the princess snapped. "I wasn't aware these were your private gardens." She pointed to Grace's neck. "What is the meaning of this?"

It took her a moment to realise what the princess was talking about. Then she realised she was pointing to the ribbon. Instantly, she felt guilty. "It belongs to my friend—" she began.

The princess cut her off. "It matters not to whom it belongs," she sniffed. "I take great exception to you wearing it in that fashion."

Grace frowned. What was she *talking* about?

"Please," the princess said, reaching out to undo the bow. "Please, take it off. Take it off at once!"

"All right," Grace said, blocking the princess's hands and gently unfastening the ribbon herself. "All right, if it upsets you." She folded the ribbon carefully and closed it in the palm of her hand.

"That's better!" the princess said, more calmly. She sat down beside Grace and arranged her tattered skirts. She appeared to be making herself comfortable. Grace sat beside her, impatiently. She felt deeply frustrated that the princess had interrupted her vision. It had been fascinating seeing herself through Lorcan's eyes and she felt she had been on the verge of discovering something important.

"I'm sorry I was angry before," the princess said, more amiably. "Of course, you didn't intend to upset me. You didn't know. How could you?" She snorted. "Why, you don't even know who I am, do you? My poor, ignorant child." She leaned towards Grace and pushed a stray strand of Grace's hair behind her ear. Her touch was surprisingly gentle.

"I was a very powerful person once," she continued. "Companion and confidante to Marie Antoinette. The Queen of France." She twisted her head, the glare from her necklace dazzling Grace for a moment. "I suppose you do know about Marie Antoinette?"

"Yes." Grace nodded. "Last term at school, they taught us about the French Revolution . . ."

"Ah," the princess said, smiling. "So you *do* know about me?"

Grace shook her head. "I know a bit about your friend, the queen."

The princess frowned. "Perhaps you should have read around the subject more widely. I happen to know I make most of the better history books. I was her closest friend, superintendent of the royal household. Why, she gave me this necklace." The princess lifted her hand to her throat, where the cluster of finely-cut diamonds glinted in the moonlight. "It's beautiful, isn't it? But I don't wear it for its beauty alone." Her eyes locked on Grace, she reached to the back of her neck and unclasped the necklace. The jewels rained down into her hand. As they did, Grace gasped. There was a livid, jagged scar running all the way around the princess's neck.

"This is my eternal necklace," she said, her fingers gently touching her flesh. "The misguided mob cut off my head, stuck it on a pike and paraded it around the cafés, where people drank to my death. But worse, worse than that, they paraded it past the queen's balcony. Can you imagine? Can you imagine my indignity? Her horror?"

Grace shook her head. The way the princess spoke so objectively about the terrible violence inflicted upon her was amazing. It made her view the woman in a whole new light.

"Their cruelty, their barbarism knew no limits," the princess said. "One man ripped out my heart and ate it."

259

Grace gasped, but the princess shook her head and gave a bitter laugh. "He had a shock when I paid him a visit a night or two later. He suffered more than indigestion that night. I think he was a little *surprised* to see that I had managed to collect up the pieces of my body . . . well, most of them anyway. The royal seamstress sewed me back together. There was no one to rival her craft. There were tears in her eyes, of course, but the needle in her hand was steady."

Grace shook her head. Once more, she found herself stunned by a vampire's crossing story. "But why did my ribbon upset you?" she asked.

"At the time I was killed, there was a ritual," the princess said. "Each night, the aristocrats, those who were spared, staged a grand ball. They were lavish affairs – imagine the drink, the food, the dresses. They were determined to dance until dawn because they knew the party was coming to an end. You could only attend such a ball if you lost someone to the mob. And everyone who attended, they wore a ribbon around their necks, just like you wore yours."

"But wasn't that to honour their friends and families?" Grace said. "Wasn't it a sign of respect?"

"Honour? Respect? Pah!" said the princess, her face angry again. "They should have been *fighting*, not *dancing*. If there had been fewer balls, perhaps things would have worked out differently for me, for many of us." She slipped the diamond necklace back around her neck. "Please, help me to fasten this." Grace did so. "That's better," the princess said, rising to her feet. "Well, I am tired now. This lack of blood is so draining." She stared at Grace and the hunger was all too visible in her eyes. Grace wondered if she should be on the alert for an attack. But the princess only reached out and took Grace's hand – the one in which she clasped the ribbon.

"I know whose ribbon that is," said the princess.

"You do?" Grace said.

"Of course. It is that boy. The one who has lost his eyesight. You came with him. You are a little in love with him, I think."

Grace flushed.

"Be careful," said the princess.

"What do you mean?"

"I know what you're trying to do. You're looking for some kind of answer in that ribbon."

"Yes, I suppose—" Grace began but the princess cut her off again.

"Be careful. I have lived a lot longer than you and there's one lesson I have learned well."

"What is that?" Grace asked, hoping that the princess would loosen her grip.

"Do not ask questions that are you are not yet ready to hear the answers to," said the princess. *"Comprenez?"*

Grace nodded.

The princess finally released her hold. "Listen to me, child. I know about these things. I'm a good confidante. The very best, so the queen said."

"Thank you," Grace said. "Thank you very much for the advice."

"*Mon plaisir*," the princess said. "Goodnight for now, child. I shall make one final circuit of the gardens and then, to bed." With that, she wandered off beyond the fountain. As she disappeared into the shadows, her livid scars receded and the tatters in her skirts looked like fine lace. She moved like the most elegant of ladies.

Alone once more, Grace felt a growing warmth in the palm of her hand. She looked down and saw the ribbon curled there. Was it asking to begin again? But perhaps the princess was right. Was it dangerous to return to the vision? Was she on the verge of a discovery she was not yet prepared for? She hesitated, thinking that perhaps she should just call it a night and return the ribbon to Lorcan's bedside.

But it was just too tempting. The first vision had already told her that there was a deeper connection between her and Lorcan than even she had realised. Perhaps this was also the clue to his sickness and therefore his healing too. She had to find out more. Even if it was diving into dangerous waters, she had to do it. For his sake. And her own.

Lying back again on the bench, she gripped the ribbon in her palm and closed her eyes. Instantly, the vision journey began anew. It was dark again, misty. Grace wondered if she was being given the same part of the story. But no, she was not underwater this time. Instead, she was on the deck of a ship . . . *The Nocturne*. She turned and saw herself running out into the night. She realised she had become Lorcan once more. And, at the same moment, she knew the moment they had reached. Now, she was going to learn something!

"Connor!" she hears the other Grace cry. Then she sees Connor, but not as a sister views the brother she has seen almost every day of her life. She is viewing him as Lorcan does. And now, as he sees Connor, he looks at him with the same wonder as when he watched Grace open her eyes on the deck. The boy is taller, broader, his hair a shade darker. But they share the same emerald eyes. He watches as they embrace each other. Their reunion is joyful but his joy is cut through with pain and fear.

He glances away. He is aware of the light beginning to puncture the darkness. Like grains of sand in an hour-glass, his time is running out. He begins to panic. And not only on account of the time. He realises that the boy has come, not from thin air, but from a ship. A ship which now becomes visible through the mist. Along its edge are hordes of men and women, armed with swords. What kind of trick is this? What kind of danger? He must protect Grace! He must protect them both. He made a promise long ago.

The Dawning Bell tolls. He hears Darcy's cries to go inside. He knows he must, but he feels paralysed. He cannot go. Not without her. Not without both of them.

The light is disorientating to him and only just in time does he see a pirate running towards him. He draws his cutlass. The pirate counters with a broadsword. The girls cry out. Darcy begs him to go inside. Grace shouts that he has done no harm but now Lorcan realises that they *are* all in danger. He cannot run from the fight. He draws upon his energy and lands a direct hit on the pirate's arm. There are more cries but now Lorcan knows his fate.

"I said I'd protect Grace and that's what I mean to do," he cries. He'll protect her, protect them both. Just as he did once before. Until his last breath, he'll protect the twins. Else, what are promises worth? And now there are new emotions mixed in with ancient promises. Feelings he doesn't want to admit to, not even to himself. Too dangerous.

The light gets the better of him. He has to close his eyes. Still, he lashes out with his sword, but it is pointless. They tell him that there is no attack. But he can't believe them. Not at first. Only when the boy, when Connor, speaks, does he believe it. He hears such strength in the young man's voice. It's not a surprise that he should have inherited such strength. This, this is enough to convince him he can go inside.

From the crack in the door, he watches them. It is painful. Painful in so many ways. He feels a searing sense of loss. As he closes his eyes, he has a sudden image of two babies, swaddled in soft blankets. They are being given to him, one placed in each arm. He looks down at them, glancing from one to the other and back again. They really are two peas in a pod.

Now he sees them again, hugging. She will go with her brother. She *must* go with him. Away from here. They are safe away from here, away from this ship and its crew. And yet . . . and yet, he doesn't want her to go. Is it so wrong to admit this? Is it so wrong to want something for himself? Some*one*. Her.

Suddenly, the image fractures and he is looking down upon the girl on the deck once more. She opens her eyes. Green light is emanating from them. It is dazzling.

Then, as his vision becomes clear once more, the twins are hugging one another still.

Then, babies in swaddling clothes again. In his arms, as he steps into a small boat and prepares to sail.

"They must never know," he tells himself. "They must never know."

The vision dies there, turning to blackness. Silence.

Grace opens her eyes. They are wet with tears. What has she learned? Too much, and yet not enough.

CHAPTER THIRTY

The Guilty Party

Molucco Wrathe paced up and down his cabin furiously. Connor had never seen him so angry. "So," he began, eyes blazing. "Would someone care to tell me what's going on?" He glared at Connor and Bart. "And let's have the truth, the whole truth and nothing *but* the blinkin' truth." At last, he came to a standstill by Cate. Her face was hard to read, a direct contrast to the fury visibly emanating from Molucco.

Connor looked uncomfortably at Bart. Bart glanced nervously back. Before either dared to speak, Molucco exploded again. "Why don't I speed this up for you, gentlemen? I know that you took one of my light boats and sailed off into the night. And I know that you visited some strange place where they sell BLOOD and then went off to find that ship of . . . of . . . VAMPIRES!"

Connor was stunned. How *could* the captain know all

this? No one had seen them. They'd been so careful about that. He could tell Bart was thinking the same thing. But they couldn't exactly ask Molucco how he knew. It would only send his fury soaring up to a new level.

"Well?" Molucco persisted, stepping towards them again. Cate frowned. Even Scrimshaw seemed to cower as the captain continued. "Speak to me! What on earth were you up to?"

Finally Bart spoke. "We were helping out Jez, sir," he said quietly.

"Louder!" Molucco boomed at an ear-piercing volume.

"We were helping out Jez, sir – Jez Stukeley," Bart repeated, a little more loudly.

"Jez Stukeley?" Molucco looked deeply confused. Evidently his mysterious informant hadn't mentioned Jez. "But Jez is dead."

"Yes, sir," said Bart. "He's dead, but not gone."

"I don't understand," said Molucco, his forehead creased in a deep frown.

Connor took up the story. "We all know that Jez died in the duel on *The Albatross*. We buried him at sea. But afterwards, he was found by one of the Vampirates, Sidorio, and he was transformed into a vampire himself."

"Yes, yes, I know all *this*," Molucco said, darkly. "Jez was one of the vampires who murdered my brother and his crew—"

"No!" cried Connor, more passionately than he had intended. "Yes, he was *with* them. He had no choice about that. But he didn't know about the attack – the terrible attack – until it was underway. He didn't even go aboard your brother's ship. He wasn't a proper part of it—"

"You've certainly changed your tune, Tempest!" Molucco snapped. "That night we hunted the vampires down, you said that he was one of the guilty. What's more, you led the attack on him. You threw flaming torches through the air and killed him a second time."

"Yes." Connor nodded. "Well, no, actually."

"Which is it?" Molucco thundered.

"I *thought* we'd destroyed him, but we hadn't. He survived." He paused. "He's the only one that survived."

"And he's in pain," Bart said. "He feels terrible guilt for what he was a part of . . ."

"I should hope so," Molucco said.

"And he hates this thing . . . this vampire, he's become. He wants to become mortal again. He begged us to help him out, sir. We couldn't say no."

Molucco was silent, his arms folded as he awaited the rest of their story. Cate nodded at Connor to continue.

"We took him to the Vampirate ship, sir," said Connor. "The ship that rescued my sister before. The captain is a merciful ma— a merciful being. He's not bloodthirsty like Sidorio. We think he can help Jez."

"Well, isn't that nice?" Molucco said in a more amenable tone. "What was it you used to call yourselves – the Three Buccaneers?"

Connor nodded. Bart smiled.

"And you were just reuniting one last time for the good of your old buddy?"

"Yes!" Connor nodded, relieved that he understood at last.

"Exactly!" Bart said.

There was a pause, then Molucco let out a cry. "You have no idea what damage you've done! I had just about persuaded my brother to drop the idea of avenging Porfirio's murder. That we'd dealt with his murderers, taken our revenge. Now, you go and do this and he knows that one of Porfirio's killers is alive and well . . ." He broke off, his face so red that Connor wondered if he was going to pass out.

"Excuse me, sir," said Connor, "but how does Barbarro know about this?"

"Isn't it obvious?" Molucco snapped, "You were followed."

"I'm sorry," Connor said, glumly. "I'm sorry to have caused you all this bother."

"We were just trying to help out an old friend," Bart said.

"Don't interrupt me!" roared Molucco. "You two need to wake up and smell the seaweed! Jez Stukeley died on the deck of *The Albatross*. End of. I don't care to concern myself with this zombie-after-death nonsense. We lost Jez in that duel on Drakoulis' ship." He paused. "It was terrible sad, but these things happen."

Connor and Bart both winced at this casual summation of their friend's death.

"I'm not interested in what happened to Jez after we conveyed his coffin into the ocean. I don't want to know about these Vampirates. I certainly don't want to encounter them again. And, as long as you are members of my crew – *and correct me if I'm wrong, but you have both signed up to articles binding you to my service for the rest of your days* – as long as you are both members of my crew, you will not so much as speak the word *vampire* – or *Vampirate* – aboard this ship. Is that understood?"

"Yes, Captain." Their voices were weak.

"I'm sorry. Did someone say something?"

"Yes, Captain Wrathe," Connor and Bart declared, more loudly this time.

"Then that's an end to this matter," said Molucco. "And now, we will put all our energies into trying to salvage this situation and persuading my brother to focus on the raid in India." He turned to his side, and adopted a more measured tone. "Cate, I'm going to see Barbarro now. I'll leave you to sort out a suitable punishment for these two."

He turned back to Connor and Bart. "You've disappointed me greatly, both of you," he said. Connor could barely look at the captain as he continued. "You were like sons to me. But now, I don't know. I just don't know. I trust in future you'll remember where your loyalties lie." Then he raised his voice once more to shout a final word. "Dismissed!"

Cate stepped forward and ushered Connor and Bart out of the captain's cabin. They all looked battle-weary as they walked out onto the deck. The sun was a bright, unwelcome guest, dazzling their eyes.

They walked the length of the deck in silence, each brooding on the captain's fierce and uncompromising words.

"What's up?" said a voice from behind the mast. Moonshine Wrathe jumped out in front of them. "You three look like you've been to a funeral."

"Not now, Moonshine," said Cate.

"Shouldn't you call me *Lieutenant Wrathe*?" Moonshine said.

"I'm Deputy Captain of *The Diablo*," Cate said, severely. "You're on my turf now."

Moonshine raised an eyebrow. "You're quite aggressive, aren't you, Catie? I wonder why that is? Do you sometimes feel you can't measure up?"

"OK, Moonboy," said Bart. "That's enough. Don't you have a fly to de-wing or some other nasty habit to keep you busy?"

Moonshine laughed. "That's very amusing, Bartholomew. We had you down as brainless muscle but I can see we're going to have to revise our opinions."

Bart sighed and shook his head, exasperated.

"What about you, Connor?" Moonshine continued. "What's eating you? Are you missing your vampire friends? You're looking a little pale. Perhaps you need another trip to the Blood Tavern?" Mooshine's eyes bulged. Connor and Bart were dumbstruck.

271

"It was *you*!" Connor said. "You followed us! And then you came back and told Captain Wrathe."

Moonshine shrugged. "It's about time Uncle Luck got wise to the weird predilections of his crew."

Bart glared at him stonily.

"What's the matter?" sneered Moonshine. "Don't you understand what 'predilections' means?"

Bart shook his head and swung out with his fist. "*Understand* this!" he cried.

But Cate raised her arm and took the weight of Bart's blow. "No," she said. "He's not worth it, Bart. You're in enough trouble with Captain Wrathe as it is. Don't make it worse."

Moonshine smiled. "Quite right, Catie," he said. "At least one of you three amigos has an ounce of brainpower."

"All right," Cate said, the steel back in her voice. "I think we've heard quite enough from you. Off you go. And be thankful I saved you a pummelling."

Moonshine opened his mouth once more but seemed to think better of it. He sauntered past them along the deck. He walked a few strides, then twisted his head before waving. "See ya! Wouldn't wanna be ya!" Laughing to himself, he continued on his way.

When he was gone, Bart turned to Cate. "Thanks," he said. "I sure would have liked to introduce his face to my fist but I'm glad you stopped me."

Cate managed a weak smile. "No trouble," she said. Then she sighed. "Oh, what a mess all this is!"

"So," Connor said, gloomily, "are you going to give us our punishments?"

Cate put her hand on his shoulder. "Punishments? Now why would I want to do that? Oh, I'll come up with some story for Captain Wrathe, but I think you've suffered enough already. We all have. Let's just put this behind us, eh, and move on as best we can?"

"You'd have helped Jez, wouldn't you, Cate?" Bart said. "You'd have helped out an old buddy?"

Cate sighed deeply. "I'd have done *anything* to help Jez. Anything in my power, *whatever* he's become. It was my fault he died. I messed up on our attack strategy. I should have realised there was something wrong with our intelligence. I should have known that we were being lured to that ship intentionally . . ."

"No," said Bart. "It wasn't your fault."

Cate shook her head. "I know you're being supportive, Bart, and I appreciate that. I really do. But I'm Deputy Captain of this ship. It was my job to prepare us *fully* for the attack. I stuffed up. If Jez's death wasn't my fault, then I don't know whose it was."

"Well, *I'll* tell ya," said Bart, his eyes dark. "We wouldn't have been lured onto *The Albatross* in the first place if it wasn't down to an old grievance between Molucco Wrathe and Captain Drakoulis. And once the situation became clear, Captain Wrathe didn't exactly pour oil on troubled waters, did he? No, as usual, he made things a whole heap worse."

"He couldn't have stopped the duel," Cate said. "There was no talking Drakoulis out of it."

"And," added Connor, "there was no stopping Jez from volunteering."

"Ah," said Bart, "that's all understood. But someone *should* have stopped him. It was a feud between the two captains, and it was the captains who should have fought that duel. Only Captain Wrathe isn't known for doing his own dirty work, is he?"

"Bart," Cate said, a strong note of warning in her voice. "You have to leave this behind. It won't serve you well to even *think* these thoughts, let alone—"

"No, Cate," said Bart stubbornly. "I'm not going to beat about the bush any more. There's only one person on this ship who's responsible for my buddy Jez's death. It isn't me and it certainly isn't you. It's Molucco Wrathe!"

CHAPTER THIRTY-ONE

The Block

"Where's Mosh Zu?" Grace asked.

"And good evening to you too," Olivier said, looking over from the stove, where he was brewing a fresh quantity of berry tea.

"I'm sorry," said Grace. "I didn't mean to be rude. I just wanted to speak to him, but I can't find him."

"He's meditating," Olivier said. "He cannot be disturbed." He stirred the pot. "But I'll certainly tell him you were looking for him when I next see him."

Grace's head was racing with thoughts. The visions she had channelled from Lorcan's ribbon were playing over and over in her brain. She badly wanted to talk to Mosh Zu about it.

"Grace, are you all right?" Olivier looked into her eyes. "You look a bit shaken up. What's wrong?"

"Nothing," she said, realising he knew she was lying. "Nothing – really. I just wanted to talk to Mosh Zu."

"You know," he said, turning down the heat on the stove and walking over. "You can talk to me, if you like. About anything. Trainee healer to trainee healer."

She considered the possibility for a moment. But her experience with the ribbon had been too personal. She didn't yet feel comfortable enough with Olivier to confide such things to him.

"It's kind of you," she said. "But I'll wait and talk to Mosh Zu when he's free."

Olivier kept staring at her. She could tell from his expression he was displeased. But he simply nodded and said, "As you wish."

"Thanks." Grace slipped out into the corridor.

She was torn as to where to go. She felt tired, but she was certain that sleep would not come with all these thoughts swimming in her head. She could go back outside and try to walk off her anxiety. She could go and find Johnny and talk to him about this. She weighed up all these options but she knew, deep inside, that there was only one way she was going to feel better.

She pushed open the door. "Lorcan?" she said softly. "Lorcan, are you awake?"

"What?" he mumbled.

"It's me, Grace," she said. "Are you awake?"

"Well, I am now," he said. He didn't sound *too* displeased.

"I'm sorry, I didn't mean to wake you."

"It's OK," he said. "You sound a little off-kilter, Grace. Is something wrong?"

"Yes," she said, sighing deeply.

"What is it?" Suddenly, he was the old Lorcan again, the one who had looked after her during her first days on *The Nocturne.* "Come and sit up here and talk to me."

She pulled the chair up to his end of the bed and sat down. He reached out for her hand. "You're trembling," he said. "Whatever's wrong?"

The touch of his hand was reassuring. "Oh, Lorcan," she said. "I've done something bad."

"You?" He smiled. "Grace Tempest, do something bad? I find that somewhat hard to believe."

"Lorcan, I read your ribbon."

"What?" He jolted with surprise and his hand fell out of hers.

"I know I shouldn't have done it. But I took it with me by accident. It was in my book and Johnny thought it was a good idea."

"Johnny?" Lorcan said. "The guy we met in the room? What does he have to do with this?"

"I'm sorry," Grace said. "I was telling him how worried I was about you, how I wanted to help you but didn't know how . . ."

"You were helping me just fine," he said. "You shouldn't have done this, Grace."

"I know," she said. "I know that now. I just thought I'd find some answers in the ribbon."

"And did you?"

Grace nodded. Then remembered that he couldn't see her. "Yes, I did."

"I think you'd better tell me about it," he said. "Tell me what you saw."

"I had two visions," Grace said. "They were of you and me. The first was of when we met, when you rescued me from drowning that night . . ."

She relayed the scene to him, as she'd experienced it in his vision. He remained as still as a statue as she spoke. When she had finished, he paused, then asked simply, "What was the second part of the vision?"

"It was the night you were blinded," she said. "When Connor came to *The Nocturne* and you thought we were in danger . . ."

Once more, she relayed to him what she had seen. When she finished, he had one final question for her. "And this is all you saw? Just these two moments?"

"Yes," she said. "I couldn't go on after that. I put the ribbon back. It's on your nightstand." She glanced over to it.

Lorcan reached out his hand and felt for the ribbon. His arched fingers resembled a white spider, seeking out its thread. Finding it, he took the ribbon and placed it under his pillow. "It stays there, now," he said.

"I'm so sorry," Grace said. "The last thing I wanted to do was upset you."

He sighed. "How did you think I'd feel, having you spy

into my private thoughts like that? How would you like it if someone did that to you?"

"I was only trying to help," she said. "I know I did a bad thing. But I was only trying to help you get better."

"Better?" he said.

"Mosh Zu said that your wounds are only partly physical," she said. "That your deeper wound is mental, emotional. I thought if I read your ribbon, I could help you to pinpoint whatever the block is."

"The block . . .?"

"Yes," she said, feeling on more solid ground again. "If we know what's holding you back, we can break down the block."

"Can *we* now?" he said. There was a trace of bitterness in his voice.

"We can try," she said.

"Grace, I've told you before, warned you. This is not your world. There is so much here you don't understand."

"Yes," she said. "And I'm new to this world. But I want to understand it." She paused. "I want to understand *you*. Perhaps that's what I want most of all."

"I see that," he said. "I do see that, but there are things I cannot tell you."

"About yourself?" she asked. "Or about me? Or about you and me?"

He paused. "About all of those."

She felt deeply frustrated at the way he was closing down again, shutting her out.

"But Lorcan, if it's about me – at least some of it – don't I have the right to know it? I have so many questions."

"Yes, I know. But here's the thing, Grace. I'm not ready to answer them. I was getting there in my own way, in my own time, but now you go and do this." He shook his head.

"You knew me." She couldn't keep this inside her any more. "When you rescued me, when you saw who I was. It wasn't the first time we'd met. You knew who I was. And Connor too. You'd seen us as babies. But how can that be?"

Her question hung in the air.

"Please, Lorcan, I have to know."

He shook his head. "Not from me. Not now."

Grace felt as if her head was splitting. "Please," she repeated.

"I know what it must feel like, Grace," he said. "I know how your mind works. These questions are like an itch to you and you have to scratch it. That's why you took my ribbon in the first place. But don't you see? It's like Pandora's Box. You've begun something now that cannot be stopped. And it will have a terrible end for all of us."

She contemplated his words. What did he mean? Everything he said only prompted more questions. Bigger questions.

"Please, Grace," he said. "Please leave me."

"I can't," she said. "I can't leave now. You have to talk to me."

"No," he said. "No, I don't. Just leave."

"Don't shut me out like this."

"I have to," he said. "For both our sakes."

She was shaking as she stood up and began walking to the door. But she couldn't bear to leave without one last try. "But I know how much you care for me. I read it in the ribbon."

Lorcan sighed. "Did you really need to read the ribbon to know that I cared for you?" he said. "Really, Grace, don't you know me at all?"

"I thought I did," she said, turning and pushing open the door. She rushed out into the corridor to spare him the sound of her sobs.

"Hey." Johnny glanced up from the chessboard as Grace hovered at the door the rec room.

Seeing her tear-stained face, he immediately stood and went over to her. He reached out his arms and hugged her, pushing the door to closed behind them.

Grace felt better from the hug but, as her tears stopped, she realised the irony of the situation. Johnny was the one who had pushed her to read Lorcan's ribbon, and now he was the one she was turning to for comfort.

"You did it?" he said, pulling away from her. "And it went badly, didn't it? I'm so sorry, Grace. I shouldn't have suggested . . ."

She shook her head. "No, it didn't go badly exactly. But I found things out. And I went to talk to Lorcan about it and he's angry with me."

"I guess we might have expected that," Johnny said. "I know it's hard, but I don't think you should have told him just yet."

"I had to," she said. "The stuff I read in the ribbon . . . It was so personal. About him and me."

"Ah," Johnny said.

"It's complicated," she said. "I don't think I should talk about it with you."

Johnny nodded. "Of course," he said. "I respect that. But if you change your mind, you can always come and find ol' Johnny. You know that, right?"

She nodded.

"Let's dry your eyes," he said, reaching into his pocket and producing a red polka-dot handkerchief. Grace couldn't help but smile at the sight of it.

"There," he said. "See how ol' Johnny's already brought a smile to your face?" He put the handkerchief in her hand. "Why don't you hang onto that for now? Just in case you make any more face rain tonight."

She slipped the handkerchief in her pocket. He pulled out a chair for her and sat down alongside her.

"You were right about one thing," she said.

"Yes?" He arched an eyebrow.

"Reading that ribbon told me why Lorcan's not healing. It's my fault. It's all my fault." She felt the tears prick her eyes again and hastily lifted the handkerchief to mop them up. Johnny waited patiently. She took a deep breath, then continued.

"Lorcan's blindness can't be cured by physical healing alone. Mosh Zu told me that there's another element to it, if anything the stronger part. He says that it's psychosomatic – that it's brought on by stress and fear and that, on a certain level, it's self-inflicted."

Johnny frowned. "He's *choosing* not to see?"

"Well, not consciously. It's not like he just thought to himself 'I'd rather be blind', but on some level, yes, he's blocking his body from healing."

Johnny shook his head. "I ain't never heard nothing like that before."

"Mosh Zu says it's not unheard of," said Grace. "He says that he can work with Lorcan on whatever it is that's holding him back."

"Well, that's good news, ain't it?" Johnny said.

Grace shook her head. She hardly knew what to think any more.

"Grace, I know you want him to heal fast, but I reckon that you have to give something like this time. Remember, on this side of the fence, we got a whole lotta time to play with."

"It's me," she said. "*I'm* responsible for Lorcan's blindness. He wouldn't have gone into the daylight if it wasn't to protect me. I always knew I was responsible for his physical blindness . . ."

Johnny gently interrupted her. "Even if there's a kernel of truth in that, you said yourself that his physical wound was healing."

She nodded. "Yes, but now I know I'm also the cause of the deeper wound. I had my suspicions before. But now I've read the ribbon, I'm sure of it. The reason he's refusing to get better – the block – is connected to me." There, she had said it. It felt better to have given voice to the dark thought. It still felt bad, but better.

"Like I say," Johnny answered, "you've just gotta give this whole situation time. Lorcan couldn't be in better hands than Mosh Zu. I mean, he's the Vampirate guru! He's the man! If anyone can get Lorcan through this, it's him."

"But what if he *can't*?" Grace said, feeling the icy waters of her fear rising up again. "What if Lorcan chooses to stay blind? You should have heard him, Johnny. He's pushing me away now. What if I've wrecked everything by doing what I did?"

"Hey," said Johnny, putting his arm around her shoulder. "Hey, hey, you just gotta take a piece of advice from ol' Johnny. Something I learned on those long cattle drives. Grace, you gotta learn to cross one river at a time."

CHAPTER THIRTY-TWO

The Passage to India

Connor watched with some sadness as the familiar skull and bones flag was lowered from the mast of *The Diablo*. The mast looked naked without it.

"It's only temporary," Cate said, as Gonzalez folded the flag away and sent a different one up the ropes. "It's all part of our disguise, Connor. We can't allow the Emperor or any of his team to think, for one moment, that this is a pirate ship. They're doing the same over on *The Typhon* right now. There'll be a few other changes too – cosmetic of course, nothing that will impede our usual operations. And the captains will be barred from the operation. Their faces are too well known!"

Connor looked up again as Bart, high in the crow's nest, lifted the new flag into position. It was deep blue with a white logo on it – a pair of outstretched hands carrying a ship. Beneath the picture were three letters – O.R.C.

"Do you like it?" Cate asked.

"What is it?"

"It's supposed to suggest security and safety. It's the logo of the Oceanic Removal Company." She turned to Connor once more. "Us!"

She gave Bart the thumbs-up. "Good work, Bart. Now hurry on down and we'll begin our combat training session."

In the build-up to the raid, Cate had increased the level of combat training on-board. There were daily practises. Such was Cate's reputation that Barbarro and Trofie had sent their crew-members over to *The Diablo* for the duration.

"It's important that, for the purposes of this attack, our two crews are one," Barbarro had said, when they'd announced the news.

So now there were, temporarily, twenty-five extra crew-members on *The Diablo*. They trained together, ate together in the same mess hall and bunked down in the same dormitories. Mostly, they were good guys, thought Connor as he arrived on deck, ready for the day's combat session.

"Hey, Tempest! How's it goin'?" Two of his new mates high-fived him as he joined them to begin the warm-up.

Bart arrived just ahead of Cate. It was good, amidst all the current changes, to have his best buddy at his side.

"OK," Cate announced. "Let's begin with a physical warm-up. Keep your weapons on you and we'll do three circuits of the deck."

Connor heard someone laugh behind him. "I mean,

really," he heard a dark murmur. "Could she be any more like a gym mistress?"

Connor glanced over his shoulder and saw Moonshine Wrathe sniggering away with one of his flunkies. He gave Connor a malicious glance, before turning and setting off on Cate's warm-up jog. Connor ran off alongside Bart.

"I gather little Moonshine is on top form again today," Bart said, as they ran.

"Oh, yeah," Connor agreed. "Remind me, exactly how did he make the attack squad?"

Bart laughed. "I don't think there was ever much doubt that he'd be given the nod. But did I tell ya what I overheard Barbarro tell Molucco?"

"No." Connor shook his head.

"Just that he wished Moonshine was a bit more like you – that he needed toughening up if he was ever going to be a *real* pirate."

"Wow!" Connor said, flattered and a little surprised that Barbarro Wrathe had made such a comparison.

"Of course," said Bart, as they pounded across the foredeck, "I'm sure Trofie Wrathe has very different reasons for putting mummy's little darling in the squad. No doubt she sees it as his rightful place as heir to the kingdom."

"Yeah," Connor agreed. "It's just a shame that he isn't a bit more reliable with his sword."

Bart nodded. "You're not wrong there, Tempest. Vicious? Yes! Reliable? No!"

*

"OK, everyone, great stuff!" Cate said, as the last of the crew made it back to the central portion of the deck. "Now, let's break into our pairs and work on some attack sequences."

This was the point in the day that Connor dreaded. Because, of course, they had paired up him with Moonshine. "But why?" Connor had pleaded with Cate after the first gruelling workout. "Just because we're the youngest? I'm taller than him, and way more experienced."

"I know, Connor," Cate had said. "But my hands are tied. The request, or should I say *command*, came from on high. Very specific instructions from Barbarro Wrathe that you and Moonshine should be paired up together."

As Connor had walked off, shaking his head, Cate had called after him. "You should be flattered by this. Evidently Captain Wrathe thinks his son has something to learn from you."

That was all well and good, but the reality of his day-to-day sparring with Moonshine was that the pirate prince wasn't open to learning anything from anyone. Instead he was intent on doing it all in his own unique and unpredictable fashion.

"Right," Cate said, clapping her hands. "Let's pick up from the manoeuvre we began working on yesterday. I hope you've all put in some extra practice hours between duty shifts!"

Connor and Bart had worked on the manoeuvre together long into the early hours. Out of the corner of his eye, he saw Bart and his partner from *The Typhon* execute a step-perfect sequence of attack and defence plays.

"A-hem! A-hem!" he heard Moonshine's plaintive cry. "Any chance you could peel your eyes off your beloved Bart for just a moment so that we can get down to this?"

Connor turned to him. "Ready when you are!"

Moonshine lunged at Connor with his sword and Connor effortlessly positioned his blade to repel the attack. They managed a few basic parries but it was soon clear that, as usual, Moonshine was hopelessly out of his depth.

"You haven't practised this at all, have you?" Connor said, as they tried to begin the sequence for the fourth time.

"I *would* have," Moonshine said. "Naval Scouts' honour and all that. But, the thing is, I had a really busy evening."

Connor could imagine. Moonshine, alone of the guest crew, was allowed to return home to *The Typhon* at night. Clearly the thought of sharing a cabin was a step too far for the pirate prince. So instead . . . a nice five-course dinner with Mater and Pater, then off to his dungeon to play Pirate Pinball and have quality time with his beloved pet rats.

"Besides," Moonshine said now. "It's *weeks* until the raid! There's plenty of time to practise."

But as the days and weeks went past, Moonshine's swordplay showed little sign of improvement. Some days, he was all right. But on other days, it was as if he was starting from the beginning again. There was no denying, when it came to vicious instinct, that he was right at the front of the line. Connor had the scrapes and scars of varying vintages to prove *that*. But, in a complex team attack, vicious could only carry you so far. Connor knew from his experiences with his mates on *The Diablo* that working as a team was vital to success in the heat of battle when the deck was crowded. You could certainly improvise to a degree but you had to keep rigorously focused on your own piece of the jigsaw, otherwise – with fifty men and women on your team – it was all too easy to descend into utter chaos.

He voiced his ongoing fears one night, during dinner, to Bart.

"He's a loose cannon," Connor said. "There's just no telling what he'll do next."

"I know, buddy," said Bart. "I hear you. But when we're actually engaged in the raid, it won't matter. If the operation goes to plan, we won't have to draw our swords at all. It's more of a hustle than a rumble, when you think about it. We'll only have to draw our swords if our cover is blown. And so much time and effort has gone into planning this, that I really can't see that happening."

Connor shook his head. "I know all that. But what does Cate always say? *Expect the unexpected!* I'm not just worried about Moonshine. I'm losing the edge on my own technique because I'm not getting any decent practice with him."

"Is that your way of saying you'd like an extra sparring session with yours truly later?"

Connor nodded. "That would be great! If you don't mind."

Bart shook his head. "Just get me another beer and I'll be happy to oblige."

Connor frowned. "You really shouldn't drink and draw," he said, thinking of Cate's rules.

Bart laughed. "I'm way under the limit, buddy. Just need a little tonsillary lubrication and I'll be fine!"

Later, they spent another forty-five minutes up on deck, sparring as the sun set around them – a raging fire of orange and red. It ended with Connor throwing himself from the mast into Bart's general direction. In an attack situation, he would have winded Bart, but he signalled his intent so that his friend could dive away. As they both dusted themselves down, Bart slapped Connor on the back.

"You have zero to worry about!" he said. "There's nothing wrong with *your* technique. Nothing wrong at all."

With just a few days to go until the raid, the biggest challenge became seamanship. As the twin galleons ploughed across the waters towards the Sunset Fort, they encountered the roughest sailing conditions Connor had ever experienced on *The Diablo*. Combat training had to be set aside as all crew-members worked together to navigate through the turbulent waters.

Below decks, there was a lot of throwing up and dark

murmurings about whether they'd actually reach their destination before the ocean just swallowed them up.

Cate called Connor to her cabin. He found her sitting at her desk, calmly drinking a glass of milk and nibbling a cheese sandwich.

"Aren't you feeling just the least bit queasy?" he inquired.

Cate shook her head. "I never get seasick," she said. "I'm lucky that way."

As she spoke, they heard a chorus of moans on the other side of the cabin wall, indicating that others were not so lucky.

"So," Cate said. "How are you feeling about the attack? Ready to rock?"

Connor nodded. He and Bart had managed a few further bouts before the seas became too unruly. His confidence in his own abilities had returned. Now, he was pumped with adrenaline and keen to get on with things. He told Cate so.

"Great stuff," she said, tapping the grid she had laid out in front of her. "I'm just allocating the final pairings now," she said, pen in hand. "And I've decided to pair you up with Moonshine Wrathe."

Connor immediately groaned.

"I know it isn't what you'd choose, but you must have seen this coming. You've been partnered with him all these weeks. In his way, he's comfortable with you. And you, better than any of us, know his strengths and his weaknesses. You can protect him if push comes to shove."

"*Protect* him?" Connor said. "I thought this was a raid for profit. Isn't that the goal we should all be working towards? Not protecting the weaklings!"

Cate shook her head. "Connor, I'm going to level with you. You're a highly valued colleague — and a good friend. Yes, of course, the overall aim of our operation is to get in and out of the fort as cleanly as possible, and return with as much of the Emperor's treasure as we can. But, make no mistake about this, your role is to ensure that, if we move into a combat scenario, nothing happens to Moonshine."

Connor shook his head. "Why didn't you tell me this earlier?"

"Because I'd have had you on my case day in day out, imploring me to rethink," Cate said. "But surely you must have guessed. Why else would I pair one of my strongest swordsmen with my weakest?"

Connor frowned. "So all that guff about Barbarro expressly asking for me . . ."

"Not guff — charming expression, by the way. Not guff at all. He did say that. I don't think he's under any illusions about his son's martial abilities. I can't quite say the same for Trofie. Who knows what goes on in her head?"

"Let me get this straight," Connor said. "You're telling me that my prime role in this attack is to look after Moonshine?"

Cate shook her head. "Not your *prime* role, Connor. Your *only* role. You can let the others take care of the main business. Just bring Moonshine Wrathe back to this ship alive and in one piece. Or it will play very badly for all of us." With that, she picked up her sandwich and took another bite.

"Now," she said, chomping down a mouthful of gorgonzola and seaweed, "if you don't have any further questions, I'd better get on with finalising this strategy document. I have to have it ratified by both captains tonight."

Connor shook his head. As he walked out of her cabin, her words kept swimming around his head. *Just bring Moonshine Wrathe back to this ship alive and in one piece.* He couldn't believe the injustice of this mission.

As he began descending the stairs to the mess room, who should he bump into but Moonshine himself? He looked even paler than usual – a ghostly white tinged with just a hint of pale lime.

"Are you all right?" Connor asked. As he spoke, the ship lurched dramatically to one side. Moonshine slipped on the stairs, his arms flailing.

Connor reached out and grabbed him firmly by the arm. "It's OK," Connor said. "I've got you."

Moonshine looked at Connor strangely then opened his mouth as if to speak. He seemed to think better of it and closed his mouth again. Then, he opened it once more and threw up all over Connor.

Connor stood there, frozen in disbelief, as the semi-masticated remains of Moonshine's dinner – curry, if he wasn't mistaken – slowly dripped down his head and chest.

"I'm sorry," Moonshine mumbled and, for once, he did seem to mean it. Then he lurched forward again and a fresh spray of vomit hit Connor square across the face.

CHAPTER THIRTY-THREE

The Berry Pickers

The door to Olivier's rooms was ajar. As Grace stepped inside, he looked up and smiled. "I got your message," she said. "What's this urgent business? Is everything OK?"

"Everything's fine, Grace," he said. "I just had this idea. I have to go on an errand and I thought you might like to come."

Grace shook her head and sighed lightly. "An errand? *That* was the urgent business you interrupted my precious sleep for?"

Apparently oblivious to the note of sarcasm in her voice, Olivier pointed to the pile of panniers on the counter. "We're going berry picking! Now grab a basket in each hand and follow me! Oh, you might want to take one of those jackets too. It can get very cold out there."

*

After ferreting around in one of the storerooms on the edge of the external courtyard, Olivier emerged with a small pushcart. "You can put the baskets on this," he said. "They're light enough now but once we're done, you'll be very glad of it!"

"Exactly how *many* berries are we planning on picking?" Grace asked.

"Quite a lot!" Olivier said, as they waited for the heavy gates of Sanctuary to be opened for them.

"Do you go out every day?" Grace asked.

He nodded. "I have to. The vampires get through a lot of our berry tea. But you know what? It's no hardship. I'm still mortal, after all. Just as you are. As much as we might accustom ourselves to the darkness, we still have need of occasional forays into the light."

Grace noticed that the early afternoon sun was high and the mountainside was bright and pretty warm, though there were still clumps of snow on the grass. It was lovely to be out in the air and to see the countryside surrounding Sanctuary in the light of day. The mountain looked so different to how she remembered it from the arduous climb that had brought her here. She tried to work out the route they had taken.

"Come on, slowcoach!" Olivier chided her. "If you're running out of puff already, you won't be much use to me at all."

Grace shook her head and ran over to catch him up. "I'm not out of puff," she said. "I was just trying to work out the route we took to get up here from the shore."

Olivier laughed. "I really wouldn't give that too much thought."

"Why not?" she said, not liking the edge in her voice.

"It's a very changable mountain," he said. "It never looks quite the same from one day to the next."

"How can that be?" Grace said.

"It just is," Olivier said. "Everyone finds their own way up here. For some, the journey is intensely gruelling. For others, it's a simple hike."

Grace pondered these words as they continued along the snaking path, Olivier trundling the pushcart loaded with their panniers. They were approaching an area closed in by dense bushes. When they reached it, Olivier brought the cart to a standstill. "This is our first stop," he said.

Grace could see that the dark, green-black bushes were heavy with fruit.

"Now," said Olivier. "There are seven panniers. One for each kind of berry. It's very important that we don't mix them up."

Grace nodded. "I understand," she said. "But how do I make sure?"

Olivier lifted the lid of the first pannier. Attached to the inside of the basket was a detailed picture of one of the berry plants. It looked like something you'd see in a naturalist's book. It was a beautifully detailed and precise piece of pen-work.

"Did you do this?" she asked.

He nodded. "I thought it might make it easier for you."

"Thanks," she said. "You're very talented. I had no idea."

He shrugged. "Sometimes Sanctuary is a lonely place for us in-betweens. When I can't sleep or when time just weighs heavily on me, I like to draw."

He began opening up the other panniers. She could see that he'd attached an equally detailed drawing to each of them.

Olivier sighed but smiled. "Come on," he said. "Stop admiring my doodles and let's get these berries picked. Otherwise we'll be here until sundown."

In the event, they *were* on the mountainside until sundown. Not because of Grace's slowness but because they were having such an agreeable time. Grace didn't find Olivier the easiest of people to talk to, which puzzled her when — as *in-betweens* — they seemed to have so much in common. But, as the sun warmed their backs, he gently thawed and they chatted away agreeably about Sanctuary, about Mosh Zu and *The Nocturne*, and about drawing, all the time moving from one bush to the next, trundling along the cart and filling the panniers.

"Let's just fill this last basket and then we'll head back," Olivier said at last.

"All right," Grace said, nodding. She was tired and a little hungry but nevertheless it had been lovely to spend the afternoon out on the mountain, and she was sad in a way to have to head back.

"Don't look so down in the mouth," he said. "You've been a real help to me. You can come and help with the berry-picking whenever you like."

It was a cheering thought and, smiling, she set about the final batch of picking. As she did so, Olivier brushed past her. "There's someone on the mountain," he said, his voice suddenly businesslike once more.

"Where?" She stood up but couldn't see anyone.

"He was over there," Olivier said, pointing, "but he's hidden behind that cluster of trees now. I'll go and have a word with him. We're not expecting anyone new tonight."

"I'll come with you," Grace said, setting down the basket.

"No, no, you finish up here. It won't take a moment." He began walking away.

"I thought you said you let people find their own way up the mountain?" she called after him. "I don't understand!"

"You don't need to understand," Olivier said, a little sharply. "Just finish packing the basket!" He strode off across the path.

The view down the mountain always intrigues him. Each time he comes here, it summons so many memories. Memories that take him back, all the way back, to the beginning of his story. But the mountains of his beginnings were not cloaked in grass and heather or dusted with snow. The Taurus Mountains were parched by the sun – so high, with a climate so extreme, that nothing good could survive there.

Cilicia Tracheia – "Craggy Cilicia" – they called it. He remembers taking his first, wobbly steps to the very edge of his father's lands – his steely ambition constrained only by the limited capability of his two-year-old limbs. Even then, he was more ambitious than anyone had a right to be. Some things never change. Still, he managed to get there – half-walking, half-crawling to the cliff-edge – hands caked in the red dust of the dead earth. Even now, he remembers that first glance down the cliff, to the turquoise ocean far below. He was drawn to the water instinctively, like a jackdaw glimpsing a glittering jewel. He remembers reaching out with pudgy arms, almost falling but caught – just in the nick of time – by his father's strong, encircling hands.

One memory triggers the next. No longer a boy now, but six feet tall and then some, in the first flush of early manhood. Standing firmly, determinedly, on the same rocky edge. Now he knows something of the cruelty of the world. Knows that if he stays, the harshness of this land will wring every last drop of life from him and drive him to join his mother and father in their dry, hot graves. Now, as he looks down to the shimmering sea below, it seems to him like a much-needed drink of water. He is parched from this dessicated land. He has a desperate thirst . . .

301

"Hello! Hello!"

He turns. Someone is scurrying down the slope towards him, waving. He recognises the figure and grins to himself. The first time he saw him, he mistook him for a young woman on account of his robes. Now, he knows the man's face. And his name.

"Good evening," Olivier says, extending his hand. "It's good to see you again!"

Sidorio shakes the hand but says nothing in return.

"How are you this night? Have you thought any more about my proposal?"

"Remind me," Sidorio says. They have played this game before.

Olivier smiles and glances up at the peak. "Why, for you to come to Sanctuary, of course. We could do so much for you there."

"So you say." Sidorio shakes his head. "So you *keep* saying."

Olivier pauses. "I want to help you," he says. "And I think you want to be helped." He pauses, more daring than usual. "Else why would you climb this mountain each night?"

Sidorio grins, his twin gold teeth exposed in the moonlight for a moment. "Maybe I just like the view from here."

"The view's even better up there." Olivier points. "It gets better the higher you climb."

Sidorio shrugs. "This view's good enough."

"Come on," Olivier urges. "What have you got to lose?"

"Nothing to lose, nothing to win," Sidorio says.

"I hear you, friend. But why not follow me? You're halfway up the mountain already."

Sidorio smiles, but his eyes are dead. "Am I halfway up, or halfway down?"

Olivier returns the smile. Are they destined to play this game every night? He glances over his shoulder. Then Sidorio sees that tonight he is not alone. A little further up the mountain, the man's companion is busy packing up baskets. Sidorio sees it is a girl. Not just any girl. *That* girl! How is it that they seem to cross paths wherever he goes?

"Grace!" Olivier calls over his shoulder. *Grace!* That was her name. The girl who has no fear of him. The one who only asks him questions. Sidorio turns away. It will be better if she doesn't see him.

"Take the cart and start walking back!" Olivier calls to her. "I'll follow you shortly."

"All right!" she answers. There is no question now. It is her voice.

After she has gone, Sidorio asks. "Who is that girl?"

"Her?" Olivier says. "Her name is Grace. Why do you ask?"

"What is she doing here?"

"She's like me," Olivier says. "An assistant to Mosh Zu Kamal, the great Vampirate guru."

"Really?" Sidorio's eyes widen. "She's young for such a job."

303

"Yes," Olivier says, unable to remove a certain bitterness from his voice. "Yes, she's young. But she has a talent for healing." He pauses. "So my master says."

"You disagree?" Sidorio looks deep into Olivier's eyes.

Olivier gazes back, suddenly needing to articulate his feelings and sensing this is someone he can trust. "Have you ever felt like you were being replaced?" he asks.

Sidorio nods. "Go on," he says. "Tell me."

And Olivier tells him. It feels good to let these words out – like lancing a boil. There is no one he can confide in at Sanctuary, no one to tell dark thoughts like these. But here, on the mountainside, he is free to speak his mind. The stranger – for, in truth, this man is no more than a stranger to him – is a good listener. He might even be a healer of a kind. He seems able to draw out the darkness from deep within you. When Olivier finishes, the stranger nods and places a reassuring hand on his shoulder.

"If I were you," says Sidorio. "I'd do something about this."

"You would?" Olivier says. A flicker of something – instinct? – tells him that this is wrong. But once more, he looks into the stranger's eyes and that fragile instinct disappears. Replaced by a deep hunger for the stranger's advice.

"You *must* do something about this," Sidorio says. "Before it gets out of control."

He's right. Olivier nods. Of course, he's absolutely right.

"What do you suggest?" Once more, he eagerly searches the man's face.

Sidorio appears to ponder the matter. "Give me time to think," he says. "Meet me here tomorrow night. We'll talk some more."

Olivier is bereft. Must he wait until tomorrow?

Sidorio begins walking off into the darkness.

"Wait!" Olivier calls. "What's your name? I don't know your name."

Sidorio turns, gazing back at him. "Until tomorrow, my friend."

Olivier is left hungry by these words, both spoken and unspoken. "Just one more thing before you go . . ." he calls.

Sidorio stops in his tracks once more, an eyebrow raised in expectation.

"It's just that I hope you'll consider my proposition," Olivier says. "That one night you will come to Sanctuary."

"Oh yes," Sidorio says, reassuringly. "One night, I shall. And that night is drawing ever closer."

Olivier smiles at this. At last, a breakthrough! After all their meetings on the mountainside. He feels better than he has in a long time, as he strides back up the path to catch up with Grace.

Olivier has withdrawn into himself again, thought Grace, as they made their way back to Sanctuary. He had grown affable out on the mountainside, as if mellowed by the sunshine. But now, as they approached the gates, he was closing down again. No, she thought. No, it had started when he'd seen the stranger.

"Who was he?" she asked.

"Just a traveller," Olivier said.

"A vampire?" Grace asked. "Someone seeking help? Why didn't you bring him along with us?"

"You ask too many questions," said Olivier, frowning.

"What do you mean?"

"What I say. I've tried to be patient about this, I really have. But, you know what? If you're so gifted that you're going to be Mosh Zu's first assistant, then you're going to have to work some of this out for yourself!"

"His first assistant?" Grace was dumbfounded. "What do you mean? *You're* his first assistant."

"For now," Olivier said. "But that will change soon. *You* must be blind if you can't see it. Mosh Zu is training you to take over from me. Or rather, he's having *me* train you. And once I've done my job, I'll go back to being a regular assistant and you'll take my place."

"No," Grace said. "No, that's not fair. It's not what I want."

Olivier gave a hollow laugh. "It hardly matters whether it's fair or what you or I think about it," he said. "It boils down to this. You have been chosen."

They had reached the gates. Olivier gave the signal for them to be opened. Grace walked on ahead, dumbstruck by what he'd told her.

CHAPTER THIRTY-FOUR

No Heroes

On the morning of the raid, the fifty-strong attack crew gathered on the deck of *The Diablo*. Connor looked from side to side. They were all dressed alike, in fake uniforms – boiler suits and baseball caps bearing the ORC logo. The suits cleverly concealed the weaponry beneath. With one easy tear, each pirate would have access to his standard armoury of cutlass, rapier, épée or dagger. No trouble or expense seemed to have been spared in this operation. But then, as Cate had said, "You have to speculate to accumulate. If all goes to plan, we're going to be very rich after this mission. Very rich indeed!" However, it hadn't yet been explained how the riches would be divided between the captains, their deputies and the crews.

Now, Connor looked up as the two captains – Molucco and Barbarro – and their deputies – Cate and Trofie – came out onto the deck. Behind them, looming ever closer into view, was the majestic Sunset Fort itself. It was, thought Connor, as if their very destiny was coming forward to meet them.

Molucco opened proceedings but swiftly gave way to Cate to run through the strategy one last time. "You've trained long and hard," she said, by way of a conclusion. "Each of you is a credit to your ships and to your captains." Connor glanced over at Moonshine. Out of his customary black leathers, dressed in the same uniform as everyone else, he looked younger and curiously vulnerable. Perhaps, at the eleventh hour, he was finally facing up to just how far out of his depth he was.

Connor turned his attention back to Cate. "If you stick to our strategy today, this should be a very straightforward operation. So keep disciplined and focused and look out for each other!" Her eyes sought out Connor's through the crowd.

The attack squad applauded Cate. It was known that she had worked just as hard as they had to get this attack ready. Cate had always been popular aboard *The Diablo*. Now she commanded the respect and affection of those from *The Typhon* as well.

As the applause for Cate subsided, Barbarro Wrathe stepped forward. "I just wanted to say, on behalf of myself, my precious wife and my beloved brother, how proud we are of each and every one of you. It's been some time since the Brothers Wrathe staged a joint operation, but I am confident that this will not be the last!"

Wasn't he being just a little premature? Connor wondered.

"I have little more to add to what my colleagues have said this morning," Barbarro continued. "Except this. As we keep saying, this should be a straightforward operation. It's been said before but I can't emphasise it enough – *stick to the plan*. We're not looking for anyone to get heroic up there." He pointed to the fort. "No heroes. Just comrades – following the excellent strategy of their leaders, looking out for their fellows."

Once more, Connor turned to Moonshine. Cate's words were fresh in his head. *Just bring Moonshine Wrathe back to this ship alive and in one piece.* Just then, Moonshine turned his head and his eyes met Connor's. Connor couldn't believe it but he actually felt sorry for the boy. Moonshine Wrathe was many things, but the one thing he most certainly wasn't was stupid. Even if he didn't know about Connor's specific mission, he'd almost certainly know that someone had been assigned to protect him – that behind closed doors, there had been hushed conversations about how to keep him out of real danger. Such conversations were, to Connor's mind, a self-fulfilling prophecy. If you were forever preventing Moonshine from encountering real danger, you were forever denying him the chance to see how he'd measure up. How could you ever be a hero if you were never tested?

These thoughts were spinning around his head as the attack squad divided up, half returning with Barbarro and

Trofie to *The Typhon*. Molucco went with them – he and his family would see out the attack in one of *The Typhon*'s elegant state rooms. Of the four senior personnel, only Cate would be integrally involved in the raid. She was the public face of the Oceanic Removal Company and she would lead her team of removal specialists into the fort.

Connor marvelled at the beauty of the fort as they made their final approach. The last stretch of water was as still as a mill pond in contrast to the rough ocean they'd sailed through these past few days and nights. And, he reminded himself, that they would be sailing back through very soon.

When the Sunset Fort had been built by Prince Yashodhan, it hadn't nestled on the waters as it did now. Instead, it had perched majestically atop a high hillside. It must have been quite impressive then, Connor thought, but somehow its current proximity to the water magnified its beauty, reflecting back every stained-glass window, every turret, so that you had two forts for your money.

The two removal ships docked and Cate led the way across one of the wishes to the harbourside pontoon.

It appeared that the Emperor had come down to meet her himself. He was, Connor noted, a small man. He was framed by two much taller men, who presumably were responsible for his security. Right now, it looked as if they were in position in case a stray gust of wind blew and knocked the Emperor, like a feather, into the water.

"Good morning, sir!" Cate said, all bright and breezy, shaking him by the hand (her other now bearing the official ORC clipboard). "I wasn't expecting the honour of being met by your own good self today."

The self-styled Emperor spoke, his voice thin and reedy. "I always like to make sure a job is done well," he said. "Besides, you are the last guests I shall ever welcome to the Sunset Fort." His voice was saturated with sadness.

"Yes." Cate nodded, still smiling. "But we are the first guests you'll be taking to the Sunrise Fort, your new home."

"I suppose so," the man said, a weak smile momentarily crossing his face. "Now, you've got the map, haven't you?" he inquired.

"Oh yes." Cate lifted some pages on her clipboard and tapped a coloured navigation chart. "Don't you worry about anything, sir. It's all here. I have everything absolutely under control."

"That's why we chose the ORC," said one of the Emperor's sidekicks. "You come very highly recommended."

"I'm glad you checked our references," Cate said, smiling. "Anything that gives you confidence in our service and removes a layer of stress on a day like today can only be a good thing."

She was giving a brilliant performance, thought Connor. She came across as relaxed and efficient; ready to get things moving, but in no suspicious hurry.

"Well," said the Emperor. "I suppose you'll be wanting to get started?"

"Absolutely!" Cate said. "Why don't you lead the way and show me how everything is organised? Then I'll brief my teams." She turned and indicated the fifty men and women, dressed in their blue and white uniforms.

"Such a lot of them!" the Emperor said.

"Well, you do have a lot of goods," Cate said. "And we wanted to take the very best care of each and every item."

"That's why we ordered the deluxe service, remember?" one of the security guys reminded his boss. The Emperor shrugged and began leading the way up the green slope to the entrance of the fort.

"Don't mind him," the other security guy whispered to Cate. "He's very antsy today. I love your uniform, by the way. It's so nautical."

"Yes," Cate said, with a smile. "Yes, I suppose it is."

Connor and Moonshine climbed the pathway towards the fort together, following several other pairs of "removal specialists", with the rest making their way behind them.

Once inside the fort's enclave, they were led away from the more opulent living quarters towards the vast stores where the treasures were kept. Connor remembered Cate saying that the Emperor's rare treasures hardly ever saw the light of day. It made him feel a little better about the significant redistribution of wealth which was about to occur.

He could still hear the Emperor's security aide chatting away to Cate. "I think I told you before, Catherine, that the main store was originally the giant bathing house Prince Yashodhan created for Princess Savarna."

"Yes," Cate said. "I remember that very well."

"Well, here we are!"

Led by the Emperor and his two aides, they walked into the vast store. Connor glanced up. The building still held onto some signs of lingering grandeur. Certainly, the bathing house had been built on an epic scale. When the prince fell in love, he'd obviously wanted to leave his intended in no doubt about it whatsoever.

Now the bathing pool had been drained and filled with many numbered crates. It would be back-breaking work collecting up each and every one of these and carrying them to the ships. But that was why Cate had focused on increasing everyone's fitness levels in the run-up to the raid.

"The bulk of the Emperor's collection is divided between the bathhouse and the music gallery across the courtyard," said the security guard. "I'll stay and assist you here and Alessandro will do the same on the other side."

"Thank you," said Cate. "That would be very helpful, Mr Esposito."

"Please, Catherine, I'd be more comfortable if you called me Salvatore."

"Salvatore, then," she said. "As you know, the ORC is committed to making you feel as comfortable as possible at all times."

"I think I'm going to leave you to it," the Emperor said, his voice – if it was possible – lighter than ever. "I'll just get too anxious seeing my treasures lifted and carried."

"Quite so," said Salvatore. "Why don't we take you up to the main complex to rest and then we can return and help out Catherine and her team with any queries?"

The Emperor nodded. He turned and reached out a bony hand to Cate. "Please," he said. "Please tell them to be careful."

Cate held his hand lightly, careful not to break anything. "Sir, my team are specialists in the field of removals. Trust me, we'll take the very best care of your treasures. We'll treat them as if they were our own precious heirlooms."

"That's very reassuring," he said. Then he held out his arms and Salvatore and Alessandro propelled him away.

"OK," Cate said, calmly turning to her assembled crew. Without dropping her performance for a moment, she tapped her clipboard. "Right then, I hope everyone is fit and ready."

"Yes, boss," came the well rehearsed response.

"Excellent. Well, we'll split into teams now. Team A stay here and get started. Any questions, Bart's your man. Team B, follow me to the music room . . ."

Three hours later, the job had proceeded without a hitch. It was a blisteringly hot day, and under his boiler suit, Connor was sweating buckets. So too was Moonshine. Connor knew that his partner was finding it very heavy going. He was doing his absolute best, but Moonshine was thin and wiry where Connor was muscled and he could see that the lifting and carrying, combined with the heat, was taking its toll.

"I'm fit to drop!" he confided to Connor.

"I wonder," said Salvatore, who had overheard this exchange, "would your teams like to pause for some refreshment?"

Cate smiled and, rifling through the papers on her clipboard, appeared to consider the matter. "That's very kind of you, but I think we're so near to completing the loading that we should power on through."

"As you wish," said Salvatore. "But I insist that we prepare some fresh lemonade for your crew before they depart. They've worked so hard, and in such merciless heat." He fanned himself. "It's the least we can do."

"That's very kind of you," Cate said. "My crew certainly love a glass of lemonade."

"Excellent!" Salvatore said. "I'll go and arrange it now."

As he hurried out of the bathing house, Cate caught up with Connor and Moonshine. "Everything all right with you two?" she asked. Her voice gave nothing away but Connor recognised the concern in her eyes.

"Everything's fine," Connor said.

"I'm so hot," whined Moonshine.

"We all are," said Cate, briskly. "But we've almost finished up here. Just take that crate to the ship. Then I reckon it's one more load apiece and we're done."

"Yes, boss," Connor said, with a wink.

"Keep up the good work!" Cate said, refusing to step out of character for a moment. "Not long now!" she called over her shoulder as she walked away.

The pairs of pirates-turned-removalists carried the last of the treasure crates from both storehouses to the ships. The operation had, as predicted by the senior personnel, gone strictly to plan. All the fitness training and the other preparations – from the fake uniforms to the fake references – had paid off brilliantly.

Now, Cate watched from the front of the fort as Salvatore set up a table and glasses of lemonade on the green leading down to the pontoon.

"This is very kind of you," she said.

"Not at all," he said, smiling. "Your guys have worked their fingers to the bone. And it's a good hour's sail from here to the Sunrise Fort. This is our small way of saying thank you."

Cate gathered her fifty-strong team on the pontoon. "Excellent work, guys," she said. "A hot day, I'm sure you'll agree, but nothing stops the ORC from getting the job done. We'll get on the water again shortly and continue on to the Sunrise Fort to unpack the Emperor's precious cargo. But before we leave here, Mr – that is to say, Salvatore – has kindly provided some fresh lemonade for us all, so please come forward, enjoy a glass, and then let's get back on the ship and keep to schedule!"

"Lemonade!" Connor heard Bart cry. "How lovely!"

Several other members of the crew were similarly getting into character as removal men and women. Connor could see the slight anxiety on Cate's face. He knew that she would sooner have got them all back on the ship and out of danger.

As the crew stepped forward to pick up their drinks, Cate sought out Connor once more. "Everything in order?" she asked.

"Yes, boss," he said, sipping his lemonade.

"And where's Moonshine?"

"He's right here," Connor said, looking round. "Right beside . . ."

But as they turned, they both found themselves gazing into thin air.

"Where is he?" Cate asked, careful to keep her tone light and jovial.

"I don't know," Connor replied, with a fake grin. He felt his pulse starting to race.

"Connor, this was your primary job," she said, under her breath. "Find him! Fast!"

"Is everything all right?" Salvatore asked, appearing at Cate's side.

"Yes, everything's fine," she said. "Delicious lemonade, by the way. You must give me your recipe."

Salvatore smiled. "The secret is a few mint leaves," he said, with a wink.

Connor headed off to search for Moonshine. Where on earth had he gone? They'd come back out of *The Diablo* together. So he couldn't still be there. He had to be somewhere in the fort, but where? Connor scanned the crowd but, with fifty people dressed exactly alike, it was not easy to pick him out. Where *was* he?

Suddenly his question was answered. There was a scuffle at the top of the green and the heftier of the Emperor's security aides, Alessandro, came into view, appearing to help Moonshine along. Connor's first thought was that the boy had fainted in the heat. Then he realised that Alessandro wasn't helping Moonshine so much as dragging him.

"What's going on?" Salvatore called to his compadre.

"Yes," Cate said, glued to his side. "What on earth is going on?"

"I'm afraid there's been an unfortunate incident," Alessandro said. "Involving one of your team."

All eyes turned to Moonshine, then to Alessandro. "It would seem that our confidence in the ORC has been misplaced," he said with a frown.

CHAPTER THIRTY-FIVE

Girl Talk

Grace couldn't get to sleep. Whether it was her natural circadian rhythms asserting themselves or the events of the past night, she wasn't sure. But one thing she *was* entirely sure of was that however long she lay on the bed, closed her eyes and willed herself to sleep, the more wakeful she became.

Deciding to seek other options, she got up and changed her nightclothes for the clothes she'd been wearing before. She walked out of her room and into the corridor. It was utterly silent. She wanted to see if Lorcan was awake. If so, she could talk to him or even read some more from *The Secret Garden* to him. They had just got to the part where Mary had found the key to the locked, walled garden in the manor grounds. She hoped very much that by now he'd have had time to get over his anger about the ribbon.

She came to Lorcan's door and decided it would be

unfair to knock and wake him up if he was sleeping. Instead, she pushed open the door and stepped into the darkened room. His eyes were dressed and bandaged, of course, just as she'd left him a few hours before. He was still as a rock. She walked closer, but there was no doubt he was fast asleep.

What bad luck! All these nights dealing with Lorcan's insomnia and the one time she couldn't get to sleep, he was dozing happily away. Oh well, she was pleased for him. It must augur well for the healing process. She picked up the copy of *The Secret Garden* from his bedside table. It wasn't any good to him without her to read it to him, but it might be a welcome distraction for her.

She continued along the corridor, still not passing anyone, and took the turning towards the rec room. Perhaps Johnny would be there and they could chat or even play some chess. But, as she turned the corner, she could already sense that the rec room was empty. As she poked her head around the doorway, she saw that Johnny's chessboard was there, but he was not.

Sighing, she sat down and opened the book. She started to read, but part of her didn't want to get ahead of Lorcan's place in the story. Besides, she really wasn't in the mood for reading. She put the new bookmark – a feather she'd found while berrying with Olivier – back in place and closed the covers once more.

She looked down at the chessboard. It appeared to be mid-game. She knew that Johnny sometimes played himself at chess, out of sheer boredom. Maybe she should take a page out of his book. She surveyed the spread of pieces on the board.

"I'd say Knight to C4 is your best bet."

Grace jumped at the voice. She had been so focused on the chessboard that she'd had no inkling anyone else had entered the room. She glanced up, but the place appeared to be empty.

"Or maybe use your Bishop to threaten the Rook."

Recognising the voice, Grace was smiling as she turned around. "Darcy!" she exclaimed. "Darcy! How brilliant to see you!"

Darcy Flotsam stepped over from behind Grace and beamed at her. Grace got up to hug her hello. She reached out her arms, but Darcy shook her head. "Sorry, Grace," she said. "I'm not here for real. I'm on one of those astro-thingies!"

"Astral journeys?" Grace said, helpfully.

"Yes, that's the one," said Darcy. "Like when I came to see you at the pirate ship that time."

Grace nodded. "I remember." It didn't matter to her whether she could touch Darcy or not. It was just great to have her here to talk to. She sat down again, grinning from ear to ear, and indicated a chair for Darcy.

"I hope you don't mind me coming like this," Darcy said, hovering above the chair. "I couldn't sleep and there was no one about to talk to on *The Nocturne*. Besides, I missed you, Grace. I miss our girlie chats."

Grace nodded. "I know *exactly* what you mean. And you couldn't have picked a more perfect time to come. I couldn't sleep either. Lorcan's dead to the world . . ."

"How *is* Lorcan?" Darcy asked, her voice and eyes brimming with concern.

"Oh, he's doing better and better," Grace said. "The physical damage is beginning to heal. It's going to take time, though. But Olivier – he's one of Mosh Zu's assistants – well, he made up this special salve and it seems to be working. But the wound isn't just physical. Mosh Zu thinks that Lorcan's blindness might be psychosomatic – in part, at least."

"Cycle-so-what-ic?" Darcy said, going virtually cross-eyed.

Grace smiled. "Psychosomatic. It doesn't make the condition any less real, but it means it's caused by mental rather than physical factors. The most usual cause would be stress, so Mosh Zu thinks Lorcan's stressed about something."

"Well, it must be something big if it's made him go blind," Darcy said.

Grace nodded, thinking about the discoveries she had made through Lorcan's ribbon. Part of her wanted to confide in Darcy. Darcy had always proved a most understanding listener. But she knew that the conversation would only bring them both down. It could wait for another time. For now, she was in the mood for chitchat and, for want of a better phrase, "girl talk".

"So tell me," Grace asked. "What's been happening on board *The Nocturne* since I left?"

Darcy's eyes bulged. "SO much, you wouldn't believe!" she said.

"Well, go on," said Grace. "Start talking. I don't want you being summoned back to the ship before I've heard at least *some* of the good stuff."

"Don't worry about that," Darcy said. "I think I'm getting better at this astral travel thing. The captain gave me a few pointers. But look, here's the thing." She looked fit to burst. "Grace, I think I'm in love!"

"*In love?* Wow! That *is* major news. Who's the lucky man?"

"Why, Mr Jetsam," Darcy said. "You know that I've been waiting all this time for Mr Jetsam, my one true love?"

Grace nodded. "Well, yes, but you don't mean to say that someone actually called Mr Jetsam has come into your life?"

Darcy shook her head and then tucked her hair behind her ears. "No, no, I don't expect that to happen. But I know, deep in my heart – or the place where my heart used to be – what kind of man my Mr Jetsam would be, and I think he's come on board the ship."

Grace was thrilled. "Well, what's his name then?"

"He's called Stukeley," said Darcy, her voice suddenly dreamy. "His full name is Jez Stukeley."

"Jez Stukeley," Grace repeated.

"What's wrong?" Darcy asked.

"Nothing." Grace shook her head. "Nothing at all."

"Don't lie to me, Grace. I may be on an astral visit, but my mind is as sharp as a tack. There's something in your voice. A warning."

"No," Grace said. "I'm just surprised, that's all. I knew a Jez Stukeley. He was a good friend of Connor's, on board *The Diablo*. He died a few months ago."

"Why yes," Darcy said. "I know that. And it's the same Jez Stukeley. I mean, it's not like it's that common a name! There's nothing common about my Jez. And it was Connor who brought him to the ship."

"*Connor* came to *The Nocturne*?"

"Yes!" Darcy said. "Him and that big muscly friend of his . . . I've forgotten his name."

"Bart," Grace said with a smile.

"That's the one! Bart. Connor and Bart came to *The Nocturne*, with Jez. They brought him to seek the captain's help. You see, Jez crossed over during a duel."

"Yes," said Grace. This was starting to make some sense. "I know. It was during my time on the ship. I was at his funeral."

"Oh yes," Darcy said. "Of course, you would have been there. I'm sorry."

Grace shook her head. "No problem. Carry on!"

"Well, it seems that after the coffin was thrown into the ocean, Sidorio found it and broke into it and sired Jez to be his assistant. He's a vampirate now, just like me."

"Jez is a vampire now?" Grace exclaimed. This was big news indeed.

"No, silly. Not a vampire. A *Vampirate*! Just like me!"

"I see." Grace said distractedly. She was still reeling from the news that Connor had visited *The Nocturne*. How had he known where to find it? Did he share the same kind of bond with the ship that she did? This was a surprise, and no mistake. "You said that Connor and Bart brought Jez to seek the captain's help. What kind of help?"

"Well, you know that Sidorio's missing, presumed dead? Certainly, that's a blessing in so many ways. But not the least of it is that Jez was completely under his control. Well, you can imagine, can't you? Being a sire to another vampire is like being a parent . . . and you can imagine the kind of parent Sidorio would make." Darcy's eyes bulged once more. Grace shuddered at the thought.

"After Sidorio went missing, Jez was all alone in the world. He did some bad things. But how could he have stopped himself? It's hard adjusting to the Afterdeath. And he had no one to help him. Not like us, on board *The Nocturne* with the captain, or them what's here with Mosh Zu. Jez was so lost he was . . . well, he was thinking of ending it all."

Grace was wide-eyed once more. "Is that possible?" she asked. Her knowledge of vampires dying – or whatever the next stage after dying was – was minimal.

"I don't know," Darcy said. "But I think there's no end

of ways to torment yourself in this world – that is, in your world and in mine."

Instinctively, Grace reached out her hand to Darcy's, though it only slipped through the phantom wrist. "We live in the *same* world, Darcy."

"Well, yes," Darcy said. "But you know what I mean."

"So how is Jez since he joined the crew?"

"Oh he's much better. Really happy, I think. In fact, he's been a breath of fresh air aboard *The Nocturne*."

"And is he taking to the Feast and the donor relationship all right?" Grace asked.

Darcy frowned at this. "You did have to go and bring that up, didn't you?"

"Sorry," said Grace. "Is he having trouble with his donor?"

Darcy shook her head. "No, he isn't. But I am! The captain's only gone and given him that Shanti as a donor."

"*Shanti?*" Grace was initially surprised, but then it made sense.

"Yes, well, after she came back from Sanctuary with him, she had no vampire partner of course, and that wasn't doing her any good so I'm sure it seemed like the obvious solution. But I really wish it hadn't been. Truly, Grace, I do. She's so jealous of us. We all know that there's a special bond between vampire and donor. I have a very special relationship with my Edward. But it's different to my relationship with Jez. It's different to a love relationship."

"What does Jez say about all this?" Grace asked.

"Oh he says that it's all in my mind. He says that there's nothing between them, that it's just a business relationship. But you know what Shanti's like. You've seen how possessive of Lorcan she was."

"Yes." Grace nodded. "Well, be careful, Darcy. I know you think you're in love, but I'd hate to see you get hurt."

"I don't *think* I'm in love, Grace," Darcy said, airily. "I *know* it. I feel it. Jez *is* my Mr Jetsam. I felt it from the moment he stepped aboard the ship."

Grace wasn't so sure. She'd have to keep an eye on this situation, as best she could. But she wasn't about to rain on Darcy's parade. "I'm really thrilled to see you so happy," she said. "He's certainly put a spring in your step and a glow on your cheeks!"

"Oh no he hasn't!" Darcy smiled. "That's my own very special new rouge. I'll let you borrow it when I next see you for real . . . Yes, hello. Who's there?"

Grace was confused. "I'm sorry, what did you just say?"

"Oh it's you, darling! Just a moment! I'm just in the middle of something . . . Grace, I have to go. He's outside my door. I'm sorry, but I'll have to cut this astral visit short. It was great seeing you!"

"You too!" Grace said, standing to say goodbye. But as she looked up, Darcy had already faded into the ether. Typical! thought Grace. The minute she finds a man, Darcy disappears from view. Grace sat back down again, glumly surveying the chessboard.

"Have you been messing with my pieces?"

"Johnny!" She looked up to find him grinning down at her. He was dressed in a towelling dressing gown, his customary bandana still knotted loosely around his neck.

"Couldn't sleep," he said.

"Me neither."

He sat down on the chair beside her. "Were you talking to someone? Just now, before I came in?"

Grace shook her head, deciding it was simpler to tell a white lie. "No," she said. "No, I was just chatting away to myself."

Johnny spiralled his finger close to his head. "I won't be friends with you any more if you lose your marbles," he said. "Just thought you should know that, Grace."

"Thanks for the heads-up, cowboy," she said. "Now, sit down and make your move. You're black tonight."

CHAPTER THIRTY-SIX
Complications

All eyes remained on Alessandro and Moonshine. Cate stepped forward. Connor could sense her thought-processes. It was vital that the crew could see and take the lead from her at this point. Things seemed to have moved into the danger zone but, depending on what happened next, a combat situation could still be avoided.

Alessandro kept hold of Moonshine, but turned to address Cate. "Your boy here asked to use one of the conveniences. Of course, I was happy to direct him to one. But on the way back he took a detour through the Emperor's own quarters and pocketed a souvenir or two."

Now, the security aide reached into Moonshine's pocket and withdrew a handful of items. Connor, like the others, was transfixed. It appeared that a fascination for sapphires ran in the Wrathe family.

Moonshine didn't even try to deny it. He just looked

peeved to have been caught. Connor wondered if he realised the extent of what he'd done. He hadn't just placed himself in danger but Cate and the entire attack squad as well.

"I am terribly sorry," Cate said now. "Of course, I will want some time alone with my staff member to look further into this. But I can assure you this is an isolated incident."

Alessandro was not easily mollified. "Frankly, we expected better from the ORC."

"Of course," Cate said. "And at this stage I can only offer you my sincere apologies. But I can assure you, there will also be a significant discount off the fee."

Alessandro shook his head. "It's not as simple as that," he said. "Security has been breached and I no longer feel comfortable using your company. This contract is terminated. We'll expect a full refund of the deposit. And I'd like all the Emperor's items removed from your ships."

"Removed?" Cate's expression said it all, but she spoke calmly. "Can't we talk about this? I'm not for one moment understating the seriousness of the offence, but the rest of my crew have been completely professional."

Alessandro shrugged. "We only have your word for that," he said. "And, as I say, that word is now called into question."

Connor held his breath. What would happen now? He couldn't bear the thought of having to carry everything back out of the ships and into the fort. Surely Cate wouldn't agree to it.

"Of course," she said. "If you're at all unhappy, then we must do whatever we can to make you happy again."

"Alex," Salvatore stepped forward. "Don't you think you're being a little hasty? One bad apple, and all that!"

"No, Salvatore, I don't think so. Our trust has been misplaced. Who knows what other misdemeanours this lot might have planned?"

There was a hubbub from the ranks. Connor was impressed by the acting abilities of the crew to get into character as disgruntled removal guys.

"Please," said Cate. "I appreciate that you are disappointed, terribly disappointed, with the actions of this one . . ." she surveyed Moonshine intently, looking for the right word. "This one member of my staff. But I will not stand here and have the rest of my team – who have worked tirelessly and in good faith – I will not have them slandered."

"Try to understand," Alessandro said. "Your feelings have very little importance in all this. What matters is that the Emperor's considerable personal fortune has been placed in grave danger. Now, tell your crew to put down their glasses of lemonade and to start bringing the loads back out and into the fort."

Cate looked close to tears – whether genuine or not, Connor couldn't ascertain. "All right," she said. "All right, everyone, listen up! We'll do exactly as we are asked. Go back into the ships and begin unloading the cargo. And do it carefully. Excuse me, for one moment," she said to

Alessandro and Salvatore. "I just need to brief my second in command." She strode after Bart. Connor overheard her as she passed on instructions quickly and precisely.

"Get everyone back on the ships," she said. "And get ready to sail off. Understand?"

Bart nodded. "Yes, boss!"

"I'll deal with Moonshine and follow. But no one else is to come back, you understand?"

"Yes, boss!" he repeated. Then he began moving the teams back towards the ship, calmly passing on the orders.

In a matter of moments, only Alessandro and Salvatore, Moonshine and Cate were left on the green. Well, only the four of them, plus one other person.

"Connor?" Cate said, noticing him for the first time. "What are you waiting for? Go back to the ship and join your team. It's all hands on deck if we're going to get that cargo unloaded."

"But boss," he said, without missing a beat, "he's my work partner." He nodded towards Moonshine. "I can't lift stuff on my own, can I?"

Cate smiled at Connor. Her smile conveyed a number of thoughts and emotions that they didn't have time to work through then and there.

Now she turned to Salvatore. "You have apprehended the thief," she said. "Be assured he will be disciplined most severely. But, in the meantime, the most important thing is to get your cargo out of the ships. It'll take us just that bit longer with a pair down. Would you consider releasing this boy so that he and his partner can proceed while we three agree suitable reparations for this mess?"

Salvatore nodded. "Yes, I think that would be accept—"

"No." Alessandro stepped in between them. "No, I don't think so."

At that moment, Moonshine took a decision. Connor could see what he was about to do as if in slow motion. And, if he'd dared to open his mouth, he'd have cried out, "*Nooooooooooooo!*" Instead, he could only watch as Moonshine shoved Alessandro to one side and began to run. Alessandro fell heavily against Cate and Salvatore and the three of them tumbled to the ground.

Moonshine ripped open the flap in his boiler suit and produced his weapons of choice – starfish *shuriken*. He began throwing these at the security aides. It was a typical Moonshine attack – instinctive, unplanned, vicious.

The two guards were swiftly on their feet. "I told you!" Alessandro shouted, running towards Moonshine. "I told you, Salvatore. We've been conned!" He pointed to the water, where both ships were lifting anchor.

For a moment, Salvatore looked crushed. Then he grabbed a jewelled dagger from inside his pocket and threw himself at Cate. His small talk now all used up, he swung the dagger in the direction of her heart. As he did so, she unsheathed her épée and expertly parried the throw. Then, as he prepared to strike, she delivered an expert épée blow to his ribcage. As he fell to the ground, stunned, Cate looked down at him. "Your lemonade wasn't all *that*!" she said.

Meanwhile, Connor watched as Alessandro caught up with Moonshine and tackled him to the ground. Like his fallen colleague, he was carrying a small, jewelled dagger. This he positioned across Moonshine's neck. "I'm going to enjoy this," he said.

"No!" Connor leaped forward as Alessandro lowered the dagger. He threw himself upon Alessandro, driving the blade of his rapier in between the guard's shoulder blades. Immediately a pool of blood erupted from the wound, soaking the guard's shirt in an ever-increasing circle, like a setting sun. Alessandro's body slumped on top of Moonshine, pinning the lad to the ground. The dagger blade, which moments ago had spelled certain death, was now plunged only into the Emperor's manicured lawn.

"Get him off me!" Moonshine cried. "Get him off me!"

Connor had fallen onto Alessandro, his hand still clasped about his rapier. Now, he raised himself up from the lifeless body of his victim. On one level, he knew exactly what he had done. Cate had ordered him to protect Moonshine at all costs and, as he had seen the guard attack with the jewelled dagger, instinct and training had joined hands and taken over.

Connor realised that he had killed Alessandro and saved Moonshine. But he had made no conscious decision to kill. There hadn't been time for that. Nor had he had time to weigh up whether he could safely wound Alessandro or just kill him outright. In fact, as he'd seen his rapier plunge through Alessandro's shirt and into the flesh between his shoulder blades, it was as if he was watching someone else make the attack. As if someone else had seized the sword from his clutches and done his dirty work. His head raced with these thoughts. *This isn't happening to me. I didn't do it. I'm not a . . . I'm not a . . .* But there, in his hands, was the indisputable truth. The blood-stained rapier.

"Get him off me!" Moonshine cried once more.

It was as if everything until now had happened in slow motion, but what happened next occurred in double-quick time. Cate was suddenly at Connor's side, reaching out her own hands and helping him haul the dead weight off Moonshine. Later, Connor would remember that weight and think of a haunch of meat or a sack of potatoes. Then, all he thought of was the effort it took and how much blood there was. It seemed to soak from every pore of the dead man's body. All three of the survivors now had Alessandro's life-blood on them. Moonshine lay stock still, bathed in it.

"Run!" Cate cried to him, pulling him up. "Quick as you can! Onto the ship!"

Now, she turned and pushed Connor forward. "You too," she shouted. "Run!"

But Connor was unable to move. "I killed him," he said, looking down at the pool of blood which had turned Alessandro's shirt from white to crimson. Reality was sinking in. Fast. "I killed him."

"Yes," Cate said. "I killed one and you killed the other. What do you want, a medal? Get back on the ship. NOW!"

She pushed him forward and they both ran towards the pontoon. Connor's heart was racing wildly, a terrible cocktail of adrenaline and fear. He made it across the wish as *The Diablo* began to make its hasty exit from the harbour.

Stumbling onto the deck, he was growing more and more confused about what had happened. He wanted to rewind time, not so much to change what he'd done but just to see it as it had happened, slower than it had happened, in order to understand it. But there was no way to turn back time. Not for him. Nor for the two fallen security aides, who lay on the green sward in front of the fort, fast disappearing from view as *The Diablo* continued on its way.

Connor glanced down to his side. His rapier was still clasped tightly in his hand. Its blade was coated with the fast-drying blood that, until moments previously, had pumped around Alessandro's body. How long was it since Alessandro had been alive? Five minutes? Ten? Exactly the same amount of time that Connor had become a killer.

He had known that one day he might kill. But he had expected that day to be far ahead in the distance. When he had had time to prepare for it. But that wasn't what life had in store for Connor Tempest. With no real preparation, he had made a journey he could never return from. In a matter of seconds, he had travelled from pirate to assassin. Now, he had a whole lifetime to come to terms with what instinct had made him do.

As the ship raced away across the ocean, Connor stole one final glance at the guards splayed out on the lawn, then back to his blood-stained sword. His hand began to tremble and he felt the rapier slip from his grasp and tumble onto the deck. As he reached down for it, he had a sudden image, not of the sword, but of Alessandro lying there, looking up at him, blood pooling around his prone body.

"You killed me!" exclaimed the security aide, half in surprise and half in anger. "You killed me! But why?"

"I had my orders," Connor said.

Alessandro looked up at him in disgust. "You can't explain away what you did in terms of orders."

"Yes I can," Connor said. "I was protecting my comrade."

"*Him?*" Alessandro said, disparagingly, glancing across the deck. Connor twisted his head and saw Moonshine stripping off his blood-covered shirt and reaching for a towel. Alessandro's words rang in his ears. "But you don't even like him. In fact, you loathe him." This wasn't far from the truth, Connor realised, turning from Moonshine. "I'm sorry," he said. "But I only did what I had to do."

Alessandro shook his head. "I'm going now," he said. "But you'll never forget me. You never forget your first kill."

Suddenly, the guard's image was gone and Connor was crouching on the deck, looking down only upon his sword. He picked it up and wiped away the blood on his trousers. For a moment, the sword was clean. Then, he saw that the blood had returned once more. How could this be? The sword was coated in blood. He wiped it clean again. And for a moment, it remained clean. Connor sighed with relief. Then, fresh blood coated the surface of the blade. It was as if the wound was in the blade itself.

"No!" he said. First dead men were talking to him. Now, his own sword was playing tricks on him.

CHAPTER THIRTY-SEVEN

Stukeley's Feast

Stukeley is grinning from ear to ear. How he is enjoying his fourth Feast aboard *The Nocturne*. The captain — ahem, that is to say, Sidorio, for now he has (or at least pays lip service to) a new captain — Sidorio did not tell him about these delights. He wouldn't, of course, have appreciated such things. He'd have been bored by the ritual — by the dressing up in your best finery, as if you were setting off to a summer dance; bored by the formal dinner during which no food touched your lips, because what need had you for food? And perhaps, most of all, Sidorio would have been bored by the need to make small talk with his donor. But everything which would have bored his master is a source of rare delight to Stukeley. From the tuxedo and dress-shirt he is wearing — with its starched white collar — to the glow of candles which stretch the length of the vast table; from the way Shanti curtseyed before him and he bowed to her as they took their places at the long table; yes, for all these reasons and more, Stukeley could not be happier.

Shanti, it seems, is happy too. She chatters away, under the impression he is hovering like a fly upon her every word. He nods and makes small noises from time to time, smiling when she smiles. In this way, she seems convinced he is paying her his complete attention when, in fact, his mind is elsewhere altogether. He has much to think of. He dares a quick glance along the table. The rows of vampires and donors stretch out almost to infinity on both sides. He remembers his mission.

"Excuse me, my dear," he says to Shanti, reaching forward and taking her glass in one hand.

She watches him curiously as he grabs her unused knife in another. (Shanti eats everything with her fork and fingers. It's not entirely ladylike but he can forgive her.) Now, rising to his feet, Stukeley strikes the glass with the knife – once, twice, three times.

"Ladies and gentlemen," he says. "Ladies and gentlemen, if I might crave your indulgence for the briefest of moments."

"Sit down, Stukeley!" He hears the whisper inside his head. He smiles indulgently at the captain but continues.

"Ladies and gentlemen, I do not intend to keep you from this delicious Feast. I simply wanted to say—"

"Sit down and be quiet!"

"I simply wanted to say a heartfelt thank you to our generous host, the captain. Tonight is my fourth Feast aboard *The Nocturne* and a very fine time I am having, too."

"Sit down *now*, Stukeley!"

"Forgive me if I appear a little gauche – I am still new to all these things. I know it is not traditional to make speeches on this occasion. And this, indeed, is hardly a speech. More a toast. If you have a glass before you, then please raise it now. And, for those of us who do not have glasses, well, we – in our own way – will drink this toast later."

Some laughter at this.

"But please, whether you have glass in hand or no, please join me in a toast of thanks to the captain. In gratitude to the one who grants us all safe harbour. To the captain!"

He raises his glass. The donors follow suit. Some of the vampires, amused by this deviation from the norm, raise their hands as if clasping imaginary glasses. Together, donors and vampires exclaim, "The captain!"

"And now, ladies and gentlemen, I wonder if you'd care to join me in a dance?" At his words, the soft percussive music of the Feast grows louder and faster. Stukeley nods at the musicians in the corner. They smile back. At last, some new music to play.

"Sit down, Stukeley!" the captain says once more, but already Stukeley has swept Shanti into the centre of the room. He begins twirling her around the floor. The music grows louder.

"Come on!" Stukeley calls to the others, ignoring the captain's protests. The so-called leader of the ship stands still as a statue as Stukeley and Shanti dance around him. "Join us! This night is cause for celebration."

"No," the captain says once more. And now not only Stukeley hears him. Now, not only Stukeley defies him. Others amongst the Vampirates lead their donors into the centre of the room and begin to dance. Their faces reveal a mixture of fear, delight and rebellion.

Shaking his head, the captain pushes through them and strides out of the room. Many of the vampires rise and follow with their donors. They will not play any part in this.

But others join the dance, intrigued that the ritual of Feast Night can change like this. They watch Stukeley with true admiration. He is so new to the ship – a much needed breath of fresh air. Hands reach across the table. Feet scurry to the centre of the room. Has there ever been music so sweet and tempting as this? Why, it is impossible to stand still!

The style of dance varies from couple to couple. Dances of different eras play out alongside each other. Not all of the vampire-donor pairs are composed of a man and a woman, so there are men dancing with men and women with women. No one thinks anything of it. From above, they resemble the petals of a giant flower. At its very heart is Stukeley and Shanti.

"Well," she says, as they turn once more. "This is irregular to say the least."

"I thought I'd shake things up a bit," he says.

"Did you now?" As she speaks, she becomes aware that someone is watching. She turns quickly, meeting Darcy Flotsam's eyes. Darcy has her donor by the hand. They are about to leave the room, *of course*, but there is something in Darcy's eyes. A longing to stay, perhaps? A longing for something else besides. Darcy's eyes meet Shanti's. Embarrassed, Darcy turns and walks out of the room. Stukeley watches her go.

"That figurehead is a pest!" Shanti says, drawing Jez closer towards her.

Stukeley laughs. "Now, now, my dear. What harm has she ever done to you?"

"What's her game anyway?"

"Game?"

"She's got her sights on you," Shanti says, as he spins her around again.

"Darcy and I are friends, that's all."

"Friends?"

Stukeley nuzzles the curve of Shanti's neck. "She can't give me what I need." He looks her in the eyes. "Only you can do that."

"Yes," Shanti says. "You'd do well to remember that."

Later, they are alone in his cabin. Now at last he can drink his toast to the captain. And he does, lingering over the taste of her blood.

"Stop!" she says. "Stop!"

343

He looks up at her face. She is frowning. He draws back for a moment and stares up at her, the picture of innocence, his lips wet with her blood.

"Is something wrong?"

"You're taking too much! You've had enough!"

"Nonsense." He smiles. "Your blood tastes great, by the way!"

"You've had enough," she repeats, pulling away from him.

"How can you tell?"

"I've done this many times before. Or have you forgotten? I was Lieutenant Furey's donor for a long time before I was switched to you." He can hear the hurt in her voice – the demotion from a lieutenant to a non-ranking officer.

"I don't expect the good lieutenant had much of a thirst. He was only a young lad, so they say. I'm a full-grown man."

"He had a very healthy thirst, until his current . . . difficulties."

"Yes," Stukeley says, his words edged with a sneer. "And now he has no taste for your blood at all."

"It has nothing to do with me."

"I'd have thought you'd be grateful," he says. "There you were, shrivelling up like an old prune and here I come along, bang on cue, to drink your blood."

"Oh lucky me! Lucky, lucky me! Remember, Stukeley, you need me."

"Yes, Shanti, and remember that *you* need *me*. Without each other, we're nothing."

He bends down to her thorax again and, though she tries to fight it, she feels his mouth clamp down on her skin once more.

The deck is almost empty. Stukeley has come to get some air. He is elated with the intake of fresh blood in his veins. Shanti's blood is as spirited as she is. They are a perfect match. He enjoys the element of cat and mouse in their relationship. And if he sometimes feels like the mouse and lets her feel like the cat, well, where's the harm in that?

He sees a familiar figure, leaning against the deck-rail.

"Hello, beautiful!" he says.

The woman turns. Darcy Flotsam directs her large eyes towards him. "Hello," she says, holding something back in her voice.

"You're disappointed in me," he says, joining her at the guard-rail.

"Disappointed?"

"Because of the dance," he continues. "I know I was impulsive, but I felt such joy. Before, I was so full of despair. But now, since I came here, things are so different. Can you understand that?"

Darcy nods. "I do understand, as it goes. But you must be careful. Try to contain that joy of yours sometimes. Out of respect for the captain."

He laughs. "But, surely, the captain wants us to be happy."

"The captain wants what's best for us," Darcy says. "We must respect his wishes."

"Wishes?" says Jez. "Or rules?" He sees he has pushed this as far as he should. He doesn't want to upset her. Not her. "It's a lovely night, isn't it?" he says, his voice much softer. "Rather balmy. And would you look at those stars?"

Together, they turn their eyes up to the heavens. True enough, the stars are out in force tonight.

"But you know what?" Stukeley says, looking at Darcy sadly. "You know what, Miss Flotsam? There's one star missing from the skies tonight."

She sighs. "Please don't use that cheesy old line on me."

"What line?" he says, innocent as ever.

"You know the one – about how I fell from the skies."

"No," he says, lifting his clenched fist towards her. "Not you, this."

He opens his fist and there, sitting in his palm, is a glittering diamond brooch in the shape of a shooting star.

"For you," he says.

She gasps, then, reluctantly, "No, really, it's lovely, but you mustn't."

"Mustn't what?"

"You mustn't give me things."

"Why not?"

"Well, for one thing, it will make Shanti jealous."

"Shanti? Why ever would it? I'm grateful, of course I

am – *deeply* grateful for what she does for me. But she can only fill one of my needs. Whereas you, Miss Flotsam . . . Well, I'm embarrassed to speak further. May I? May I pin this brooch onto your dress?"

Darcy bows her head. "All right. If you insist."

He comes closer, reaches out and carefully pins the brooch onto her bodice, mindful not to snag the fine material. "There," he says, stepping back. "Quite beautiful!"

"Yes it is! Thank you, Mr Stukeley."

"Please," he says, "you must call me Jez. And I wasn't talking about the brooch."

Darcy shakes her head from side to side. First the dance, then this. He is like a force of nature. Unstoppable. She shakes her head again. "What *are* we going to do with you, Mr— I mean, Jez? What *are* we going to do with you?"

CHAPTER THIRTY-EIGHT

Hero of the Hour

Connor's crew-mates were in jubilant mood. By all accounts, the raid on the Sunset Fort had been a great success. Both *The Diablo* and *The Typhon* were loaded with more precious treasures than either had carried before. And it had all been accomplished without loss of life – amongst the two crews, anyhow. And no one seemed in any doubt as to who was responsible for this victory.

"You were amazing, man!" said Gonzalez, slapping Connor on the back. "We were all watching from the deck. The way you brought that guy down!"

"It would all have fallen apart if it wasn't for you," said one of *The Typhon*'s crew. "That idiot Moonshine nearly ruined the whole operation, but you saved the day!"

"You did good, Connor," said Cate, who had remained at his side since they'd returned to the ship. "You did exactly what was asked of you."

He looked at her, trying to frame the words but he found he was shaking uncontrollably. He tried once more to speak. "I k . . . kill . . . I killed . . ."

Cate shook her head and brought her arm around him. "You did your duty, Connor. If you hadn't killed that guard, Moonshine Wrathe would be dead now. You were only doing your duty."

But Connor couldn't seem to see it that way. In his mind, his hands were outstretched, like the two sides of a scale. Moonshine sat on one palm and the security guard – Alessandro – on the other. Who could say who was more deserving of life – or death?

"Where *is* Moonshine?" Connor asked.

"I'm not sure," Cate said. "He must be here somewhere. Oh yes, here he is! Moonshine!" she called. "Moonshine, over here!"

No! thought Connor. He hadn't wanted to see him. But it was too late. Moonshine Wrathe was ambling across the deck towards him. He had already changed out of his fake uniform and was now dressed in his more regular uniform of skinny jeans and a T-shirt.

"Hey," he said, as he came over to Connor. "Thanks for the helping hand over there."

Connor tried to smile. "It's OK."

"Seriously," Moonshine said. "That security guard was one mean dude. I owe you one." He flicked his fingers at Connor then turned and sauntered off again.

I owe you one. Was that all this meant to him?

Moonshine had nearly been killed. His actions had placed both Connor and Cate in extreme danger. He'd nearly blown the entire raid. And now Connor had taken a life on his account. But all this was like so much water off the back of the pirate prince. He was all cleaned up and ready to put the incident behind him.

"I know what you're thinking," Cate said. "I can see it in your eyes. We've all been there. It's going to take time for you to deal with this. But you will, Connor, you will." She hugged him again.

More members of the attack squad came up to offer their thanks and congratulations. Their words and faces began to blur. He felt like a fog was coming down, separating him from them. They reached out and touched him, squeezed his hand, punched his shoulder. And yet they could have been in another world altogether. He felt like he was utterly alone, cold and exposed. He couldn't stop shivering.

"Hey," Cate said. Connor turned, to realise she wasn't talking to him but to Bart, who had appeared at their side.

"Hey guys, how are you doing?"

"Connor's not doing so good," Cate said. "But it's no surprise under the circs."

"No," Bart agreed, sitting down on Connor's other side. He put his arm around Connor's shoulder. "We've all been through this. And now we'll get you through too. It's a difficult journey, but we'll get you through."

"He didn't deserve to die," Connor said. "He didn't *need* to die. If Moonshine hadn't gone off like that . . ."

"You can't think that way," Cate said. "You can't rewind the scene. It happened the way it happened. It's regrettable that we had to do what we did. But you saw how readily those two guards pulled their daggers. That's the world they live in, the world we live in. Live by the sword, die by the sword."

Was that it? Was that the extent of Cate's philosophy? Because it wasn't giving Connor any comfort. No comfort at all. Suddenly, he felt like a dead weight, as if all the adrenaline had completely drained from him and he was ready to drop.

"I'm so tired," he said, finding he was barely able to get the words out.

"Here," said Bart. "Why don't I take you down to your bunk? We'll get you cleaned up and then you should rest. There's bound to be major celebrations tonight and you'll be the hero of the hour."

"No celebrations," Connor shook his head. "There's nothing to celebrate. I'm a kill—"

"*No!*" Cate said. "You can't think like that. There *will* be celebrations tonight, Connor. And the best thing you can do is to be a part of them. So off you go –clean up and get some rest. And we'll see you at dinner." She turned to Bart. "Take him to my cabin," she said. "He'll rest better behind closed doors. Stay with him if you think it's helpful."

"Come on," Bart said, rather more gently. "Come on, Connor. Let's get you downstairs." He helped him up onto his feet. Connor's body felt like clay – heavy, formless and awkward. He hadn't any injuries but still he leaned on Bart as they made their way across the deck.

As they passed amongst the high-spirited attack squad, his comrades turned and continued to pass on their thanks and congratulations.

"Good goin', buddy!"

"Man, you got *cojones*!"

"Moonshine Wrathe owes you his life!"

The words washed over him. They meant nothing. In his mind, he could only see his hand reaching for the rapier and plunging it between Alessandro's shoulder blades. And then the blood – the blood spraying up and soaking Alessandro's shirt and his own, binding them together. The eternal union of the killer and the killed.

"Connor! Connor! Connor!" Bart turned him around to face the crowded deck as each man and woman joined in chanting his name. Connor's eyes swept across the deck. There was something feverish in their chants. In his head, their words and expressions suddenly changed. Now, their eyes were angry and they were chanting, "Killer! Killer! Killer!"

"Stop!" he cried. "Make them stop!"

"Come on," Bart said. "Let's get you out of here."

Connor was back in the lighthouse. He was seven years old and he was surfacing from a deep, comfortable sleep. As he forced open his eyes, he saw that there were presents at the foot of his bed. It was like his birthday or Christmas – no,

352

both, rolled into one! There were presents everywhere – bright packages bound with ribbon, occupying nearly every space on the floor.

Somehow, his dad and sister made it through the sea of presents to the side of his bed.

"See, he's awake!" Grace said. She was carrying a glass of milkshake. At the top was a thick scoop of ice-cream and a chocolate flake and a sprinkle of hundreds and thousands. Carefully, Grace set it down at Connor's bedside table.

Then his dad joined them. In his hands was a big plate of lamingtons – thick, chocolate-dipped squares of sponge cake, dusted in fluffy white coconut. They were his absolute favourite!

"We made these for you!" Grace said.

"To help you celebrate!" his dad added, with a smile. "We're so proud of you!"

They both leaned forward. "Congratulations on your first kill!" they said.

As their faces leaned closer, Connor let out a cry. Opening his eyes, he found he was in unfamiliar surroundings. It took him a few moments to adjust. *I'm on a pirate ship.* The Diablo. *This is Cate's cabin. I'm a pirate now. I'm a . . .*

He couldn't say the word, not even to himself. If only he could go to sleep and not wake up – though if his last dream was anything to go by, even sleep wouldn't offer him any solace.

He stretched up in bed and that was when he saw it, lying on the blanket beside him. It was a small wooden carving in the shape of a man. He reached out and grabbed it. As he drew it up to his eyes, he saw that the figure was stained with blood, right where its heart would be.

Connor's own heart started racing again. His head suddenly felt like it was going to crack. What was this carving? Who had come into his cabin, while he was sleeping, and put it there? What did it mean?

CHAPTER THIRTY-NINE
The Blood Captain

Connor's hands began to shake as he stared at the crudely carved figure. Rough-hewn as it was, there was no doubting that it had a human shape. Nor was there any doubt that the red mark was right where the figure's heart would be. As Connor stood transfixed, he became sure that the dye was blood. Blood changed its shade from wet to dry. Connor's head was filled with the sight of Alessandro's blood spraying out from the open wound onto his own shirt. He'd never forget that colour. Trembling, he gripped the wooden figure tightly. He had to focus. Danger was imminent. Someone was sending him a message. This was voodoo – or, if not exactly voodoo, then some other kind of curse. Someone was planning revenge, and not only had they signalled their intent very clearly, but they had managed to get onto *The Diablo*, and into this cabin. Maybe they were still on board now . . . A hand came to rest on his shoulder. He froze.

Suddenly, somehow, Connor drew all his attention to his fists. He swung around and whacked his opponent in the face. He heard a cry of pain, felt the hand release and heard the body slump heavily to the deck. As he turned, his heart sank. Lying on the floor, his nose bleeding profusely, was Bart.

"I'm sorry," Connor cried.

Bart shook his head. "It's OK, buddy," he said. "I should have known better than to come up behind you like that." He lifted his sleeve to staunch the blood-flow. "You were trembling. I wanted to comfort you. I didn't think."

Connor shook his head slowly. He didn't know who he was any more. Everything was out of kilter. Adrenaline was pumping through his veins. His body felt foreign to him, out of control. He had delivered a nasty blow to Bart. What might he do next? Had becoming a killer unleashed a previously unrealised blood-lust in him?

"What's that?" Bart asked, pointing to the figure Connor clasped in his hand.

"I don't know," Connor said, crouching down and bringing the figure closer to Bart. "It was on the blanket when I woke. Look, it's got blood on it. It's voodoo or something."

"Give it to me," Bart said. He reached out for the figure but, as he did so, his head began to roll and he slumped back against the deck.

"Bart! Bart, are you OK?" Connor knelt down and began patting his friend's face. "Bart, Bart, wake up!"

"*Whaaaat?*" Slowly, Bart's eyes opened again. "What happened?"

"You fainted. But only for a second. You're back now." Connor's eyes roved around the floor for something to prop under Bart's neck to make him more comfortable. He reached for one of Cate's pillows. As he squished it under his friend's neck, his thoughts turned to his first ever night aboard *The Diablo*. Bart had given up his bed for him that night and slept on the floor, using his kitbag as a pillow. Connor trembled. That was only four months ago, but so much had happened since. He had been a boy then. Now, he was something else. A man? He wasn't sure about that. Did killing someone automatically make you a man? It didn't feel that way. If anything, he felt more like a wild animal. So much had changed.

"I'll get help," Connor said.

"It's OK," Bart replied. "I'll just rest here for a bit. Here, pass me my water bottle, would ya?"

Connor grabbed the bottle and unscrewed the cap for his comrade.

"Thanks," Bart said, thirstily swigging from the bottle. "Ah, that's better."

Connor looked across at his buddy. "I'm really sorry," he said. "I didn't mean to hurt you."

"Of course you didn't," Bart said, raising a smile. "No need to apologise. You're going through a tough time right

357

now. I know that." He reached out his hand and grabbed Connor's. The strength of Bart's grip instantly pulled Connor together.

"Connor," he said. "What you're going through. It's the hardest thing you'll ever have to deal with. But we've all been there. We can help."

His words were clear. He might just as well have said, "You're a killer, now. We're all killers on this ship. But now you've killed once, it will be easier next time. And the time after that. Soon you'll be dispatching death without so much as blinking your eye."

"One for all," Bart said.

Connor was lost in his reverie.

"One for all," Bart repeated.

Connor looked at their joined hands. He couldn't look into Bart's eyes, couldn't show him the mixture of fear and sudden repulsion that was there.

"All for one," he mumbled.

"That's right," Bart said. "We look out for each other. Just like we always did. Just like we looked after Jez, in life and afterwards."

Suddenly, Connor needed to be free of Bart's grip. He needed to get out of this claustrophobic cabin. Feeling the carving in his other hand, he came to a swift decision. "I have to go," he said. "I have to go and see Captain Wrathe."

"Sure," Bart said, smiling as if nothing had happened. He released Connor's hand with a final squeeze, then lay back and closed his eyes. Is this how easily he could dismiss death? Well, Connor wasn't there yet and he wasn't sure he ever wanted to be.

The door to Captain Wrathe's cabin was open. Connor darted inside, pushing forward through the familiar assortment of treasures Captain Wrathe had acquired on his voyages and raids.

Connor could hear voices, including Molucco's. They were coming from the back of the cabin. Sure enough, as he walked past a familiar jewelled elephant, he found Captain Wrathe and Cate sitting drinking wine, surrounded by their fresh booty. Scrimshaw was lazily entwining himself around a Michaelangelo statue as though checking out the quality of the goods.

"Aha!" said Molucco, glancing up with a grin. "The man of the hour! Some wine for you, Connor?" He lifted a silver flask but Connor shook his head.

"What's the matter, Connor?" Cate asked. "You're shivering."

"What's this?" he said, holding out the figure towards them.

Molucco took it from him and turned the figure around in his hand.

"Where did you get this?" he asked.

"It was on my blanket," Connor said. "I was sleeping on Cate's bunk and when I woke up, I found it there. Someone must have come in while I was sleeping—" he broke off. "It's real blood on it, isn't it?"

Molucco lifted the figure nearer to his eye and nodded. "Yes, that's definitely blood."

"It's voodoo," Connor said. "They're coming to get revenge on me for what I did. For killing that guard. How did they find me? How did they get on board the ship?"

"Calm down, Connor," said Cate.

Calm down? How could she talk about being calm when there was an enemy aboard the ship? When at any time, not just Connor but the rest of the crew could be under attack?

"Sit down, Connor," said Molucco.

"But—" he protested.

"Sit down!" commanded the captain and this time it was clear it was an order.

Connor sat on one of the floor cushions. His legs refused to stay still though, jiggling away as if at any time they would be ready to make a break for it.

Molucco cradled the carved figure in his hand. "I know what this is," he said. "And I know where it came from. I know whose blood it is." He smiled. "Now . . ." He lifted the flask of wine and poured a small amount into a goblet. "Drink this. It will calm your nerves."

Connor took the cup in his hand. One glance at the red liquid made him feel nauseous, reminding him once more of blood, but he could tell that Molucco would not tolerate any refusal. He took the smallest sip, then set the cup down.

"OK?" Molucco asked.

Connor nodded.

"Right then. This figure, my lad, is called a Blood Captain. It's not a curse. Quite the opposite. It's a gift, an ancient pirate tradition which some ships still maintain. When a young pirate makes his first kill, he or she is given a Blood Captain. As you can see, it's carved in the shape of a man – though," he glanced across to Scrimshaw, "it's clearly no Michelangelo! But the blood is genuine enough. And it's the blood of the ship's captain."

Connor frowned. "This is *your* blood? *You* gave it to me?"

Molucco shook his head. "No," he said. "I don't continue this tradition. This came from my brother. The blood is Barbarro's."

"But why?" Connor said.

"It's an honour," Cate said. "Captain Wrathe and his wife are both acknowledging your bravery and thanking you for saving their son's life."

Connor shook his head. "They're honouring me for killing?"

"It's not as simple as that, Connor. You didn't simply kill that guard. You performed an act of true courage and bravery. You took only what action was necessary to save your comrade . . ."

"Moonshine?" Connor said, laughing in spite of himself. "I don't even *like* Moonshine. In fact, I loathe him."

"All the more reason," said Molucco, "for us to thank you. For putting aside those understandable, personal

361

feelings and acting for the good of your crew." He held the figure out to Connor. "Take it," he said. "Take it, boy, and keep it with you. It will remind you of the day you became a true pirate."

Connor's head was spinning. He had had such romantic ideas about piracy. He had dreamed of captaining his own ship. And, in those dreams, there had been plenty of fighting. He loved the fighting, the bravura display of athleticism and swordsmanship. But not once, not once in those dreams had he stolen another man's life. Not once had he stood and watched as a dark river of blood gushed out of another man's veins. This was not what he had sought. It was not what he wanted.

He looked down at the carving, stained with Barbarro Wrathe's blood. A gift. He had no desire for such a gift. The evil figurine would only be a daily reminder of the single most terrible deed of his young life. As he took hold of it once more, he felt hot tears prick the back of his eyes. He couldn't cry, not in front of them. He closed his eyes. As he did so, he had the clearest image of his sister's face. She was looking at him with an intensity only she could muster. There was no escaping her stare.

"I'm sorry," he told her. "I've done something terrible. I've let you down."

There was no mercy in Grace's eyes. They met his with icy pools of emerald-green as she nodded. "Yes," she said. "Yes, you have."

CHAPTER FORTY

Two Letters

Dear Captain Wrathe,

I'm sorry but I have to go away. I know that it's breaking the articles but I don't know what else to do. I've lied to you and all my friends on board <u>The Diablo</u>. I didn't mean to deceive you. I thought I could make a go of being a pirate but now I know that I was kidding myself all along.

After what happened at the fort, people are acting like I'm some kind of hero. But I'm not any kind of hero. I know what I am but I can't bring myself to write down the word. I can't even find it in me to say it. Cate and Bart told me that I'd come to terms with this in time. Maybe I will, but right now that feels an impossibility. I wouldn't be any use to you if I stayed so it's better I go away and work this out somehow if I can.

I don't know where I'm going. I guess that's kind of the point.

Thanks for everything,

Yours truly,
Connor Tempest

p.s. Cate and Bart – thanks for all you've done for me. You're the best friends I've ever known. I should have written you both letters too, but I don't have time. I have to get away from here. I hope you understand. I hope you know what you both mean to me. C

Connor scanned the note then folded it into an envelope and addressed it "Captain Molucco Wrathe". Next, he took up his second letter and read it a final time.

Dear Grace,

I really don't know why I'm writing to you. It's not like I know how to get this letter to you. But somehow, something's compelling me to put this down on paper so I will go with it.

You never approved of me being a pirate but I was so gung ho, I ignored your concerns. But as usual, you were right. I think I have a talent for burying my head in the sand, for only seeing what's here now. Whereas you, it's like you get the bigger picture. You see further along the road. And I reckon you saw what would happen to me – where this road was leading – long before I did.

Well, in a way you have your wish. I'm leaving <u>The Diablo</u> now and I'm not coming back. I'm no pirate.

What am I? Right now, I only have one answer to that question and it's not an answer I can face, certainly not one I dare share with you.

I'm going away – I don't know where or for how long. There's a lot of ocean out there and I'm sure it's easy to find a patch of it in which to hide.

I hope you are doing well – better than me, anyhow. I feel in my heart that you are. Maybe you chose a better path. Again, I couldn't see beyond my nose. But you've always seen more than me.

Like I said at the beginning, I don't know why I wrote you this letter. It's not like I can send it to you.

365

Think of me kindly. Take care of yourself!

Your brother,
Connor x

Connor picked up the second letter. He folded it in three, then placed it in its envelope and addressed it to Grace. He took the two letters, swung his kitbag over his shoulder and began heading up to the main deck. It was quiet up there. Everyone was getting ready for the night of celebrations ahead. *The Diablo* had moored, alongside *The Typhon*, at a small harbour. The light boats had been lowered into the water.

Connor walked quietly across the deck. Molucco's cabin was shut tight. He slipped the envelope under the captain's door then walked as quickly as possible across the deck. Still unseen, he began descending the ladder down to the pontoon below.

It was as if the light boat was waiting for him to steal it. He really should have apologised for this in his letter. Too late now! Captain Wrathe might already be stumbling through his cabin and picking up the envelope. Connor jumped into the small boat and began unfastening the moorings. Then, he slipped out of the harbour and began his getaway.

Tears were streaming down his eyes as he turned back and saw the twin hulks of the pirate ships. One of them had felt like his home. But that had been a delusion. It had all been one giant delusion.

As he headed out into the open ocean, he had one final task to do. He took the letter addressed to Grace in his hands. Then he ripped through the envelope. He tore it again and again, until its tiny pieces were like confetti, showering over the side of the boat and into the waters below. He watched as his truncated words blurred in front of him, unsure if the seawater was loosening the ink or if it was just the tears in his eyes.

Grace was walking along the corridor when it hit her. She closed her eyes and reached out for the wall, steadying herself against it. Her head was filled with a torrent of water. She closed her eyes, hoping to focus more clearly on the image. It worked.

Now she could see that the water was not as rough as it had seemed at first. Not a raging torrent but merely the ocean.

She could see scraps of something moving within it. Paper. Then she saw the marks on the paper and thought she understood.

I have to bring them together, she thought. *It's some kind of test.* Perhaps Mosh Zu had sent it to her. Her eyes tightly closed, she began scanning the waters for the scraps of paper. As she found each one, she pulled it into the centre of her mind's eye. After a while, she was unable to find any further pieces. That must be it, she thought. Time to assemble the jigsaw!

This was harder than she thought. The motion of the water was not violent but it was strong. Just as she got one scrap of paper into place, the tide threatened to drag another away. No! She wouldn't let it. She knew it was taking all her energy but she was determined. As she brought two pieces of the paper together, she recognised the handwriting. Now, with a terrible jolt, she understood. This was not a test. This was the real thing.

Her head ached with the effort. It was so tempting to open her eyes and relieve the pain for an instant but she knew that if she did that, the vision might be lost to her for ever. She was almost there. The jigsaw of paper scraps had just about been assembled. Now, she simply had to hold them there as she read the letter.

Dear Grace

Just seeing her name written in her brother's distinctive handwriting moved her. He hardly ever wrote letters. She knew this was serious. She read on.

As she read the deep feelings encapsulated in the letter, it became harder and harder to maintain the vision, to keep all the pieces together. But she couldn't give up now. This was too important.

Think of me kindly

She was almost at the bottom of the letter and the pain in her head was searing. It was compounded by her growing sense of dread at what he'd written.

At last, she gave in to the pain in her head and allowed the pieces of the letter to scatter once more. They raced away on the tide, leaving her mind filled only with water. The noise of it was growing louder and louder, the water darker and darker. She felt like she was drowning.

She realised that this must be what was happening to Connor. She had been sent the letter and now she was being given this vision into what he was experiencing. But she had no clue where he was. There was nothing she could do to help him!

The vision of the water gradually diminished. Suddenly everything was quiet. Perfectly quiet and pitch black. The end.

Grace opened her mouth and screamed.

"*No!*"

CHAPTER FORTY-ONE

The Boat on the Water

"How are you feeling now?" Mosh Zu asked, as Grace stepped into the meditation room.

"Calmer," she said. "I'm sorry about before. I lost control."

Mosh Zu shook his head. "You have a very close connection to Connor. When he suffers, you suffer. That's part of what makes you so powerful as a healer. But we need to work with you more so that you can use the power to help him — and others — rather than being consumed by it."

She was a little puzzled by his words. He beckoned her to come and sit with him.

"Think of it in this way. We know that Connor has some kind of emotional burden. It's like a very heavy weight he's carrying. Now think of a heavy object he might conceivably try to lift. Tell me. What are your thoughts?"

Grace searched around the room for ideas. "A table?" she said, with a shrug.

"Very good!" Mosh Zu nodded. "Let us imagine that Connor is struggling to carry a table. He's strong, we know that. But it's not a regular table. It's made from very heavy wood. Maybe even heavier than that. Made of stone. Of course, he is going to struggle with it."

Grace nodded.

"Well," said Mosh Zu. "You want to help him, don't you?"

Grace nodded once more.

"So, tell me, what's the best way to help him carry the table?"

"By taking one end of it," she said, instinctively.

"Exactly! By sharing the load. Not by taking the table out of his hands altogether and transferring the burden entirely to yourself." Mosh Zu's eyes were bright. "Do you understand?"

"Yes, of course. That makes perfect sense."

"It's one of the most important things we must learn as healers," Mosh Zu said. "We cannot carry everyone else's burdens for them. At times, it can be tempting to try, but it makes us ineffective. When we start to swim in other people's emotions, there's always the danger we may drown in them."

"So what *can* we do to help Connor?" Grace asked.

"Oh, there is much," Mosh Zu said. He stood up and padded across the room towards a high counter. He turned and came back bearing a wide, shallow bowl made from beaten copper. He set it down on the floor between them. As he did so, Grace saw that it was filled with water. Next, Mosh Zu removed a small bottle from his pocket and emptied it into the bowl.

"Squid ink," he said, as he dipped his fingers into the bowl and lightly mixed the ink into the rest of the liquid. "We want the surface of the water to be as dark and reflective as possible for this," he explained.

Grace was intrigued.

"And now," Mosh Zu said, drying his hands, "I need your help. We need to ensure that these candles are reflected in the water. Can you help me to move them?"

Together, they walked back and forth across the room, adjusting the positions of the tall candlesticks until the flame of each candle was indeed reflected in the dark pool of water. Looking down, Grace's eyes were tricked for a moment into thinking that she was looking into a bowl of fire.

"And now," said Mosh Zu. "We sit." He settled himself close to the bowl and gestured to Grace. "You sit here," he said. "But make sure you cannot see your own reflection in the water."

She sat down and nodded.

"All right, then," he said. "And now we turn our eyes to the surface of the water and we begin to take deep breaths. In and out. In and out. In and . . ." As he continued to speak, his voice soft and rhythmic, Grace felt her breathing grow deeper and deeper. She knew she was entering a state of profound relaxation. In itself, it felt good, but she knew that there was more to this. This was only the beginning of one of Mosh Zu's journeys.

"That's good, Grace," he said. "Keep your eyes gently lidded. Your vision should not be too fixed, too intent. Keep it on the water but allow it to blur." She adjusted her vision. "And now, simply relax and we shall see what we shall see."

All sense of time was lost to her. She had no sense of how long they had been sitting there, eyes gently focused on the water. But suddenly, she was no longer looking at a dark surface reflecting flames. Instead, she was gazing on a dark sea and at a small boat tossing and turning on it. She must have smiled, because Mosh Zu said, "Yes, I see it too. Now, keep your eyes relaxed and we'll take a closer look."

As he spoke, the image of the boat came closer and closer to them. It was like a camera lens zooming in. Now, they could see that the boat had one sole passenger.

"Connor!" Grace whispered. "You're safe!" She felt relief flood through her body.

"Yes," Mosh Zu said. "We've found him."

"What do we do now?" Grace asked. "Just watch him?"

"For now, yes," said Mosh Zu. "Keep breathing, keep the focus of your eyes soft."

She obeyed his instructions and felt the image of Connor grow crystal clear. She could see his face and it was as easy to read as a book. He looked tired and troubled. His forehead was etched with worry lines and there were dark circles under his eyes. He didn't look as though he had slept in many nights. His eyes were empty, distant.

"He looks in great pain, doesn't he?" Mosh Zu said.

"Yes." Grace nodded, but then steadied her head once more. "But where is he? Is he really on this boat?"

"Oh, yes," Mosh Zu said.

"But why has he left *The Diablo*? What's happened?"

"Sssh," said Mosh Zu. "These are not the questions we must ask if we want to help him. Let's look, instead, more closely at his pain."

"All right," she conceded. "But how?"

"I'm going to dip my hand, very gently, into the water. And I want you to do the same. Very gently though. Try to disturb the surface as little as possible."

Grace watched as Mosh Zu eased his hand into the water. He made hardly a ripple on the dark surface. Carefully, she extended her own hand and did the same. It was harder than it looked. There were a couple of bubbles. She hesitated.

"It's all right, Grace, you're doing fine. And you're nearly there."

Spurred on by his words, she plunged her hand a little lower into the water.

As she did so, she felt a jolt of sensations.

"That's excellent, Grace. The most important thing now is to remain as still as possible. Keep breathing, but try not to move even a muscle. Be as strong as stone but let the sensations wash over you, as if you are a rock in the centre of the ocean."

And truly it felt like a wave of emotions was being unleashed on her.

"Can you feel them, Grace?"

"Yes," she said, focusing intently on keeping as still as possible, as the rogue emotions crashed over her.

"Tell me what you are feeling," Mosh Zu said.

"I feel angry, betrayed, disillusioned."

"Yes," he said, a note of excitement in his voice. "Yes, Grace. What else?"

"I'm drained, so tired and . . . no, wait! I feel guilty. That's bigger than the others. I've done something terrible and I feel *so* guilty."

"This is really excellent," said Mosh Zu.

She was grateful for his praise but this was overshadowed by a deeper concern. "Are those the feelings Connor has?" she asked.

"Yes," he said. "You read them perfectly!"

Reading them was one thing, but Grace had something else on her mind. "But I want to *help* him," she said. "How can I do that?"

"We're getting there," Mosh Zu said. "Now, I'm going to remove my hand to give you more room. Keep your hand under the water. OK?"

Grace nodded.

"Now, I want you to take your hand and place it under

the boat. Very gently. Place it under Connor's boat as if you want to pick it up and carry it out of the water. Be careful, though. Imagine it's a slippery bar of soap that you're lifting out of the bathtub. You must do it as gently as you can. It won't be easy."

She moved her hand into position.

"All right? Lift the boat out of the water."

Grace brought her hand up and was stunned as the image of Connor in his boat rose out of the water's depths, changing from two dimensions into three as it was cradled in her palm like a living toy.

"Keep raising your hand out of the water," Mosh Zu instructed.

She kept raising her hand.

"All right, that's perfect. Now hold it there."

Grace marvelled at what she was seeing. Connor was sitting before her eyes. He was tiny but he was clearly Connor.

"Now ask him what he wants," Mosh Zu said. "Ask him how you can help him. You don't need to say the words out loud. Just look into his eyes and ask the question."

Once more, she followed Mosh Zu's lead. *What do you want, Connor?* she asked. *How can I help you?*

He did not give her a clear answer. She couldn't hear his voice. But something compelled her to the sword he was holding.

"What does he say?" Mosh Zu asked.

"It's not clear," she said.

"No, it might not be. Keep listening. Keep feeling the answer."

She waited. "It's something to do with the sword," she said.

Mosh Zu waited. "If it still isn't clear, then ask him. Ask him, 'Connor, how can I help you with the sword?'"

Once more, she gazed into Connor's eyes. She asked the question.

The answer came to her like a charge of electricity.

"He wants to let it go," she said. "He wants to let it go but something is holding him back. It's as if it's glued to his hands."

"All right," Mosh Zu said. "Then take your other hand and, very gently, try to loosen the sword. Don't pull it away entirely. Just loosen it for him."

Very, very carefully, Grace raised her other hand. She brought her thumb and forefinger to the tiny sword and pulled it gently towards her.

"That's probably enough," Mosh Zu said. "Wait and he'll tell you."

"Yes," she said. The moment she had moved the sword, she had felt a shiver within herself, then a sense of tension easing. Did this feeling emanate from Connor?

"You're doing so well, Grace," said Mosh Zu. "Now, you can lower your hand again and return the boat and Connor to the water. When the boat is safely in the water, you can bring your hand away again."

Grace lowered her hand as carefully as she had raised it.

She returned Connor and his boat to the waters within the bowl. As they dipped below the surface they turned from three dimensions to two once more.

"Now, take your hand from the water," Mosh Zu instructed. "And sit still and watch what happens."

Out on the dark ocean, Connor felt a sudden inrush of energy. He didn't know where it had come from. He had been so tired, his thoughts circling around and around on themselves like wild dogs. But now, suddenly, he had a sense of purpose. He knew exactly what he had to do.

He walked to the side of the boat, holding his sword high in the air. Then he let out a wail that seemed to come deep from inside his very soul and, as the sound broke out across the ocean, he threw the sword out of his hands. He watched it fly through the dark sky, then pierce the water's surface and slip into the void below.

Looking down at his empty hand, he sighed. Throwing away the sword didn't take away the terrible deed he had performed with it. But he felt lighter – as though he had thrown away more than the sword alone. For the first time since the killing, he realised there might be an onward journey.

"He threw away the sword!" Grace said, excitedly.

"Yes," Mosh Zu said, nodding. "You enabled him to do that. I don't think he could have done it without you. Not at this point."

"That's amazing!" Grace said.

Mosh Zu smiled. "You're a healer, Grace. And there are many ways to heal. But you did good! Really good!"

He began to sit up, reaching out for the bowl of water.

"Wait!" she said. "Can't we watch him just a little longer?"

"Best not," Mosh Zu said. "For now, we should let him make his own journey. Remember what I told you before about the table?"

Grace nodded. She understood. Nevertheless, she felt a sudden sense of loss as Mosh Zu lifted the copper bowl and took it to the sink to empty it. As she heard the mixture of water and ink swirl away down the drain, she couldn't help but think of her brother, on the small boat, out there all alone on the dark, dark sea.

Where are you? She couldn't help but ask. *What made you leave* The Diablo? *What is it that you feel so terribly guilty about?*

But this time, there were no answers forthcoming. Whatever connection they had formed was broken for now.

"Travel safe!" she said, without opening her mouth. Then she scrambled to her feet and went to help Mosh Zu reposition the candles.

CHAPTER FORTY-TWO

Magic Night

"Ah, there you are! I've been looking all over for you!"

At his voice, Darcy turned and smiled to see Jez – *her* Jez – walking towards her across the deck. She sighed. Every night, he seemed to grow more handsome. She had fallen for him the very moment he had stepped aboard *The Nocturne* but, on reflection, he had been only a shadow of his current self then. He had bloomed under the spell of her love – and she, no doubt, under his.

"What are you thinking about?" he asked, flashing her his irresistibly cheeky smile.

She grinned back. "Wouldn't you like to know?"

"Oh, yes," he said. "I want to know every one of your secrets, Darcy. I'm a man on a mission!"

"Stop it!" she said, though she never grew tired of hearing his sweet nothings. No, it wasn't fair to describe them that way. This was *the real thing*. She knew it. He was the one she had waited for – her Mr Jetsam. He'd taken his time making his way to her, but it had been worth the long wait.

"You're positively glowing tonight," he said now.

She shrugged prettily and turned around, leaning forward against the guard-rail and letting the delicious ocean breeze rise up and cool her flushed skin. Her sheer chiffon scarf floated out in the breeze. It began unfurling itself loose from her neck.

"Oh!" she said, as it came undone and began floating away.

Not missing a beat, Jez jumped up and caught it in his hands. He wrapped it back around her porcelain-white neck. They both stood looking at each other for a long moment.

"You make me so happy," she said.

"And you me," he said, grinning at her. "I never thought I'd be happy again. You've given me the kiss of life, Darcy Flotsam, and no mistake!"

"Have I?" She leaned forward and planted the daintiest of kisses on the tip of his nose. Then he held her close as she turned and looked out to sea. Glancing out at the dark, star-filled sky, she couldn't quell the excitement she felt. Tonight was a magic night. There was just something in the air. It was on nights such as this that questions were asked and answers were given and lives changed inexorably.

"You've gone all quiet again," he said, his soft voice interrupting her thoughts.

"Just thinking some more," she said.

"Well, how about I give you something new to think about?" he asked.

She felt a shiver at these words. "Go on," she said.

"I have a question for you, Miss Flotsam."

"Do you, Mr Jetsam?"

He grinned at this – he always did when she used her pet name for him. "I was just wondering," he said, "whether you would ever consider leaving *The Nocturne* and coming away with me?"

Here it was, then. Here was the turning point she had dreamed of for so long. *Don't rush this, Darcy*, she thought. *Savour every moment, every sensation.*

"I suppose that tells me your answer is no," he said. His jutting mouth and disappointed eyes made him look like a helpless puppy. In that moment he was more appealing to her than ever before. She couldn't prolong his agony.

She shook her head. "Darling Mr Jetsam, I'll go wherever you want to go. Just the two of us. I never thought I *could* leave *The Nocturne*, but since you arrived here, everything's changed." She gazed at him in wonder. "Why, I think I'd follow you to the very ends of the earth."

"Well," he said. "It wouldn't *quite* be just the two of us. Not at first, anyway."

"No?"

"Oh, don't look so troubled, my sweet Darcy. Look, there's some business I must attend to now, but could you, that is, *would* you be willing to leave tonight?"

"Tonight?" It was so soon. Was she to have no time to plan, no delicious anticipation? Well, if this was how it was to be, *c'est la vie*! He was so romantic, so impetuous. She had waited so long for him. Why wait a moment longer? "Yes," she said. "I'll pack up my things and we shall leave tonight!"

"Good girl!" he said, reaching in his pocket. "This is for you."

"Not another gift. You really shouldn't!" But then she watched – barely believing it – as he dropped to his knee and held the small satin box out towards her. As he opened it, she could scarcely focus on the ring through the blur of her tears. But she knew it would be beautiful. His gifts always were.

"What are *you* doing here? You're not supposed to come to my cabin. You know the rules."

At her voice, Jez grinned. "That's not much of a welcome for your blood partner, now is it?"

"It's the only welcome you're going to get," Shanti said. "Seeing you once a week is more than enough for me these days." Studiously ignoring him, she continued rifling through her wardrobe.

He shook his head. "*Touché*, darling. But whatever's changed? Time was, you couldn't get enough of Jezzie boy."

Shanti frowned and tossed away one blouse, then picked up another. "You really are delusional," she said.

"Oh I'm not under *any* delusions, darling," he said,

coming to stand behind her. "I know exactly what the deal is between us. You brought me back from the brink and I'll always be grateful for that."

She scowled at him as she held the blouse up against herself and appraised her reflection in the mirror. She did look truly beautiful – if she said so herself. Her old colour was back. Her skin was smooth once again, like silk.

"Yes, I'll always be grateful to you, Shanti. But it wasn't a one-sided arrangement, now was it? When the captain brought you back from Sanctuary, you were a dried up old donor, on a fast train to oblivion. It was Jezzie boy who restored you. You were a dessicated old thing then, remember? Not like now! Now, you've certainly got your glow back." She was still appraising her own reflection in the mirror. "And you'd think you might be a little more grateful for that."

"If it's grateful you want," Shanti said, without turning, "then go and seek out that simpering figurehead. She's pathetically grateful for every glance you send her way. But then, if I was a rotten old lump of painted wood, I suppose I might feel that way too— oww!"

She cried out as he grabbed her arm and twisted it savagely back behind her. "Don't!" he hissed in her ear. "Don't talk about my beautiful Darcy that way. A splinter of her is worth ten of you."

In spite of the pain she felt, Shanti laughed. "Oh don't tell me it was all for real! All that time I had you down for playing her like a fool! So, was it authentic vampire *lurve*?"

She laughed once more – a cold, cruel laugh. "Well good luck to you both. I'm sure you'll be very happy together."

"Yes, we will," he said. "It's just a shame you won't be around to see it."

"What?" At his words she tensed up. Suddenly, she was frightened. Instinctively she tried to hide it, but he could sense it.

"Things are about to change around here," he hissed into her ear. "Tonight, everything changes. Big time. I'm going away. And Darcy's coming with me. Others too. We've been making plans."

"I'm very happy for you," she said, seeming to gain some new strength from within. "Well, off you run then, *dearest*. Off you scamper to your new ship. But, if it's all the same with you, I think I'll stay put right here."

"Oh yes," he said, his hand closing tight around her neck, the other spinning her around towards him. "Yes," he repeated, tearing away all obstructions to her chest. "That was always the plan."

Darcy was standing on the deck, a small case at her feet, her favourite evening coat draped over it. Most of her elegant clothes were left hanging in her wardrobe. In the end, it had seemed pointless to pack more than a few things. They were too much a part of her life here – her old life. She was about to begin again. She'd have new things. Beautiful new things. Mr Jetsam would see to that.

"Darcy!"

She glanced up and saw the captain walking towards her. As he passed the ship's sails, they flickered briefly with light but soon fell to darkness again. He seemed tired. Lately, he seemed more tired each time she saw him.

"Captain," she said, shivering. She had been dreading this moment.

"I see your bag is packed," he said. "Are you embarking on a journey?"

She nodded, feeling the tears already sliding down the slope of her nose. "Captain," she sniffed. "Yes, you've been so good to me. But something's happened, something wonderful. And it's time for me to sail away."

He seemed to smile at her. "Why are you crying, child? It sounds as if this new journey is a cause for great happiness."

"Oh yes!" she said, nodding. How could she ever have doubted that the captain would have been pleased for her? He had always taken such good care of her.

"Of course, we'll miss you," he began. "You know you're so much more than the ship's figurehead."

But his whisper was drowned out by the first scream. Then the second. And the third. They overlapped with each other, a tortuous symphony. A fourth, fifth and sixth scream followed. Then footsteps, pummelling the deckboards.

The captain and Darcy turned to find the deck suddenly swarming with a crowd. The donors!

"Captain!" one rasped, his clothes torn, his chest

exposed and dripping blood. "Why did you let this happen?" Having released the words, the donor fell to the deck, bringing his hand to the gash.

In their panic, his companions surged over him, towards the captain.

"We're being attacked!" another cried, his face a picture of terror. His shirt was torn too, and spattered with blood. His skin was pale as milk.

There were fresh screams and more of the donors rushed out onto the deck. They all looked like they had staggered off a battlefield. Their clothes were torn, the puncture wounds evident on each and every chest. There were further signs of struggle in the streaks of blood on their faces and arms.

"Not attacked," one of them cried, "massacred. They're trying to kill us. They're taking too much blood, with no care."

"I don't understand," the captain said.

As he spoke, the panicked cries of the donors grew louder, rising into a horrible cacophony. This was accompanied by fresh screams. The donors drew on the last of their dwindling energy to race to the edge of the deck, flinging themselves upon the guard-rails and hovering in the darkness.

"Let's jump for it!" one cried. "It's our only hope!"

"Don't be stupid!" another cried. "You'll drown! The captain will help us." His eyes turned plaintively towards the captain.

"Yes," shouted another, at his side. "The captain always helps us." Her eyes too turned towards the captain.

Darcy herself now looked at the captain. He would lead them out of this crisis, just as he had led them out of every crisis before.

But the captain was frozen and his words gave little reassurance. "Stop speaking! Stop speaking all at once. Please!"

Darcy watched all this in terror. And the thing that terrified her the most was the sudden sense that the captain was not in control. She had never seen him this way before. He was always so composed, always in charge. Now he seemed . . . He seemed vulnerable. She couldn't bear to watch him.

Turning away, she saw that a fresh crowd of people had arrived on the deck. The renegade Vampirates! Their eyes were aflame and their lips and teeth smeared with the blood they'd taken before the donors had broken free. There was no question that their hunger was still strong. They were on the hunt for more blood.

Now the donors' screams grew louder and more urgent. More climbed up onto the guard-rails. One did jump into the ocean. Another fell after him, though it was hard to tell if this was an accident or intentional.

The captain, who appeared to have gathered his strength now, held up a gloved hand and addressed the renegades. "Stop!" he said. "What have you done? What on earth have you done?"

"We were hungry," came a voice from the heart of the crowd. "We were peckish so we helped ourselves to a bit of what we fancied."

"Who speaks to me so wickedly?" said the captain, his whisper sailing about the deck like an icy wind. "Who rebels against my rules? Show yourself!"

But Darcy had already recognised the voice. It came as no surprise to her when Jez Stukeley stepped out from the crowd. By then, her heart had already been smashed into a million little pieces.

"You!" the captain said, evidently surprised. "You, whom I brought back from the depths?"

"Erm yeah, that's right," Jez said, "only you missed out the part where you told Connor and his pirate chums to set fire to me!"

"You survived. What does it matter now?" the captain said.

"Well, anyway – no hard feelings," Jez said. "I bounced back. I'm a resilient little fella, me."

The captain shook his head. "You . . . you've brought terror to this ship, to this community. You've made a mockery of our world. You've brought fear and panic where there was calm. You've broken the bonds of trust. You're no better than . . ." He broke off, seemingly unable to even speak the name.

"Maybe I *have* shaken things up a bit," Jez said. "But I wasn't the first. And, as you can see, I'm certainly not the last. Isn't that right, guys?"

The other vampires nodded and turned their angry gaze upon the captain. Darcy wondered if they might actually attack him. She felt fear slice through her.

"We have a message for you, oh Captain, my captain," Jez said. "Here, give us a leg-up, would ya?" With that, two of the others hoisted him onto their shoulders. "That's better," he said. Then, from this lofty position, he looked down upon the captain and began chanting, "Need more blood! Need more blood!"

The others joined in. "Need more blood! Need more blood! Need more . . ."

The chant was the most horrible thing Darcy had ever heard. It was a hiss like fire. The tight crowd of vampires were like a horrible fire-breathing creature, with Jez – *no, she must think of him only as Stukeley now* – with Stukeley the creature's eyes and tongue.

By no means was the entire crew involved in the rebellion but there must have been thirty or more who were. Before, the biggest revolt aboard the ship had come from just three vampires. This was something else altogether. Darcy watched Stukeley as he led the chant. She remembered, hours earlier, thinking that this was going to be the night everything changed. She had been right, but not in the way she had hoped. Her silly little dreams were ripped to shreds now. This was *not* a night of magic, it was a night of evil. As she pondered this sudden, cataclysmic change, Stukeley caught her eye and grinned. She turned away, feeling sick to the core.

"Need more blood! Need more blood! Need more . . ." The hissing continued.

"Stop!" the captain said. "Stop! There will be no more blood taking aboard this ship. Not until the next Feast."

"All right then," Jez said, with disarming acquiescence. "Then I guess we're going to leave you now. I think we're all a bit bored here, to tell you the truth. No offence and all that."

"You know the rules," the captain said, his whisper as cold as steel. "Either obey them or—"

"Or what?" came a fresh cry. The voice roared out across the waters. The captain turned. Darcy turned. The weakened, terrified donors clinging to the guard-rail turned. The mob of blood-hungry rebel vampires turned.

They all saw the same thing. A ship, sailing up alongside *The Nocturne*. Another galleon. And, on the deck, standing prouder and taller than ever, a face from their past. A face from all their pasts – and now, perhaps, from their future too.

Sidorio.

He waved at the captain.

The captain stared back, shaking his head. "I thought you were gone for good."

Sidorio bared his teeth in a grin. "Let's save ourselves some time here, shall we? You're never going to destroy me, so you might as well stop trying and get used to having me around."

"Never," said the captain. "While there is breath in my body, I will stop at nothing to eliminate you."

Darcy smiled. There was strength once more in the captain's whisper.

Sidorio shrugged. "Sounds like someone's a sore loser," he called.

Stukeley laughed at that. And his laughter proved infectious. Darcy clamped her hands over her ears. Hearing them making a laughing stock out of the captain, after *everything* he had done for them, was just too much to bear.

"Nice work, Stukeley!" Sidorio called. "I knew you were the man for the job! You have the charm of the devil! Now, let's not waste any more time. You've all been waiting far too long as it is. Come, friends. Come to me! Your new ship awaits. It's only temporary, mind you. We'll be getting something bigger soon!"

As he spoke, he beckoned them to him. Stukeley led the way. He stood on the guard-rail and launched himself high in the night air, somersaulting and landing on the deck beside the renegade captain.

"You see that?" Sidorio cried to the rest. "You can do that too! Each and every one of you. Come on, give it a go. You don't know the true extent of your powers!" He pointed at the captain. "He's deprived you of blood, kept you weak like pet dogs, when you should run wild like wolves. Now you will learn what I have learned. That the more blood we take, the stronger we become. The things we were told to reject are the very things we should embrace!"

"No," the captain said, shaking his head. "No, this is all lies. You'll see!" His cape momentarily flickered with light.

"Who do you believe?" Sidorio asked. "The one who hides behind the mask; the one who cowers in his cabin; the one who whispers like a frightened child? Or me?"

With that, the renegade vampires moved towards the edge of the ship and began launching themselves into the air.

"That's it!" Sidorio cried, obviously delighted. "That's it! And this, this is only the beginning!"

Darcy turned to the captain, waiting for him to do something more to stop this. He seemed frozen. His cape was dark now. She watched in horror as they each jumped ship, every last one of the rebels.

Until only she and the captain remained on the deck of *The Nocturne*. Only them and the donors who clung onto the guard-rail, still paralysed with fear.

On board the other, nameless, galleon, the rebels were in a high state of excitement. Stukeley pushed past them to the guard-rail and called out to her. "Aren't you coming then, Darcy? Won't you join us?"

She shook her head. This time she had no tears. She wouldn't let him see her cry.

"Are you sure?" he called. "We could have a beautiful future, you and me!"

"*Beautiful?* You don't know the meaning of the word!" she cried angrily.

Aboard the rebel ship, they were laughing at her. "Don't

393

mind her," she heard one call to Stukeley. "She's only a plank of wood!"

"Yes," cried another. "If you've got a thing for driftwood, there's plenty more where that came from!"

She'd had enough. She wasn't going to stand here and take these insults. She turned to the captain but he seemed too stunned to speak. His gloved hands were crossed over his chest.

Looking back across the deck, she saw more Vampirates arrive on the scene. Her first thought was that the rebellion would continue but she was heartened to see that these crewmates were as shocked and bewildered as her. Their eyes were clear and they showed no traces of having taken blood tonight.

"What *happened* here?" one asked.

Darcy turned to the captain, waiting for him to pull the crew together, just as he always did. But he seemed to have run out of words. He stood, still as stone, staring at the other ship. Urged on by Sidorio, the renegade Vampirates shouted abuse as they sailed away.

Darcy turned and found the deck of *The Nocturne* crowded once more. The arrival of more Vampirates had clearly terrified the donors, who clung frantically to the edges of the ship. But the danger had passed.

"It's all right," she called, her eyes taking in the donors and the vampires. "It's all right. There was a terrible scene up here and some of the crew have left us. But we're better off without them."

She saw the nods from across the deck.

"OK," she said. "Let's get back to our cabins." She turned to the donors. "Come on, let go of the guard-rails. No one's going to hurt you now. You are quite safe."

She watched as, somewhat to her surprise, the donors began to obey her instructions. The remaining vampires helped them through, shaking their heads and offering comfort and reassurance.

At last, only Darcy and the captain remained on the deck. He was drawn into himself, still looking out to sea, though Sidorio's ship had already sailed off, deep into the night. Darcy reached out her hand to his arm. "Was that all right, Captain?" she asked. "Did I tell them the right thing?"

He waited a time before speaking. "Yes, Darcy. Thank you."

"Why didn't you do something?" she asked. "To try to stop them."

There was a moment of silence. Then the captain's head dropped lower and his whisper was so faint it was barely audible.

"I tried, Darcy." His whisper was growing faint. "I tried, but I didn't have the strength."

"But you . . ." She was almost speechless. "You never fail us."

"I'm growing weak, Darcy." His voice was distant. "I don't know how much time is left."

"No!" she said. "I'll help you. Just tell me what to do."

"I don't know," he said. "I don't have the answers this time."

Darcy watched in horror as the Captain keeled over and slumped on the deck, his cape splayed out around him. There was a brief spark of light in the cape. Then darkness.

"It's over," he whispered. "It's all over now."

Terrified, Darcy looked up at the sails. They too were utterly devoid of light.

CHAPTER FORTY-THREE
Return to Pirate Academy

The sun was setting in a blood-red sky as Connor sailed towards the stone arch marking the boundary of the Pirate Academy. Already, the large torches had been lit beneath it, their flames licking the stone and illuminating the academy maxim:

Plenty and Satiety,
Pleasure and Ease,
Liberty and Power.

Only a couple of months before, he had sailed through the arch for the first time and asked Cheng Li the meaning of "satiety". "Taking everything you want, and then everything else besides," she had said with a smile. Remembering that moment, it seemed a lifetime away. He had been a child then – full of excitement at what the

Academy had to offer him. During his days at the Academy, he had been flattered by the staff – the headmaster especially – into thinking that a career as a great pirate lay ahead of him. Now, those dreams had been torn to shreds. So much had changed. Around him and within him.

The maxim promised such a happy life as a pirate – a life of infinite wealth and pleasure but also power and freedom. It all sounded great in abstract but the one thing the maxim omitted to tell you was the price you had pay. Oh yes, all those riches could be yours, if you could only resign yourself to the act of killing. No, not even *resign* yourself, but learn to embrace it. Kill. Kill. Kill. Again and again and again.

The bright crimson sky was a livid reminder of the blood spraying from his victim's wound. *Don't go there*, he thought, closing his eyes. But, as usual, that only made it worse. Inside his head, the scene was more vivid still – like a loop of film, ready at a moment's notice to play over and over. He opened his eyes again, grateful to see that the sunset was fading fast and darkness drawing out the sting of the red.

He sailed on, gazing up the hill at the Academy buildings. The windows were bright with light against the dark sky and he could see the silhouettes of the students and teachers moving about inside – on their way to and from dinner, no doubt, then back for the final lessons of the day. He had better wait a while before landing the boat and making his way across the lawns. Wait until the final bell was rung and the weary students crashed in their dormitories.

As he sailed towards the dock, seeking out a place to wait under the cover of the willow trees, he was assailed by memories of his brief time at Pirate Academy. He remembered his first meeting with Commodore Kuo and his first glimpse of the gallery of swords in the Rotunda, or "Octopus" as the kids had nicknamed it. He thought of his own sword – now rusting at the bottom of the ocean. Knowing his luck, it had probably speared a dolphin on its way down to the seabed. He remembered the classes – Combat Workshop and SSM – the dawn run led by Captain Platonov. The crunch of the gravel underfoot and the salt tang of the early morning air. The sense of belonging he'd felt jogging through the Academy grounds, with Jacoby and Jasmine at his side. Jacoby Blunt, his new best mate . . . or so he'd thought. But Jacoby had betrayed him, urged on by the headmaster. He thought back to the staged fight on the "Lagoon of Doom", where Jacoby had tried to wound him for real. Jacoby had bottled it when push came to shove. Connor wondered if that had sealed his fate at the Academy. The Pirate Federation wasn't looking for protégées who bottled it.

It had been a strange and confusing time for him but, although it had ended badly, Connor still couldn't help but feel a certain excitement about the place. The sense of energy and optimism was so tangible here you could almost reach out and touch it, holding it in your hands like the abundant pomegranates which ripened in the Academy's fertile soil. Kids came here with dreams of being great pirates. Kids like those in Captain Quivers' Knots class, who had gazed wide-eyed at Connor and Grace, bombarding them with questions about what it was like to sail on a real pirate ship. Then, he had spoken with enthusiasm about life aboard *The Diablo*. Now, he might answer their questions very differently. "*Forget about your knots and your navigation skills,*" he'd say. "*Forget about niceties like thinking up names for your ship and sewing your version of the skull and classbones. Just focus on one question. Are you prepared to kill? That's really all there is to it.*" All things considered, it was probably not a good idea to crash Captain Quivers' Knots class during his return visit and share this newfound wisdom.

Suddenly, Connor heard voices, laughter. Instantly, he ducked down, low in the boat, then raised himself cautiously so he could look over the side. Between the willow branches, the garden lanterns illuminated two figures, racing down to the water's edge. As they came to a standstill, Connor's heart sank. It was Jacoby Blunt and Jasmine Peacock. Of all the people to come across! They mustn't see him. He slipped back into the boat, hoping that they would continue on their way. They were quiet for a moment and all he could hear was a strange rustling sound. Then more laughter. Then a definite splash, followed by a cry.

"I've done it! Now it's your turn!" It was Jacoby's voice. No question. He was in the water – alarmingly near Connor's boat, by the sounds of it. "Come on, Jasmine. A dare's a dare!"

"Is it cold?" Connor recognised Jasmine's voice and had to fight hard not to steal a sneaky glimpse at the prettiest girl at Pirate Academy.

"It's fine once you're in and move about a bit," Jacoby called, over some more splashes.

"OK – here I *cooooooooooooome*!"

Another splash and then a squeal and lots more laughter.

"You're a liar, Jacoby Blunt! It's *freeeeeeeeezing*!"

"Come for a swim, then. You'll soon warm up."

Connor's heart was thudding. *Don't swim this way*, he willed them. *Swim out into the harbour.*

"Race you to the willows!" Jacoby called.

Great! Just great! Now, it was only a matter of time. Connor lay there trying to decide what to do. There was no time to sail further along the dock. Any movement would only alert them more quickly to his presence. The best plan he could come up with was to just lie there, keeping himself and the boat as still as possible. That way, there was a chance – albeit a slim one – that they'd swim off in blissful ignorance.

"*Yessss!* The winner!" Connor heard Jacoby's voice cry out. He must have reached the willows.

"Not fair! You started swimming before I was ready."

"Oh Jasmine, that's so lame!"

"Rematch! First back to the dock."

Yes! Connor could have punched the air.

"Wait a minute! Is that a boat?"

"Looks like it."

"What's it doing here? There are no mooring points here."

The next thing Connor knew, he was looking up as Jacoby Blunt's square shoulders and inquisitive face loomed over the side of the boat. Connor lay there, unsure what to do, as Jacoby pulled himself up into the boat and landed, dripping wet, on Connor.

"*Whaaat?*" Jacoby reeled in confusion.

Connor pushed Jacoby's slippery body him away from him.

"Connor!"

"Hello, Jacoby."

"What are *you* doing here? You're the last person I was expecting . . ."

Suddenly Connor realised that Jacoby was stark naked. He turned his head. "Could you . . .?" Embarrassed, he began waving his hands. "Could you?"

"What? Oh yes!" Suddenly Jacoby realised too and looked around for something to cover his embarrassment with. "Do you have, er, anything?"

His eyes averted, Connor reached around the bottom of the boat and found a spare flag. He held it out.

"Thanks," Jacoby said, fastening it around his waist. "OK, the coast is clear."

Opening his eyes, Connor was relieved to see that Jacoby had wrapped the flag around himself like a sarong.

"Connor!" said Jasmine, her face bobbing up over the side of the boat. He assumed she must be naked too by the way she was careful to remain submerged in the water.

"Hi Jasmine," he said. In spite of himself, he smiled. "So, when did you two start skinny-dipping together?"

"Oh, you know, it just kind of . . ." Jasmine blustered.

"It was a dare!" Jacoby announced. "She said she'd do it if I did."

"I see," said Connor.

"So," said Jacoby, sitting down amiably in the boat. "What brings you back to the ol' Academy, bro?"

Bro? Did Jacoby not remember how they'd parted company last time? Or was he just unremittingly cheerful? Connor wasn't sure.

"Yes, Connor," said Jasmine. "We didn't think we'd ever see you again. Not here, at least."

"I had to come back," he said. "I have to talk to Cheng Li about something." He sighed.

"Sounds serious," said Jasmine.

"Yeah," said Jacoby. "I've got to say, Connor, you're looking pretty rough, ol' buddy."

Connor hung his head. Seeing them only reminded him further how complicated his life had become. "Things haven't been going so well for me," he said.

"What's up?" asked Jacoby.

"The thing is," Connor said, "I'm not sure I can trust you."

Jacoby nodded. "I know. I know. After last time. Of course you'd feel that way. But I was your friend, Connor. I know I let you down but I was your friend and, like I told you before you went away, I'd do anything to make things right with you."

Connor looked into Jacoby's eyes, weighing up his decision. Jacoby looked as innocent as a puppy dog. It was hard to believe he had a bad bone in his body. Even so, he'd done the headmaster's dirty work for him.

"He means it," Jasmine said, imploring Connor with her bewitching eyes. "He's always talking about how he regrets what he did. How he'd do anything to regain your trust."

Connor turned back to Jacoby and made his decision.

"All right," he said. "I need you both to help me. I don't want to go into detail, though. Not yet. I just need to get to Cheng Li's rooms. But no one else must know I'm here. You understand?"

Jacoby nodded. "That's so straightforward, we don't even need a cunning plan." He smiled. "Seriously, Connor. This doesn't even register on the favourometer. We'll get you up there in no time. Just let us get some clothes on."

"Now that's the best idea you've had," said Connor, grinning. "Your abs are giving me a serious inferiority complex."

*

Once Jacoby and Jasmine had quickly towelled off and dressed, the three of them made their way up the hill towards the sprawl of Academy buildings. Jacoby strode ahead, with Connor keeping to the shadows and Jasmine covering the rearguard.

"Watch out!" Jacoby suddenly hissed. "Captain Quivers at two o'clock."

"Jacoby!" came Lisabeth Quivers' distinctive cut-glass voice. "Jacoby Blunt? Is that you?"

"What ho," he cried jauntily, pushing Connor into a nearby rhododendron bush and grabbing Jasmine by the hand.

"Ah, Jasmine. What are you both doing out here?"

"Why, Captain Quivers," said Jacoby. "You make it sound like there's something wrong with taking a walk around these fine gardens on a beautiful night with a lovely young lady."

Captain Quivers gave a light laugh. "Nothing wrong with that. Nothing wrong at all," she said.

"What about you?" Jacoby persisted, leading them both away from the rhododendron.

"Me? I always take a post-prandial stroll," she said.

Jacoby grinned. "I have no idea what that means," he said. "But it sounds lovely."

"It means 'after-dinner'," said Captain Quivers. "It's a great shame they didn't include Latin on the curriculum here. I've always found it rather useful." She sighed. "Anyway, I'll let you two on your way. You look wet,

Jasmine. Was there, perhaps, a spot of localised rain on the dockside?" With a little nod and an enigmatic smile, the eccentric teacher continued on her merry way.

When she was out of range, Connor darted across the path to rejoin Jacoby and Jasmine.

"I think the coast is clear now," Jacoby said. "But we'll walk over to Mistress Li's quarters with you, just in case."

Straying from the gravel path, they headed straight across the dark, manicured lawns towards the building which housed Cheng Li's rooms.

Her light was on and they could see her working away at her desk, in front of the window. She was intent on something or other, scribbling away furiously with her distinctive pen.

"Mission accomplished!" Jacoby said, placing his hand on Connor's shoulder.

"Good luck!" Jasmine said, planting a small kiss on his cheek. Her touch was as light as a butterfly's but it swept through him like a wave. It was a good thing he was only making a passing visit here. Otherwise things could get complicated.

"We'll leave you to it," Jacoby said, already backing away. "But if you ever need anything . . ."

"Yes." Connor nodded, his eyes fixed on the window ahead.

"It was good seeing you again, Connor," said Jasmine, turning away and following Jacoby back to the path. "Look after yourself!"

Connor stood there for a moment, watching Cheng Li, wondering if this was such a good idea after all. Then he stepped forward and lifted his hand to tap on the window. As he did so, she looked up. Never one to give anything away, she registered neither fear nor surprise. Instead, she smiled, set down her ink pen and, with a neat flick of her fingers, beckoned him inside.

CHAPTER FORTY-FOUR

Collapse

"Let me in! Let me in! Please, let me in!"

The young woman threw herself at the gates, her cries subsiding into sobs.

"Who are you?" asked the guard.

"I'm Darcy Flotsam," she said. "I come from *The Nocturne*. The captain . . . the captain has collapsed. He needs Mosh Zu Kamal's help."

The guard opened the gates and Darcy ran through them. She ran right past the guard and into the courtyard, crashing into a young man and his pushcart. The two of them, and the cart, tumbled to the ground. The cart had been loaded with baskets and these flew across the courtyard.

"Are you all right?" Olivier asked, helping Darcy up.

"No!" she cried. "No, I'm not all right! I need your help. I need the help of Mosh Zu Kamal!"

"All right," Olivier said. "You've come to the right place." Seeing the urgency in her eyes, he dropped the pushcart. "Come with me!" he said, taking her hand. Over his shoulder, he called to the guard. "Luka, please put the pushcart away, rescue what you can from the baskets and saddle up two of the mules. Fast as you can!"

Luka nodded, springing into action, as Olivier raced away with Darcy.

"I was here once, long ago," Darcy said as they stopped running and slowed to a fast stride down the corridor towards Mosh Zu's rooms.

Olivier nodded. "And since then you've been travelling aboard *The Nocturne*?"

"Yes," she said. "The captain's been so good to me. So good to all of us. I can't bear to think . . ."

"Try to stay calm," Olivier said. "You need to tell Mosh Zu what's happened. Look, his rooms are just ahead."

The door was ajar and, knocking briefly, Olivier pushed it open. He saw Mosh Zu and Grace beginning, or perhaps finishing, a meditation. They broke off and rose to their feet as the others entered the room.

"I'm sorry to interrupt," Olivier said.

"It's all right," Mosh Zu stepped forward. "Darcy Flotsam." He smiled warmly at her. "Welcome back to Sanctuary."

"Darcy!" Grace exclaimed. She ran to hug her friend. "How good to see you!"

"Oh Grace, it's good to see you too!" She glanced up at

Mosh Zu. "And you as well, Mr Kamal, of course! But I'm not here on a social visit. I have terrible news. Simply terrible!"

"Sit down," Mosh Zu said, helping Darcy to a chair. "Have you come up the mountainside alone?"

Darcy nodded. "I had to. I had to! The captain couldn't. Oh, it's so horrible. Just so horrible!"

"Can we get you some tea?" Mosh Zu asked. "Something to restore you after this journey?"

Darcy shook her head. She looked on the verge of collapsing into tears again but managed to stop herself. "I must tell you what has happened," she said.

"Yes," said Mosh Zu. "In your own time."

"There's been a rebellion on *The Nocturne*. Not just one or two Vampirates this time. It was bigger, much bigger, than that. Thirty or more of them. Sidorio set it all up. He sent one of his . . . one of his lieutenants, I suppose you'd say, onto the ship. Jez . . . Stukeley . . ."

At his name, Darcy and Grace exchanged a look. Grace instantly realised the depths of Darcy's pain.

"He came on board the ship and pleaded with the captain to help him. The captain made him welcome and we all thought Jez was a good . . . well, a good guy. He was very charming. I was taken in by him. I was so stupid! It seems all the time he was talking to other members of the crew, seeing which of the vampires were most likely to rebel, planting seeds of discontent in their weak heads, telling them about this other ship where things would be different."

410

Mosh Zu shook his head grimly. "I feared this day would come. But I hadn't expected it so soon." Grace shivered. It must be a grave threat indeed to have taken both the captain and Mosh Zu by surprise.

"It all came to a head tonight," Darcy continued. "Jez . . . I'm sorry, Stukeley – Stukeley killed his donor, Shanti—"

"Shanti is *dead*?" Grace was deeply shocked. There was no love lost between her and the donor but still, it was a terrible jolt to think of her as dead.

"Killed for her blood. And another twenty of the donors, massacred by their own blood partners. Others escaped with bad wounds. They came up onto the deck. I was there with the captain. At first, we didn't understand. It was just awful. Then the Vampirates followed, the ones Stukeley had recruited. You could see they'd taken too much blood. They said terrible, vicious things to the captain." She took a deep breath. "And then this other ship pulls up alongside . . ."

"Sidorio!" Grace said.

"Yes." Darcy nodded. "The exiled Lieutenant Sidorio. He shouts out to the others to come and join him. And so they do, flying through the air to him, like he's put a trance on them or something. It was one of the worst things I've ever seen, and I've seen plenty."

"And the captain?" Mosh Zu asked.

"That's the very worst of it," Darcy said. "I thought the captain would take charge. But it's like he's been wounded, very deeply. He seems so weak. He collapsed on the deck. He's barely spoken a word since. He told me to bring the ship here . . ."

"*You* navigated the way here?" Grace asked.

Darcy nodded. Grace was at once tremendously proud of her friend and now even more deeply concerned for the captain.

"He gave me the directions, but when we arrived, he was too weak to climb up here, so I came alone."

"The other Vampirates," Mosh Zu said now, "the ones who remain on the ship. Is there any danger that they will rebel too? That they might try to harm the captain?"

Darcy shook her head. "No," she said. "No, they are looking after him. They love the captain. We all love the captain. The rebels are gone. It will be a better ship now. If only . . . if only you can help him."

"Yes," Mosh Zu said. "Of course we will." He turned from Darcy. "Olivier, take Dani and go and fetch the captain. Saddle up the mules!"

"Already done," Olivier said, turning and running out of the room.

Her story out, her work done, Darcy slumped back in the chair, utterly exhausted. Grace went over and held her. Darcy's body felt limp with exhaustion.

"Darcy Flotsam," Mosh Zu said. "You have been a real hero tonight."

"I only did what I had to to help," she said.

Mosh Zu shook his head, "you did more than that, Darcy. You may just have saved the captain from the end. Thank you!" Now, he turned to Grace. "I think Darcy should rest. Perhaps you would take her to your room and make her comfortable? Some berry tea might be a good idea too."

Grace nodded. "No problem."

"Thank you, Grace. I'm going to prepare the healing chamber for the captain. We may need to act very fast when he gets here. Once you've settled Darcy, come back to me if you will. I'd be grateful for your help."

"Yes," Grace said, nodding. Then she took Darcy's hand. "Come on," she said. "Let's get you somewhere you can rest."

When Grace returned to Mosh Zu's rooms, she found him busy in the healing chamber, lighting candles and strewing the edges of the room with sweet-smelling herbs.

"How is Darcy?" he asked, turning as Grace entered.

"She's sleeping now," Grace said. "I gave her a little tea and we talked for a bit. Then she quickly fell asleep."

"Good," said Mosh Zu. "It's what she needs after her ordeal."

"She did good tonight, didn't she?" Grace said.

Mosh Zu nodded. "I think she surprised herself," he said. "But not me."

"Nor me," said Grace. "I always knew she had it in her."

She glanced around the room, her eyes taking in the

413

long bench on which the captain would lie for the diagnosis. She felt a sudden panic. "Do you think you can save him?" she asked.

"I must be honest with you," Mosh Zu said, "I just don't know. I won't know what I'm dealing with until he arrives."

Grace shuddered. "You said that he was in danger," she said. "You said that a new time was coming and that he needed to be stronger for it."

"Yes," Mosh Zu said. "But even I hadn't realised how quickly things were going to change."

The preparations complete, they walked out of the healing chamber into Mosh Zu's meditation room.

As they did, they heard sounds out in the corridor.

"Is that them?" Grace asked. "Are they back already?"

They stepped out into the corridor and found Olivier striding ahead, while three of the others carried the captain. Grace could hardly bear to look. Just the sight of the captain's cloaked body, slumped over their shoulders, was terrifying to her. He looked so weak. So near the end.

"Good work," Mosh Zu said. "Bring him to the healing chamber."

Grace watched as they carried him away. She lingered in the corridor. It was then that she heard a bell. It was the tiniest of sounds but as her ear tuned into it, she heard it more and more clearly. It was Lorcan's bell – the one which sat on his nightstand in case he needed help.

She turned to Mosh Zu. He nodded. "It's all right, Grace. Go to him. See what he wants and report back to me." She nodded and set off. "Wait!" Mosh Zu called after her, stopping her in her tracks. "One thing, Grace. Whatever's wrong with him, don't tell him about the captain, you understand?"

She nodded, then turned and began running. The ringing of the bell was growing more and more urgent. What fresh trouble was he in? Had he sensed the chaos happening on the floor above? Had his wound somehow deepened? She couldn't bear to think of him suffering more. But she had to put all such thoughts out of her mind. She gritted her teeth and ran along the corridor down to his room.

She passed the rec room. Was Johnny inside? She saw the chessboard set up for a game but her brief glimpse indicated no sign of Johnny. She didn't have time to go in and look. The bell rang again. She had to get to Lorcan, to save him from whatever new hurt he was feeling.

At last, she made it to his door and pushed it open.

"Lorcan! I came as quickly as I could. It's me, Grace."

He was sitting up in bed. As she entered the room, he let the bell fall from his hand. It landed on the bedclothes, next to his torn bandages.

"I can see who it is, Grace," he said with a smile. "I can see exactly who it is."

"You mean?" She couldn't believe her ears.

"Hasn't your hair grown long since I last had a proper look at you! Very pretty!"

"Oh, Lorcan," she said, rushing to embrace him. "You can see me! You can see me!"

"Yes," he said, taking her hand. "And now I think I finally understand that old expression – a sight for sore eyes."

CHAPTER FORTY-FIVE

The Mentor

Connor stepped into Cheng Li's room and immediately ducked out of the light. "Can you close the shutters?" he asked. "I don't want to be seen."

Without missing a beat, Cheng Li drew down the shutters. "I can dim the lights too, if you feel that's necessary," she said.

"I just don't want anyone to know I'm here," Connor said.

"I'll try not to take that personally," she said, staring intently at him. "I must say, you're the very last person I expected to walk into my study tonight."

He stared back at her, remembering the last time he had seen her, shortly after his fight with Jacoby on the Lagoon of Doom. He had been angry with Cheng Li. He had felt betrayed by her. She and Commodore Kuo had toyed with him — with his ambitions and his emotions. He remembered the words she had spoken back then. "*You may not like me very much at the moment but there are things you don't understand.*"

"What are you thinking about?" she asked him now.

"The last time we met," he answered.

She nodded. "You were angry with me then, Connor," she said, matter-of-factly. "Tell me, are you still angry?"

He shook his head. "No, not with you." It was true. Somehow the issue of whether or not she had betrayed him back then was of little consequence now.

"Good," she said. "But just for the record, there *was* no dark and devious plan to maim you. All we were doing was testing your fighting skills, seeing what you were made of. Commodore Kuo thought – indeed, he still thinks – that you'd be a great asset to the Pirate Federation."

"Yes," he said. "I see that now." It didn't mean he liked it one bit, but he accepted what she was saying as the truth.

"And, in fact, it did tell us what you were made of," Cheng Li said. "You not only proved your ability at combat. You also showed how important loyalty and honesty is to you." She smiled. "You might say *you* taught *us* a lesson."

Connor was a little taken aback, both by Cheng Li's words and her smile. She was so changable. Every time he met her again after a separation, she seemed to have shed one skin and evolved into something just a little different. It was impossible to predict quite what she'd be, where she'd go, next. It made her fascinating and not a little dangerous.

"Are we done with the past then?" she asked.

He nodded. "Yes." He had much more important things to talk to her about now. If only he could find a way to begin.

She smiled once more. "Well, whatever's brought you here, Connor Tempest, it's good to see you."

Connor was still searching for the right words. But glancing around the room, he found himself distracted – drawn into Cheng Li's world. It was, in many ways, a welcome distraction. He had been wrestling with his inner demons for a long time now. It was good to be thrown into someone else's world – a world where, as usual, there was so much going on. Looking about the room, there were piles of paper everywhere – jottings, charts, notes pinned onto the wall and piled up in stacks on the floor, table and sofa. Organised chaos – *very* organised chaos.

"It looks like you're busy," he said, indicating the papers.

"That's an understatement," she said. "You're lucky to catch me. I'm about to take a week's leave. I have a business trip tomorrow. Well, to be more accurate, a shopping trip."

A shopping trip? This didn't sound at all like the Cheng Li Connor knew.

He raised his eyebrows in surprise. "Commodore Kuo's giving you a week's leave from the Academy to go *shopping*? I'm surprised the Academy can even spare you for a week."

Cheng Li leaned back against her desk. "They're soon going to have to spare me for a lot longer than that. I'm leaving the Academy, Connor."

"But you've only just come back here!"

"So I move fast. Get over it! You know me, Connor. I'm ambitious. This was only ever a temporary teaching post. A stop-gap, really. Besides, the Pirate Federation prefers Academy staff to have been captains." She paused. "Can I get you some tea?"

Suddenly, Connor put together the jigsaw of papers strewn around the room – the charts, the plans, the pile of CVs right under his nose.

"You're going to be a captain, aren't you?" he said. "The Federation's giving you your own ship!"

Cheng Li nodded, unable to keep the smile from spreading across her face.

But Connor didn't need to see her smile to know how happy she must be at this news. It was the goal she had been working towards all her young life. Her post as Deputy Captain of *The Diablo* was supposed to have been her apprenticeship, but that had ended badly and now, he realised, the Federation itself had called her away to the safe harbour of Pirate Academy. But teaching had never been Cheng Li's forte, not on land at least. She was itching to get out onto the oceans and build a reputation as glorious as that of her father – the great Chang Ko Li, "the best of the best". And now, she was poised to set off on that epic journey. In spite of his own torpor, he felt overwhelmingly happy for her. He had a sudden urge to reach out and hug her. If she had been Grace or Jasmine or even Cate, he might have. But somehow hugs and Cheng Li didn't quite go together. Instead, he lightly punched her shoulder and said, "Well, that's great. Really great! Have you decided what to call your ship?"

"I'm still thinking," she said, pointing to a small notebook labelled *Ship Names*. "If you have any good ideas, I'll add them to the list."

"Wow!" he exclaimed. "This is *big* news. So when do you take up command?"

"In another couple of weeks, maybe sooner. It all depends when the ship is ready. That's out of my hands, which is a good thing because there's so much else to get organised." She barely drew breath before continuing. "And, right now, I have no crew, so everything falls to me. Well, at least that way we know it will all be done properly. That's why I'm leaving the Academy early tomorrow morning. I'm setting sail for Lantao Island to collect the weapons the swordsmith has made for me . . ." Cheng Li broke off for an instant and looked him up and down. "Where is *your* sword, Connor?" she asked.

He glanced away, feeling awkward again. "Actually," he said, "I think I *will* have that tea."

"Excellent," she said, not pushing further for answers. "A break from my work will do me good. Clear a place for yourself on the sofa, but *don't* mess up any of those piles." She padded off towards the small kitchenette, but turned back and smiled uncharacteristically warmly at him. "Oh, it's very good to see you, Connor. I do so love it when a friend pops by unannounced." Then she disappeared around the corner to prepare the tea.

After relocating Cheng Li's meticulous towers of notes, Connor sat down on the sofa. This meeting wasn't going anything like he had planned it out in his head. After the way he'd exited Pirate Academy, he'd expected a difficult atmosphere between them. He certainly hadn't expected her to make him tea and call him her friend. But then Cheng Li didn't operate the way other people did. She was honest, often to the point of brutality. She didn't cling onto unnecessary emotion. Instead, like a ship, she sailed on. She had said it herself – she moved fast. So fast that, sometimes, it was hard to keep up with her.

He picked up the notebook of ship names and began scanning her list. Typically, there were not just three or four names but pages and pages of them, all written in her immaculate script. Some had been crossed out; others given one, two or three stars. Clearly, it was very important to her to choose exactly the right name.

He was still poring over the list when she returned to the room, carrying a tray bearing a small iron teapot, two tea-bowls and a plate of temptingly chunky cookies. "I'm so going to miss the cooking here at the Academy," she sighed. "I did think about doubling Chef Hom's wages and taking him with me but I don't think that would put me in the Kuo's good books, do you?"

Connor shook his head, removing another two stacks of papers to create a space for the tray on the low coffee table.

"So," said Cheng Li, sitting down on a floor cushion and neatly folding her legs into the lotus position. "Do any of the names leap out at you?"

Connor glanced at the book again. "Hmm." He began to read. "*The Avenger. The Tormentor. The Renegade. The Despair of the Seas, The Wastrel, The Holy Terror, The Miscreant, The Viper, The Larrikin, The Assassin, The Hellcat.*" He glanced up, smiling. "There's a bit of a common thread here, wouldn't you say?"

"Whatever do you mean, Connor?" Cheng Li began pouring the tea.

"Well, they're all a bit aggressive, aren't they?"

Cheng Li giggled. "That's rather the point, isn't it?" she said. "So that when one draws up alongside another vessel, they know from the get-go that it's my way or the highway. Here's your tea. Be careful, it's hot."

"I suppose so," said Connor, taking the bowl. "All the same, these all sound a bit macho and *thuggy* for you."

Cheng Li nodded. "I hear what you're saying. Turn the page. You'll see I've tried some other tacks."

Connor turned over the page. "What's this? *The Aetolian League?*"

"Ah yes," said Cheng Li. "It's a historical reference to a Greek military and pirate confederation in the fourth century BC."

Connor shook his head. "Too *historical*," he said, "and not scary *enough*."

"I agree," she said, nodding. "Cookie? They're macadamia nut and goji berry."

"Thanks," Connor said, taking one of the cookies and dipping it in his tea.

"What do you think," Cheng Li paused, "about *The Blood and Compass*?"

Connor shook his head. "Sounds more like a pub than a ship!" he said, laughing.

Cheng Li laughed with him. It was the most natural laugh he had ever heard from her.

"This one's not bad," he said. "*The Teuta*. I don't know what it means but it sounds tough without being macho."

"Ah, yes," said Cheng Li, snapping her cookie in two. "Give that an extra star, would you?" She passed him her pen. "Teuta was a Greek pirate queen in the third century BC. Caused a lot of problems for the Romans. I've always found her to be *quite* an inspiration."

Connor set the notebook down and lifted the tea-bowl to his lips. A spiral of fragrant steam warmed his face. He took a sip. It tasted good.

"Fresh mint," said Cheng Li. "There's a bush of it growing rampant right outside my window." She had set down her own tea-bowl and was watching him intently, her eyes as bright and clear as a mountain stream.

"So," she said, "I have an idea."

"An idea?"

"Yes." She nodded. "I think you should come with me to Lantao tomorrow. It's a two-day voyage out. You can keep me company."

Four days of sailing in the Academy sloop – it wasn't an unpleasant thought.

Cheng Li nodded again. "And on the way, we'll have plenty of time to talk – or *not* talk – about whatever's on your mind."

"I . . ." Connor began. He wanted to tell her, but all his well-rehearsed words were jumbled in his head now.

"It's OK, Connor," Cheng Li said with a smile. "Drink your tea. Then I'll clear the sofa and you can have a rest. Your eyes look very tired and you know what they say – the eyes are the mirrors of the soul. We'll set off early in the morning. That way no one will see us depart together. And we'll make excellent sailing time to Lantao."

CHAPTER FORTY-SIX
Eyes Wide Open

"How is he?" Grace asked. It had been twenty-four hours since the captain's arrival at Sanctuary.

"I think you should come and look," Mosh Zu said. "You may find it a difficult, possibly painful, sight. But his condition is stable. And, if you are to be a healer, you must open your eyes to sights such as this."

Nervously, Grace followed Mosh Zu into the octagonal-shaped healing chamber.

The Vampirate captain lay on a slab-like table, low to the floor. The drifts of his cape spilled over the table and brushed the floorboards. It was shocking to see him like this. Grace knew he was only sleeping – sent by Mosh Zu into a healing trance – but he might just as well be dead. She was immediately transported back to her childhood. She had never felt comfortable watching her dad sleep. Indeed, she would do everything she could to avoid witnessing it. But, every once in a while, she'd walk into the lighthouse living room and find him sprawled on the ratty old sofa, quite motionless. The sight was enough to bring on a cold sweat. Catching her own breath, she would have to walk up to her dad and check for the sound of his breathing or else look carefully for signs of the gentle rise and fall of his abdomen beneath his shirt. Only then could her own breathing return to normal.

Seeing the captain lying motionless like this was similarly uncomfortable. During the time Grace had spent with him, the captain had emanated such power. Now, he seemed stripped of all vitality and authority. Strange because his face was still masked and his hands were still gloved. There was no outward difference in his appearance, and yet there was no question he had undergone a profound change.

"Come on," Mosh Zu said, leading her back out into his meditation room. "I think that's enough for now."

When they were out of the healing chamber, Grace couldn't disguise her shock. "I hadn't . . . I hadn't expected to see him like that."

"I understand," Mosh Zu said. "And you do well to acknowledge those feelings, Grace."

"How is his treatment proceeding?"

Mosh Zu gestured for her to sit down. "I must be honest with you, Grace. He's not doing as well as I would wish. I've stabilised his condition for now but it's becoming clear to me that this kind of gentle healing will only help him so far. Something more radical is called for, and soon."

"What's wrong with him?" Grace asked.

"It's simple, in a way," Mosh Zu said. "It comes back to our earlier discussions about healing. To be an effective healer, you must develop the ability to draw out pain from others without absorbing it into yourself. This is not nearly as straightforward as it sounds, especially when we are working with those who mean a lot to us personally. We're so determined to help those we love that we lose all perspective. We misread signals and, in doing so, our treatment becomes less effective for them and dangerous to ourselves."

As he spoke, Grace reflected on how hard it had been to confront Connor's pain and to help him to heal.

"The captain is utterly dedicated to helping people," Mosh Zu continued. "He is, without doubt, the most selfless being I have ever met. But there's the problem. He has been too ready to carry the burdens of others. In doing so, his own self is growing weaker and weaker. If I do not act to remedy this, we are in danger of losing him altogether."

Grace was chilled at the thought.

"I'm sharing these opinions with you, Grace, because I believe in your own healing powers. But you must listen carefully to what I'm saying and not fall into the same trap that the captain has done. As much as you want to help others – and you can help them in very powerful ways –

you must learn not to absorb their pain and carry it around for them. Do not allow their darkness to take you over."

She nodded.

"I can see the worry in your eyes," he said. "And I know that in part I'm responsible. You are worried about the captain. Of course, you are. But I *will* heal him, Grace. It will not be easy or straightforward, but I can do it."

His words were somewhat reassuring.

"Let's talk about other things," he said. "Have you seen Lorcan today?"

"Not yet," she said, "but perhaps I could go and see him now?"

Mosh Zu nodded. "I think that's a very good idea," he said. "But Grace, there is something I must ask you. Although Lorcan's sight is restored, given the psychological aspect of his blindness, he is still not quite out of the woods. He remains in a delicate balance. If he becomes overly stressed or fearful, there is every chance that he will retreat back into blindness. If that happens, it will be harder for me to lead him back a second time. Do you understand?"

"Yes," she replied. "I'll take good care of him. I won't do anything to upset him."

"Off you go then!" Mosh Zu said. He smiled again. "Don't look so anxious, Grace. I know he is very keen to see you."

*

429

"Grace!" said Lorcan. He was lying on the bed but now he swung his feet down onto the floor and stood up to greet her. He opened his arms to hug her, but she hesitated, wanting their eyes to meet.

As they did, she found tears welling up in her own eyes. "I'm sorry," she said, trying to blink them away. "I'm sorry! I just had to check again. I'm still getting used to the idea that you can see again, that I didn't dream this!"

"It's no dream," Lorcan said, wrapping his arms around her. "I can see you, Grace! And I've never been happier to see someone in all my days."

Lorcan released Grace and sat back on the bed. She sat down opposite him. For a moment they sat there, smiling at one another.

"How does it feel?" she asked.

"It feels amazing," he said. "It's not just that I can see again. Things seems brighter and crisper than before." He squeezed her hand and gazed deep into her eyes. "Things seem even more beautiful than I had remembered."

The depth of Lorcan's gaze was disconcerting. It had been quite a time since Grace had felt his eyes upon her. So much so, that though she was already growing used to it, in some ways it was like the very first time their eyes had met. She was cast back to the moment that she'd opened her eyes on the deck of *The Nocturne*. At first, she had thought she was looking into the sky – so blue were his irises. But then she had realised. And nothing had quite been the same since. For him too, she pondered,

430

remembering her vision of him looking down into her green eyes. Looking down and recognising her. But how?

"What are you thinking about?" he asked. "You seemed very far away for a moment."

She shook her head. "No, I'm right here. I was just remembering the first time we met."

He smiled. "When I fished you out of the water?"

She nodded.

"I've been thinking a lot about that too," he said.

"Have you?" She was excited to hear it.

He nodded.

"I've been doing a whole lot of thinking while I've been lying here. Well, there hasn't been much else I *can* do."

"No," she acknowledged, squeezing his hand. "No, but that's all over now. You have your eyesight back and you'll soon get your strength back." She paused, remembering Mosh Zu's instructions. "And soon, we'll be back on *The Nocturne*," she said, hoping that she sounded bright and breezy. "And everything will be back to normal."

Lorcan frowned. Grace felt a flicker of alarm – had she let slip some shadow of a doubt about their return?

"Grace, there's some things I need to say to you," Lorcan began. "You may not like them or find them easy to understand at first. But please hear me out and know that I'm saying them because I care about you very much."

Now it was her turn to frown. His words were ominous indeed.

He took a breath then continued. "When I go back to

The Nocturne, I don't think you should come with me. That ship, well, it's not a fit home for you."

"I like it there," she said. "I know it's crazy, but it's true."

He shook his head. "I know you do," he said. "And, speaking for myself, I like having you there. I more than like it. But it just isn't good for you. You could go to join Connor . . ."

"No." Grace shook her head. "No, that wouldn't work out."

"I know you don't feel a connection to the pirate world," Lorcan said. "But I'm sure in time . . ."

"No." She shook her head again. Hot tears were pricking her eyes once more. "No, it doesn't matter how long I stay on a pirate ship, it will never be my home. It's different on *The Nocturne*. I feel a connection there."

"I know you do, Grace. And I feel responsible for that."

As well he might. A good deal of why she felt so at home on the ship was because of him.

"But I was wrong to drag you into this world. It's not right for a mortal. It's not safe."

"Safe?" she said. "I think I've taken pretty good care of myself so far."

She thought back to how she'd repelled Sidorio's attack. Others would have been driven to terror by being trapped in a cabin with only the most bloodthirsty of vampires for company. But she had kept her nerve and kept him talking, drawing him out on the subject of his life and death – a subject he was only too keen to revisit for a while.

In this way, she had bided her time until the captain came to rescue her. If she could deal with Sidorio, she could deal with any of them.

"Grace, it's only a matter of time before your luck runs out. You're not a vampire and you're not a donor."

No, she thought. I'm an in-between. And at that moment, being an in-between was just about the worst thing she could imagine.

"You look so sad," he said. "And it's my fault."

"Yes," she said, her sadness turning into anger. "It *is* your fault. You told me that I should stay, remember? You said there were a million secrets for me to discover on the ship. Don't you remember? *You* said that."

He nodded. "I remember. I think I remember every word we've ever said to one another. And, since I've been laid up here, I've replayed each and every one of them." He sighed. "When I said that to you, I was being hopelessly romantic. I thought that somehow we could find a way to cross the bridge between our worlds."

"And now?" she said. "Why have you changed your mind now?"

He looked at her very intently. "I've opened my eyes," he said.

CHAPTER FORTY-SEVEN

To Lantao

It would take the better part of two days' sailing to journey from the Pirate Academy to Lantao Island. Plenty of time, thought Connor, as they set off in the early morning light. Plenty of time to talk to Cheng Li about the things on his mind.

But as their journey got underway, Connor found himself busily engaged with Cheng Li on the sailing of the Academy sloop. There was no time for heart-to-heart discussions. Instead, their conversation was limited to an exchange of instructions and confirmations as they navigated the boat through the choppy waters.

The strange thing was that Connor was starting to feel better, without even saying a word. Perhaps it was simply losing himself in the physical challenge of sailing the boat with Cheng Li. Ever since he was a little kid, he had found comfort in physical activity. When dark thoughts started crowding in your head, there was nothing better than going and shooting some basketball hoops or pounding down the saltwater pool, length after length in perfect freestyle.

Cheng Li was the ideal companion, too. She wasn't someone who needed constant conversation. Rather like Connor himself, she kept to the mantra of only speaking when she had something to say. He could tell that she was lost in her own thoughts – her head, no doubt, filled with all the various lists and decisions she was making in the run-up to becoming a captain. Even without speaking, she radiated optimism, and this too was infectious. Combined with the sun, which had pushed back the clouds and added to the pleasure of their trip, it all made for the perfect day's sailing.

As the sun finally began to set, they dropped anchor and at last gave their weary bones some rest. Cheng Li disappeared down into the hold for a moment and returned with a hamper of food packed up by the chef at Pirate Academy.

"Dive in!" she said. "I'm sure you're as ravenous as I am."

They both opened up the various containers – filled with cold meats and fish, salads and sauces – and piled their plates high with tempting goodies. After a day of physical effort, their appetites were large. Once more, conversation was limited, as they devoured each tasty treat Chef Hom had provided for them.

"I'm going to sleep well tonight," Connor said at last.

"Me too!" agreed Cheng Li. "Actually, Connor, you do look dog-tired." Trust Cheng Li – always a ready compliment at hand.

"I'm going to make some tea," she said, heading below-stairs once more.

Connor busied himself clearing up the debris of their supper, then ferried the empty cartons down to the galley where Cheng Li was brewing up a tempting blend of green tea with ginger and ginseng.

"That smells great!" he said.

"Take it up onto the deck," Cheng Li said. "Give it time to brew. I'll join you in a minute."

He carried the tray and set it on the table up there.

Then he stretched out on the cushioned bench to relax while the tea brewed. He propped his head on a life-jacket and settled back, gazing up at the star-filled sky. He searched the heavens for his favourite constellations. He always drew comfort from this game. It took him back to the lighthouse, to Grace and his dad. But tonight, by the time he'd found Aquila, his eyes were heavy and he had no strength to keep them open any more.

When Cheng Li came back up on deck, she found him fast asleep, his breathing long and deep. She unfolded a blanket and draped it over his body. She padded around the deck, quietly, lighting the lanterns. Then she sat down again and began to sip at her tea.

*

436

Connor awoke with a start. Immediately, he was fully alert. He felt a chill through his bones. The sky was black and the night air was empty of the warmth of the sun. But it wasn't just that. His dreams had given way to memories and the last thing he had seen, a second before waking, was his rapier slicing into Alessandro's flesh.

"What is it?" Cheng Li said. He looked up and found her sitting opposite him, making notes by lamplight in one of her books.

"There's something I need to talk to you about," Connor said.

She set down the book and the pen and waited for him to begin. He imagined that this was what it might be like sitting in a psychiatrist's chair.

There was no point in delaying things any further. This was what he had come to her to talk about, seeking her out at Pirate Academy and embarking on this voyage with her. He had allowed himself to be distracted by her news. He had let the sunny day and the business of sailing wrap a comforting blanket around him – almost persuading himself that he still lived in the old world. The world before this terrible thing had happened. But there was no longer any place to hide.

"I killed a man," he said.

She nodded.

Instantly, he understood. "You already knew, didn't you?"

"Yes," she said. "News travels fast. It's why you came to

find me, Connor, isn't it? To hear what I had to say on the matter?"

He nodded. "Yes. I didn't know where to turn. I couldn't stay on board *The Diablo*. Not after they gave me the Blood Captain. I sailed around, going nowhere. I threw my sword into the ocean. Finally, I knew that there was one person who just might be able to help me."

"Me," she said. It wasn't a question.

He nodded again.

"All right, then," she said. "Well, you'd better tell me all about it, don't you think?"

She was a good listener. He could tell she was taking in every word, every emotion that the words gave rise to. And she didn't interrupt. She was patient, even when he had to break off to think of the right way to express his feelings clearly to her. It was important to tell her exactly what he felt. She sat and waited for him to get there in his own time.

When he was done, she nodded, then remained silent and still for a time, as if her head was still computing the information, sifting through the various facts he had presented to her.

"Well?" he asked, hoping to nudge her into speaking.

She seemed surprised. "I can't take away your feelings of guilt," she said. "You killed a man. He awoke that morning with a life stretching out ahead of him, who knows how far? And you cut that short. There's no denying or getting away from that fact."

Connor listened. He had thought he'd derive comfort from her words but, if anything, she was making him feel worse.

"None of us can remove the guilt we feel when we take another's life. But, in my opinion, nor should we try to. Guilt is a reasonable price to pay, I think. There's nothing satisfying or rewarding about taking someone's life from them. Nor should there ever be."

"You've killed?" Connor said.

"Yes." She nodded. "Several times."

"How do you come to terms with it?" he asked. "How do you move on and get on with your life? How do you continue to enjoy life as a pirate?"

Once more, she considered his words before framing her answer. "When I kill, I feel exactly as you do now. They say that the first time is worst, that you become numb to it after that. But I reject that philosophy. I don't want to feel numb. Why should I? There's no strength in denying the feelings that are racing through you, the feelings that make you human. We feel guilt for a reason. Just as we feel fear or joy or fatigue. They are signs. We are not *supposed* to kill each other. But, in the world we live in – like it or not – it happens."

"OK," he said, wondering where she was going with this.

"The way that I move forward is by not killing unnecessarily. You've seen me in battle, Connor. I believe in precision. I'm not into wanton violence; I'm into results.

439

During your rather brief spell as a student at Pirate Academy, I believe you heard John Kuo's lecture on *zanshin*. Do you remember?"

"Yes," he said, nodding. "*Zanshin* is the state of super-alertness in which you are ready to defend and attack in all directions."

"Yes," Cheng Li said. "But it's a state of alertness I believe in maintaining at all times – outside of battle as well as in the heart of it. The more alert you are as a pirate, the fewer life and death situations you will find yourself in. Being a pirate captain is not about being a killer. Sometimes you are forced into a situation in which you have no other choice. It's you or them. Or it's them or your comrade. It seems clear to me that you acted in this way. If you had not killed the security guard then most certainly Moonshine Wrathe *would* have been killed. You were given your orders and you followed them. In terms of the combat situation, you displayed a great mastery of *zanshin*."

He felt somewhat flattered by her words, but she had not yet finished.

"Where you are less capable of *zanshin*, Connor, is in life away from combat. The raid on the Sunset Fort was a typical Molucco Wrathe ploy. A deed of derring-do for mercurial gain. There was no higher motive, no strategy. Oh, I understand that Cate's action plan was quite clever – what I mean is, there was no overarching strategy at the end of the day. You allowed yourself to be caught, once more, in a situation where the dangers were quite unnecessary."

"You mean, like the attack which resulted in Jez's death?"

"Exactly." Once more she nodded.

"So what are you saying?"

"I'm making an observation," she said. "That's all. You will never find that killing becomes any easier. There's not a thing you can – or should – do about that. But what you *can* do is make sure that you reduce being in situations where you need to kill. You don't need to leave piracy behind. You just need to think more about the kind of pirate you want to be. And the kind of pirates you want to be with."

Her words had not comforted him in the way he had hoped or expected they might. It wasn't even comfort he felt right now. But he did feel somehow different about what he'd done. And, just for a moment, he had a sense that he might be able to go forward. But then it disappeared, drowned out by the familiar tide of dread rising within him.

"What is it?" she asked, quick to notice the change.

"I understand what you say," he said. "It's just that I've never felt so scared before. I don't understand it. I'm not in any danger now. In every moment of danger, I've done what was asked of me. But now here – on this calm night, in the middle of the ocean – I'm absolutely terrified. Why is that?"

Cheng Li considered his words, then smiled at him. "It's

441

very simple, really," she said. "The greatest terrors aren't out there on the oceans. They're not hiding in the shadows." She leaned closer and put her hand over his heart. "They're deep inside you. They're in your blood." She removed her hand and shook her head. "You're no different. It's the same for all of us."

442

CHAPTER FORTY-EIGHT

The Lariat

"I'm only saying these things because I care so much about you," Lorcan said to Grace. "We all do. Mosh Zu, the captain. We only want what's best for you."

"And the best thing for me is to never see you again?"

Lorcan nodded. "Yes. I know it's difficult but, in time you'll come to see I'm right."

She was torn between laughing and screaming. Instead, her voice was measured when she spoke again. "I don't think so," she said. "I don't think I'll ever thank you for this."

There was much more she might have said but she remembered Mosh Zu's warning. As much as Lorcan had hurt her, she didn't want to cause him a relapse. She realised she'd have to get out of the room. If she stayed a moment longer, if this conversation continued, she'd be sure to mention the rebellion aboard *The Nocturne* or the captain's collapse.

"I'll leave you," Grace said.

He kept hold of her hand. "Don't go now," he said. "Don't run away while you're upset."

She removed her hand from his clasp. "I just need some time to myself," she said. "To think this through."

"Oh," he said, sounding a little surprised.

She couldn't even look at him as she stood up and stumbled towards the door and then out into the corridor.

It was only once she'd closed the door behind her that the tidal-wave of emotions really hit her. She could feel the sobs coming but she was determined to be far away from him when they broke through. She began running along the corridor, racing to get back to her room.

Along the way, she passed a few of the vampires. They glanced at her and no doubt noted the state of distress she was in. She could hear hushed voices behind her. She didn't care what they were saying. She kept on running.

Somewhere along the way, she must have taken a wrong turning because she wasn't on the corridor leading back to her room. Instead, she'd gone down to a lower level. It was unfamiliar territory, but at least the corridor was deserted. Drained and tired of running, she stopped and collapsed in a heap. The sobs broke through her.

Through her tears, Grace looked along the corridor. She remembered the awe she had felt on entering Sanctuary. This great place of healing. Well, it was true – Lorcan's eyesight had been returned to him. But now that he was healed, he was pushing her away. She was happy for him that he had got his sight back, but utterly devastated that he should now tell her to leave him and *The Nocturne*.

Her whole world seemed to be crumbling. The news from *The Nocturne* was so bad. A fresh rebellion and the most serious so far. What made it even worse was that it had been provoked by Jez Stukeley. In life, he had been such a good man, but after death – and under Sidorio's tutelage – he had firmly embraced his dark side. It seemed incredible to think that the captain had weathered revolts by Sidorio but been broken by Jez's rebellion. But, from what Mosh Zu had said, it wasn't simply the rebellion in itself that had laid the captain low; he had been fighting a long war of attrition with himself, trying to keep harmony on board *The Nocturne*, trying to help the vampires manage their blood hunger.

It seemed like everything Mosh Zu and the captain had been working towards was failing. Maybe you just couldn't manage the vampires' appetites and it would only bring you grief to try. Grace knew that this was a defeatist attitude, and yet it seemed that, at every turn, the work of the captain and Mosh Zu was being *defeated*. It was such a shame, such a terrible shame. They were trying to give those who had been cursed with immortality a way to bring meaning to their interminable existence. But most of the vampires couldn't see beyond their own immediate cravings.

Grace shook her head. Things couldn't be much worse. Jez had caused fresh unrest aboard *The Nocturne*. It now seemed clear that Sidorio was not gone but had only been resting, lurking in the shadows. How much longer, she thought. How much longer until he stepped out once more and launched a fresh attack?

When he did, it might be the end of the Vampirate captain. He had fallen terribly ill and now his very survival depended on Mosh Zu's healing. Perhaps it would be the ultimate test of the guru's powers.

And then there was Connor. She had done her best to heal him but she had no idea where he was now or what he was going through.

And last, there was Lorcan. Lorcan, whose healing seemed to have gone well. And yet that moment of elation had been all too brief, any sense of happiness snatched away by his cruel pronouncement that she must leave *The Nocturne*. Little did he realise that there might be no ship for either of them to return to.

What a mess, she thought. What a terrible mess! Images of them all flashed inside her head. Jez and Sidorio. The Vampirate captain and Mosh Zu. Connor and Lorcan. It seemed that her fragile world was collapsing on all sides. She had no idea how – or even if – they could all find their way out of this.

She could hardly motivate herself to get up from the dusty floor. What was the point? She let her head sink into her hands.

After she'd been sitting like that for a while, she heard the sound of whoops and cries in the distance. She lifted her head to listen. The cries were not so distant, she realised. Perhaps only around the corner. And she thought she recognised the voice. Maybe this was the one person who could raise her spirits.

Drawing herself up to her feet, she dusted herself down and, following the sounds, continued along the corridor. It twisted and turned and then led into a large internal courtyard. Standing in the middle of it was Johnny Desperado, lariat in hand, crying and whooping as he threw the rope and deftly lassooed his tea flask.

Grace smiled. He looked like he had some life to him. He was just the person she needed to see. Johnny would cheer her up.

She stepped into the courtyard. He was busy pulling in the rope and releasing the flask again. As she stepped forward, he turned and smiled.

"Here!" he threw her the flask. "Set this down for me, anywhere you like. And ol' Johnny will lasso it for you."

"OK," she said, laughing, and placed the flask on the dusty ground. She stepped back to watch Johnny perform his throw. She could see there was a real art to it. The lasso flew up and spun through the air, then seemed to float down over the flask. At that moment, Johnny drew in the rope and it tightened right about the flask. Grace had a sudden vision of Johnny lassoing a horse. She could tell how good at this he was.

As he reeled in the flask again, he chattered away. She couldn't be sure if he was talking to her or to himself.

"When you break in a bronco, it's all about confidence building. You gotta take it a step at a time. Like building a friendship. You figure out what you can do with the horse to make her like you. No confrontation. Nothing good ever comes from confrontation. Not in the beginning, anyways. It's all about knowing just how much pressure to apply, and when. Applying a little pressure, then relieving it, well that's the most important message you can give a horse. You're telling her she's not trapped. There's something she can do to relieve the pressure she's feeling."

Johnny shot Grace a glance as he threw her the flask again. He continued to chatter away as she went to place the container in a fresh position. "When a lariat tightens around a horse's neck, even a trained bronco will want to fight. And an untrained horse, well she'll want to fight even harder. When she feels the lariat tighten, there's nothing she can do short of total collapse to relieve this pressure she feels. Right then, right there, she'll fight for her life."

Johnny took the lariat in his hand once more. He raised his hand to throw it. As he let go of the rope, he winked at Grace. She watched the lasso sail up into the air. But the wink must have set him off balance because the noose wasn't falling anywhere near the flask. Instead, it was high above her. Grace turned to Johnny. He had a strange expression on his face. Suddenly she felt a slight breeze as the loop of the lariat fell over her head and neck. It hovered

448

there, then dropped a little lower to her elbows. Then she felt the pressure tighten.

Something told Grace that this was no longer a game. She looked nervously over at Johnny.

"Looks like I roped me a real wild one this time," he said proudly.

CHAPTER FORTY-NINE

The Swordsmith and his Daughter

They approached Lantao from the South. Raising his head from the navigational chart to the island itself, Connor saw Lantao Peak, its highest point. It was wrapped in a thick blanket of lush green forest. He remembered Cheng Li saying that the swordsmith lived high above the water. He had a grim feeling that they would have to journey up that mountain – and down again – to fetch the weaponry Cheng Li had ordered for her crew.

The sloop was skimming past a long beach. Sheltered between two cliffs was a long stretch of sun-baked sand. If he'd still been travelling alone, he'd have been tempted to drop anchor and swim from the boat to the sand. But he only had to look at Cheng Li's face to remind himself that they were on a mission. They had come to Lantao on business and there was no time to waste. He crossed the deck once more to join her at the steering wheel.

"Lantao has something of a pirate history," Cheng Li said, when he was back within earshot. "It has always been a popular base for pirates and smugglers."

"Really?" said Connor, still gazing wistfully at the beach and thinking that the pirates and smugglers had chosen well.

Cheng Li nodded, her eyes fixed on the sweep of emerald-green in the distance as she continued, "In the nineteenth century, the island was a base for Chang Po, an exceptionally gifted pirate." She glanced at Connor briefly, as if checking he was paying attention, before continuing. "Chang Po was born a fisherman's son, in the Xinhui on the Pearl River Delta. His life might have been very different – long, hard and uneventful – but when he was fifteen years old, he was captured by a pair of pirates. Not just any pirates! These were the famed Cheng I and his wife Cheng I Sao." Connor hadn't heard the names before, but he sensed that they were deeply etched upon Cheng Li's psyche.

"Fate had smiled on Chang Po," she continued. "His captors were two of the most successful pirates of all time. This wife and husband team operated a whole fleet of pirate ships called the Red Flag Fleet. A few years after Chang Po joined their crew, the husband drowned and Cheng I Sao took over all his duties. She empowered Chang Po to manage the day-to-day operations of the fleet.

451

He was just a year or so older than me at that point. Under Chang Po's leadership, the pirates of the Red Flag Fleet defeated every force sent to challenge their power. For ten years his power seemed invincible. All the pirates of those times – whether his own or those of rival captains – believed that the gods protected him. They talked of him as if he was superhuman."

"That's impressive," Connor said. "But you said he was invincible for ten years. What happened then?"

Cheng Li turned the wheel, keeping her eyes on the curving rock as they sailed around the south-west tip of the island. "The empire they had founded started to show cracks from within. Their captains and admirals began to bicker. Crews mutinied. There was a dismal battle with the Red Flag Fleet. Chang Po and Cheng I Sao decided to get out of piracy while they could."

"Really?" Connor said. Somehow the two pirates Cheng Li had described did not seem cut out for a quiet retirement.

"Yes," said Cheng Li. "Chang Po became an officer in the navy. He had an illustrious career there too."

"What about Cheng I Sao?" Connor asked.

Cheng Li smiled. "Although she gave up the fleet, she never quite left piracy behind. She ended her days as the director of a large smuggling operation."

"She sounds like quite a character," Connor said. "Him too."

"You don't know the half of it," Cheng Li said. "But I'll

tell you the rest of their story some other time. We're almost at our destination."

"Why *did* you tell me about them?" Connor asked.

"Just a little local history," she said, but there was something in her smile that made him suspect that wasn't the whole story. Connor knew that Cheng Li did not waste her words any more than she did her sword-strokes. This was not simply a colourful historical anecdote. She was laying out his options before him. Better the life of a fisherman or the admiral of a pirate fleet? That's what she was asking him to consider. She might just as well have asked him to consider two other possibilities. *Better a pirate prodigy or the orphan of a lighthouse-keeper in a dead-end town?*

He was still pondering the question as Cheng Li began turning the sloop tightly around and slowing their speed as they approached land. Connor could see a small fishing town coming into focus. It was not the grand harbour he had expected to arrive at. There were rows of simple stilt houses constructed right over the waterway, with brightly-painted fishing boats bobbing in the silvery waters beneath them. As Connor helped Cheng Li to anchor the sloop, he wrinkled his nose. The air was filled with a distinctive smell.

"Salt fish and shrimp paste," Cheng Li said, breathing in deeply. "A speciality of the stores on the front here. We'll have some while we're here. It's quite delicious."

Almost the moment they had anchored their boat, they

453

found one of the fishermen had brought over his craft to ferry them the rest of the way to dry land.

Cheng Li nodded to the oarsman as she and Connor climbed inside the boat. A few strokes later and they were climbing out again. Cheng Li tossed some coins into the fisherman's leathery palm, then joined Connor on the wooden pier.

"So, how do we get to the peak from here?" he asked.

"Why would we want to go to Lantao Peak?" asked Cheng Li.

"Isn't that where the swordsmith is? You said he lived high above the water, so I assumed . . ."

Cheng Li shook her head and pointed at one of the stilt houses. "He lives up there. I know you're none too keen on heights, but I think you can cope with this. Come on!"

She began walking across the pier towards the stilt house. Following her, Connor thought that it didn't seem a grand enough residence for the renowned swordsmith of Lantao. He had expected something more akin to a great temple. Instead, he found himself climbing a short, rickety flight of steps and waiting in an open doorway while Cheng Li drew down a bird-shaped bell-pull.

Almost immediately, a girl appeared. Her hair was close-cropped but Connor was in no doubt that she was a girl. Her soft Chinese features were not dissimilar to those of Cheng Li but her face was somehow gentler.

"Mistress Li," she said, putting her hands together and

bowing. As she did so, her eyes closed and her long lashes cast shadows down her face.

"Mistress Yin," said Cheng Li, mirroring the gesture. Rising, she pointed to Connor and spoke a few words which Connor didn't catch, except for "Tempest". He realised he was being introduced and he put his hands together and bowed as the two young women had.

"Connor," Cheng Li said, "this is Bo Yin, the swordsmith's daughter."

"It is a great pleasure to meet you, Connor Tempest," said the young woman.

"And you," Connor said, immediately captivated by the girl's natural grace and beauty.

Bo Yin blushed and extended her hand. "Please, come inside. My father is working but I will tell him you have arrived."

They entered the swordsmith's home. And it *was* homely, in the best sense. A humble dwelling but filled with everything you could possibly want – a cluttered but well-organised kitchen, an inviting seating area and shelves of books and artefacts. And then Connor noticed that on the wall were hung just a few swords. Compared to the display of swords at the Pirate Academy, this was minimal indeed but, even from a distance, Connor could sense that the swords here were ancient and precious, with stories to tell. He stood in the centre, taking it all in, while Bo Yin disappeared into another room to confer with her father. She emerged a moment or two later.

"My father is just finishing one of your pieces," she explained to Cheng Li. "He asked me to offer you some soup and to say that he will join us shortly."

"Excellent," said Cheng Li, smiling softly as Bo Yin lifted the lid on a small pan. Again, Connor's nostrils were tantalised by saltfish and shrimp. This time, it smelled even better, and all the more so as Bo Yin ladled out bowls of her tempting broth and carried them over to a low table.

"There's no need to stand on ceremony," Bo Yin said with a smile. "You must both be hungry after your long journey."

"Actually," said Cheng Li, "Connor's eaten continuously ever since we left the Academy."

"I always have a big appetite out at sea!" he protested.

"Boys," said Cheng Li, exchanging a knowing look with Bo Yin.

They drank their soup hungrily and when Bo Yin offered them more, both Cheng Li and Connor gratefully accepted. She was ladling more broth into the bowls when a door creaked open and the swordsmith walked into the room. All eyes turned towards him. He was a little shorter than his daughter, with white hair tied back in a pigtail. His eyes seemed to dance about the room, Connor thought, as if he was a mole who had emerged into the daylight after a long spell underground.

"Father," called Bo Yin from the stove. "Some soup after your labours?"

He nodded, then spoke in a soft voice. "If you please, Bo

456

Yin." Then he turned to Cheng Li, who had risen the moment he had entered the room.

"Mistress Li," he said.

"Master Yin," she said.

They came to stand before each other and bowed.

"Your own ship!" he said. "To think you are to have your own ship."

She nodded. "It was only a matter of time."

"This is true," he said. "Your father . . . he would be *so* proud of you."

"Thank you," Cheng Li said, nodding. She turned and extended her hand. "Master Yin, this is Connor Tempest. Connor, Master Yin is the most talented swordsmith of his generation."

Connor came to stand before Master Yin and they bowed to each other.

"I've heard much about you, sir," said Connor.

"And I just a little of you also," Master Yin said.

Connor was surprised at this and all the more so when the swordsmith added, "He is the one, Mistress Li, is he not?"

Cheng Li nodded.

"Come, drink your soup, Father," said Bo Yin, beckoning him over to the table.

Connor was left to ponder the swordsmith's enigmatic words as Bo Yin set a wicker chair up close to the table. Clearly the old swordsmith could no longer bend sufficiently low to sit on the cushions.

The others all returned to the table and sat around it. Connor watched as Master Yin dipped his spoon into the bowl, savoured the taste, then swallowed. He nodded and smiled. "Just like your mother's," he pronounced. "Very good, Bo Yin."

Connor looked at the dutiful Bo Yin and wondered if, in spite of her father's love, she perhaps felt constrained by her life here. He had a sense that she wanted more from life than this. In her eyes, he saw something – a certain fellow-feeling. He was still weighing up in his mind the two options Cheng Li had presented to him – the fisherman or the pirate. But it was no longer a true contest. In his mind, the scales were already tipping firmly in one direction.

"So," said Bo Yin, breaking through his reverie. "Tell me, Connor, what is it like to be a pirate?"

Before Connor could respond, her father gave a short laugh. "She always asks that," he said. Then, imitating his daughter's voice, "*What's it like to be a pirate? What's it like on a pirate ship?*"

Bo Yin's eyes flashed with pain and something else, but only for an instant. Connor wondered if anyone but he had noticed it. "And maybe one day I shall find out for myself, Father," Bo Yin said.

He shrugged. "That's right. Off you go and be a pirate and leave your poor old father to wither away in his house of swords."

Bo Yin shook her head and sighed. "I'll never leave you, Pop," she said. She turned to the others, her eyes wide and wistful. "Still, in another lifetime, perhaps I too shall know the glory of being a pirate . . ."

Was that how long she'd have to wait? Connor wondered. A whole lifetime of making soup and pulling up her old father's chair seemed too limited for a girl like Bo Yin. Suddenly, he realised just how free he was. Free to make his destiny.

He became aware of Cheng Li's eyes upon him and looked away, his gaze settling on one of the swords on the wall behind Master Yin.

"Impressive, isn't it?" Cheng Li said.

Master Yin turned in his chair, his own eyes travelling to the sword. "Ah, yes," he said, turning back to Connor. "That sword belonged to the great Chang Po. It's inscribed with a dedication from Cheng I Sao. You know of these great pirates, I assume?"

Connor nodded. "May I have a closer look?" he asked.

"Of course!" Master Yin waved his spoon freely.

Connor stepped towards the sword. It was evident it had been through many battles, given the nicks in the blade and the hilt. But the blade was still sharp. With a rub of oil, it would be ready for use once again.

"Take it off the wall-mount," said Master Yin. "Swords are not meant for display alone. Give it a try!"

Connor was surprised that the swordsmith would be so cavalier with such an ancient and important artefact. Hesitantly, he reached towards the sword and lifted it down from the wall. As his fist closed around the hilt, he realised it was the first time he had held a sword since he'd thrown his own rapier into the ocean.

"It's a perfect fit!" declared Master Yin. He turned to Cheng Li. "This is most auspicious."

Connor gripped the sword and immediately began slicing the blade through the air. It felt as if the ghost of Chang Po was moving alongside him, guiding his hand. Suddenly, he was no longer in the stilt-house but on the deck of a great ship, commanding the Red Flag Fleet on another successful raid on the Pearl River. He could smell the cannon and hear the melee as the battle got underway. He felt a sudden surge of adrenaline. Then he heard a cry.

"Bravo for Captain Tempest!"

He turned and realised that this was not Chang Po's ship, but his own. His crew were approaching. They were smiling and laughing and clapping him. He could sense that they had won a great victory that day.

Before he knew it, they had lifted him onto their shoulders and were parading him about the deck. He was laughing. "Put me down! Put me down! By order of the captain, put me down!"

But they only laughed. And he didn't care. In that moment, he felt deeply happy and peaceful. He knew he was a popular captain. He knew he had done a good job. He lifted the sword above his head and there were great cries.

"Captain Tempest! Bravo for Captain Tempest! Bravo . . ."

Suddenly, his focus came back into the room, aware that three pairs of eyes were watching him intently.

460

Embarrassed, he turned and was about to hang the sword back in its mount. As he lifted it, he caught sight of the Chinese characters engraved on the hilt.

"What does it say?" he asked.

"It is a dedication from Cheng I Sao to Chang Po," said Master Yin. "Bring it here and I will translate."

He pulled a pair of glasses from his shirt pocket, opened them out and set them on his nose. Then Connor extended the sword towards him and the old swordsmith balanced it upon his lap.

"Ah yes," he said, taking a cloth and wiping the surface of the hilt. "That's right! It says, 'You've come a long way from the river delta, little fisherman!'"

The swordsmith smiled, the loose skin around his eyes crinkling. "She had a good sense of humour, I think, that Cheng I Sao."

"Yes," smiled Cheng Li, her eyes never moving from Connor, "didn't she?"

CHAPTER FIFTY

The Danger Zone

"OK, Johnny, very funny! Now let me go!"

It had been an expert throw. The lariat had trapped both Grace's arms, minimising her range of movement. Now the rope was starting to dig into her bare arms. But he showed no signs of loosening the lasso. Instead, he looked at her with distant eyes and drew it even tighter.

"Come on, Johnny, you're hurting me! Please let me go."

"Not just yet," he said. "I'm not done with you yet, little lady." He shook his head slowly.

What did he mean? He began pulling the rope towards him, as expertly as once he would have pulled cattle. She had no choice but to follow.

"What's wrong with you, Johnny?" she asked as they drew face to face.

"*Wrong* with me?" he said, grinning. "Nothing's wrong with me! I feel better than I have in a good long while!"

One look in his eyes confirmed her worst fears. "You've taken blood, haven't you?" She looked down at the flask he had dropped onto the dusty floor. "There was blood mixed in with your berry tea. But how? Where did you get it from?"

"The usual place," he said, with a grin.

"You've taken it before?"

He shrugged. "I'm a vampire, Grace! There's only so long I can survive on herbal tea and group meditation."

Grace winced to hear Mosh Zu's complex treatments dismissed so scathingly.

"But the tea is a *substitute* for blood! You're supposed to be learning to manage your hunger. You were doing so well."

"Gee, thanks," he said. "That's very encouraging. Now, stop trying to loosen those ropes. Don't you know that the more you struggle, the tighter they're gonna get?"

Grace realised he was right. The more she struggled, the more tightly the ropes dug into her flesh. Looking down, she could see red welts forming just above her elbows. She was close to tears from the pain alone but she didn't want him to see it. She bit down hard on her lip to pull herself together. "Why are you acting like this?" she asked. "This isn't you!"

"Sure it is," he said. "What's wrong? I kept telling you I was bad news, baby, but all you saw was this rumple-haired geek with a late-night chess habit."

"No," she said. "There's more to you than that. Don't

give up, Johnny! Just because someone's given you blood you don't need. Don't throw it all away! You've been running for so long. But you don't need to run any more. You could have a home on *The Nocturne*."

"Yeah," he said. "You'd like that, wouldn't you? You, me and Lorcan. Very cosy! Very exciting for you, I'm sure." She could see the transformation gathering pace now. His teeth were sharpening. His eyes were losing focus. Soon, they'd be pools of fire. She had to delay that moment as long as she could. She had to keep him talking. Even if it was hard stringing together a coherent sentence when the pain was cutting into her deeper and deeper.

"What do you mean?" she asked at last.

"I just think it's kinda creepy, the way you like to hang around guys like us. It's like you're flirting with the dark side or something. But we're not animals in a petting zoo. You can't just come and visit us when you like. There are consequences to hanging out with us *lost boys*."

He leaned in close and she could feel his hot breath on her. "Why are you fighting this? You know deep down that you want it just as much as I do – maybe more! The Blind Boy of Connemara won't give it to you, but I will. It's what you've been wondering about, isn't it? All that time on the ship and now here. You've watched Lorcan with Shanti. And you want to know for yourself – what's it like to share?"

"No," she said. "That's not what I want. You've got it all wrong."

He shook his head. "I don't think so, Grace. I think ol' Johnny's right on the money this time."

Keeping hold of the lasso in one hand, he raised his other hand to her neck. It clamped her as tightly as the rope. Now, he let go of the lariat and reached out for the collar of her shirt.

"No!" she cried as she heard the material tear, but the pressure of his hand on her neck reduced her cry to a dull croak.

Suddenly, she heard footsteps.

"What's going on here?"

"Lorcan!" Grace rasped in relief.

"Oh great! Right on cue, it's good ol' reliable Lorcan," sneered Johnny. He still had his hand clamped firmly around her neck.

"Let her go!" Lorcan cried, attempting to prise Johnny's arm away. But the *vaquero* was too strong for him.

"Why should I?" Johnny said, his face dark and angry. "So *you* can get a piece of the action?"

"Just let her go!" Lorcan repeated.

But Johnny showed no sign of releasing Grace.

Grace shut her eyes. There was nothing Lorcan could do to save her. Nothing she could do to save herself.

When she opened her eyes again, she saw Lorcan lift his hand once more. Why was he even bothering? He knew that Johnny was far stronger.

But then Grace noticed something strange. Lorcan's Claddagh ring was glowing deep red as if it was heating up like a branding iron. The skull shape on it seemed to grow. No, it wasn't *seeming* to . . . it was *actually* growing! She watched as the head grew large and started moving – the small mouth grinding its teeth. Now Lorcan brought his hand up close to Johnny's neck and the glowing head came into contact with the flesh just beneath Johnny's ear. The skull's mouth opened and two fangs extended, like long, burning needles.

Johnny hadn't seen any of this. He was too lost in his hunger. He didn't notice until the glowing needles were embedded deep in his neck. Then he froze, his hands suddenly paralysed, his face wracked with pain.

Lorcan took advantage of the moment to pull Johnny away from Grace. This time, the *vaquero* put up no resistance. But Lorcan was merciful. The needle-like fangs retracted and he withdrew the ring.

While Johnny was still out of action, Lorcan busied himself loosening the rope around Grace's arms.

"Wow!" she said. "I never knew it could do that. All that time I had the ring around my neck . . ."

Lorcan shrugged. "I've told you before, Gracie. I've a few surprises up my sleeve yet." As he pulled the rope away, he saw the extent of her bruises and winced.

"Is it bad?" she said. "I hardly dare look."

"It's pretty bad, I'm afraid. You're going to need pots of that elder salve."

Johnny, meanwhile, had staggered to his feet. "Those wounds will heal," he said. "They're only surface cuts." He

466

drew himself up to his full height. "They're nowhere near as deep as the hurts you've inflicted on her."

"What are you talking about?" Lorcan said. "I've never hurt Grace. Not once."

"Oh, really?" said Johnny, with a smile. "Because that's not the way she tells it."

"Grace?" Lorcan looked at her in horror. She couldn't hold his eyes. She dropped her head. How could she have made the mistake of confiding her deepest feelings to Johnny? But he'd been a different Johnny then.

And now it was Lorcan who was raging. "What are you talking about? I never hurt Grace. Grace, tell him—"

"Oh, stop whingeing," Johnny said, his hunger momentarily abated after Lorcan's attack. "It's time for you to grow up and be a man. It's time you made up your mind about Grace. It's like you're hot one minute, cold the next. She doesn't know where she stands with you. None of us do."

"My feelings for Grace . . ." Lorcan began. Grace was surprised that he'd risen to the bait. Suddenly, she felt her heart racing in an entirely new way as they both waited for him to continue. "My feelings for Grace are . . . complicated."

"Complicated!" Johnny laughed. "*Complicated?* That's as lame as we might have expected from you."

On this point, Grace was inclined to agree with him, though it utterly enraged her to do so.

Johnny wasn't finished with Lorcan yet. "Look at the

467

facts, amigo. She came all this way up the mountain to help you. She's been living amongst vampires for months now. Why, the way *she* tells it, she even offered to be your donor. And how do you repay her? You tell her that it's all been a big mistake and she should go back to her regular little life and forget you!"

"No," Lorcan said, his eyes darting from Johnny to Grace. "It wasn't like that."

"Then tell us," Johnny continued, clearly enjoying himself. "You tell us how it is. And while you're at it, tell us what you want from Grace. Because if you really *do* want her, I'll step aside. I'll concede that the best vampire won. But if not, I'll take her. Maybe not today, maybe not tomorrow, but someday. Someday real soon."

"I'm not a prize!" Grace said angrily.

"No," Lorcan said. "No, you're not. Don't listen to him, Grace. It's the blood-hunger talking."

"At least I *have* some hunger," Johnny said. "At least I got some fire left in my belly!" He turned to Grace. "You know what they call it when a vampire feeds from a mortal?" She looked blankly back at him. "No? They call it a vampire kiss. I think you got a head full of dreams about loverboy over there, but I'll tell you something for nothing, that's the only kind of kiss he'll ever give you. The only difference between him and me is that I'm being honest with you."

Grace looked at Lorcan, her heart suddenly weighed down with emotion. Could it be true? Was that all their relationship could be? Was that what he'd been trying to tell

468

her himself, the struggle he'd been going through? Simply that he saw her as a potential donor – nothing more?

"No," Lorcan said. "No, you don't know what you're talking about. I told you before, my feelings for Grace are—"

"Yeah, yeah, we know – *complicated*!"

Suddenly Lorcan pulled Grace towards him. He held her tightly in his embrace and looked into her eyes. The pressure on her bruised arms was painful but she didn't care. She'd waited a long time for this moment.

"I do have feelings for you, Grace," he said. "The very strongest of feelings. But I'm not going to be forced into a corner like this. We need to talk – and soon – but we're *not* going to talk about this while he's here. What I have to tell you is too important. Is that good enough for you?"

"Yes!" She nodded, tears of pain and relief streaming down her face. "Yes!"

"Good!" With that, Lorcan leaned forward to enfold her in his arms and planted a kiss on her forehead. She felt his cool lips brush her skin. It sent shivers coursing through her entire body.

"Wow!" Johnny laughed. "A kiss on the head! You really are a passion wagon!"

"What on earth's going on here?"

They turned and saw Olivier striding towards them, kicking the discarded lariat. He had seen Grace's wounds too. He rushed over and lifted her arm with a gasp.

"It's Johnny," Grace said. "Someone mixed blood with his berry tea. He's gone psycho on us."

Olivier let go of Grace's arm, grabbed Johnny and held his arms behind his back. "It's OK," said Johnny. "It's OK, amigo. I'll play nice." Olivier let him go but kept his eyes firmly upon him, alert to further trouble.

"How could this have happened?" Lorcan asked.

"I don't know," Olivier said with a frown. "But we don't have time to discuss this now. Mosh Zu commands all vampires to join him in the Assembly Hall immediately!"

"Oh, really?" said Johnny. "What's up? Did he have a sudden overwhelming urge for group therapy?"

"Shut up!" Olivier said.

Johnny shrugged. "All right then. Come on, gang, let's all hightail it to the Assembly Hall!"

Olivier shook his head. "Not you, Grace. You need to go back to your chamber and lock the door."

"No way!" Grace said defiantly.

"These are Mosh Zu's express orders," Olivier said.

"Grace stays with me," said Lorcan, gripping her hand firmly.

"All right," sighed Olivier. "I haven't got the time or patience to argue with you. But Grace, you're putting yourself in the danger zone this time."

"Of course she is!" said Johnny. "Don't you know that there's no place Grace would rather be?"

470

CHAPTER FIFTY-ONE
The Journey On

"You are happy with my work?" Master Yin asked, as he lifted a swathe of cloth and revealed the gleaming swords beneath.

Connor was taken aback by the modesty of the master craftsman. Cheng Li had said he was the most gifted swordsmith of his generation and yet he watched as nervously as an apprentice as she took one of the swords from its case and held it up in the air. When she declared, "It's perfect!" the old man beamed from ear to ear.

Cheng Li laid the sword back down in the case. Master Yin covered it again with the cloth, as gently as if he was drawing a blanket over a baby in its crib. "Seventy swords and seventy daggers, as you requested," he said, placing the wooden lid on top.

"Excellent," said Cheng Li. "Connor, start taking these down to the pier while I sort out Master Yin's payment."

"Sure." Connor grabbed the first box of swords.

"I'll help you," said Bo Yin, grabbing the second box and following him out of the room.

When they were gone, Cheng Li turned to Master Yin. "Well?" she said. "What do you think?"

Master Yin smiled. "I think you are right," he said. "There *is* something about him. The way he handled the sword. I've only seen it very few times before. The last time, it was you."

Cheng Li smiled at his compliment, but then her smile faded.

"Something is troubling you," Master Yin said.

Cheng Li nodded. "I'm sure of Connor's talent. But he worries me. He is vulnerable. He just killed for the first time and it's left him in turmoil. I really think he might choose to leave piracy behind."

"Easier said than done." Master Yin nodded. "You do not choose to become a pirate. Piracy claims you. Just like it claimed Chang Po and the great Cheng I Sao." He sighed. "The first kill is a deep shock for anyone. It should be. To be a great pirate, you must appreciate the value of life and death. You do not want a killing machine on your crew."

"No," she said. "No, you're right, of course you are."

There was the sound of laughter as Connor and Bo Yin returned to the chamber to collect another two boxes. They reined in their giggles as if Cheng Li and Master Yin were teachers.

After they had gone, Cheng Li smiled at the

swordsmith. "There might be more than one pirate prodigy in this house today."

Master Yin shook his head. "We will not talk of this."

But Cheng Li proceeded, undeterred. "You know how Bo's face lights up at the mere mention of the ocean. She's strong and smart. And I've seen her handle swords before."

"Please," said the old swordsmith. "Please don't say such things."

"I don't want to upset you," said Cheng Li. "But think about your own words. *You do not choose to become a pirate. Piracy claims you.* And I think it's claiming . . ."

"Bo Yin," her father called, through the door.

"Yes, Pop!"

"Be careful with those boxes!" he called down. "You're not transporting fruit and vegetables!"

"Yes, Pop," she called back again.

Seeing his expression, Cheng Li decided not to push him further. But she had seen a certain look in the young girl's eyes. She recognised the fire there. You didn't have to be a seer to know how this was going to play out. Looking back at the swordsmith as he busied himself with another case, she realised that he knew it too. It was only a question of time.

"Here," he said, opening up a smaller case than the others. "Here is the special commission you requested." He opened the case and revealed the single sword and dagger, lying side by side.

Cheng Li leaned forward and let her finger trace the

length of the sword. "Superb," she said. "Exactly what I was hoping for."

"Good, good," the swordsmith said, closing the case again and setting it on top of the others for collection.

When the sloop was loaded with all the sword cases, Connor and Cheng Li taxied back to the pontoon to bid farewell to the swordsmith and his daughter. Bo Yin led Master Yin down the wooden stairs to meet them on the dockside.

"Thank you so much," Cheng Li said to the swordsmith.

"Thank *you*," said Master Yin. "And remember my advice."

Cheng Li nodded. "I shall. And remember mine." She turned to Bo Yin. "Thanks for all your assistance, Bo Yin."

Bo Yin nodded. "It was good to see you again, Cheng Li. And you too, Connor."

He grinned and nodded to her.

"Take good care of your father," Cheng Li said.

"We shall take care of one another," Master Yin said, drawing his daughter protectively towards him. "Just as we always do."

"It was a great pleasure to meet you, sir," Connor said, bowing before him.

"And you," said the swordsmith. "Enjoy your new weapons. Oops!" He clamped his hand over his mouth.

Connor turned and found Cheng Li shaking her head.

"Come on," she said to Connor. "Time we were setting sail."

She jumped down into the taxi boat. He followed and they journeyed back across the harbour. Soon, they had climbed from the smaller boat back onto the Academy sloop and were raising anchor, bound for the return journey. As Connor prepared the boat for departure, he saw Master Yin climbing back up to his house. But Bo Yin was standing on the harbourside, still watching. He waved to her, but she didn't seem to notice him. She seemed mesmerised.

"Bo Yin wants to be a pirate, doesn't she?" he said to Cheng Li.

Cheng Li nodded, pausing in her tasks. "There's an old saying. Perhaps you have heard it? The saying asks, how can you tell a true pirate?"

"And what's the answer?" Connor asked.

"Because when you look in their eyes all you see is the ocean." Cheng Li nodded. "Well, I've looked into Bo Yin's eyes and I see a whole lot of ocean."

The sail back was similar to the journey out. They talked little during the day, each focused once more on their own thoughts. Proper conversation was again delayed until dinner, over which Connor had many questions about Master Yin, his workshop and his pretty and spirited daughter.

"Now, *I* have a question for *you*," Cheng Li said.

"Something happened when you lifted Chang Po's sword. It was as if you had left us for a time and gone somewhere else entirely."

Connor nodded, putting down a chicken bone. "I had a vision," he said. "At first, I was on Chang Po's ship, or at least I thought I was. Then I found myself on the deck of my own ship . . ."

"Your *own* ship?"

"It was a vision of the future, I guess," he said. "People were calling me Captain Tempest."

"How did it feel?"

"It felt good," he said. "But it isn't the first time I've seen my future."

"No?" Her eyes compelled him to continue.

"No, it happened to me before at Pirate Academy. Twice. The first time was in the Rotunda, standing under all the captains' swords. Then it happened again, during one of Commodore Kuo's lectures."

"And, tell me, is it always the same vision?"

Connor shook his head. "No, the vision I had at Master Yin's was happy. It was a time of celebration. In the ones I had at Pirate Academy, I was wounded, bleeding. In fact, I think I foresaw my own death."

Cheng Li was wide-eyed. "You think you've seen your own death as a pirate captain?"

"Yes," he said. "It's another reason why I think I should leave this world behind."

"Easier said than done."

"Yes," he agreed.

"Connor, do you want my advice?"

"Of course."

"These visions, as vivid as they are, may not be actual flashes of your future. Perhaps they are more like glimpses into *choices*."

"You mean that it's all about the *kind* of pirate I become? Like you said before?"

She nodded.

"I've been thinking about that," he said. "I was thinking about it a lot when we were at Master Yin's. I think I *am* ready to go back to being a pirate. But not on Molucco Wrathe's ship." He looked up, his eyes bright once more. "I want to join *your* crew."

"I see." Cheng Li nodded. As usual, her face gave away little emotion.

"I thought you'd be pleased," Connor said.

"I'm flattered, of course," Cheng Li said. "But things are more complicated than you perceive or perhaps care to acknowledge." She fixed him in the eye. "You are not yet a free man, Connor. You are still bound to Captain Wrathe's articles."

"He'd let me go," Connor said. "I know he would. He'd understand I need a fresh start."

Cheng Li shook her head. "He'd think I poached you from under his nose. Let's not beat around the bush, Connor. We all know there's no love lost between me and Molucco Wrathe."

"Are you saying you won't consider me for your crew? For your deputy?"

"My deputy?" she smiled. "I see the old Connor Tempest is back and no mistake."

"No," he said, firmly. "This is the new Connor Tempest talking. Older, wiser . . ."

"Prove it to me," she said. "Go back and make your peace with Molucco. Whatever I think about him as a captain, he's been good to you. You should honour that. Go and talk to him, tell him how you feel. If he agrees to release you from his articles then I'll be pleased to have you on my crew."

They arrived back at the Academy under cover of darkness. In the Academy harbour was a galleon. Lit by the moon, it shone majestically.

"So it's here already," Cheng Li said, unable to keep the excitement out of her voice.

"Is that our new ship?" Connor asked.

"*My* new ship," Cheng Li said, with a smile. "It's my ship. And it's time you set sail for *The Diablo* and had your little talk with Molucco."

"Yes," he said, his heart once more heavy at the thought. He began gathering his things together and getting ready to run down to the light boat, still in its hiding place.

"Wait!" Cheng Li said. "I have something for you."

She disappeared into the hold and returned carrying a small case. She passed it to Connor. He looked at her questioningly, though he was already pretty sure what was inside. "Can I open it?" he asked. She nodded.

As he flipped back the twin locks and opened the case, his face was bathed in light. Lying there, looking up at him, were two new weapons – a rapier and, alongside it, a dagger.

"You needed a new sword and I thought it was about time you learned to fight with two weapons," Cheng Li said.

"They're beautiful!" Connor exclaimed. He reached in and lifted the sword. Immediately, he felt the same sense of connection he had with Chang Po's sword.

"Is it a good fit?" Cheng Li asked.

"Oh, yes," he said nodding. As he turned it in his hand, he noticed that there was an inscription on the hilt, just as there had been on Chang Po's sword. "What's this?"

"Read it," she said.

"*To Connor Tempest, a pirate of extraordinary promise. Given at the beginning of an outstanding career. From Cheng Li.*"

Connor was overwhelmed.

"Thank you," he said, forgetting about decorum and hugging her. "Thank you so much!"

"You're welcome," Cheng Li said, clearly a little thrown by this display of emotion.

"And thank you for your advice too," he said, returning the sword to its case.

"I rescued you from dark waters once before, remember?" She mused. "In fact, I seem to be making a habit of it, don't I?"

CHAPTER FIFTY-TWO

The Storming of the Citadel

Grace, Lorcan and Johnny were amongst the last to arrive in the Assembly Hall. The room was crowded with vampires, many of whom Grace had not seen before during her stay at Sanctuary. She realised that these were the vampires from all three blocks – from each stage of Mosh Zu's treatment. There were, as Olivier had indicated, no donors. Grace imagined they must be locked safely behind doors in the donor block.

She realised with a shudder that she was one of the very few non-vampires in the room. She had rejected Olivier's pleas to go to her own chamber and barricade herself in. But now she wondered if she had been right to do so. There was a difference between braving danger when it came at you and wilfully throwing yourself in its path. A squeeze from Lorcan's hand went some way to reassuring her that she had made the right decision. Besides, she wanted to be here to support Mosh Zu.

She looked up now as he took to the stage. "Is everyone here?" he asked Olivier.

Olivier nodded, closing the doors at the back of the hall and taking his seat beside Dani.

The hall was alive with murmurs but Mosh Zu silenced these by raising his hand. At once, all eyes turned to him.

"I have gathered you all here today to talk to you about a new state of danger." In response to this, whispers began circulating around the room. They soon died away as Mosh Zu continued. "But first I want to remind you all why you are here and what we can offer you at Sanctuary." He paused. "Being a vampire in society has its difficulties. I hardly need to tell you that. In your time here, I have talked with each and every one of you and heard your experiences – often deeply painful experiences – during your years of wandering. We have all been given the great gift of immortality. But, as we all know, that gift can also become a burden. It can become a burden if it means we are caught in an endless spiral – a spiral of hunting and feeding, then hungering, hunting and feeding, and hungering more. The danger of an existence such as this is that all we ever feel, all we are concerned with, is our own hunger. It blinds us to the rare beauty of the gift we have been given. It compels us to hurt others. It makes us exiles in this world. And I know that all of you here are familiar with this sense of exile."

Grace listened, gripped, as he continued. "When you come to Sanctuary, it marks the end of those years of wandering and the beginning of your coming out of exile. We work with you to manage your hunger. When our work is done, you are able to feed without hurting others. Our ultimate goal is for you to sail away on *The Nocturne*. Some of you may choose to return to the land. But when you leave here, so long as you continue our teachings, you will have a system for managing your hunger and for embarking on a more meaningful immortality. Then you are truly free to embrace the gift."

Now Mosh Zu's face grew dark. "However, there is now a new state of danger. You are going to be pulled in different directions by outside forces."

There were murmurs at this.

"A new, growing faction of vampires is actively encouraging the abandonment of our teachings," continued Mosh Zu. "They would sooner waste away their eternity than give up the constant hunt for blood. They are wanton in their employment of violence, flagrant in their disregard for mortal lives. Even now, they are preparing to come at you and tempt you to join them. And make no mistake – you *will* be tempted. It will be hard work to resist. As I said before – our work here is not easy. But joining them is *very* easy and that makes it even more inviting."

He looked up and swept his eyes across the ranks of vampires. "I want you to know two things. Firstly, if you do make the decision to join them, you will never be able to return to Sanctuary. Our gates will be closed to you for ever . . . and I do mean *for ever*. That may sound brutal but I will not take the risk. The second thing to know is that, as inviting as their promise seems, it is an invitation only to your own oblivion."

With that he stepped back. "That is all."

A hand rose from the centre of the crowd.

"I have nothing further to add at this point," Mosh Zu said. "Later, if you have questions . . ."

But this vampire wouldn't be stalled. There was a hubbub in the crowd and Grace could see he was pushing through his row to get to the gangway. As he made it, she gasped. It was Sidorio. How on earth had *he* got in here?

Clearly Mosh Zu was thinking the same thing. He stared at Sidorio in disbelief as he came striding along the gangway, up towards the stage.

"It's all right," Sidorio said. "I don't have a question."

"Then go," said Mosh Zu.

"Won't you let me have my say?"

Mosh Zu hesitated. Grace could see he was unsure of what to do for the best. That hesitation proved fatal. Sidorio leaped onto the stage beside him and began addressing the crowd.

"Some of you may be wondering who I am. Others will already know. I am Sidorio, a former lieutenant on board *The Nocturne*. I'm here with news of my own. The first thing to know is that there is no longer only one Vampirate ship. *The Nocturne*'s time is over. There is a second ship and soon there will be others. And on these ships, we will do things a little differently."

"You must leave!" Mosh Zu told him.

"But they want to hear from me," Sidorio said, nodding at the spellbound crowd. "Can't you see how interested they are? You've had your turn at the stump. Am I to have no chance to put across my manifesto?" He bared his teeth in a smile.

Mosh Zu stepped forward again. As he did so, a voice from the crowd called out. "Let him speak!"

"Yes!" cried another. "Let him have his say!"

Mosh Zu shook his head but Grace could see that it was a shake of despair. Now, as Sidorio took centre stage, Mosh Zu climbed down from the platform.

"That's democracy for you, eh?" Sidorio laughed. "He won't even share the stage with me!"

Some of the vampires laughed back. Grace could see that he had already begun to win over part of the audience.

"I come from the new faction, as your *guru* calls it. But there's nothing new in my thinking. It's not very complex, either. You could sum it up in two words. *Be yourself.* You are vampires. So am I. You need blood. So do I. Why fight it? *Be yourself.* Why complicate your existence with trying to 'manage' your supply? We need blood and we always will. We already have the gift of immortality. *Be yourself.* Do you really want to spend eternity measuring out your portions? Or do you want to just get on with the business of living, really living? We're not under threat, by the way, from the mortal community. We are growing in number. We *are* the threat! No mortal in their right mind would mess with us. *Be yourself.*"

As he spoke, his eyes scanned the room and fell upon Grace. She sent him a look of disdain. She saw to her satisfaction that he seemed momentarily perturbed, but then he continued.

"My ship is waiting for any of you who would like to come and join. All you have to do is follow me down the mountain. A new voyage awaits you there. And, I can assure you, it's going to be the voyage of your lives! So what do you say? Who's with me?"

Grace felt her heart sink to new depths as she watched a number of vampires raise their hands and call out their support. Amongst the voices, she heard Johnny's familiar accent. "I'm with you, man!" Grace shook her head sadly. It was his hunger talking. It was the same for all of them. Sidorio knew exactly which button to press as he signed them up to their doom.

"Excellent," Sidorio said. "In a moment, I'll walk out of here. All you have to do is follow me. But I have one further message for the rest of you, for those of you still sitting on the fence. You have been told that *The Nocturne* is ready to welcome you when you have completed your studies here. That the captain will take you off on a jolly voyage into eternity. Well, I'm sorry to be the one to burst the bubble but the truth is that, as of this moment, *The Nocturne has* no captain."

There were gasps around the room.

"No," roared Sidorio. "Because he's collapsed and is fighting for his life up here. And, between you and me, I don't rate his chances."

"Is this true?" one of the vampires cried.

Mosh Zu stepped back onto the stage.

"Tell us the truth!" cried another.

Mosh Zu raised his hand. "It is true that the captain is unwell . . ."

"*Unwell*?" Sidorio cried. "I think that's a bit of an understatement."

But Mosh Zu's confirmation had been enough to increase the discontent in the hall and to raise the number of new recruits for Sidorio.

"Why didn't you tell us?" another vampire yelled.

"Yes! We should have been told!" called out another.

"Don't you see?" Sidorio said. "That's how they do things here. They keep secrets from you."

"It's your fault!" Mosh Zu cried. "It's you who *caused* the captain's collapse."

Ignoring this comment, Sidorio continued. "How long has he been here? How long has he been laid out in your healing chamber while you fight to save his life? An hour? An afternoon? A night?"

Mosh Zu shook his head, refusing to answer.

"Well, *you* may not be willing to tell them, but I am," Sidorio roared. "He's been there for two days. Two whole days under lock and key, his life draining out of him. And with it, any hopes you lot might have had for sailing off with him on that ship."

"That's not true," Mosh Zu cried to the audience. "You don't understand! It's all lies."

Sidorio shook his head and folded his arms. "I'm not the one telling porky pies round here and well you know it." With that he jumped down from the stage.

"Olivier, open the doors!" he called.

How did he know Olivier's name? Grace turned towards Olivier and saw Mosh Zu's head swivel at the same time. So, there had been a fresh betrayal. They watched as Olivier leaped up and did his new master's bidding, pushing open the doors.

"This, by the way, is the man you have to thank for the way you're feeling tonight!" Sidorio said, drawing Olivier towards him. "He's the one who put a little extra kick in your flasks earlier. In fact, he's been gradually increasing your blood levels for days now. We reckoned you'd had your fill of berry tea."

Grace felt sick. So it was Olivier himself, Mosh Zu's trusted number two, who had tampered with the tea mixture and given the healing vampires an increased dose of blood. No wonder Sidorio had found such a susceptible audience.

"How could you?" she asked Olivier. "How could you do it? You were Mosh Zu's first assistant."

"Yes," Olivier, "I was. Until *you* came along. But then everything changed, didn't it?"

487

Grace was shaken to the core. Was she in some way responsible for what was happening?

"Ignore him," Mosh Zu said. "His mind has been poisoned."

"No!" Olivier said. "No, Sidorio listened to me, heard my concerns." He looked to Sidorio for reassurance. "We made a pact."

"A pact!" cried Grace. Her eyes travelled from Olivier to Sidorio. "What *kind* of pact?"

"I paved the way for Sidorio's arrival here," Olivier said. "And he promised me . . ."

Sidorio chuckled. It was chilling. Olivier faltered.

"*What* did he promise you?" Mosh Zu asked. "A position on his new ship?"

"What's the problem?" Olivier said. "I was your first assistant. Now I'm his!"

Sidorio shrugged. "Not *necessarily* my *first* assistant, buddy . . ."

"What do you mean?" Olivier said. "We talked. We agreed—"

"You've been a great help," Sidorio said. "And I'm grateful. From the bottom of my . . . well." He pushed Olivier away. "We'll talk later."

"You see," Mosh Zu said. "You see how he uses you and then pushes you aside?" Mosh Zu's eyes swept across the rooms as he addressed the others. "Make no mistake! This is how it will be for each and every one of you. He does not have your interests at heart, only his own evil scheming."

Grace felt a flicker of hope. She could see Mosh Zu's words had struck home with some of the crowd.

But as Sidorio cleared his throat, all eyes turned to him once more. As if he was exerting some dark hold over them. Some terrible charisma.

"We've allowed ourselves to get sidetracked," he said. "Now, where was I? Oh yes . . .

"Follow me if you want a new life on a new ship. A ship where you'll get the blood you want when you want it. And, I can promise you, there'll be no more pathetic heart-searching, no more touchy-feely stuff like meditation or group hugs!"

As he reached the door, a large number of vampires rose from their seats and swarmed excitedly around him. They began talking to each other in raised voices. Sidorio marched out of the room, and they followed him. Like rats following after the Pied Piper, thought Grace, grimly. She watched as Johnny surged forward, his eyes bright with a new purpose. He had always said he was a bad judge of character. Well, he'd hit the jackpot this time.

Grace rushed over to Mosh Zu. "We must stop them!" she said.

"No." He shook his head. "They are already tainted. My trusted assistant has seen to that." They both turned to watch as Olivier ushered the new recruits through the doors. Grace wondered why he was still helping Sidorio. Didn't he understand that there was no place for him in the renegade crew? She turned back to Mosh Zu, wishing that he could have foreseen Olivier's weakness, his betrayal.

"It's always the ones closest to you," Mosh Zu said. "They're always the hardest to read. You lose perspective."

Grace watched in despair as the chairs emptied. By now, about a third of the vampires had followed in Sidorio's wake. The rest lingered, reeling at the news of the captain, distraught at their safe harbour being invaded.

"Can't you stop him?" one asked Mosh Zu. "Can't you bring them back?"

Mosh Zu shook his head. "Whatever Sidorio might accuse me of, I'm not in the business of brainwashing. *I* don't heal you when you come to me. I work with you so you can heal yourself. You come to Sanctuary of your own volition and you leave here in the same way. It's about the choices *you* make. And they," he nodded towards the doors, "they have made their choice."

"What about us?" one of the others asked. As she turned, Grace recognised her as the Princesse de Lamballe.

"Nothing has changed," Mosh Zu said. "Our work continues. There may be fewer of you here but that only means we can work harder with those of you who choose to stay."

"What about the captain?" the princess persisted. "Is it true that he is dying?"

"The captain is in some distress," Mosh Zu said. "But he is responding well to treatment. He will recover. And he *will* return to *The Nocturne*. And now, if you'll excuse me,

I am going to check up on him. Grace, perhaps you would like to join me?"

She nodded.

Mosh Zu turned. "The rest of you, those of you who have chosen to stay, please go back to your rooms and think about what has happened here today. Think about what you really want out of your eternity. And, if you are in any doubt, then leave us and follow that camel train down the mountain."

With that, he marched angrily out of the room. Grace followed in his wake.

As they walked along the corridor to Mosh Zu's rooms, they passed the rec room. Glancing inside, Grace paused. Mosh Zu marched on ahead, oblivious.

"I'll catch you up," she called. She was unsure whether he had even heard her.

Stepping inside the rec room, she watched Johnny move one of the chess pieces. "Checkmate," he said, looking at her with a grin as he knocked down the white King. He began packing up the chessboard. She wondered whether he'd find any willing chessplayers amongst the departing vampires.

"Don't go with him, Johnny," she said. "I know you're tempted. They put blood in your tea, so you would be. That's why you attacked me before. You couldn't control yourself. But if you stay here, things will get better for you. I know they will."

He looked at her sadly. "I told you before, Grace, it's

491

hard here. The truth is, today wasn't the first time I took blood. Olivier was always open to a little deal." He sighed. "I tried, Grace, I really did. But I've made my decision. I'm going with that Sidorio dude."

Grace watched disconsolately as he picked up the chessboard and pieces and threw them into his kitbag. She had one final idea of how to stop him.

"Remember everything you told me?" she said. "About your life and death? You admitted it yourself. You're a really bad judge of character."

He smiled. Clearly he remembered the confession.

Grace continued. "You've made bad choices before, Johnny. But if you walk out of these doors tonight, that'll be the very worst choice you've ever made."

He shrugged. "I hear you, Grace. I hear you, but the way I figure it, what more have I got to lose?" With that he swung his bag over his shoulder and came over to her.

"I tried being good. I really gave it my all – and then some. And you know what, it ain't that I *can't* be good. It's just that I'm so much better at being bad." He took up his Stetson and angled it low across his brow. "I'll be seeing you, little lady," he said as he slipped out of the room.

Grace shook her head, tears rolling down her cheeks. This was all so awful. Her whole world was crumbling around her. And not just *her* world.

Suddenly she had a fresh thought. Where was Lorcan? She hadn't seen him since the Assembly Hall. As the crowd had surged forward and she'd sought out Mosh Zu, she'd lost him. Where had he gone? He couldn't have followed Sidorio too, could he? If he had, then all her hope, all her faith was gone. Tears in her eyes, she turned and left the rec room.

As she entered the corridor, she began running. She wasn't sure exactly where she was going. But she had a sudden desperate urge for air.

Outside, she saw Johnny racing off to catch the back of the line descending the mountain. Shaking her head, she stood alone in the courtyard. The air was cold and she realised it was starting to snow. She looked up at the eddy of snowflakes swirling down to meet her. She remembered the vision she'd had of Johnny's life and death, of falling snow. She shut it out. It was too painful to think about him now.

Remembering the kitchen garden where she'd retreated once before, she decided to go there now, to get away from them. To get away from all of them. She darted away from the main square and took the path to the garden. It was a relief, at first, to be alone there. It looked even prettier than she remembered it, as snow fell over the fountain and the benches surrounding it.

She thought of the time she had lain there, Lorcan's ribbon around her neck and then, after the princess's interruption, in her hand. She had been searching for answers that night, searching for a way to help Lorcan. Now, any such thoughts were banished. Lorcan had gone, presumably following Johnny and Sidorio's other fresh recruits. Now, all Grace sought was peace. But although this place might offer it, it was too cold. She'd have to go back inside else catch her death by staying here. Sadly, she retraced her steps out of the garden and into the main courtyard. She dropped her head to keep the snow from falling into her eyes.

By the time she saw a figure walking towards her through the falling snow, he was almost upon her. She glanced up for a moment. He was dressed in a military greatcoat, its shoulders already dusted with snowflakes. As his intense blue eyes met hers, he quickened his pace.

"Lorcan!" she cried.

"Grace! You're covered in snow! You must be freezing!" He opened his greatcoat and drew her inside it.

"You're shaking," he said. "How long have you been standing out here?"

"I thought you'd gone," she said miserably. "I thought you'd followed Sidorio and I'd lost you all over again."

"Are you crazy?" he said. "You think I'd choose Sidorio? Over *you*?" He shook his head. "Never!"

She sighed with relief and relaxed into Lorcan's chest. This more than made up for Johnny. This gave her some belief that things might once again be right in the world.

"Come on," Lorcan said. "Let's get you inside before you catch your death."

Together, they hurried back into the warmth.

CHAPTER FIFTY-THREE

The Ties that Bind

"Hello stranger!" Sugar Pie smiled as she entered the booth. "How many nights in a row is this? Six?"

Connor shook his head. "Nine."

"Maybe tonight's the night, eh?"

"I hope so," Connor said. He was growing tired of waiting for Molucco and his crew. The burden of his impending discussion grew heavier the longer it was delayed. After returning from Lantao, it had been impossible to try to track *The Diablo* at sea. Coming back to Ma Kettle's had seemed the obvious idea. The moment the ship was back in these waters, they'd be sure to hit the tavern.

"Let me get you another drink," Sugar Pie said.

"Thanks."

"Are you sure I can't tempt to you to anything stronger?"

He shook his head. Shrugging, Sugar Pie turned to exit

the booth. Before doing so, she glanced back at him. "I'm worried about you," she said.

"Please don't be."

"It's just that you look so much older, Connor. The first time you came in here, you were just a boy. Now you're a man. But you're not a happy man. And you know what they say about a pirate's life. It should be short but merry – with an accent on the merry!"

"I have some things to sort out," Connor said. "Once they're done, I'll be the same old Connor you always knew."

"Don't make promises you can't keep . . ." Sugar Pie said. "Right now, I'd settle for a smile."

He did his best.

"Well, that's a start," she said. "There's something I want you to know, Connor. You're always welcome here at Ma Kettle's. Whatever the future has in store for you." She paused. "You're one of the good guys."

It was just what he needed to hear. When he looked back at her, there were tears in his eyes. Suddenly all the pain and sorrow and guilt swimming around inside broke through him like a wave.

"Oh, Connor," Sugar Pie said, seeing him struggling with his emotions. She sat down and wrapped her arms around him. He didn't fight it, just let her hold him. It felt good to let everything out.

"Better?" Sugar Pie asked.

He pulled back from her and nodded. This time, he felt

the muscles in his face relax and he was able to give her a proper smile. He'd often dreamed of finding himself in Sugar Pie's arms, but in somewhat different circumstances.

"OK, then," Sugar Pie said, standing up again. "Now, I'm going to get you that drink."

After she'd gone, Connor leaned over and pulled back the velvet curtain, looking out across the dance-floor and the rest of the tavern. It was quiet tonight but, then again, it *was* a Tuesday. He wondered if Ma's new security procedures had deterred some of her regulars. In the wake of Jenny Petrel's murder, Ma had banned all weaponry from the bar. Even now, her head of security – a nice guy who went by the name Pieces 08 – was busy frisking newcomers and putting their swords, daggers, *shuriken* and other accoutrements into the cloakroom for the duration of their stay. It was ironic, thought Connor. Because it wasn't a sword or dagger or *shuriken* that had put an end to young Jenny's life. It was a pair of teeth and a hunger beyond all human understanding. And that was a whole lot harder to prevent.

"What's all this then?" Connor heard a familiar voice. "What an indignity! Whoever heard of such a thing as a pirate being stripped of his daggers!" There was no doubting that voice. Connor's heart began to race. He looked down over the edge of the booth and there, sure enough, was Molucco Wrathe, in the centre of the tavern, his face a picture of bewilderment as Pieces 08 gently but firmly explained that there were no exceptions to Ma Kettle's new security rules.

As the debate continued, Connor exited the booth and made his way down the narrow staircase to the ground floor.

By the time he got there, Pieces had succeeded not only in taking Molucco's twin silver daggers off him but a few other smaller weapons which he'd evidently secreted under his vast coat. Connor watched from afar as Pieces collected up the armoury and loaded it into a metal box, handing Molucco a numbered ticket.

"Where's Kitty?" Molucco was asking. "Someone tell Kitty Kettle that I'm here. And tell her I'll have no truck with numbered tickets unless there are good prizes to be won!"

He was poised to set fly with another protest when his eyes met Connor's. His mouth dropped open, but he was unusually silent. Then he smiled and said Connor's name, beckoning him closer.

"Dear boy, is it you? We've been so worried!" Molucco held out his arms and Connor hugged him, more out of protocol than the desire for any warmth. There were things he needed to say to Molucco Wrathe and he couldn't get sidetracked by the captain's overblown displays of sentimentality.

"Let me look at you!" Molucco said, holding Connor's face between his jewelled hands. "You've lost weight! Have you been eating? Oh, Mister Tempest. How good it is to know you are safe and well and have come back to us!"

Connor looked up at him through his vice-like grip. He

could see that Barbarro, Trofie and Moonshine Wrathe had followed Molucco inside. They looked a little less enthusiastic about this reunion.

"Good evening, Connor," said Trofie, at least putting on a display of concern. "We've all been so worried about you, *min elskling*."

As Captain Wrathe finally released him from his grip, Connor nodded to Trofie. "Thank you," he said. "But I'm fine. I've been travelling."

"Yes, yes," Molucco said. "And we must hear all about it. It's a night of comings and goings, and no mistake," he said. "My dear brother and his family are bidding us farewell, for now."

Moonshine grinned at Connor. "You know how it goes. Places to raid, people to maul."

"Actually," said Trofie, smiling indulgently at her son, "I had a yen for cooler climes."

"And," added Barbarro, "what my dear wife wants, my dear wife gets." He placed one arm on Trofie's shoulder, the other on Moonshine's.

Molucco beamed at Connor. "So it is with us nautical families. Our ships are for ever sailing. But, as one ship voyages out, so another returns to safe harbour. Come along, Mister Tempest. Your dear friends Bartholomew and Cate will be here soon. Let's go into the VIP area."

"Yes, let's," agreed Trofie. "I'd give my left hand for a glass of champagne."

"Actually," said Connor, addressing Molucco alone, "I'd

like to talk to you alone, sir, if that's all right. I don't want to keep you from your party but perhaps we could step outside for a walk?"

"A walk?" Molucco boomed. "Well, yes, why not? So long as it's all right with the head of security."

"It's fine by me, sir," said Pieces 08 with a smile. "And don't worry. Your private arsenal will be quite safe with me."

Shaking his head, Molucco gestured for Connor to lead the way back out of the tavern and onto the boardwalk. As Molucco had said, Bart and Cate were in line at the door. They both turned, surprised, then grinned and waved at him. He nodded and mouthed, "I'll see you later!" He couldn't allow himself to be distracted from this important task. He had already walked on as they turned back to each other, their faces etched with expressions of concern.

Connor and Molucco walked to the end of the boardwalk but it was louder out here than inside the tavern, not least as word spread down the queue of the newly imposed security measures.

"This is no good," said Molucco. "We can't talk here." Connor grimaced. He had to have the captain alone. "We'll go aboard the ship," Molucco said. "In fact, we'll take a sneaky rum in my cabin before rejoining the others."

"Perfect!" Connor nodded, thinking that he'd forego the rum.

*

It was strange being back in Molucco's cabin. It was at once a familiar yet foreign place to him. He recognised the treasures contained within and yet he saw it with different eyes. The eyes of a stranger, he realised. Already, he was distancing himself from the captain and the ship. Already, he was stepping back from the crew.

"There!" said Molucco, placing a large glass of rum in front of him and pouring the remains of a decanter into his own. "Sit down, take the weight off your feet!" They both sat at a highly polished table that Connor decided must be a new acquisition, perhaps from the raid on the Sunset Fort.

"So, Mister Tempest. Tell me, where have you been?"

"All over," said Connor, trying to keep his tone as measured as possible. "I've been sailing around, thinking about everything that's happened, everything I've done."

Captain Wrathe nodded, taking a draught of rum.

"I'm sorry I left you like that," Connor said. "I didn't mean to worry you or anyone else. I just had to deal with what I'd done."

He waited for the captain to say something encouraging but he simply sipped his drink and nodded. "And now you've made peace with yourself and come home." Molucco lifted his glass. "Welcome back, Connor!"

Connor frowned. "I *haven't* made peace with myself," he said. "I'm not sure that I ever will. I killed a man. In cold blood."

"You saved my nephew's life!" Molucco said. "And the

Wrathe family will always be grateful to you for that. Take a drink of your rum, boy. You'll feel better."

Connor shook his head. "I acted to save Moonshine and I'm not sorry I did that. But I can't let go of the fact that I killed that security guard."

"The first time's never easy," Molucco said. "But you're a pirate, lad. It was bound to happen sooner or later. Especially with your prowess at swords. It will get easier, you'll see."

"I don't *want* it to get easier," Connor said.

Molucco's face was a picture of confusion. "You want it to get more difficult?"

"Yes," Connor said. "No. No, I just don't want to become accustomed to killing. For no good reason."

Now Molucco frowned. "You think that saving my nephew's life was no good reason to kill?"

Connor paused. He'd have to choose his words very carefully now, very carefully indeed. "I think," he began, "I think that Moonshine could have avoided getting himself into that situation in the first place."

"Oh," said Molucco, swigging more rum. "You do, do you? Suddenly, you're the expert on attack strategy."

Connor shook his head. "You don't need to be an expert."

"No," said Captain Wrathe. "*You* don't need to be an expert. You're a junior ranking pirate, Connor Tempest. In some circles, they call the likes of you *rapier fodder*. You're paid to fight, not to think. You can comfortably leave that to the senior members of the crew."

Connor was silent but his expression said it all.

"Unless," continued Molucco, "you're not happy with what the senior crew decides. In which case, you had better *get* happy, and fast."

Connor had known that he'd have to contend with Molucco's anger at some point and now he could see it had arrived, like a rogue wave rising from a calm sea. Connor gritted his teeth and prepared for the emotional white water ahead. With Molucco Wrathe, it was ever thus.

"I'm surprised," said Molucco, "that if you're so ill at ease with the way I run my ship that you came back from the wilderness at all. Why not just sail off into the sunset?"

Connor shook his head. "That wouldn't be right. Or fair. I'm so grateful for everything you've done for me . . ."

"I should think so. I rescued you from the ocean with my bare hands!"

This was a bare-faced lie, rather typical of Molucco's myth-making, but it was hardly the moment to remind him that in fact it was Cheng Li who had fished him out of the water.

"You gave me a home," Connor said simply, "when I had none. And I can never fully repay you for that." He sighed. "But *The Diablo* no longer feels like my home. I just don't feel I can be the pirate you want me to be."

Molucco shook his head sadly. "A pretty pass this is, Mister Tempest. A pretty pass. You were like a son to me."

Connor had expected him to trot out this well-worn phrase. "But I'm *not* your son," he said. "And when the

503

chips are down, I'll always come second to Moonshine, to your real family."

Molucco seemed surprised at his words. "So that's it, then? You've come back to tell me thanks but no thanks. After all I've done for you."

"Yes," Connor said.

They sat in silence for a good while longer. To say it was uncomfortable was an understatement.

"So is that all?" Molucco said at last. "Or is there more?"

Connor took a deep breath. There was one more thing he had to tell Molucco. It would be safer not to but he owed him the truth – the whole truth. However explosively Molucco reacted now, he had to hear it from Connor.

"There *is* one more thing," Connor said. "I saw Cheng Li."

Molucco's eyes widened. Surely he wasn't going to enforce his petty rule of not having her name spoken in his cabin? They were way past all that.

"She's to be given her own ship," Connor continued.

"*Muchas gracias* for the newsflash," Molucco said. "But I was aware of that fact. And I can guess where this is going. You want to join her crew, don't you?"

Connor nodded. There was another prolonged silence. He expected the captain to unleash another torrent of rage but, instead, he shook his head and sighed. "I might have expected that Cheng Li would have been at the root of all this. She's poisoned you against me. Got at you when you were at your most despondent and vulnerable and—"

"No," Connor said, daring to interrupt his captain. He had so far overstepped the mark that now there was no going back. "No, it wasn't like that. She took me to Lantao. She was collecting weapons from the swordsmith there. We talked . . ."

"Oh, I'm sure you had plenty to talk about," Molucco said bitterly. "I'm sure she was full of advice, as she warmed you up to the idea of betraying me."

Now Connor was angry. Or, rather, he realised quite how angry he'd been all along. He could no longer batten it down. "Actually," he said, "she told me to come back and make my peace with you. I would have sailed with her then and there but she told me to come and talk to you. She said that you were my captain, whatever I felt, and that my first duty was to you. That I must honour my articles."

It was the *coup de grâce*. They both knew it. Every card Molucco Wrathe had to play had been played. Now, he stood up and drained the last of his rum. Then he staggered over to a heavy wooden filing cabinet and ran his hands over its three drawers. "A to I, J to R, S to Z!" He heaved open the bottom drawer and started rummaging through the files inside. Finally, exclaiming "T for Tempest," he lifted out a green card file and began flicking through the leaves of parchment inside. The papers covered the colour spectrum from cream to yellow to beige to brown. Such was the length of time that some of Captain Wrathe's crew had been articled to him.

"Here we are," the captain announced with no joy. "Tempest, Connor." He took out the creamy sheet of Connor's articles and stuffed the rest of the file back in the drawer. He walked back to the table where they had been sitting. A candle was burning in its centre and the captain brought the paper into the glow of the candlelight as he began to read. "*On this, the sixth day of the sixth month in the year two thousand five hundred and five, I, Connor Tempest, being of sound mind and able body, do solemnly swear my allegiance in perpetuity to Captain Molucco Wrathe . . .*"

He stopped reading and glanced up at Connor. "You know, of course, what *perpetuity* means?"

Connor nodded. "I know that the articles are binding for ever. I know what I'm asking is unprecedented. I could pay you. I don't have much now but we could come to an arrangement."

Molucco's hand trembled for a moment. In the candlelight, his sapphire rings glittered like the ocean. When he spoke, his voice had taken on a new tone. "An arrangement is impossible."

What did he mean? Was he going to refuse point blank to let Connor go? His eyes gave nothing away. They were distant, empty.

Suddenly, Connor smelled burning. He looked down and saw that the sheet of paper bearing his articles was alight. His contract with Captain Wrathe was literally going up in smoke.

He opened his mouth to alert Captain Wrathe to the

accident. Then he realised it was no accident. The captain was feeding the paper into the hungry fire. It was incredible how quickly the paper burned. Connor watched as the flames licked away at his signature and the spot of his own blood he had spilled beneath it. Now, Captain Wrathe held up the last jagged edge of paper as it duly turned to soot. He blew it off his fingers and, taking a silk handkerchief from his breast pocket, carefully wiped the soot from his skin. He looked up at Connor coldly.

"There are no longer articles binding you to this ship. Which begs the question, why are you still sitting here in my cabin?"

He turned and walked away from the table. As he did so, Scrimshaw uncoiled himself and glanced back at Connor. Connor expected the snake to hiss, out of loyalty to his master, but, if anything, he seemed to be regarding Connor with some sadness.

"Thank you, Captain Wrathe," Connor said.

There was a pause as if the captain hadn't heard him. Then he spoke, without turning around. "Don't thank me, boy. Don't talk to me. You're nothing to me now."

Connor could take no more of this. He turned and walked as fast as he could out of the cabin and across the deck. He had got what he wanted, had secured his freedom, but it didn't feel anything like victory.

As he climbed down the ladder and jumped down onto the pier, his heart was pumping wildly. He looked up and saw Bart and Cate walking towards him.

He couldn't stop the tears from flowing again.

"What's the matter, Connor?" asked Cate, anxiously.

"I'm leaving," he said. Seeing their surprise, he added, "for good this time. Captain Wrathe has released me from my articles."

He saw the expression that passed between Bart and Cate. They knew how serious this was.

"Where will you go now, buddy?" Bart asked, tears welling in his own eyes.

"I'm signing up to Cheng Li's crew," Connor said. "I need a fresh start. But before I do that, I've got one more important journey to make. One more person I have to see."

Cate nodded and managed a stab at a smile as she spoke. "Grace."

Connor nodded too. He couldn't bear to draw this out. There was so much he wanted to say, such a strong bond between him and the two people before him. "I'm really bad at goodbyes," he said, gesturing vaguely towards the jetty, where his small boat lay waiting for him.

"Then let's not make it goodbye," Bart said, stepping forward and hugging his friend. "Make it *hasta la vista*. This isn't the end! We'll see you soon, buddy!" He gripped Connor tightly then stepped back, tears flowing down his face.

"He's right," said Cate. "Just because you've left *The Diablo*, nothing changes between *us*. Our friendship goes deeper than that. You can always count on us. *Always*."

Connor nodded but his eyes were streaming now and he couldn't stay there and let it get any worse. "I really have to go now," he said, as much to himself as to his friends. As he turned away, he glimpsed Bart put his arm around Cate's shoulder.

His legs threatened to buckle but he kept walking down the boardwalk until he reached his small boat. He let slip the mooring line, jumped aboard and began manoeuvring it away from the harbour, out onto the dark sea. He didn't look back, *couldn't* look back, but the bright light of Ma Kettle's neon sign flashed over him like the rays from a setting sun.

CHAPTER FIFTY-FOUR

The Liberator

"Now this," says Sidorio, eyes bright, "*this* was a great idea! Good work, Stukeley!"

Stukeley shrugs. "You wanted a bigger ship *and* more crew. I thought we'd kill two birds with one stone."

"A prison ship!" Johnny D says. "You know, they used to call these hulks."

"Like the Incredible Hulk?" Sidorio asks, grinning.

"Not exactly," says Johnny. He and Stukeley exchange a look. In a few short weeks, they have become firm allies — each recognising their need for the other as the future dawns. They stand, on either side of their captain — his two trusty lieutenants. The power — the brains — behind the throne.

Their own hijacked ship looms close to the prison hulk. The hulk will do them much better, they all agree. It's bigger, for a start, and it looks ugly, barren, like some kind of sea-monster. "It sends out the right message," Stukeley says. Johnny D nods.

"Not long now, lads," says Sidorio. In a short time, they will board the hulk and take it for their own. A new era – for all of them – will begin. No more false starts, thinks Sidorio. Everything's coming together. He thinks briefly of three former comrades – Lumar, Olin and Mistral. Those who perished in the fire. They were weak. There can be no weakness in his team. He turns from side to side, observing his twin lieutenants. There's a darkness about these two. No weakness there. He addresses them both. "Is everyone ready?"

The two lieutenants turn and survey their teams. Behind them on the deck are ranked the two halves of the newly forged crew – those who Stukeley lured from *The Nocturne* and those who came alongside Johnny D from Sanctuary. Out of them, it was Johnny D's enthusiasm that had marked him out for a senior role.

"Yes, Captain!" Stukeley and Johnny D answer in unison.

"Excellent! We'll go in first. And each of you, pick five of your crew – ones you know to be bloodthirsty. They'll come in with us. The rest should be poised to follow once we've taken out the guards."

Stukeley and Johnny D quickly make their selections. The chosen men and women step forward. The others are ready to follow. There's a sense of energy and purpose as the ship draws level with the prison hulk. Everyone knows that tonight marks the beginning of something.

"OK, crew!" Sidorio cries. "Follow me!" He jumps from one ship to the other, somersaulting in midair. He has the athleticism of a teenager, Stukeley thinks. The captain is at his best in these situations. Turning, Stukeley sees that Johnny D is already ushering the rest of their team forward. One after another, they take flight from one deck to the next. Thirteen pairs of feet drum across the upper deck of the prison hulk.

Sidorio summons them over. He has found the stairs leading down. But why bother with stairs when you can simply jump? "Follow me!" he says to his lieutenants. In a single motion, the three of them descend into the depths of the ship. As they land, they face three stunned guards. It's like a mirror, but a distorted one such as you'd find in a carnival tent.

"Who are you?" asks the bravest of the guards. "Where did you come from?"

"Didn't you see?" Johnny D replies. "We floated down from the sky like angels."

"Yeah, I saw that, but how did you get on board?"

Stukeley smiles. "Looks like you made a mistake. You were so intent on no one breaking *out* of your prison, you didn't do too much to stop anyone breaking *in*."

"Who'd want to break in here? Do you know the category of prisoners we're carrying?"

"Yeah," says another of the guards. "Category D – for doomed."

The third guard now finds the confidence to speak.

"When they locked up this lot, they really did throw away the key. These guys ain't never gonna see the light of day again."

Sidorio shrugs. "The light of day is overrated." Smiling, he lifts his head and surveys the lines of cells above them. Behind thick white bars, the prisoners are watching them. They look like row upon row of caged birds at a street market. That's all about to change, thinks Sidorio. *Sidorio the Liberator*. Has a nice ring.

"Sir, I think it's about time you stated your business or moseyed back to where you came from," says the first of the guards, stroking his moustache.

"My business?" Sidorio stares at him blankly.

"What is it that you want?" The guard speaks slowly, as if Sidorio is stupid or something. Bad mistake.

"What do we want?" Sidorio appears to ponder the question. His hand rests on his jawline and he pats his finger against his lips. "What do we want? What do we want? Oh yes! That's right!" He looks straight into the eyes of the guard. "We want this ship."

"No can do!" the guard says, drawing strength from his two colleagues, who now stand on either side of him. "This prison ship is state owned and operated. I'm not aware of any instructions to pass over control. No one briefed me on this." He turns to guards numbers two and three. "Did either of you guys see a memo or anything from HQ?"

They shake their heads. Guard number two speaks. "We ain't had a memo from HQ since Christmas!"

"Details!" says Sidorio. "I'm not what you'd call a *details* kind of a guy." With that, he approaches the first guard. The moustached one opens his mouth to speak but something stops him.

"Sorry," says Sidorio, "I didn't hear that." He knows that the cocksure guard has seen the twin gold teeth. The argument has now taken on a whole new dynamic.

Thinking fast, the guard concedes. "You know what? I think I *do* remember a memo. The ship is yours. The prisoners too!" He tries to detach the keys on his chain but his hands are trembling.

"Here," says Sidorio, "let me help you with that!" He reaches out and tears the bundle of keys clean off the guard's belt. The other guards watch him, surprise and terror visible in equal measure on their stricken faces.

"You see how they're all numbered," the first guard says, his voice at least an octave higher than before. "Each little bitty number there corresponds to the numbers on the cells."

"Thanks for the tip!" Sidorio says, tossing the bunch of keys to Johnny D, who catches them in his palm.

"Okey dokey," says the guard. "Well, me and the boys'll just leave you to your business." He grips the others' arms and starts to move away.

Sidorio glances up at the ranks of cells ranged along the vast deck. From every side, the prisoners look down upon him. They are silent, watchful. Sidorio smiles up at them. "What do you think?" he asks. "Should we let your guards go free?"

"No!" cries one of the prisoners. The word echoes around the ship.

"Nice acoustics!" says Johnny D, nudging Stukeley. Stukeley nods and smiles back at him.

The first prisoner's shout is taken up by another. And another. Soon, the whole ship is thronging with the chant: "Don't let them go! Don't let them go!" Feet drum against the metal floors.

The fear on the guards' faces is clear now. It's like their old faces have been stripped away and all that is left is a pool of raw terror.

Sidorio shrugs and turns to the guards. "Sorry, boys, but these guys in the cages are going to be working for me soon and I need to keep them on side." With that, he tears the guard's shirt and undershirt in one brisk movement. Holding the guard still with one hand, he brings his gold teeth to the man's thorax. He punctures the skin and begins to feast.

As he does so, the prisoners start cheering. Sidorio is reminded of the stadium back in Rome. He went there once or twice. In another lifetime, he might have been a gladiator. Maybe he has become one now – of sorts.

The two other guards are as still as statues, watching the shell of the man who used to be their superior brought down lower than they knew it was possible to go. One of the guards digs deep and manages to ask, "Who are you?"

Sidorio lifts his head and beams. "I'm the stuff of your

nightmares . . . Actually, I'm the stuff your nightmares wake up screaming about."

The guard trembles at this. So does his companion.

"We really shouldn't drag this out," says Stukeley to Johnny D.

Johnny D nods his head. "That would be bad manners," he agrees.

Together, they move towards the terrified guards. There is the tearing of cloth and the puncturing of skin. The lieutenants take their fill.

The prisoners are going mental now. There's a strange combination of celebration and trepidation in the air. The noise is intense. In these airless quarters, it bounces back upon itself. It's like a wave building and building. The cheers border on hysteria. But don't they realise? They must realise. What started with the guards will end with them.

As Sidorio drops the husk of the guard to the deck, all sound ceases. The drumming of the feet stops too. All the prisoners are waiting to hear what happens next. Sidorio allows Stukeley and Johnny D to finish feasting, then raises his head and smiles a bloody grin.

"OK, everyone," he begins. "As you may have gathered, we – like you – are from the wrong side of the tracks. We're here to take this prison hulk and turn it into a pirate ship – but a special kind of pirate ship; a ship of Vampirates. That's vampires who are pirates. Is everyone following so far?"

There is no response. Fear has started to take over.

"I can't hear anything." Sidorio turns to address Johnny D. "Johnny, I can't hear my crew."

Now Johnny shakes his head and looks up at the rows of barred cells. "When your captain asks you a question, you answer him," he says. "And he just asked you if you were following his gist. To which you gotta reply either yes or no, but preferably yes."

There was a moment's pause and then a muted cry of "Yes!"

"Good call," said Johnny. "I'll hand you back to the captain, then. Oh, and I'm his deputy – ahem, *joint* Deputy, Johnny D – by the way. I'm looking forward to meeting y'all properly later!"

"As I was saying," Sidorio continues. "This ship today ceases to become a prison. It becomes a Vampirate ship and I'm the captain. Now, this being a Vampirate ship, it's important that all crew-members are vampires." He nods to Johnny. Johnny looks up to the top of the stairs and clicks his fingers. At this sign, the waiting ranks of vampires begin descending the gridwork stairs.

"Here are some more of my crew," announces Sidorio.

Everyone watches as the vampires begin filing down the central gangway.

"That's right, people, come on down!" Sidorio says. He glances up once more. "But hey, good news for you people in the cages! We're still recruiting. Yes, there's a place for each and every one of you on the crew. The only thing we have to ensure is that each of you is a vampire . . . oh and don't worry if you're not yet a vampire because my crew will be passing amongst you and you very soon will be."

He spins around. It has been centuries since he addressed this size of audience. He thinks back. The last time he had this many people waiting on his word was in Cilicia. Before Caesar. That was when he last had this much power. Too long ago. Much too long ago. But now, the wait is over. He turns to his lieutenants.

"What are you waiting for?" He points to the key-chain in Johnny's hand. "Let's get busy!"

Johnny slides the keys off the chain and splits them with Stukeley. They hand a key in turn to each of the vampire crew. Soon, every vampire in the ranks has the key to a numbered cell. They begin climbing up the gridwork stairs to complete their first mission.

Sidorio stands, his two lieutenants on either side. "I think this is going to prove a very effective recruitment drive," he says. "Good work, boys." He rests his arms around their shoulders.

Johnny D turns to him. "Shouldn't we have a name for this ship?"

"Absolutely!" says Stukeley. "I was thinking the same thing."

"Your captain's one step ahead of you," says Sidorio with a grin. "Welcome to *The*—"

But his voice is drowned out by a scream. The crew has reached the cells. The recruitment process has begun.

"I'm sorry, captain," says Stukeley. "I think I missed that."

"I said, *The Cilicia*," says Sidorio.

Stukeley and Johnny exchange a look.

"What?" Sidorio says. "You don't like it?" He seems crushed.

"It's not that I don't like it," Johnny D says. "It just doesn't quite state our business, if you know what I mean."

"It's the place I came from," says Sidorio.

"Maybe that's the problem," says Johnny D. "It's backward-looking. It's all about where you came from. Maybe what you want as the ship name is where you're *goin'*."

Sidorio hesitates. He hasn't thought of it this way before but the kid has a point. "So, have either of you got any suggestions?"

Johnny D shakes his head. "I'm terrible with names," he says.

Stukeley speaks. "I did have one idea," he says to them both.

"Well," says Sidorio. "We're all ears."

Stukeley clears his throat. "*The Blood Captain*," he says.

"Nice!" says Johnny.

"There's this pirate tradition, you see—" says Stukeley. But his words are drowned out by Sidorio.

"*The Blood Captain*. I like it! Yeah, let's go with that!"

CHAPTER FIFTY-FIVE

The Collector of Souls

"I've called you all here to tell you about the captain," Mosh Zu said, standing in the centre of the meditation room and addressing Grace, Darcy and Lorcan. "I need your help to heal him. We don't have much time. I've begun the preparations but I want to explain as best I can what we're going to do and why.

"The captain was in a very bad way when you brought him here, Darcy. If it hadn't been for your quick thinking and courage, he might have perished on that deck. But by bringing him here, you gave him a chance. I managed to stabilise his condition and, for the past two nights and days, he has been resting. I had hoped that rest, combined with some gentle healing techniques, might prove sufficient. Alas, that is not the case. The time for gentle healing is past. I'm going to have to try something more radical.

"As you all know, the captain is deeply committed to helping people, often people who refuse to help themselves. It's as if he is hard-wired never to give up on them. Not until the very end. The captain has put a good deal of strain upon himself carrying the burdens of others." He locked eyes with them, making sure they were following, before he continued.

"All three of you have, at one time or another, experienced the ribbon healing we practice here. You'll recall that in the healing ceremonies, I draw the pain out from each tormented vampire and channel it into the ribbon. Each time I do this, there's a danger that I myself absorb their pain. Once it's there, it can become trapped and is very hard to remove. Well, over the years, the captain has allowed too much of others' pain to accumulate inside him. It is weighing him down. But the captain has not merely carried the pain of others. It goes deeper than that. He is what is known as a Soul Carrier or a Collector of Souls. This means that, in some cases, when trying to rescue someone, he hasn't just taken their pain away; he has drawn their whole soul into him. He is, if you like, a ship within a ship.

"It is a sign of the captain's great strength that he is able to carry souls in this way. It should only ever be a temporary measure, used *in extremis*. After giving the vulnerable souls shelter for a time, he should release them and allow them to become strong in themselves once more. But the captain has harboured too many souls inside him for too long. This is the reason he has grown so weak. Together, we must work to release those souls from him. It is neither straightforward, nor free from danger. We risk losing not only those souls but also the captain himself."

"And what if we *don't* take that risk?" Grace asked.

"Then we'll almost certainly lose him, and them, in any case."

"Then we have no choice," Grace said.

"That's my feeling," Mosh Zu said. "I think we must proceed with this healing and we must do it now, without further delay."

"Yes," Darcy said. "But I don't understand. How can *we* help?"

"Perhaps the greatest danger of all," Mosh Zu said, "is that the captain will choose not to release the souls. I need to gather around him the people he cares most deeply about, and those who care most deeply about him. Only then can I show him that he *must* release the souls, or else journey with them into oblivion."

CHAPTER FIFTY-SIX

Behind the Mask

The door opened. "The preparations are over," announced Mosh Zu. "We will begin."

Mosh Zu beckoned Grace, Darcy and Lorcan to join him in the healing chamber. As they stepped inside, Grace's senses were overwhelmed with the smell of beeswax from the candles and the sweet herbs with which Mosh Zu had earlier strewn the floor.

Judging by their expressions, Darcy and Lorcan were clearly shocked to see the captain laid out on the slab. And, even though Grace had seen him like this before, she still felt a fresh jolt of panic at being reminded how weak and vulnerable he was. *But we're here to heal him*, she told herself. *Together, we're going to bring him back.* The thoughts helped to strengthen her resolve. Even so, she was keen to get on with the healing process.

"Grace," said Mosh Zu, "I'd like you to sit at his feet."

Grace did not hesitate but went to the end of the slab and knelt down before it.

Now Mosh Zu turned to Darcy. "You come over here, by his right hand," he said. "And you, Lorcan, you sit by his left hand."

The three friends took up their positions. Mosh Zu approached the captain's head. Grace watched him. He had told her that she had a talent for healing —one day, perhaps, she would lead a healing such as this. It was exciting to contemplate but she filed this thought, returning her sole focus to the work at hand.

Before he began, Mosh Zu addressed the others once more, his voice soft and precise. "We are all here today because of our love and respect for the one who lies here before us. We want to help the captain and it is in our power to do so." He looked at each of them in turn. "We come together from different worlds, from different sides of life and death. We bring together all our unique experiences, thoughts and feelings and unite them and gather our diverse energies to this task of healing. We may be worried or even scared by what we witness during the healing process but we must remain steadfast for the good of the one who lies before us, our dear captain."

Mosh Zu placed his hands on the Vampirate captain's head. He nodded to Grace, who reached out with both hands, each touching the tip of the captain's boots. "That's it," whispered Mosh Zu, "just the gentlest of touches will suffice – you're simply allowing your energy to connect with his." He turned to Darcy and Lorcan. "And now you."

Darcy and Lorcan each reached out and cradled the captain's gloved hands in their own. Mosh Zu nodded, then opened up his palms to cradle the captain's skull. He closed his own eyes.

"Begin to let it out," he said, softly. "Begin to let go of the pain that weighs you down."

He fell silent and waited, his hands lightly but firmly supporting the base of the captain's skull. The others maintained their points of contact. Grace suddenly felt a jolt as though the captain's foot had lashed out at her. She glanced up and saw that the foot was stone still. Then she felt it again. It was a very definite sensation.

"It's a good sign," said Mosh Zu. "Maintain the hold, Grace. It's beginning."

Suddenly Darcy felt a charge pass through her from the captain's hands. She looked up, seeing that Lorcan was looking equally surprised. Once more Mosh Zu nodded, without opening his eyes. "This is good, everyone. Our contact is working. It's going to get bumpy, but just focus on holding him. Hold him in your heart spaces as you do with your touch. Give him the reassurance to shed his deep burden."

Mosh Zu adjusted his own hold. Almost immediately, Grace had the sensation of the captain's legs buckling. And yet, he still had not moved. She could see from Lorcan's face that he was experiencing something similar. Just as Mosh Zu had promised, the energies within the captain were beginning to realign. It was becoming harder to keep her hands on his feet but she knew that it was vital she did so.

There was a fresh surge of energy. The captain began flailing about. Grace saw Lorcan and Darcy adjust their holds. She found herself struggling once more. They each only had a hand, but she had both his feet and they were each moving in different directions. It was becoming too much for her. She started to panic. If she let go, she might break an important part of the healing process.

Suddenly, she felt an arm at her side. It brushed hers aside and took hold of the captain's right foot, enabling her to set both hands on his left one. It was still pulsing with energy, but now that she had only one foot to focus on, she could manage.

After a time, she grew used to the strange movements emanating from the captain's body. The movements themselves became more regular, like waves breaking on a shore.

She turned to see whose hands had come to her aid. And could scarcely believe her eyes.

"Connor!" she gasped.

He smiled back at her. "Looks like I got here just in time," he whispered.

Grace was amazed. There was so much she wanted to say to him, to ask him. But now was not the time. It felt so right to have Connor with them at this moment. She glanced up at Mosh Zu, wondering if he had somehow brought Connor to join them. He nodded at her, smiling.

526

Whether through Connor's intervention or because of the healing work they had done together, the captain's internal movements became steadier.

"Can you feel the change?" Mosh Zu asked.

"Yes," Lorcan answered softly.

"Me too," Darcy said.

"It's like the ocean's moving inside him," said Grace.

"Yes, Grace." Mosh Zu smiled softly. "I hadn't thought of it like that before, but you're quite right." He paused. "All right, he's comfortable now. You can release your touch. One at a time. Lorcan first."

Lorcan let go of the captain's hand. It remained stretched out towards him.

"Now you, Darcy." Almost reluctantly, Darcy too let go. Both the captain's arms remained extended, as if he was floating on the salt-rich ocean.

"Next you, Connor." Connor took his hands away from the captain's foot.

"And now you, Grace," said Mosh Zu, nodding. Grace lifted her hands from the captain's boot and rocked back gently onto her knees. She reached out and gripped Connor's hand, as if to reassure herself he was actually there.

Now, Mosh Zu himself stepped away from the captain. "Your burden is ready to be lifted," he said. "Feel how much lighter you are becoming."

At these words, the captain began to rise into the air, his cape floating up beneath him, fluttering at the outskirts of his body, glimmering with soft light. The captain's body rose about a metre and a half off the slab, then stopped in midair, floating within the circle created by the others.

It was an extraordinary sight. Grace, Darcy, Lorcan and Connor were all transfixed. None of them sensed how much time had passed before Mosh Zu spoke once more.

"All right," he said. "I think he's steady now. We are ready to begin."

To *begin*? Grace was surprised by the choice of words. She had thought the treatment must nearly be over. What did Mosh Zu mean by "begin"?

"It is time to let go," Mosh Zu said, gazing down upon the captain. "For so long, you have carried the hurt of others. You have taken hold of their pain in order to heal them. But now you have nothing left to give. You must let their pain out. As you do so, the weight upon you, within you, will lift again."

Grace noticed that the veins within the captain's cloak were glowing brighter and brighter at Mosh Zu's words.

"Come," Mosh Zu said. "It is time to remove the mask." He beckoned the others towards him. "There are three buckles here. Lorcan, come and unfasten the first of them."

Grace, for one, needed little reminder that the captain's mask was fastened at three points, which came together in a silver pin shaped like angel wings at the back of his skull. So many times she had seen that silver pin, bright against the deep brown skin at the back of the captain's head. So many times, she had wished that he might unfasten the buckles and show her the face behind the mask. Now, it was actually going to happen. At last, she would stand face to face with the Vampirate captain. At last, she could begin to truly know him. If only, she thought sadly, it could have been in different, less dangerous, circumstances.

Lorcan came to Mosh Zu's side and let the guru's hand guide him towards the first strap.

"All you need to do is to touch the strap," Mosh Zu said.

As Lorcan did so, Mosh Zu began chanting.

"Like the flower blooming in the sun,
Open and release!
Like the cloud letting loose the rain,
Open and release!"

As he spoke, the first buckle unfastened and gently floated out to the side.

"Thank you, Lorcan," said Mosh Zu. "And now you, Darcy. Come and help with the second."

Now Darcy approached, with some trepidation.

"Touch the strap," instructed Mosh Zu.

As she did so, he chanted once more.

"Like the shell liberating the pearl,
Open and release!
Like the chrysalis releasing the butterfly,
Open and release!"

Once more, the strap released itself and floated out to the side.

"Good work, Darcy." Mosh Zu smiled. "And now, Grace, the final strap is for you."

Connor gave Grace's hand a supportive squeeze before letting it go. She stepped over to Mosh Zu's side. Her heart was racing with anticipation. Ever since she had first encountered the Vampirate captain, she had waited for this moment. Now, her deep fascination was tempered by the heartfelt longing that her actions would help him, heal him. She reached out for the final remaining strap.

Once more, Mosh Zu chanted.

"Like the mouth setting free laughter,
Open and release!
Like all these things, great and small,
Open and release!
Open and release!
Open and release!"

She heard the buckle release. As it did, the wings on the buckle began to flap, as gently as the wings of a butterfly. The mask flew up above the captain's prone body. It continued its flight up towards the ceiling. None of them saw where it went next. Their gaze was fixed downwards. None of them could quite believe their eyes.

"I don't understand," said Grace.

"Nor me," said Lorcan. "Is this some kind of trick?"

Mosh Zu's voice was calm and steady. "There's no trick. Just observe it. Do not try to understand it."

Grace's heart was racing faster than ever. At the same time, she felt a chill through her very insides. The captain's body floated before them, but he had no face, no head. There was nothing beneath the mask at all.

CHAPTER FIFTY-SEVEN

Reunion

"There's nothing there," Grace said.

"See with your mind," said Mosh Zu. "Not with your eyes."

They all looked down at the gap above the captain's shoulders. There was still very clearly an absence of anything. You could see straight through to the thin pillow Mosh Zu had placed on the slab.

As they looked down, Grace realised that she could no longer see the floorboards. They were hidden from view under a layer of smoke. Her first thought was that a candle had fallen and set one of the tapestries alight. But there was no smell of burning. Nor was the room warm with fire. Indeed, if anything, it had grown cooler. The smoke thickened and Grace realised that it was not smoke but mist. She looked across at Connor. He stared back at her, confused. She smiled faintly, hoping somehow to reassure him, though she was no more certain about what was happening than he was.

The mist reached up to the level of the captain's prone body but no higher. Instead, it began to thicken and take shape, rolling back and forth like waves on the shore. Now, more than ever, the captain appeared to be floating.

Grace looked once more towards Mosh Zu. His eyes were tightly shut and he was chanting softly once more.

"Like the flower blooming in the sun . . .
Like the cloud letting loose the rain . . .
Like the shell liberating the pearl . . ."

Grace felt herself trembling. Connor came and stood beside her, resting a hand gently on her shoulder.

Grace turned her gaze from Mosh Zu down to the captain once more. As she did so, she caught her breath. There, where previously there had been nothing, a face was beginning to form. It was very faint at first – no more than an outline – but slowly it came into focus as if it, too, was rising through a deep mist. Grace was transfixed. It was a face she had seen before.

As the features began to sharpen, she remembered her first meeting with the Vampirate Captain. Talking to him, she had suddenly had a vision of a man's face, his deep brown skin marked with a crimson scar. This was that face. The captain had congratulated her for seeing behind the mask. And now, so much further on in her journey, his mask was removed and here was his face, visible at last.

"It's him," she gasped. "That's the captain."

Connor gazed down in amazement. Lorcan was transfixed. Mosh Zu's eyes remained closed and he continued to chant.

"Like the chrysalis releasing the butterfly . . .
Like the mouth setting free laughter . . ."

"Look!" Connor whispered in her ear.

They watched as the face began to rise up. A body followed. A man was climbing out from the captain's familiar armour. But he was clothed in stained and tattered rags. He looked up at Grace.

"Hello," she said, smiling. She realised she was crying. Something amazing had happened in this room. It was as if a baby had been born.

The man gazed back at her, but he did not smile. He cowered from her.

"What's wrong?" asked Grace. She turned to Mosh Zu. "He seems frightened of me. Doesn't he know me any more?"

Mosh Zu shook his head. "He *doesn't* know you. He is *not* the captain."

"What? I don't understand . . ." Grace began.

"Wait," Mosh Zu said softly. "Wait and watch."

Confused, Grace watched as the man stepped away from the shell of the captain's body and began walking off through the mist.

"It's happening again," Connor whispered.

They all watched as a second face began to take shape in

the void above the captain's shoulders. As the features became clearer through the mist, they saw a woman's face. She looked old and frail, her eyes flickering around her. It wasn't clear whether she was looking *at* them or through them. Now she too rose, as if pushing back the sheets of a bed, and stepped out from the captain's body, making her way into the mist.

"Who *are* they?" Connor asked, as a third face began to take shape.

"These are lost souls," Grace whispered, suddenly realising. "The captain has been carrying them. They need to be released." Mosh Zu nodded, never wavering from his chanting.

The third soul – that of a young man – began to rise.

Together, they watched a fourth, then a fifth figure emerge from the captain's body.

"How many more?" Grace asked. She felt deeply emotional and realised tears were running down her face.

They watched in silence as a sixth, seventh, eighth and ninth figure awoke from the depths of their "sleep", rubbing their eyes and glancing about the room, then rising and stepping out into the mist.

Throughout, the captain's husk of a body lay there, still floating. And Mosh Zu continued his chant, his voice unwaveringly strong and melodic.

Grace realised that the souls who had risen had gathered around them, watching as they were joined by their fellow travellers.

"Will they survive?" she wondered. "Are they real people? Or just ghosts? Will they survive now they have been released from the captain?" She ached to ask Mosh Zu these questions but she could not disturb him from his chant.

Seeing her discomfort, Connor drew near once more. He put his arm around her shoulder. She realised she wasn't the only one experiencing this intense wave of emotion. Darcy and Lorcan were crying too. They were holding each other tightly.

They all watched as another face came into view before their eyes. It was a young woman. Grace could tell she was going to be beautiful as the first lines of her nose and cheekbones sketched themselves in the air. Her flesh was pale and lightly freckled. Shoulder-length auburn hair came into focus, tendrils floating out in the breeze. And then her eyes opened. Grace caught her breath. At the same instant, Lorcan gasped. Grace felt Connor's hand clasp hers all the more tightly. The woman's eyes were green, a deep emerald-green.

As the woman lifted her head, Mosh Zu spoke at last. "She is the last," he said, stepping back, evidently drained from his work.

Grace looked at Connor. He too was transfixed by the woman in front of them. She was sitting up now, pushing her unruly hair back behind her ears and blinking as she took in her new surroundings.

Grace could not contain herself any more. She addressed the woman directly.

"Look over here!" she said.

It took a moment for the woman to respond. It was as if she was still some distance from them and could only see and hear them faintly. But at last she turned and her eyes settled upon Grace and Connor.

Grace was crying. Connor was frowning, shaking his head in disbelief.

The woman rose. Surely she couldn't walk away, out into the mist like the others, thought Grace. She couldn't *go*.

But she wasn't going anywhere. She seemed to be growing more alive, more vibrant with every moment. And now she stood up and, rather than turning away, began walking towards them. Her emerald-green eyes were wet with tears, but they were happy tears. She held out her arms to Grace.

"Mother!" Grace said, unable to hold back the word. "Mother, it's you, isn't it?"

The woman nodded, as Grace thudded into her, wrapping her arms around her. She was surprised to feel the touch of living, breathing flesh. And then she felt the brush of the woman's lips on her forehead. She kissed her.

"Mother!" Grace said again.

"You've no idea how long I've waited to hear you say that, Grace." The woman's voice was warm and gentle.

"Mother! Mother! Mother!" Grace repeated, overcome. She wanted to carry on saying it for all those times she had thought about her or wished she was there at the lighthouse. For all the times she had dreamed of her mother, then woken to find no trace of her.

536

The woman hugged her and kissed her again, then held out an arm to her son.

"Connor," she said, looking across at him.

He was uncertain at first but then he let go of any doubts and ran to her, flinging his arms around her and Grace until they were one compact bundle.

The woman hugged her children tightly and lifted her head.

Grace noticed then that Lorcan was watching them intently.

"Hello, Sally," he said at length.

Grace was taken aback. How did Lorcan know her mother's name?

She looked from Lorcan to her mother and back again. They were smiling at each other – a smile that spoke of deep friendship, maybe more.

"It's grand to see you again, Sally," Lorcan said.

"And you, Lorcan," she said. "Thank you. Thank you for taking such good care of my babies."

Grace looked at Connor. Like her, he was gazing curiously at his mother and Lorcan.

Suddenly Grace wondered about the others. She glanced around the room for Mosh Zu and Darcy. They were nowhere to be seen. All the other souls had disappeared too. And there, visible in the thinning mist, was the slab the captain had lain on. But there was no sign of him, either. Even the pillow had disappeared. Where had they all gone? What was happening?

She would find out soon enough, she decided. She held tight to her mother and her brother, as Lorcan too came forward and joined them. As the four of them stood there, hands connecting, Grace felt a moment of perfect peace. She knew it couldn't last. Why, it might even be some kind of dream. But however fleeting the moment might be, whether a dream or no, she didn't care. It was the moment she had waited for all her life and nothing, *nothing*, was going to spoil it for her.